ISBN: 9798445338772
Imprint: Independently published

Cover illustration by Aliea Manley
Author Photograph by Ariel Lobdell

This book is dedicated to God, who inspired me to do this work. Thank you for giving me this story and the words to make it real.

To my wife, who has been both my editor and manager throughout this process. Thank you for your constant support in all of this, I couldn't have done it without you. I love you.

To all the people who read the many different stages of this book, who gave feedback and critiques, thank you for all your help.

And finally, to my mom and dad, to which one of them now owes me a steak dinner.

Love you guys!

The Purpose of After

Prologue

Somewhere off to the west, caught between rolling hills and a set of foreboding cliffs, was a small town. The town was nestled in a seemingly infinite sea of green grass that stretched to the horizon. Amidst it, gentle hills rose and fell like lazy waves swelling in the deep. Through the middle of the scene carved a single road. It curved like a river, meandering through the town only to split both north and south once drawing near to the cliffs.

These cliffs were impressive to say the least. They stood at an incredible height, making even the most adventurous soul tread with caution near its treacherous lip. Far, far below at the base of the mighty giants was a long band of white sand.

This stretch of beach was where many of the townsfolk would spend their summer days, splashing about in the frigid water until the sun would begin to lay its head down for another night. It took quite the drive up north for the road to switch back and safely deposit travelers to the pearly sands, but when there wasn't much in the way of activities, a small road trip was never too much to handle.

It was at the lip of the cliff that the first evidence of the town's general disposition could be witnessed. There, near the edge of the drop-off, was about ten feet of twisted guardrail. The sad bundle of metal, wood, and plastic had clearly fallen victim to negligence. It sat there like some miserable, broken insect nearing the end of its life.

The rail had been a project from years ago to make the town safer in an attempt to be more attractive to newcomers. There had been much fanfare about the whole thing but the people had quickly lost interest in it. Excuses were offered up, funding was cut, and soon it had been all but forgotten.

This mindset infected the very walls of the town itself, sinking its fingers into every building, every road, and every park. To someone just passing through, they may find themselves thinking the general atmosphere of the place was one of quiet living and gentle days. Yet if they were to stay for any length of time, its true nature would be revealed.

A whispering apathy had caught the whole town up in its hands. It was quiet, deadly, but not invisible. An outsider would begin to notice the fade in the color of the homes, the grime collecting upon playground equipment, and the slump in the shoulders of those trudging by. Where weeds sprung up, they would grow unabated. Where rust consumed, it would be ignored. Where rot crept in, it was covered. What was once seen as quaint would quickly turn to depressing, and those who thought perhaps they could build a life there would find themselves looking to greener pastures.

It was rare someone would choose to stay and rarer still for those who escaped to ever return. And yet, somehow, such a person did find their way home.

It was with this return a subtle change had occurred within the town. What was once neglected and forgotten was now loved and remembered. There were splashes of color scattered about everywhere within the town, popping up in the most unlikely of places.

One playground received a fresh coat of paint every month so that it gleamed cheery colors for the children that ran about it. The community center had gained a mural of a blooming garden that wrapped around the building, breathing new life into the tired windows of the once abandoned place. The statue of the founder, which used to be perpetually covered in rust and bird feces, had begun to shine once again in the sunlight, freed by diligent hands. On every block there seemed to be at least one thing that had been given new life and it was all due to the hard work of one individual.

This had not been her home, but rather her husband's who had moved them back to take care of her late father-in-law in his last days. After the older man had passed, the couple had inherited the house. Every year that rolled by, the conversation of selling the place would be brought up, but for one reason or another, the idea would never stick.

And so they stayed, building a life with the turn of every season. This choice breathed a second chance into the tired home they had been given. It was once indistinguishable from the rest of the town, but had slowly become something quite magnificent.

The building sat in a small yard covered not in a carpet of weeds or grass, but rather a sprawling garden that bloomed with every flower allowed to grow in such a climate. Dashes of brilliant color peeked out from every corner, building a perpetual rainbow as the flowers danced in the wind. It was well-maintained; arranged and cared for by someone with an artistic eye. Amidst the garden, a cobblestone path meandered from a white gate that sat at the property's perimeter to the blue front door.

The house was also meticulously taken care of. Its walls were a brilliant white with a deep, blue trim along its edges. A cute chimney poked its head from out of the slanted roof. On cold days, a steady stream of smoke would come trickling forth from the inside, but as it was the height of summer it sat more as an ornament. Instead, the great windows of the home were thrown wide to allow the cool, ocean breeze to cut through its space. Even the front door was propped open without a care to the outside world.

From out of the very heart of the home blared the upbeat sounds of big band music that was perfect for swing dancing. Such music spun its song from an old record player that seemed to never stop playing. Rain or shine, its welcoming tune could always be found gracing the halls and rooms of the building.

The entirety of the residence was like a ray of brilliant sunlight breaking through the clouds of apathy that so plagued the world around it.

This very place had become a gathering spot for many over the years. Whether it be for a cup of fabulous tea or instruction in a particular form of artistry or just for an ear willing to listen, this home was a sanctuary for some. Many more, however, would shake their heads while passing by. They pitied the outsider, speculating on why she chose to stay after everything that had happened.

This outsider, who had since moved into the middle of her life, had asked herself that very question, wondering day after day why she stayed. Yet there was something inside of her that told her to stay, a kind of Certainty that helped push her through the most difficult of circumstances. It is with this woman that the story begins.

And her name is Adda Reinhoff.

Part 1

1

Adda stood in her kitchen, humming softly in tune with the record player that sang its jaunty song. She had heard this one a thousand times and instinctively moved her hips to the swinging beat. As always, it was some big band piece that inspired many a soul to lively tap away on a dance floor. It was Adda's favorite genre of music and belonged to a time that she had wistfully imagined taking part in when she was a younger woman.

Of course, since then she had come to understand the multitude of benefits living in this modern time, but it was still fun to think about on occasion.

The kitchen around the woman was fairly standard. It had its oven with a stovetop, decent amount of counter space, a fair share of cabinets, a refrigerator, a two basin sink, and dishwasher to finish the set.

Though in many ways, the kitchen had been made for function rather than form, one could see quite a few indicators scattered around of Adda's influence.

The cabinets had once been a plain, white color, but had long since been redecorated. Adda was a painter by hobby and by trade, and as such, had gifted the cabinets with a brilliant display of designs. The woman was an expert at scenic pieces, but had chosen to do something a tad more abstract for these particular works. The swirling designs were almost hypnotic in the way they danced around one another, curving not unlike creeping vines interconnecting with one another.

The drab curtains had been swapped out for a set of deep blue ones that more often than not were hung to the sides of the big window facing the backyard. They rippled gently in the breeze of the open frame, billowing like sails of a ship ready to set out on the ocean. They added an extra dash of color to a room so consumed by grays and whites.

The door leading out of the kitchen had been fixed up as well. It had also been a stark white at one point, but had quickly been passed over by Adda's skillful hand. It now was adorned with a pattern of blue triangles that went all the way from the top of the frame to the base of the door.

The counters were the only thing left alone, as their dark gray had appealed to Adda. She felt like they added a nice tone to the room and didn't see any reason to change them.

The rest of the house had certainly received the same treatment as the kitchen, but it was the kitchen she spent most of her time in. It was here she got her best work done. She had an artist nook elsewhere, but somehow always found her way back into the kitchen with easel under arm to find inspiration. The room just felt more open than anywhere else and helped Adda think more clearly.

So Adda stood in her kitchen, easel placed and canvas set for another piece to put together. Most days she would just start painting, following the rhythm of wherever her creativity lead her, but today she found she was struggling. There were plenty of ideas in the world, plenty of things to paint, but none of them wanted to grace the woman with their presence.

Adda gazed out the windows, running a nail along its sill as she did so. It made a soft hissing sound as she trailed her hand along, eyes distant in deep thought. She sought inspiration from the flourishing garden of her backyard, hoping one of the bobbing flowers or lush, edible plants would strike up her fancy.

Though they were pleasant to look at, none of them did anything to help her predicament.

Her eyes drifted from the gardens, passing over the stepping stones carefully placed between toward a shed that sat in the left corner of her yard. The shed had once been a workshop but had been converted into a house of memories over the last year. It held many artifacts of a previous life within it and sometimes looking upon it would help loosen up the creative juices.

There was something about nostalgia that could inspire the mind.

The side of the shed had been painted with the likeness of a rising sun, a beautiful cascade of the dark colors of night forming around the brilliant ones of the coming day. Adda had painted the piece a long time ago and had taken great care to ensure a fresh coat of paint anytime it had begun to fade. She stared at it now, letting her mind wander through pleasant memories.

Her brush drifted in her hand, dipping down to lightly kiss the canvas. The act pulled Adda back to the work before her, noting the small green smear in the middle of the portrait. She cocked a head as she looked at it.

"Anything you have to say for yourself?" Adda idly asked the smudge.

The paint didn't reply.

She shook her head, frustrated that she couldn't think of anything to do yet being unable to shake the insufferable need to paint. There was this Certainty deep in her bones that pushed her to make something, but wouldn't give an answer to the itch it brought.

The woman glanced back out the window and froze.

There, sitting upon the fence that was the barrier between Adda's and her neighbor's yard, was a dove. A dove was not a strange thing to see, of course, they weren't uncommon in the surrounding region. In fact, Adda more than likely would have given it no more than a cursory glance on a normal day.

But there was something about this one that gave her pause.

It was, all things considered, a standard dove. There was nothing that made it out of the ordinary, yet Adda couldn't shake a peculiar feeling as she looked at it.

Adda was overwhelmed by the feeling that the dove was looking at her.

And not in the way of a curious animal sizing up a human as a potential threat, but as something deeply intelligent. There an understanding there in its little, black eyes as it regarded her. It seemed- sad; a feeling that Adda had never seen come off an animal in such waves.

It was haunting.

They stood there, gazing upon one another in silence. Then Adda blinked, her eyes unable to stay open any longer. In that fraction of a moment, the little bird was suddenly gone as if it had never been.

Shocked, Adda raced to the backdoor, throwing it wide as she strode into the yard. She scanned the fence and then the sky, looking for any evidence of this strange creature. No matter where she looked, the dove had simply vanished.

Adda stood a moment in shock, trying to process what had happened. Then, with a shake of her head, she let out a laugh.

"Goodness gracious," Adda said in a chiding voice, "I must be going crazy."

As the moment fell away from her, Adda was more and more convinced she had imagined the whole thing. At the very least, the bird must have just flown off, disturbed by the human staring so intently upon it. The occurrence had been too bizarre and Adda considered that she was attributing meaning somewhere it didn't belong.

Still, the moment weighed upon the woman for the rest of the morning and well into the afternoon, causing her to feel distracted and restless. Adda paced before her canvas, trying to put the moment from her mind as she tried to sate the burning hunger of creativity that continued to growl from the corners of her soul. Still no ideas came to her.

Fed up with her inability to let go of the mundane interaction, Adda finally decided it was time to change her scenery. If the house would not offer inspiration, maybe the world outside would. Adda wandered through her house, moving into the living room and toward her art nook where she kept a carrying case for all her paints and supplies.

The tv had been left on in the living room, something Adda hadn't remembered doing. The news was talking over yet another crisis that had nothing to do with her or her little corner of the world. She paused to search for the remote, intent on turning off the stream of depressing updates as she only half listened to what was being said.

"...tensions continue to rise as..."

"Where is the blasted thing?" Adda grumbled, pulling up the cushions on her couch.

"...water being tested..."

Adda finally found the remote lodged by one of the armrests of the couch. She was normally a fairly organized person so she was a tad miffed as to how the controller had ended up in such a place.

"No more tv before bed." Adda declared as she pointed the remote at the screen.

"...and the government is recommending that..."

Those were the last words out of the newscaster's mouth before the display went black. Merciful, peaceful silence descended on the living room. Adda wondered if she should be more aware of what was going on, if she should take the time to be more educated in affairs both foreign and at home, but she pushed the notion off. If the world was going to end tomorrow, she was intent on living for today.

Within a few minutes, Adda had retrieved her large carrying case from her nook. It was a piece once designed to carry luggage that she

17

had retrofitted to hold all the things she needed to paint on the go. It was large, bulky, and somewhat inconvenient to carry around, but it had a charm to it that made Adda refuse to let it go.

Once she had grabbed the case, she went back into the kitchen to collapse her easel down and grab her canvas. It was a lot to carry for one person, but she had managed to become an expert in carrying awkward loads. Now with all she needed, Adda walked from her home, kicking the front door closed on her way out.

With a bit of a struggle, Adda trudged along the curved stone path to her front gate, reorganizing herself in order to hit the latch and push her way through. After slipping by, the gate swung back closed of its own accord, latching as she walked away.

Adda did have a car, but generally chose to walk instead of drive. The vehicle sat in her driveway now, hot beneath the summer sun. It was a pleasant green color, and though she certainly liked blue more, she wouldn't dream of changing it. The car had been through a lot with her and she wouldn't disgrace its legacy.

For a moment, she was tempted to pack up all her things and actually take the car. It would certainly make things easier. In the end, she chose against it, relishing the challenge and the ability to enjoy the summer day.

As Adda walked, she formulated a destination for her journey. There were many places worthy of a visit, but none were quite as majestic as the cliffs just west of town. Her mind made up, Adda went up her street, hurrying to make the best of the remaining daylight.

Her house sat on Marigold Avenue which ran itself around into Main Street. Main shot through the exact center of town with all the notable businesses gathered on it to prey upon tourists and the odd passerby. They didn't get many of either group, but everyone did what they could.

As Adda found herself on Main, she saw there were only a handful of people still wandering about. It was a Sunday and as the evening drew closer, most were either still down at the beach with their families or were at home letting the day wrap up. There was a sense of preparation for the week to come that always manifested itself at the conclusion of a weekend. Adda wasn't surprised at this and was even glad to find it so quiet out.

She wandered beneath street lamps crafted in a victorian style. They were adorned with hanging baskets that had once held blooming flowers. The plants had since succumbed to the heat of summer, their green leaves browning as the season pressed on.

Adda made a mental note to try and organize a group to ensure the flowers were getting watered. They always brought much needed zest to the street. Already a series of names ran through her head as she envisioned breathing life back into the hanging gardens.

This is what she did; anywhere there was a problem, she found a solution. It was endearing to some and irritating to others, but Adda didn't care either way. If something needed doing, she wouldn't wait for someone else to step up to the plate.

"Mrs. Reinhoff!" A deep voice broke her from her scheming.

Adda turned about to see a portly figure marching after her. He walked at a swift pace, sweat glaring off his forehead as he waved a hand. This was Keith Baker, owner of the local grocery store.

His grandfather had founded the business, naming it 'The Grocery

Store' as he was a practical man that didn't have time for zany titles or marketing gimmicks. Once Keith had taken over, he had started putting a ridiculous amount of emphasis on the *the* in its title. He insisted that it was called *THE* Grocery Store since it was the only one that mattered.

Of course, it was the only surviving grocery store in town, so his point was hard to argue.

He was a blustery sort who always seemed to dodge around what he really wanted. It was hard to know where one stood with Keith as he almost spoke in riddles when engaging in conversation. Still, he had been a good friend to Adda and he was not without merits. He was quick to laugh and was never one to let a mishap keep him off balance for long.

Their friendship had actually started with Adda's husband, who had grown up alongside the other man. They had both attended the same school, gone to the same events, and had generally been considered inseparable. When Adda and her husband had moved back to his community some decades ago, it had been Keith who had helped them get situated.

"How do you move so fast?" Keith gasped as he finally caught up to her.

He pulled out a small cloth and dabbed at his forehead.

"Well, I once was asked to be a sprinter in the olympics." Adda replied with a chuckle.

"Well if you had, I would've bet all my money on you!" Keith said with a broad grin, playing along.

"So, is there something you needed?" Adda asked.

"Oh- yes- right! I just saw you lugging all this stuff and wanted to help out!" Keith said and began to reach for Adda's art case.

Adda neatly dodged away, putting space between the two. The movement brought a flash of disappointment to Keith's face and Adda could tell that man was a little hurt.

"Now now, Keith, I'm a grown woman and I can manage my paints, thank you very much." Adda said, "But I do appreciate the offer."

Keith reddened, embarrassed.

"Of course, anytime really!" Keith said, attempting to recover from the social blunder. "What are you working on?"

"Just a painting."

"Oh! A commission then?"

"No, this one is all for me." Adda said, her arms straining under her load.

The dipping sun caused a flare of irritation to run through Adda. She didn't have time for small talk, there was an itch that needed scratched and instead she was wasting away the day. Keith seemed blissfully unaware of all this as he continued on, hands in his pockets.

"That's- good? Is finding work hard right now?" Keith looked around and then leaned in close as if to share a secret. "Do- do you need any money? Are you doing alright and all that?"

There it was. As he spoke, a tinge of pity flickered in his eyes and tainted his voice. This pity had been hounding after her for too long now, reflected in the eyes of everyone who knew her, and in a small town such as this, that meant nearly everyone. Adda couldn't escape it, no matter how she tried. The townsfolk were determined to put her in a box and no matter how much she insisted she was doing alright, they refused to listen.

Adda hated that look, it felt so demeaning, but at the same time, she couldn't fault them. She couldn't make anyone see what happened behind closed doors. The tears that were shed, the agony that was felt, and finally, the victory that was had. She had grown so much, but to them, she had diminished.

"I make enough." Adda replied, "Besides, Isaiah put me in a spot to live comfortably for a long while, so please don't worry about me."

A shadow passed over Keith's face at the mention of the name. He cleared his throat uncomfortably and glanced to the side.

"Right, right. Where are you headed? You know, to work on this next project?" Keith deftly switched the subject.

"Up to the cliffs." Adda replied. "I just needed to get out of my house."

The statement brought forth another pitying look and Keith reached over to place a hand on Adda's shoulder. The touch was as awkward as it was tentative as if the man desperately wanted to comfort her but didn't quite know how.

"It must be hard." Keith said in a low voice, bringing himself closer to Adda.

"It is what it is." Adda replied with a smile and a deliberate step back. "I'm really sorry to cut this conversation short, Keith, but I do have to go. I need to get this painting done and we're burning daylight."

"At least let me drive you up there." Keith insisted. "It's no problem at all!"

"Thank you, but I really would rather the walk." Adda said again.

With that, Adda said good day to the man and walked away. She had only gotten a few steps before Keith called out to her once again. A barb of irritation bit at Adda's heart, but still, she turned about to consider the man. She waited, somewhat impatiently, for him to speak.

"Just- be careful." Keith said after hesitating a moment. "There's something strange in the air."

Adda turned, moving up Main toward her destination.

Those last words Keith had uttered filtered themselves into the back of Adda's mind, hanging there like ominous clouds on an otherwise perfect day. She didn't know what had prompted the man to say such a thing, but it seemed to carry some weight with it. Regardless, the woman had a mission for the day and would let nothing else get in her way of seeing it through.

So she marched on, feeling the weight of Keith's gaze resting upon her the whole way.

2

It didn't take much longer for Adda to break free of town limits. She still walked along the road, but her scenery had shifted into a view of both fields and hills stretching out to her left and right. Trees dotted the region, growing in small clusters to help break up the monotony of the surrounding world.

The road went straight toward the cliffs up ahead before cutting off to the north about a mile from her destination. There was a pull off at the curve, one made beneath hundreds of tires who had stopped there over the years to take the short hike to the cliff. A well worn path had been constructed by trailblazers with no official trailhead marker. It was easy to find and soon Adda's feet were marching against the compacted dirt.

It wasn't much of a climb, there was hardly any elevation gain and the path didn't wind or switch back on itself. All things considered, it was an easy accomplishment to complete the trail, but Adda was finding it difficult to catch her breath. She had never had any kind of issue before as she took care of herself and even took pride in her physical capabilities, yet today she found her lungs heaving as they struggled with every mouthful of air. Sweat began to trickle down her forehead and, for a brief moment, her vision swam as if she was about to pass out.

Adda stopped a moment, setting down her case and taking a few, steadying breaths. The dizzy spell passed and the world became stable once more. She straightened and wiped away the sweat on her brow.

What was that? The alarming thought strayed through Adda's mind.

She had her own share of aches and pains, but had never experienced such a powerful sense of vertigo before. It left her feeling debased and unsure. For a moment, she considered turning around and going home. After all, night was only a few hours away and she didn't want to be out here in case something were to happen again.

But the Certainty deep in her bones insisted she press on despite this. It had never lead her wrong before, so Adda obliged, gathering her supplies to resume the journey.

To her relief, the moment seemed to have been a fluke as the rest of the hike went on without a hitch. Still, she moved slowly and methodically in case something would trigger another episode. The last thing she needed was to pass out and spend the night out here.

Soon Adda reached the cliff edge where she paused to marvel at the wonder.

They were sheer things, running at a steep grade to beaches well below. The face of the cliff was dotted with a number of shallow depressions and caves where seagulls and other ocean birds rested for the night. Adda loved standing up here, watching them dive and flit along the currents of the air. How small she must look to them, those that were gifted the power to deny gravity.

Today, not a bird was in sight, causing Adda to frown. She looked to the left and right, scanning the horizon for the many birds that normally filled the sky with their shrill cries. As far as her eyes could reach, Adda saw not even a feather to indicate their presence.

This, along with Keith's cryptic warning, disturbed Adda. There were still plenty of people down at the beach, so the birds should have been swarming as they looked for opportunities to steal unguarded snacks or riffle through abandoned trash. Yet all seemed calm and quiet on the pearly sands, not a winged creature to interrupt the perfect day.

"Adda, stop." She whispered to herself, shaking her head in the process.

There were plenty of explanations as to why the skies were quiet. Whatever was going on, it didn't change her mission. Putting the oddities from her mind, Adda set up her easel and canvas, and then got to work.

Her easel had a drawer attached to it where she kept her brushes. She moved all the colors she'd be working with from her case to the drawer as well. This way, she wouldn't have to lean over everytime she needed to add more paint to her palette.

With everything situated, Adda began to paint the scenery before her, taking extra care to catch the finer details. The sights from the cliffs were magnificent and it was her job as the artist to bring the viewer to this very place.

She watched how the waves curled, crashed, and then dribbled onto the beach. How each structure of water bent over itself with white heads forming at their forefront. She worked the colors of deep blues and greens together to match the rich combination reflected in nature.

She saw a distant boat on the horizon, one that appeared to be a fishing vessel. With brush in hand, she pieced together its narrow frame, giving it form and depth on her two-dimensional space. She imagined the people who were hard at work upon the deck of the vessel. With every stroke, she imagined their stories, bringing deeper shades of color to the boat.

The sun had begun to sink into the ocean, preparing to bring its light to other parts of the world. From its decent, an amalgamation of deep and brilliant colors swirled together as day met night. Adda's hands acted fast, wanting to capture every ray of light even as they were giving away to velvety dark. As many times as she had seen the display, it still made her pause to marvel.

Gazing from the cliffs out to the very horizon, Adda found the gnawing hunger in her soul become satiated. The burning need to create had finally been met, allowing all her restless energy to settle down after a day of pacing in the back of her mind.

It was a magnificent scene and Adda was glad to have caught it. She glanced at the thin, gold watch on her wrist, noting the time. To her surprise, she found she had been up on the rise for hours though it had hardly felt more than half that. It wouldn't be long until the last pieces of daylight finally laid to rest, plunging Adda into darkness.

That was her cue she needed to go home.

She glanced at her handy work and paused, suddenly aware of it as if she had awoken from a long slumber.

It wasn't hers.

Well, it *was* hers in the fact that it shared Adda's style and was signed with a little, red *AR*, a signature she put on all her pieces.

It wasn't hers because there was no way she could have accidentally made such a masterpiece.

There was no ocean on the canvas, no abrupt cliffs, dipping sun, or distant ship. She had certainly painted those things, or at the very least, she *thought* she had, but the evidence before her told a different story. It was as if her hands and paints had conspired against her, putting together the piece they wanted, rather than the one her mind and eyes had told them to do.

On this canvas, the one impossible, was a scene that Adda couldn't remember ever seeing.

In the background, hulking like a great beast from myth, was a snow-peaked mountain range. One peak stuck above the rest, rising in the sky in a powerful image of stone and strength. These mammoth entities were like a great wall, taking up the background of the painting beneath a blue sky.

Under the shadow of these titans was a sprawling forest as thick as it was massive. It took up large chunks of the painting, spreading out with all manners of green trapped in its branches. They almost appeared to sway against one another, pine and leaf whispering in an impossible wind.

A field of light green rolled on where the forest ended, not stopping until it met the edge of a beautiful lake. The painting was only taken by part of these crystal waters, but Adda got the impression that the body of water was far larger than the canvas allowed in the way it widened into the bottom right corner of the picture.

This was all almost too much to take in, too strange to understand, but there was one other detail that stuck out even amidst this phenomenon.

Off to the left side of the scene was a lone hill. It rose up to overlook the valley and the lake below it. It was detailed and rugged, looking to not be an easy climb. On top of this hill was nothing more than a smudge of golden radiance.

It shone out to look like a dome, its edges fading and blurring into the background as if it were light filtering off of something. Like a star, there was a glimmer to its nature and it flickered and winked at Adda as she puzzled at its design. Whatever was at the heart of this light remained a mystery as Adda hadn't gotten to painting it yet.

The woman hovered a hand over the spot, her fingers wanting to brush against it in hopes that perhaps something would reveal itself.

"What on earth?" Adda whispered.

There was no possible way that she could have painted this. Throughout the process, she had checked on her work, ensuring the accuracy in what she was capturing. Every time she had glanced over, she had been met with the ocean scene. In the blink of an eye, in the fraction of a second, it had somehow changed.

It was impossible.

A chill ran down Adda's spine as the winds of the coming night ran against her. Goosebumps raised along her skin, causing her to shiver and wrap her arms around herself. She glanced around instinctively, an atmosphere of unease causing paranoia to begin building in the back of her mind. Everywhere she looked, shadows leered back at her, tumbling every which way from behind rock and brush alike. They almost seemed alive in their sporadic motion.

Adda took a step back, bumping against the easel. Her heart leapt as she felt it teeter and she whirled about to steady it so that the whole thing wouldn't come crashing down. Fortunately, she was able to grab ahold of it, putting its feet back to the earth as she once again looked over her handy work.

Her eyes rested upon the radiance.

For a moment, it almost looked like it was actually glowing.

And just like that, the strange moment ended. The mounting chill passed, the shadows were as mundane as they had always been, and the canvas was becoming more hidden in the fading daylight with no inner shine to suggest anything was used on it aside from normal paints.

Despite these return to normalcy, the painting retained its foreign shape, refusing to morph back into the ocean view Adda knew she had captured.

It was still unsettling, but Adda found now the fear had passed, she was more curious than anything.

"What are you?" Adda whispered to the canvas.

She willed it to answer, but no answer came.

If it was not for the mounting darkness, Adda would have stood there for hours in an attempt to decipher this mystery. With night now underway, she had no choice but to pack up her things and begin the trek home. Her mind whirled as she went about this chore, questions chasing questions round and round until Adda began to feel dizzy.

She turned then, stumbling down the trail toward the lights of her home with easel, canvas, and carrying case under arm. The town was some distance away which made it difficult to see the winding, dirt path. To Adda's relief, there must have been just enough moonlight peeking from the skies above to illuminate the way. The dirt almost shone beneath the reflected light, taking on a silvery glow. It wasn't much, but it was enough that Adda didn't trip as she drew closer to the main road.

The moment her feet touched the asphalt, Adda found herself finally beginning to relax. With the solid road beneath her feet and the brilliant street lamps warmly welcoming her home, she began to put all the eerie things from the day behind her. With every step, it was like one unsettling event would slip from her mind. They didn't quite escape her, but they buried themselves deep in the woman's subconscious, allowing for more immediate needs and wants to take their place. By the time Adda walked through her front door and fumbled blindly for the lights, she had all but forgotten it, no longer worried about whatever it is that might have happened on the cliffs.

She would deal with the strange canvas later, because as weird as it was, it didn't change much about her life.

That was one thing about this town Adda knew to always be true: nothing ever happened here.

At least-

Not yet.

3

Adda woke to a headache. It was a loud, sharp thing that beat itself against the back of her eyelids. She groaned, ramming the heel of her palms into both sockets and rubbed them in earnest. The thrumming pain continued on as it ignored her attempt to banish it.

With clenched jaw, Adda rose from her bed, keeping her eyes screwed shut as the barest amount of morning light was almost too much to bare. With hands outstretched, and moving with a a tentative shuffle, the woman moved slowly across her bedroom as she searched for the adjoining bathroom. It took but a moment for her fingers to find the frame of the door which she ran her hands along until she found the door knob.

With a twist, and a faint *click*, Adda stumbled into the next room.

She reached up instinctively, searching for the light switch though her eyes were still closed. It was a motion so often repeated that she had hardly thought of what she was doing. Her floating fingers found the switch to which she flipped on.

Immediately the room was filled with harsh light that caused Adda to groan. With a wince, she squinted from beneath heavy lids, her bloodshot eyes watering in pain. Through her lashes, Adda reached out and opened the mirror to riffle through a collection of bottles hidden there. She quickly identified the one she needed, a common painkiller to ward off the worst of this aggressive headache.

Adda left a glass of water next to her sink, one she had filled last night. It was a habit of hers to drink a cup before getting started with the day. She plucked it up and tossed the pills into her mouth before taking a long draught from the cup. The stale liquid tumbled down her throat, delivering the pills to help in the fight against whatever the source of this pain was.

She lingered there in the bathroom for awhile, leaning heavily against the door frame as she took in long, deep breaths. Adda focused all her attention on those breaths, letting each one wash away a little more of her pain. To her relief, the agony began to dissipate, slowly drifting away piece by piece until only the dullest of throbbing could be felt. Whether it was from the pills or her breathing, Adda didn't care as she was just relieved that she could get on with her day.

Now, back in control, Adda found her eyes flit to the other side of the bathroom. She paused there a moment longer, letting memories course through her.

The bathroom was built to accommodate two people, his and her sinks in a marble style countertop, and in the corner, a shower with a generous amount of tub space. There was a closet across the way, deep enough to house a plethora of towels and a pair of robes. It was a room designed with two in mind. Adda stood there, taking it all in as images of far flung days pushed the headache from her mind. For a moment, she even caught a whiff of something dancing on the air.

It smelled like aftershave, pine needles, and coffee.

Of course, the scent was just a figment of her imagination. It plagued her every so often when she was feeling nostalgic. As much as she would have liked to dwell in the moment, Adda felt the requirements of the day tug against her.

She let out a sigh and slipped back into her bedroom.

"Today is the only day." Adda whispered to herself in a rehearsed fashion. "And it is a day worth living."

After changing into more daytime appropriate clothing, Adda strode into her kitchen and began the task of getting ready for the day. A solid breakfast was part of her morning ritual and this headache be damned if it thought it could derail her tradition. Within moments, the home was filled with the smell of garlic simmering, bacon sizzling, and toast browning.

A record was selected and put into place, bringing a lighter tone to a heavy day. The music caused her to sway back and forth as she prepared her skillet for a couple of eggs. Adda's routine had helped her find a sense of peace in the face of difficulty. She wouldn't allow herself to give into self-pity. Too many people already pitied her; she didn't need one more person to be added to the list.

It was only as the toast became ready that she noticed all at once she was quite parched. The water from her bathroom hadn't quite done the trick. Without so much as a thought, the woman reached up, opened a cabinet with intersecting-lines painted on the door and pulled out a glass. She hummed softly along to the jaunty music as she turned on the tap and watched the water slowly fill. Her hand came up, bringing the cup to her lips as she took a long draught.

Immediately, Adda gagged as the liquid poured into her mouth and down her throat. It had a quality that made it flat and somewhat oily, though that was not the worst of it. The water brought with it a sour, metallic taste that assaulted her senses. It was like something had long spoiled in her pipes and had intermingled with a combination of dumped chemicals.

Whatever it was, it was foul.

She leaned over the sink and spat out what was left, her face crinkled into a look of disgust. The inside of her mouth was caked with the intrusive flavor as it had left some kind of film behind. Adda could feel it on her tongue, her teeth, and down her throat, coating it all like a thin layer of mold.

With a deft motion, Adda threw open the refrigerator door and pulled out a carton of orange juice. She unscrewed the lid and chugged down part of its contents, hoping it would rid the awful flavor and cloying ooze from her mouth. It did help a little, but the invader was not completely diminished, hanging stubbornly onto the fringes of her tastebuds.

Adda marched back into the bathroom where she seized her tooth brush. She squeezed a heavy dollop of toothpaste onto the bristles before vigorously scrubbing at the inside of her mouth. The taste of orange juice and toothpaste intermixing made Adda screw up her face, but still she brushed, trying to be free of whatever this was.

The brush was brought underneath the faucet, the water released to wet the end of the tool. It wasn't until Adda had brought it back into her mouth that she realized her mistake. The metallic taste had ridden the toothbrush like a trojan horse, leaping back into her mouth in an all out assault.

Adda once again spat out the liquid, thankful that this time she didn't swallow it. She glared down at the sink with a look that was a mixture between disgust and betrayal. It was now clear that her water was contaminated, but rather than being worried, Adda was frustrated.

It was nothing to be alarmed about, and she was already trying to figure out where to insert into her day the time to get it checked out. This was an inconvenience in the grand scope of life. One that would take time and money, but would be dealt with just the same.

With her breakfast still on the stove, and dangerously close to burning, Adda decided it would be something to handle later. Returning to the kitchen, Adda calmly set the table and arranged the food. Orange juice remained her beverage for breakfast as the water had insulted her one-too-many times.

After completing her morning ritual, Adda stacked the dishes beside her sink. She would wash them up once the water issue had been resolved. For now, they would sit there, a minor nuisance in the back of the woman's mind who tried hard to keep her home at least somewhat put together.

With that out of the way, Adda left her place and climbed into her car. She had a few errands to run which ended with her going to the grocery store. She would need to get bottled water after all. There was no telling how long it would take to get the situation resolved.

Off she went, slowly cruising through town as she made a few stops. Anytime Adda went out, she would always check up on a few projects around town to ensure they were still being maintained.

Negligence would often allow for things to fade or die, but Adda had made it her mission to push back against the quiet apathy of the world around her.

It warmed her heart to see these little flickers of life she had helped restore. Whether it was paint, plant, or simply fixing up a broken swing, the evidence of her handiwork was everywhere. In order to keep up with all the little things she held together, Adda made it a point to check up on things periodically.

Today was a good day after all as every stop made revealed little work to be done. Adda hoped it meant that someone else had noticed her work and had decided to take up the charge with her. Not that she minded doing it all by herself, it just warmed her heart to imagine someone else working alongside her to breathe life into their town.

Satisfied that everything was in order, Adda turned her sights to the grocery store.

Upon arriving, Adda found the parking lot was more packed than it normally was. People swarmed from their vehicles, moving in and out of the grocery store in droves. They looked like ants warring over a discarded meal, each side vying to take it back to their own nest.

"What on earth?" Adda muttered to herself as she pulled in, finding parking on the far reaches of the lot.

She climbed out of the car, picking up on a general sense of unease and tension. No one seemed to be in a panic, but there was certainly a nervous energy that hovered in the air. People grabbed their carts with white knuckles, their eyes flickering about suspiciously as if someone might come in and try to rob them. Adda noticed that those leaving the store were carrying cases of bottled water.

The thought momentarily disturbed Adda, but she put it away as she prepared herself to dive headlong into the throng.

Being as this was a small town, the crowds weren't that excessive, but it was still an unusual thing to brush shoulder to shoulder with others as they jockeyed to get access. Adda went with the flow of the mob, somehow managing to procure a shopping cart. She held onto it tightly, feeling others around her glancing her way as she walked through the front door.

The inside was equally a madhouse. It was as though the whole town showed up and had decided to pick the place clean. Aisle after aisle was stripped bare as greedy hands took more than necessary. There was no concern for others, no willingness to share in case someone else might go wanting, it was every man for themselves.

Adda paused at the door, watching all of this play out around her.

All this over water? Adda wondered to herself.

The fact that the whole town's water was contaminated was alarming, but not necessarily unheard of. What was truly disconcerting was the fact people were showing up to grab more than just that.

Did something else happen? Adda thought.

For now, it didn't matter, what mattered was that Adda procured water for her home. With the cases being shuttled out around her, she made haste through the store in hopes that there might be some left. She pushed against the throng of people, moving at a steady pace toward her destination.

The layout was simple and small, having all the necessities one might have to live off of in a forgotten corner of the world. They had the important pieces of produce, nothing that was unusual or out of the ordinary. There was an aisle for meats, cheeses, and other dairy products. On one side of an aisle were all the snacks one would care to find directly across from the few electronics that Keith was always trying to sell. Keith thought it was a clever strategy as teenagers were often the ones to buy snacks and electronics, so he thought by putting them all in one place it would garner more sales of either.

Then again, not many families with teenagers ever found themselves out this far in the middle of nowhere, so it was questionable if such a strategy worked at all.

Down from that aisle, there were self-care odds and ends that seemed to be all shoved into one place with little care for organization. Adda suspected that they were purposefully left like that to force people to stay in the store longer. Keith was always trying to get people to leave with more than they needed.

Adda rounded a corner, her heart falling as she laid eyes on bare shelves that should have been holding water. The aisle had all the appearance of a great beast that had been picked clean to the bone. There was nothing left, not even a sweet tea or sport drink.

It was mildly frustrating, but Adda kept her cool. If need be she could always drive to another town to get her supplies from them. This wasn't the end of the world, just a minor setback.

She began to turn her cart around when Keith popped up behind her. He was beaming at her with a look of triumph as customers poured around him. Someone was at his arm, asking if he had more bottled water in the back, but he ignored the question as he addressed Adda.

"Have you ever seen anything like it?" He asked, "We're going to have record sales for every hour of the day!"

"Glad to hear you're doing your part." Adda replied in a dry tone.

It bothered her that he seemed to be celebrating this panic. Then again, he was a business man trying to make his way through the world. It wasn't like he was taking advantage of anyone.

"What can I do you for?" Keith went on, ignoring Adda's comment.

He looked into her empty cart and tutted.

"Seems like you missed out on getting yourself bottled water." Keith said. "Missed the last case by about fifteen minutes."

"Really? Well I'm sure whoever got it needs it more than me." Adda said, "I suppose I'll just have to go elsewhere."

"You're right, you *could* do that." Keith said, a mischievous on his face.

He paused, waiting for her to ask.

"Seeing as I don't have much of an option, I think I will." Adda said, glancing at the empty shelves.

Keith just kept on beaming at her.

"Ok, just tell me already." Adda said, exasperated.

Enjoying his game, Keith chuckled and then looked around. He leaned in close, putting a hand on Adda's shoulder.

"Come with me, I'll show you something."

The proximity was uncomfortable, but before Adda could pull away, Keith had already began to stride down the aisle. There was a swagger to his step that she wasn't used to seeing. He breezed past people, greeting them as he went, but never stopping as he rushed by. Adda decided to follow him, knowing he wouldn't drop it until she had.

Her cart squeaked after him, one of the wheels loose from overuse. She navigated around the people and made her way into the back. Keith had moved through a pair of double doors that had a red plaque above it reading *Employees Only* in bold lettering. The cart rattled as Adda pushed her way through, assuming that it was Keith's intention for her to continue to follow him.

The back of the store wasn't much, just a series of hallways with a larger room for receiving. The room was gray concrete with little in the way of decoration. Across the room, a large door sat at the bottom of a low ramp, the entry way for products freshly unloaded from the delivery truck. There was some back stock, but not as much as the general public would be lead to believe. Palettes were stacked off to one side, sitting next to a large bailor that idly waited to be filled with more cardboard.

Keith was standing over a palette that sat off to one side. All it took was one look at it to realize why Keith had appeared so enthusiastic. There, stacked in row after row, was cases of bottled water.

The man patted the stack with satisfaction.

"The news kept going on and on about taking precautions, so I've been over-ordering on bottled water and such for awhile." Keith said, his voice brimming with pride. "At first, no one was buying any more than regular and I thought I was stuck with all this extra stuff for no reason."

He let out a laugh then. "Who could've guessed that this water problem would come at such a perfect time? It's my lucky day!"

"I don't think this is a good thing, Keith." Adda replied, taken aback by the man's euphoria.

"Sure it is! I wait awhile and then throw this on the shelves with an emergency markup. You know, since I had to special order more water in and all that." Keith gave her a knowing wink. "I'll be helping everyone out and making some extra money too!"

Adda felt sick.

"Are you being serious?" Adda asked, "These are our friends, our family. Are you really ok with taking advantage of them?"

This gave Keith pause, the light in his eyes sapping away as he became aware that she didn't approve. He cast a look downward and shifted uncomfortably on his feet, now unsure of himself. In a fit of inspiration, the man suddenly picked up a case of water and put it in Adda's cart.

"I was saving one for you before I put out the rest. You can have it, free of charge!" Keith smiled, his eyes searching hers.

"Thank you, Keith. I appreciate that, but I would rather buy it at the price everyone else is going to pay." Adda said. "How much will that be with the emergency markup?"

"Oh- well- there isn't one."

"One of what?"

"I- uh- I've decided to sell the water at a regular price." Keith said, his tone subdued.

He reached out and placed a hand on Adda's own.

She tensed.

"Thank you, for keeping me an honest man." Keith's voice came out low. "There aren't many women in the world like you."

"I don't know about all that." Adda replied, all too aware of how empty the back of the store was. "Thanks again for the water."

In a deft motion, Adda pulled the cart back and began to wheel it out toward the rest of the store. She walked at a quick pace, but not one that would suggest urgency. The woman got to the double doors that lead from the receiving area before turning to look back at Keith.

He was staring after her, his face lifting in hope as he saw her turn around.

"I'm going to tell the others that you'll be bringing more water out soon." Adda said. "Maybe put up a sign that says 'one per customer' or something? We're all in this together after all."

Keith just nodded, clearly disappointed, but made no effort to push anything else.

Adda then left, moving back into the light of the store beyond.

4

Adda felt the doors swing shut behind her and she quickly marched away, putting distance between herself and the strange conversation. She was shocked with what he had said to her- his *eagerness* to take advantage of the situation. He had spoken in a boastful tone as if this marked cruelty might earn him favor in her book.

Sure, there were parts of Keith that didn't click with everyone, but to be so unabashed of such wickedness? It stunned Adda.

For a moment, Adda debated going home until the world started making sense again. Everything had been out of sorts for so long that a break from it all sounded nice. It was a tempting thought, but Adda knew she couldn't just disappear. There were people and projects that relied on her.

Besides, she still needed to go grocery shopping. Hiding from the world was only appealing until the food ran out.

Keith was no doubt feeling the pressures of this weird life that they were all experiencing. He had made a mistake and Adda resolved to address the issue next time they could have a proper conversation. He was her friend and she believed it was the duty of a friend to keep one another on the straight and narrow.

With that decision made, Adda returned to her shopping.

There wasn't much in the way of groceries left, but she still managed to scrape together some basics that would tide her over for the time being. This situation would eventually be behind them, for now she and everyone else would just have to take it all one day at a time.

Adda then rounded a corner, looking for some bread, when she nearly ran into Candace Bailor.

The woman was a mother of five and also the owner of the local paper. She was always well in the know and enjoyed nothing more than expositing such information on others. If she had happened to live in a bigger place, she would have been a journalist of frightening acclaim.

Her eyes flickered down, devouring the contents of Adda's cart in a single sweep.

"Hello there, love!" Candace said, "Strange thing about this water, isn't it?"

"Yes, it's made for a crazy day," Adda replied, "but I'm confident we'll make it through one way or another."

"Well said, well said indeed." Candace replied, "I was really looking forward to a nice, long shower last night but the moment the water came out I knew something was wrong! I'm just lucky I let it heat up first, there's no telling what it would have done to my skin."

"Oh, did this all start last night?" Adda asked.

Adda thought back to her evening, trying to remember the last time she needed to use water. If she had, Adda couldn't recall if it had already been corrupted by that awful, metallic flavor.

Candace shrugged, "I've asked around a bit and it seems that's the case for most."

Abruptly, the woman turned to bark in a commanding voice at one of her children who were currently running amuck. "Spencer Allen Bailor! You put that back right now!"

The offending child made a face, pulling a package of desserts from the cart before running off with them. Adda watched him disappear around the corner, wondering if the spongy cakes were actually going to make it back to the shelf or if the staff would find the half eaten dessert at the end of the day.

Candace turned her attention back to Adda. "Anyway, I'm planning on badgering Kinsey's door until he gets to the bottom of this! Mark my words, I'll get this figured out yet!"

She was referring to one Martin Kinsey, who happened to be the Mayor of the town. He was a kind man, but one who was not quick in dealing with any kind of issues be they personal or professional. People often complained behind his back about his lack of urgency, but they all still voted him into office just the same. As frustrated as everyone was with him, the man had always held the position and no one was keen on shaking things up.

It was easier to complain about a lack of change than be the driving force behind it.

So, Candace would knock on his door, the Mayor would promise to look into it, but would secretly hope the problem would take care of itself. Adda had seen this dance play out a hundred times and could only hope that eventually, a solution would be found.

"So- want to hear something else strange?" Candace asked,

leaning in closer to Adda. "I was down at the beach with the family and we were having a little picnic. Normally you have to practically fight off the seagulls from stealing from you, but not yesterday. It took me awhile to even notice it, but it suddenly came to me and I realized something, there wasn't a bird in the sky."

Adda had noticed this, but Candace kept talking, leaving no room for her to speak.

"Then when we were headed home, I started to notice missing pet posters practically covering every light on the street! Even our little Doug has been acting out, barking like crazy and trying to escape everytime a door is opened."

Doug was their family dog, which had been named by one of their children who had meant to call the dog *Dog* but had sounded as if he was saying Doug. She was a mild mannered creature, so it was surprising to hear that she was acting in such a bizarre way.

"And if that isn't enough for you, get this! I was talking to Lawrence, you know, my cousin? Well, he does a lot of fishing and was telling me that over the last week or so that the fish have all left! That man could get a bite using a shoe string in a puddle, so the fact nothing is coming up is more than strange- it's down right unsettling. There's something going on around here and I don't like it! Not one bit!"

Candace may have said she didn't like it, but Adda could practically see the woman salivating. She lived for stories and gossip, and this was the most excitement this town had ever seen.

Candace would have kept going on, there was no doubt about that, when her face suddenly fell. It was as if she had abruptly realized who she was talking to. The woman reached out and grabbed Adda's hand, squeezing it in a manner that was supposed to be comforting. Pity flickered in her eyes.

"But enough about all that, how are you my dear? Is everything ok?"

"I'm fine, Candace, really." Adda answered.

"It's ok if you're not." Candace said.

"I know."

Candace gave Adda a knowing smile and patted her the hand in a maternal way even though Adda was definitely older than her. "Of course, of course. Well if you ever need anything, just give me a call, won't you?"

Adda promised she would and untangled herself from the conversation. As much as she seemed to mean well, Adda had learned to be cautious with this woman. There was no telling what words spoken to her might end up in black and white for their whole world to read.

After picking up a few more things and pushing through the slowly thinning crowd, Adda made her way to the front. She was standing in line with her cart when a magazine on a rack caught her eye. She reached down, gingerly lifting it from its resting place. *Learning to Laugh: A Guide to Self-Love!* the words exclaimed in a bold, red font. It was interesting to consider that out there, somewhere, a human being took the time out of their day to write down what they believed was the formula to living a happy life. The woman on the front cover smiled with dazzlingly white teeth, her makeup perfect, without a single blemish on her face.

Adda wondered if the woman on the cover had read the guide.

"Were you thinking of buying that too?" A voice broke through her reverie.

It was Jason Everett, who went by his last name since he claimed it made him seem more poetic and rugged. He stood at his register in uniform, drumming his fingers idly on the belt.

"Oh, no no, just lost in my thoughts." Adda said, loading her groceries to be checked out.

Everett began to slowly scan the items as they rolled toward him, apparently unperturbed or unaware of the panicked bustle that had lay siege to the store.

He was a young man, somewhere in his mid-twenties, and he had lived here his entire life. Most of his friends had all moved away to go to college or to at least find themselves somewhere a little more lively and entertaining. For whatever reason, Everett remained, still working the same job he had had in his high school days, living in a small apartment with two other men who shared in his lifestyle. Perhaps it was fear of what was out there or perhaps he had found his niche in life and had little interest to shake up the existence he had built. Regardless, he seemed to at least enjoy what he did, so who was anyone to judge?

"So- anything new in the world of Everett?" Adda asked.

The man grimaced, "Nah, not really. I mean- I think I've decided I want to learn guitar, so I guess there's that. I dunno, maybe start a band or something?"

"Well that sounds exciting. Do you have a guitar?"

"Nah, I mean I'm not sure if I'll really like playing it so I don't know if I want to spend the money. Ya' know?"

"Oh well, Isaiah's old guitar is in my shed. You could borrow it if you'd like; see how it feels." Adda said with a smile.

Everett blanched at this, "Oh, no thanks, I don't want t-"

"Nonsense, it's not being played anyway, so you might as well try and get some use out of it."

Everett cleared his throat, clearly a little uncomfortable, "I mean, I dunno, what if I hurt it?"

"It isn't alive, so I'm sure it won't hold a grudge if you bang it up a little." Adda said wryly, "Do you work tomorrow?"

"uh- yeah?"

"Perfect! I'll bring it by then." Adda's tone adopted an air of finality, cutting off any further protests from the young man.

After paying, Adda breezed out of the grocery store, pushing the cart to her Subaru. She was struck again with how thirsty she was, so she paused to pull out a water bottle. The drink was crisp and refreshing, a clear contrast to the revolting liquid she had choked down earlier.

Once the loading was completed, Adda checked her watch. Its tiny hands steadily moved forward, each *tick* announcing another second gone. Satisfied with the time, she got in her vehicle and slowly drove around the town.

The road she was on would eventually lead to the town center where an old clock tower stood, balefully sounding the hour. It was an ugly thing, but it gave the town a little extra character, so no one had ever dared even think about knocking it down. It was actually rumored that the designer of the Eiffel Tower had been hired to go about the task of designing this very clock tower. The legitimacy of such a story was easily disproved, but the people would not be dissuaded.

Travelers who happened to stay for any amount of time would be pressed to go stop by and look at the town's little piece of culture. For a while, the council had even tried to have the state approve the clock tower as a historical landmark, but nothing had ever come from it.

Surrounding the tower in a small ring were all the shops that were worth going to. There was a bookstore, three cafes, an ice cream parlor, a museum of haunted objects, a burger place, and a toy store. They were the oldest buildings in the town, matching the clock tower in the same architectural style. They had certainly seen better days, yet it added to the rustic feeling of the town center.

Adda thought that the area would be perfect for an old black-and-white film about begotten love or something of a similar effect. The entire area was just saturated in a profound sense of longing or regret.

The car followed the curve in the road around the clock tower, gently parading itself past the store fronts. There were a couple of patrons sitting outside of the ice cream parlor, but otherwise the whole lot seemed quiet. There was a red piece of paper in one of the cafe's windows. Some words were scrawled hastily in black on it, but Adda was too far away to make out what it was trying to convey. She assumed it was that the store was closed and didn't think anything else of it.

In fact, she wasn't far from the truth as most of the stores here had decided it would be better to shut down for the day. They had all discovered the same pungent problem with the water that Adda had hours before. Steaming a latte with foul liquid only but guaranteed a distraught customer, so the doors were shut for the day until the people in charge could advise them of the situation.

As she rolled past, Adda glanced at the clock tower.

It was time for her to head home.

The town was laid out in a grid-like fashion, which made getting around quick, if a little boring. There weren't many in the way of hidden roads or back alleys, everything was laid out matter-of-factly to allow easy access to any part of town. Perhaps, back in the day, the founders had been overly optimistic that their little corner of the world might someday turn into a thriving center of humanity rather than the near forgotten slate of land on the edge of the state.

Still, Adda enjoyed taking her meandering drives; there was something therapeutic about the houses passing by. It gave her time to just be still and let her mind tumble open, to relax into a moment of silence and solitude. Contrary to popular belief, Adda was quite content with the prospect of being alone, there was something about the way silence hung on the air when there's no one around to spoil it.

Taking a right, and passing by the one traffic light in town, Adda made her way back to her home. There, waiting on the front step, was a young girl in her early teens. She was looking down at her phone with a deeply perplexed look, clearly consumed with whatever had caught her attention. Adda pulled herself from the car, waving at the young girl.

"Bethany! Would you mind giving me a hand?" Adda yelled over to her.

Bethany started, torn away abruptly from her thoughts. Upon seeing Adda, she bounded across the cobblestone path to the older woman. There was a sheepish look on her face as she came and helped

Adda unload the groceries.

"Sorry I'm a little late." Adda said.

"That's ok, I didn't really notice." Bethany replied, snatching up a few of the bags. "I was kinda distracted."

"I saw that." Adda replied.

They crossed the yard, and unlocked the door before spilling inside. Bethany followed her into the kitchen, helping her unload and put away the groceries.

"So, what was it that you were reading?" Adda asked as the last thing was put away.

"Hm? Oh yeah, I dunno, just some article talking about how reality is just a simulation or something." Bethany twisted her hair between her fingers, gazing blankly out the window. "I dunno, it's kinda weird to think that maybe none of this is real?"

"Well there's an interesting thought. Do *you* think nothing is real?"

"I don't know, I think I'm real, just sometimes I'm not sure?"

Adda laughed at this, "You're not sure if you're real?"

"I mean, what even *is* 'real'?"

"Well ok." Adda said, realizing the girl was being serious. "How about this, if it were to rain while you were outside, what would happen to you?"

"I'd get wet?" Bethany answered, seeming unsure.

"It's not a trick question. Yes, you'd get wet. So why does that happen?"

"Because, water is wet?" Bethany said slowly.

"Exactly! Water is wet and it will alway be that way regardless if you're there to experience it. Even if you were to argue that it's not real, you'd still dry yourself off to not catch a cold. Doesn't that make it real enough?" Adda said, "Do you see what I'm saying?"

"So, like, you think because we experience all this stuff," Bethany waved a hand about to indicate what "stuff" she was talking about, "it makes it real?"

"I'm saying there's constants in the universe that don't care whether we believe in them or not, they're going to continue existing regardless."

"Ok, so what about stuff that you can't see or touch, or whatever? Do you think any of that kind of stuff is real?" Bethany pressed.

"Are you asking if I believe in ghosts?" Adda asked, arching an eyebrow as a smile teased at her lips.

"Yeah, I guess."

"How do I put this? Ok, so we live in and experience the physical world everyday. We have to take care of ourselves in order to continue to survive. To that extent, the physical stuff *is* real because whether we deny it or not, it will inevitably affect us." Adda walked to a closet and pulled out a couple of canvases, handing one to Bethany. "But I don't think that what's real just stops there. I think there's something deeper to it, something a little more unknowable."

Adda stopped then, turning to Bethany. The girl just returned a blank look, waiting for the woman to go on. Adda gestured to her canvas and paints as she continued to unpack the thought.

"It's like if I painted a picture and suddenly the scene came to life. To them, that life is actually real, but what they're unaware of is that their entire existence is on my canvas. They would live out their days as a reflection of our world. It would still be real, they would still have life, but it would be a shadow compared to our world."

"A world of shadows." Bethany said solemnly.

The girl now regarded her own canvas with a grave look. It seemed the teen had taken Adda's example a bit too literally.

"That's kind of a dramatic way of saying that, but yes, I suppose it would be." Adda replied.

"What do you think would happen if someone living in a painting got into our world?" Bethany asked, clearly taken by the idea.

Adda narrowed her eyes as she regarded her student, "You sure are full of questions today. Are you just trying to put off the lesson?"

Bethany flushed, "No! I was just wondering."

"Mm, I'm sure. Let's stow the questions for now, your parents are paying me to teach you art, so we should at least show them that we're using their money wisely. Yeah?" Adda walked across the kitchen and pulled out another easel.

She set it up alongside the other while Bethany unpacked her bags of her own supplies. Once they were set up, Adda began to show Bethany different techniques on her canvas before prompting her student to do the same. They talked colors and brushes and pulled inspiration from other artists as they worked. Adda looked on as the young girl fumbled through each instruction, pulling it together into her own, unique style.

Adda had known Bethany since she was a baby, having been friends with her parents for a long time. The adults used to get together every week to play board games, drink coffee, and just generally enjoy one another's company. It had been awhile since they had last all gotten together like that and Adda found herself missing those moments with the couple.

Once Bethany had gotten older and began to express interest in art, her parents had immediately called up Adda. They hired the woman to be their daughter's tutor, paying her a sum that was far too large for the level of classes she was teaching. Adda insisted that she would do such a thing for free, but the parents would not have it, refusing to back down until she caved.

Adda sometimes wondered if the couple had set these lessons up to actually help her or if it was out of guilt from not knowing how to come alongside an old friend. Honestly, a phone call every once-in-a-while would have sufficed, but Adda wasn't upset. She treasured these moments with the aspiring artist.

And so, Adda and Bethany sat side-by-side for the last few years, getting together twice a week to work on Bethany's technique and form. The girl was improving rapidly, and Adda was looking forward to introducing more complex lessons to the girl as she mastered the style.

Bethany let out a sudden sound of frustration.

"Why am I so bad at this?"

Adda put down her own brush, looking at Bethany's painting. Sure, there were some flaws, some strange and accidental choices in perspective that made the scene somewhat distorted. Even with that in consideration, it was a marked improvement from when she had first started learning to master the brush.

"For one, you're not as bad as you think you are." Adda answered, rising, "You also haven't been painting for very long. Give it time."

"I wish I was just good at it already." Bethany said with somewhat of a sulk.

"I guess that would be pretty convenient." Adda laughed, "But anything worth having in life is worth working for. The journey helps you appreciate the destination."

"That's dumb." The teenager snarked.

This pulled another chuckle from Adda. She always appreciated how up front Bethany was with everything that went on in her mind. It was a welcome change of pace.

"Yeah, life is pretty dumb, but trust me, working for it is far more satisfying in the long run. Every mistake, every mishap, every obstacle you've overcome becomes the brush you use. Your style, your skill, and your unique flair are composed of every trial you've beaten in the pursuit of life." Adda reflected on her own journey, remembering how it all was at the beginning. "To just be handed it makes the thing lose its luster. You'll come to appreciate it more if you take the time to master it."

"Is this one of those life lessons you're hiding in an art lesson?" Bethany asked, wrinkling her nose.

"Have I really become that predictable?"

"You always kinda were."

Adda rolled her eyes, but was still smiling, "My point is, your older self will benefit and appreciate the work you put in here and now. You've come a long way since you first started. Trust me, just give it time."

Bethany let out another sigh. "I guess, still kinda dumb though."

Adda looked at the girl, watching the youth as she worked. The girl's face was screwed into one of deep concentration, her lips pursed as she attempted to paint a gentle curve onto the canvas before her. Some loose strands of hair danced around her face, which Bethany would routinely reach up a hand to shoo away, only to get the paint from her fingers tangled into the strands. Adda marveled at how quickly time had passed them by. It seemed like it was only yesterday that Bethany had been a cooing baby laying in Adda's arms. Now she was a whole person, full of thoughts, hopes, and dreams.

They worked for a while longer before it came time for Bethany to head home.

"Can I ask you a question?" Bethany asked as she helped clean up.

"Nothing's really stopped you before." Adda replied.

"Yeah well, it's just kinda personal."

"Ok, shoot."

"Do you ever get lonely?"

The question drew Adda up short, causing her to freeze in place for a moment. Of all the things to ask, Adda certainly wasn't expecting that kind of question. It's not that it bothered her at all, it just wasn't the sort of thing most people would ask given the circumstance.

Adda's moment of hesitation flustered Bethany, who went back to rapidly tidying up. "I'm sorry, that was dumb."

"No, it's ok." Adda said and she reached over to place a hand on Bethany's back, pulling her attention away from her task. "No one's asked before so I think you just took me by surprise."

Bethany hesitated again, her face flushed with shame. Glancing up, the girl spoke again.

"Sometimes I just hear my parents talk and I couldn't help but just wonder and I'm really really sorry!" The words tumbled out of the girl, running together as she tried to excuse herself again.

"Hey, it's ok, I'm not upset that you asked." Adda gave Bethany a consoling smile. "To answer you though, no, I don't get lonely."

"Why not?"

Adda paused for a moment, reflecting back on her past as she considered the young girl's question. The answer was so simple on the surface, and yet it had a complexity to its depths that could only be grasped by understanding the inner workings of her life. There certainly was not enough time in a day to unpack all of that.

"There's more to a person than their circumstance or outside appearance." Adda answered slowly. "Life is difficult and some days are harder than others. With that said, I still have people."

"I guess I'm just trying to understand how you do it." Bethany said.

"By taking life just one step at a time." Adda replied. "It also helps when you know where you're going."

With that they returned to cleaning and soon everything was packed away and ready to go. As much as Adda didn't mind being by herself, she often wished that their lessons could go on for longer. She enjoyed Bethany's company and the conversations they had.

Adda walked the girl to the door and gave her a hug.

"Also, how can I be lonely when I have such an awesome painting buddy?" Adda said while they embraced.

For a brief moment, Adda felt her heart wishing that she had had a daughter. What would it be like to have moments like this everyday? She pushed the feeling away, taking solace in the fact that she could at least be involved in this girl's life.

"You never answered my other question." Bethany said as she pulled away from the embrace.

"Which one was that?" Adda asked.

"You know, the one about a person from the shadow world coming out of their painting into our world." Bethany explained. "What do you think would happen if they just popped in one day?"

"Well, I think it would be pretty overwhelming at first." Adda said. "I imagine that our world would have a lot of things in it that they'd have a hard time understanding. In the end though, I think they'd figure it out, maybe even learn how to live a life here."

Bethany made a contemplative face at Adda's response, but made no further inquiries. Instead, the teen said her goodbyes before she turned around to step down the stoop and cross the yard. She pushed through the white gate at the end of the walkway before giving Adda one, last wave. Every time she left, Adda would offer to drive the girl, but she always politely refused, as her home was only a couple of blocks away and she liked the walk.

One of the advantages of everyone in town knowing everyone else is that one didn't have to worry too much about walking home alone. Adda was never truly comfortable letting the girl go her own way as she had been raised in places with much higher populations and was ushered far more warnings about the dangers of being alone on the streets. However, Bethany would not budge and so Adda let her go, watching her disappear down the block and around the corner. Sometimes she was tempted to hop in her car and make sure the girl made it home safely, but decided that might come across as a little creepy to the teen.

Today, while standing on the porch watching that small figure with the bright, yellow backpack disappear from view, Adda was struck with an odd sensation; It was a feeling of deep nostalgia tented with an ominous finality. Perhaps it was in the sudden chill that crept down her spine despite the warm summer sun above. Perhaps it was in the quiet that blanketed her neighborhood even though it was the perfect day to be outdoors.

Whatever the cause, Adda decided to not dwell on it. She turned about, grabbing the handle of her front door and began to pull it open. With the door only half ajar, the woman suddenly paused. There, tugging against the back of her mind, the Certainty once again prompted her to action.

Adda let the door slip from her hand as she followed the sensation. It led her down the steps and around the side of her home. There, she pushed through the gate that went to her backyard. She followed the cobbled path toward the shed, walking by blooming flowers and plump strawberries. They sighed with her passing, oblivious to the change in the air.

Reaching the smaller building, Adda quickly pushed the door open which groaned in response. She made a mental note to come back out and grease the hinges, but that would have to wait until tomorrow. Today, she just stood in silence, letting her eyes rove over the walls.

There was a whole life in here, neatly organized and stored so that one would have easy access to the place. On every shelf and on every wall were many objects that each played upon her memories. Adda shook her head and powered into the shed. This was not the time to reminisce, she was here to get one thing and didn't want to be distracted.

Walking past an old, beautiful guitar, a workbench with an assortment of tools, and more than one tackle box, she approached the far wall. Reaching up, she pulled out a small, wooden box with a tiny symbol carved into the top. Her finger traced the symbol that was indented there. It had been run smooth by the motion countlessly performed over the years, the oil in her skin making the once rough edges meld near seamlessly into the surrounding wood.

With the small ritual done, she pulled off the lid of the box, revealing a book within. It was a tome, leather bound and certainly well loved. The sight of it brought comfort to her, pushing back the onslaught of unease that had been haunting her since yesterday. Adda wasn't quite sure why she had felt such an overpowering need to come get the old book, but she wasn't questioning it.

Replacing the lid, Adda turned and began to walk from the shed. As she reached the doorway, she hesitated, turning back to see what had caused her to stop. Her eyes fell once again onto the guitar, sitting unplayed for so long in its dusty corner.

Approaching it, Adda ran a finger across the strings. The sound that echoed forth was rich, but definitely out of tune. That would need to be fixed. Remembering her promise to Everett, Adda picked up the guitar in one hand and cradled the box under her arm.

Satisfied that she had what she needed, Adda turned and left the shed, making sure to secure the door behind her. Walking back across the yard, Adda was once again struck with a strange sense of foreboding. There was something inside of her that roamed about restlessly. It tried to communicate something, but it just came out as a nervous energy that set the woman on edge.

Adda was halfway across the yard when she pulled to a stop as a dizzy spell rushed through her head. She screwed her forehead together, willing away the awful sense of vertigo that was suddenly crashing against her. Fortunately, it only lasted a moment, but had left her a gift in its wake.

Adda found that she was exhausted in its passing. It was as if it had reached in and snatched away every last drop of energy. A great fatigue seeped into her bones and muscles, settling in with a weight that threatened to drag her to the ground. To make matters worse, a thick fog had rolled onto the banks of her mind, making it progressively more difficult to think.

The world became muffled and muted as her eyes grew heavy. Everything felt distant, as though it were all an endless dream. So taken by the episode, Adda almost fell over, letting her body succumb to gravity.

The sensation of almost falling made the woman jerk her head up, regaining a semblance of control as she came somewhat back to herself.

Realizing she was just swaying in her yard, Adda stumbled toward her house. It was hard to focus on anything at all and each step threatened to pitch her over. Her head swam, her body ached, and her eyes blurred. There was certainly something wrong with her, but it was hard to muster the energy to even be afraid.

Upon getting to the door, Adda pried a finger loose from the guitar to turn the knob and pushed her way into the kitchen. As gently as she could, Adda laid the guitar on the table so that she wouldn't forget it next time she left the house. The instrument was beautiful to look at, custom made for an artist who appreciated both appearance and function. She stood there for a moment, staring blankly at the craftsmanship before her.

The fog pressed in around her mind which caused her to zone out. The guitar was fascinating to stare at, and she wanted nothing more than to hear it sing again. Her eyes drooped a moment, startling the woman back to wakefulness.

How long have I been standing here? Adda thought, alarmed.

Her eyes swept to the time displayed on the microwave, but the blurry numbers were too hard to make out. Now thoroughly convinced something was wrong, Adda walked urgently from the kitchen toward her bedroom. The going was tough since every step she took felt like her feet were incased in concrete. Still clutching the box, Adda pushed the bedroom door open, flicking on the light as she did so.

Walking as fast as she could across the carpeted floor, Adda stepped into adjoining the closet. She grabbed a purse off of a hook and brought it back into the bedroom. In a motion that was far more careless than the woman normally was, she upended the handbag. Its contents spilled out onto the carpeted floor where they bounced and rolled away, lost to the recesses of the room.

Once that task was complete, the box with the book inside was gingerly placed within the purse's confines. With utmost care, Adda closed the purse and held it close to her chest. She let in a few, shaky breaths, hoping that it might clear her mind.

It was no use.

The exhaustion finally hit its final blow and Adda felt the last of her energy get sapped away. The march from the shed had drained her every reserve, leaving her empty. Adda tightened her grip on the handbag as if this would help ward off whatever was happening to her.

Another wave of vertigo made her slump into her bed. She tried to will herself into clamoring under the blankets to stave off a growing chill, but found even that to be too difficult of a task. A small part of her brain fluttered in panic like a bird caught in a trap. Even then, the woman could not find the energy to even rise to the fear, instead feeling it slide from her mind.

Her eyes flicked to the window and though sunlight still poured through unabated, the light itself seemed a muted thing, lacking a luster that an artist's eye was used to viewing. Before she could dwell on the thought anymore, Adda was blessedly taken to sleep, still gripping her purse to her chest.

5

Knock knock knock

A pounding sound rattled through Adda's dreamless slumber, causing her to stir. The ruckus also roused a building headache that crashed against the side of her mind, making it hard to think. Her eyes flickered open, only to squint against the harsh light that slipped between her curtains.

How long was I asleep? Adda thought, her mind still taken by a heavy fog.

Another series of heavy knocks pounded out, rattling against the front door with a force that demanded she answer immediately. There was a mixture of impatience and urgency in it, which pulled Adda to her feet. The movement sent a spike of pain piercing through her brain, which caused her to groan and clutch the sides of her head. There had been a number of headaches over the last few days, but this one was far worse.

It certainly didn't help that whoever was knocking continued their racket with gusto.

With a great deal of effort, Adda pulled herself up and winced as a wave of dizzying nausea rolled over her. She swayed there in the middle of her room, trying not to become overwhelmed with the intense vertigo. Once the room stopped spinning, she tried to make her escape.

But before she could make it to the front door, Adda ducked into the bathroom, falling to her knees in front of the toilet and retching up what little she had eaten before passing out. There wasn't much to release, so the poor woman could only heave as someone continued right on knocking.

After what seemed an eternity, the knot in her stomach loosened enough that Adda felt she could risk leaving the toilet. One foot after the other, she pulled herself up next to the sink. She grimaced as the taste of bile filled her mouth.

Adda grabbed some mouthwash and her toothbrush, deciding whoever was at her home would have to wait for her to pull herself back together. She went about her business, trying to rid the taste from her mouth as she brushed vigorously against her teeth and tongue. Once that deed was done, Adda grabbed some medication from the cabinet. After turning on the sink, she used one hand to act as a cup to scoop enough water to her mouth to swallow down the small pills.

From the foggy depths of Adda's mind, it struck her that the water no longer held the metallic flavor from the day before. Even the awful, cloying sensation didn't coat the inside of her mouth. She hadn't even thought about it while brushing her teeth, but she was relieved to find that one thing had returned to normal.

The woman eyed herself in the mirror, noticing that she had fallen asleep in her clothing from the day before. They were a little wrinkled but not completely unpresentable. Her hair was a bit of a mess too and so Adda reached for her brush in order to remedy the issue. The knock came again, even more incessant this time as the visitor became agitated with being left waiting. Adda glanced again at her reflection, suddenly aware of her own silly behavior.

If someone was at her door like this, it had to be an emergency of some kind. Putting herself back together would have to wait for now.

Adda gave the crazy lady in the mirror a wry smile. People in the town already thought of her as a bit of an oddity, maybe building her legend wouldn't be so bad. With that, the woman went to the front door to find what was so important for someone to linger so long in front of her home. Adda pulled open the door, preparing herself for all manner of possibilities, and yet somehow, managed to still be caught completely off guard.

A stranger stood with fist raised, startled by her sudden appearance. Adda was also startled, her confusion turning to one of fear as she took in the person before her.

The figure was dressed head-to-toe in a futuristic looking hazmat suit. It was composed in a thick, white fabric that ended in a pair of heavy gloves and boots. Around the top, the suit became a wide hood to easily surround the figure's head on all sides. On the front part of the hood, where the person's face ought to have been, was a large, tinted visor that hid away any details behind its blackened surface.

Adda stared at that faceplate, seeing her own astonished face reflected back at her. The person's suit looked almost like an astronaut's own. It was a strange thing to see in such a quiet town so many months from halloween.

"Y-yes?" Adda managed to sputter out to the alien figure.

"Ma'am," Came a clipped and deep voice, "Is there anyone else living on the premises?"

"No, it's just me."

He nodded his head, satisfied with her answer.

"I'm here to inform you that we are evacuating the town. It is of utmost importance that you leave immediately."

"W-what?" Adda asked, still confused, "What's going on?"

"The area is contaminated, you must leave immediately. The longer you stay, the greater you put yourself at risk."

"How do I kn-" Adda's question died on her lips.

So focused on the strange man, Adda had yet to notice the chaos that was spiraling around her. Even as she became aware of it, there was a part of her that struggled to comprehend it. It all seemed impossible, like some kind of nightmare from which she couldn't wake from.

Up and down the street, suited figures were ushering people from their homes. People that she had known her whole life. They had stricken looks on their faces; one of worry and fear, like sheep who had just heard a wolf lay among them. Some carried a few possessions with them, most went with just the clothes on their back.

White vans with an official looking logo that Adda didn't recognize drove up and down the street. Some of the vehicles were parked wherever they could find space, their doors open with figures swarming around them like bees in a hive. The figures carried all manner of equipment from the bellies of the vehicles to various locations. They rushed about, plugging in wires, setting up terminals, and waving around hand-held objects with little screens that flashed an ominous red.

To her surprise, Adda saw that some of the figures were even outfitted with rifles and other combat equipment. They were positioned on street corners and next to the vans. Though they didn't point their weapons at anyone, the fact that they were even holding them put her on edge.

But that wasn't the end of the nightmare.

Adda's mouth hung open as she saw, further up the street, an actual tank parked partly on someone's lawn. The military vehicle had its great barrel pointed in her general direction. Out of everything else going on, the resting tank with its instrument of death staring her down was the thing Adda found the most unsettling. Even in this scene of alien chaos, it stood out as a marker that something very wrong had happened.

"What do I need to do?" Adda asked, turning to the man on her stoop for instruction.

Even though she couldn't see his face, her question made him visibly relax. She got the sense that he had been preparing for a fight but was relieved to find her more than cooperative.

"You need to leave immediately. Take the road out East. We have an outpost set up for refugees in the next town over. We'll get you tested and sorted there. Don't stop to pack, you've gotta go right now." The man reached out and put an arm on her shoulder. "Don't worry, Ma'am, you're going to be ok."

"I need to get my keys." Adda said. "I'll be right back!"

Adda whipped around and disappeared back into her house. Her heart pounded in her chest and a rushing sound filled the space between her ears. Her body shook with the sudden influx of energy fueled by the fear of the unknown. The headache still rattled against her, but this burst of adrenaline fended off the brunt of it.

As her body went into survival overdrive, Adda's mind began to scramble for understanding in the midst of all the insanity. Already, all manner of half-baked possibilities vied to occupy the center of her focus. Adda forced herself to stop a moment and take in a deep breath. There was too much going on right now and she didn't have time to analyze everything. She would save her questions for the professionals down the road.

For now, she had to get out.

Adda went into the bedroom and marched to the bedside table where she kept all her keys in a small, glass dish. In a deft motion, she scooped them up before rapidly moving from the room. It was as she was about to step through the doorway that Adda hesitated.

There was that nagging again, that Certainty in the back of her mind. It gave her pause and caused her to turn back toward the bed. There, lying in the middle of the comforter, was the purse she had brought with her to bed. From her vantage, Adda could see the outline of the box she had retrieved from out of the shed. She had been overwhelmed with the importance of keeping it close, and though she hadn't really understood why at the time, Adda had complied.

Is this the reason? Adda thought to herself.

Without another moment of hesitation, she snatched the purse up and looped it over her neck to let it rest on her side. The box gently bumped against her, bringing a flutter of comfort to her heart. Now she was ready to go.

The man was gone by the time she went back out the front door, perhaps confident that she had understood the gravity of the situation. The true reality of what was happening was still a mystery, but the man's cryptic warning had done the job. Adda practically ran to her car, ready to put all this madness behind her.

She was tempted a number of times to stop and check on her neighbors or to interrogate the suited figures that were running around. She already had so many questions that slowly burned themselves into her mind. Yet, as tempted as Adda was, the woman didn't stop.

She didn't want to play at being detective at the expense of someone else. Whoever it was that was evacuating them seemed to have the situation under control. Adda knew that she would just get in the way if she tried to hang around. Better to keep moving and then touch base with everyone once everything had settled.

With those things in mind, Adda drove as quickly as she dared toward the edge of town.

Normally, leaving town was easy enough as there wasn't much in the way of traffic. Today, however, it had become a tedious ordeal. An entire population suddenly uprooted and forced to move with very little foresight was not one that moved quickly.

To make matters worse, tension was high as each vehicle vied with one another to get further up the road. There would be a momentary break where people would compete to get around each other only to slow down again after gaining a mere couple of feet. It was a slow chaos that boiled like a pot ready to overflow.

Above it all, there was a low buzz of uncertainty, a restrained panic. Never having to face such a thing before no one really knew how to react. As such, each became increasingly more aggressive and angry with every slight inconvenience. Horns blared almost constantly and would have frightened the birds away if they hadn't already all left.

In the defense of the people, they had gone to bed in a normal world only to be roused into a waking nightmare. There was no way or reason to prepare for such a thing as such a thing shouldn't happen. Feeling desperate and lost, every car had radios blasting and smartphones searching in an attempt to find answers. Yet, regardless of the platform, it all led back to a single, calm voice that encouraged everyone to get out as quickly and safely as possible. Through it all, the broadcast kept reminding people that the situation was under control.

Adda sat behind the wheel of her car, watching the creeping insanity roll around her. She felt oddly removed from it all as if this whole event was happening to someone else entirely. The woman had the impression that perhaps she shouldn't be driving in such a state, but made no effort to stop. Finger tips drummed on her steering wheel in an idle motion and her other hand fiddled with radio. It was like her brain was on vacation, leaving her body in restless autopilot.

It did cross Adda's mind that perhaps she was in shock, but that did little to change her course. The man back on her front stoop had told her where to go and so she would go. The fog swirled in thicker around her mind, blotting out all her thoughts until all she could do was focus on the car right in front of her. It was hard to even comprehend anything else as all the world began to melt into itself. Soon, she was driving through a tunnel of colors that all smeared and melded seamlessly into one another.

And all she could do was drive.

Adda couldn't have said how long she was in this strange twilight state. It could have been minutes, it could have been hours. Honestly, she wouldn't have been surprised to find out that days had somehow slipped by, but eventually the fog began to abate. Like coming up for air after being underwater for too long, Adda gasped as her mind snapped back into reality.

She quickly assessed what was going on around her, trying to piece together the picture of what she had missed.

Behind her, the town was already beginning to vanish, and she was startled to see that a heavy cloud of black smoke was smeared across the otherwise perfect skyline. It was as if someone had shoved their hand into a pail of black paint and ran it across a detailed canvas to ruin the careful work that had been put into it. The smear oozed and crawled across the sky like it was alive. Adda could almost taste the beast's acrid scent.

Along the road in front and behind her was a long line of cars. They honked and drove much too close together as the single lane road did little to accommodate the mass exodus. She was caught between a battered gray van and a sleek sedan. The names of the drivers popped up in her head and she was struck by a feeling of profound sadness.

Here was an entire populace, one in which everyone knew everyone else. They had all shared pieces of their lives with one another, they had all built memories together. With very few exceptions, there was not a stranger among them on this road. These were all families and friends, yet in the midst of this crisis, it was as though all those things were forgotten.

Gone were the years of bake sales, Sunday schools, dances, social events, and beach days. What replaced them was just a raw panic that changed familiar faces into those of an enemy. Anyone who got in the way of survival had suddenly become an obstacle.

The van behind let out a long, whining honk that sounded too high-pitched and comical coming from such a lumbering beast. A few other vehicles honked in response, as if any of this extra noise would help make the line move along faster. They didn't even understand what they were really fleeing from, but that hardly mattered at all.

Adda sat in silence, staring out the front windshield of her car toward the sedan ahead of her. She saw the silhouette of a man wearing a large brimmed hat who kept reaching up an arm and wiping incessantly across his brow with a nervous frequency. He sat rigid at the wheel, his shoulders tight, his head pivoting anxiously about, and a steady stream of sweat beading on his forehead.

She knew this man, he was Charles Cauldwer, owner of the children's toy store in the town center. He was a self-proclaimed inventor, his specialty was making whimsical little bubble machines. He was normally a man of quick cheer with quite an enthusiastic set of lungs, which Adda supposed was necessary when your job had you frequently working with children. Through the window, Adda saw that his cheer and gusto for life was gone, replaced instead by the same feeling that permeated the air everywhere she looked.

Fear.

She glanced into her rearview mirror again, locking eyes momentarily with the driver of the van. Scott Perkinson, an auto-shop worker, sat next to his wife, Lily, a stay-at-home mom. His eyes were as wild as they were wide, the panic being deflected by pure anger and frustration.

One side of his face was shiny and purple from what looked like a heavy hit. Blood trickled down to his jaw, evidence that it was fresh. Lily sat hunched against the door, leaning away from her husband as she cradled a child in her lap, her red and puffy eyes leaking a steady stream of tears. Behind them, Adda could make out the shapes of their other children buckled in, fingers clenching anxiously to seat belts and chairs. Their vehicle was filled with angry shouting and children sobbing, all of them filled with the uncertain fear of what had just happened to them.

Adding to the noise, their radio blared out the same repeated message over and over again, telling people to remain calm. Lily cried for the radio to be shut off, Scott roared for their children to shut-up so he could hear what the voices from the radio were saying. Not that hearing the carefully sculpted words for the thousandth time would offer any kind of solace in the madness.

Scott's mouth twisted into a hateful grimace once his eyes locked with Adda's, and after yelling something that was undoubtedly unpleasant, he slammed once again on his horn in frustration. Those eyes didn't see Adda Reinhoff, they saw an obstacle that was keeping a man and his family from safety. Perhaps on a different day, Adda would have been irritated, if not angry by Scott's aggressive behavior. Today, she just felt a deep, saddening ache for the couple so consumed with fear that they had lost themselves to the moment of panic.

Her eyes went back to the front, still somehow calm. The thought of being in shock crossed her mind again, but Adda pushed it back. She didn't think she was in shock, she had experienced truly traumatic things in her life before and had felt much different. Being evacuated in such a manner was jarring, but Adda didn't consider it the worst thing that had ever happened to her.

No, this was something else. The Certainty within her rose up as if to assure her of that fact.

Though she was comforted, there was still a streak of sadness in this feeling, a knowledge that something bigger than they could possibly understand was happening at that very moment. There was a kind of finality that seemed to float in the air around her, promising the beginning of one thing at the expense of another thing ending. Adda wondered if anyone else felt it too.

Soon, traffic began to pick up as the road broadened to allow for more vehicles to drive all at once. Cars began to dip out of line, trying to jockey for position in the available lanes. It was a miracle that an accident didn't occur within the first few moments of this change. The vehicles that had escaped the long line began to whip past Adda's car at speeds much too high. They were all racing to get to the next town over, acting as though getting there first even mattered.

Adda just went along, driving the speed limit as if it were any other day, ignoring the honking and gestures flung at her from cars racing by. Her heart beat in her chest at a regular tempo and her hands rested leisurely on the steering wheel. Though she was surrounded on all sides by the unknown, Adda didn't panic.

The Certainty kept her grounded.

The town was now far behind her, swallowed up from sight by the shifting scenery. Only the smokey blot on the skyline remained, but even it was beginning to fade. The life she had built, the only one she had ever really cared for, was now behind her. Adda had no way of knowing when she would next see her home, but even that fear rolled off of her.

The Certainty kept her grounded.

With a hand, Adda reached over to the purse that was now placed on the passenger side. While keeping her eyes on the road, she undid the flap and reached into the space beyond, searching for the box. Her fingers quickly found it lying snuggly within. She traced over the indented symbol, feeling the edges of it and drew her confidence from it. Whatever life threw her way, Adda would be ready for it.

Because the Certainty kept her grounded.

6

Eventually the other townsfolk had all zoomed around Adda's little Subaru. One by one they slipped into the distance until they were all simply gone. Their cars would turn around a bend or cross over a hill and once Adda passed it by, she would find that they were no longer anywhere to be seen. It was as if the world had simply snatched them up, leaving not a piece of evidence behind.

The road weaved ever onward, twisting between green hills and passing through quiet forests. Without the constant honking or shrieking insults, silence now permeated everything, broken up only by the low growl of Adda's vehicle passing it by. A serenity was rolling from all around, a calmness that came from an open road. The morning, and all the fear it had brought, seemed a lifetime away now as the natural beauty occupied the woman's mind.

She maintained her speed, never going much faster than what the limit declared was acceptable. There was a rhythm in motion and Adda was finding herself immensely enjoying the trip. It wasn't every day that she got to get out like this, so she wanted to savor it. There would certainly be problems at the other end of this road and because of that, Adda wasn't about to rush herself.

Around the next bend, the sprawl of nature was finally interrupted. Breaking out in the midst of a decent size of acreage was a stately farmhouse and a beautiful barn. They made a scenic pair underneath a baby blue sky with cotton candy clouds. This idyllic spot wasn't just known for being beautiful, it had also become quite famous in the local area for having the best apples one could pick.

Adda had visited the place many times over the years. The apples were delicious, the company was welcoming, and there always seemed to be an endless supply of hot cider that would be passed out in styrofoam cups. It was one of the more magical places to visit, so whenever their doors were open to the public, Adda would always find her way there.

Without thinking much of it, she swept her eyes over the scene, memories playing out in her head.

And then she glanced over it again.

Adda squinted and hunched over her wheel, trying to get a closer look as she drove by. There was something off about the buildings, but she couldn't quite put her finger on what it was. An eerie feeling trickled down her spine, causing her to shiver in response. In this normally familiar place was now a sensation of wrongness.

Had she not been driving, Adda would have quickly pieced it together but at her current speed, she only had a narrow window to observe the home. Within moments, the road snatched the property away from her, sending it into her rearview mirror. Though it rapidly vanished from sight, Adda could not shake the strange feeling that visited her. She had half a mind to turn around and investigate, but the memory of the suited man giving her orders kept her on track.

What she had seen, but not comprehended, were a hundred tiny things that all cried out that something was amiss. Like, how the once nearly cherry red barn had become sun bleached and dull. Or like how the massive bales of hay were showing signs of extreme decay, slowly collapsing into blackened husks. Or the fences that had been erected to keep in cattle had all but fallen apart.

The farmhouse itself also showed signs of neglect. Grime had collected in the windows, barring light from entering into its presumably dusty halls. The siding had become broken in places, leaving behind long scars in the walls. The beautiful, front porch sagged in the middle as the once polished wood fell victim to insects, water, and age. The thing had been reduced to a corpse, left to slowly rot and fall into itself.

But even more ominous than these was the total lack of life.

There were no chickens running around or cows lowing from their paddock on the hill. There were no ravens perched on the power lines nor on the precipice of the barn. The three big dogs that could normally be seen on the front porch, bathing in the summer sun, were nowhere to be found. The entire property was utterly abandoned.

Though Adda hadn't truly taken in the whole scene, her subconscious had absorbed every detail. Now all these tiny factors slid around in the back of her mind causing a bloom of anxiety to spring up in her chest. Icy claws sank into her and Adda found herself glancing more frequently into her mirrors. Her foot rested heavier on the accelerator and her hands gripped the wheel with intensity. She tried to quell her rising fear, but it wouldn't abate.

Then another horrifying realization struck.

Her eyes went wide as thoughts raced through her head, the sheer impossibility of it making her vision swim. In a state of near panic, Adda slammed on the brakes and pulled her car over to the side of the road. The car groaned with the sudden maneuver, protesting such mistreatment. Ignoring it, the woman threw open the door and stepped out into the summer sun, looking back down the road in confusion. The question in her eyes searched the winding asphalt, trying to divine an answer.

No answer was found.

With the car still rumbling softly and keys left in the ignition, Adda walked briskly up a nearby hill. Her feet pushed into the soil as they sought purchase on the uneven grade. The going was far from easy, yet she somehow managed to make her way to the top.

After summiting the precipice, Adda gazed back over where she had just come from, her shoulders tight and her jaw clenched as she flicked her eyes back and forth. No matter where she looked, all she could see were more and more hills spilling out in every direction. They seemed eternal with nothing to break the monotony of their emerald waves.

Atop the hill, Adda was suddenly made aware of how deep the silence actually was. Normally there was the white noise whispering behind the veil of quiet, a reminder of all the life that surrounded her. The white noise was absent here, having been consumed by a silence so complete, it was maddening. If it wasn't for her car's engine still sputtering from down below, there wouldn't be a single sound to hear.

Now aware of it, Adda could do nothing to ignore it. Her mind scrambled to understand, but understanding couldn't be found. The silence pressed against her on all sides, clenching tighter and tighter as if to squeeze the life from Adda. Suddenly feeling extremely exposed atop the hill, the woman turned about to return to her car.

Scrambling back down, Adda climbed into the vehicle and sat behind the wheel. Her foot brushed against the gas, making the car growl as it reminded her that she was still in park. Adda stared blankly ahead, her foot still fiddling with the pedals beneath her feet. Still, she did not throw the car into gear.

It was impossible.

All of this had to be impossible. The choking silence had chased her down the hill, but it hadn't been the reason for the woman to stop. It hadn't been why she'd clambered to a higher point to get her bearings.

No, what had caused her to do all these things was the realization that the farm house she had just gone by came *after* her destination, not before. The town she had been commanded to go to was a place she had driven to a thousand times, there was no way she could have missed it.

Her brain tried to piece together what exactly was happening. Did she take a wrong turn? No, there was only one road from her home to the next town, it was a near straight shot with no deviations outside of private roads that lead only to dead-end residences. Did she not notice that she had passed a whole town by? Unlikely, especially as the town would be flooded with evacuees and presumably more hazmat-clad figures directing traffic. There was no way she had spaced out so hard that she had missed all that. Was she misremembering where it was? Definitely not, the amount of times Adda had visited the place immediately ruled that out. She was no stranger to it.

Or maybe, the town was just gone?

The thought sent a shiver dancing down her spine. That couldn't be it either.

Yet no other options were forthcoming. As impossible as it was, the idea stuck. She didn't believe it of course, but it continued to run its course over and over in her mind. Every pass that it made ingrained a little more than before.

Adda considered turning back to challenge the thought, but before she could even act on the impulse, the Certainty struck once again. It brought a strange understanding that no matter how long she drove, all she would find were more hills and meandering road. Whatever was behind her was now gone, swallowed by the unfathomable. She even knew that the farmhouse would be whisked away, stranding Adda in a world she no longer understood. So, Adda did what she always did when facing the unknown.

She moved forward.

"Forget what lies behind and press ever on." Adda whispered to herself, shifting the car into gear.

The hand of fear slipped, struggling to find its hold on the woman's heart. Its once iron grip was eased back until it finally let go, fading away. Adda looked up the road, relaxing her grip on the steering wheel and letting out a long sigh as if to expel even the echoes of her fear. She didn't know what was happening to the world, but she would face whatever it was head on.

And with determination in her heart, Adda drove forward into uncharted territory.

7

The road rolled on, impossibly long as it curved a lazy course like a river though the hills. The scenery stayed near consistent, endless waves of sweeping green rising and falling around Adda. There was something hypnotic about the way the road moved, its gentle turns attempting to lull her to sleep. Her eyes fluttered so she gripped the steering wheel harder, forcing herself to focus.

It also didn't help that there was nothing to break up the monotony of her drive. No other cars came down the road, no evidence of life in the world that flew by. There were no buildings, no power lines, no paddocks, it was only the road and Adda's car that remained. Had something happened to the world?

Had something happened to her?

Those very questions tumbled around Adda's mind as she tried to make sense of it all. Yet, no amount of logic or reasoning could piece the puzzle together, leaving Adda with more questions than when she started.

Looking for a distraction, Adda fumbled around with the knobs on her console until she found the button to turn on the radio. It clicked on and greeted her with an almighty hiss. The sound screeched against her ears, disturbing the heavy blanket of silence. It startled Adda so much that it caused her to swerve on the road.

Reaching blindly once again, she found the appropriate knob and began to flip through the channels, trying to find any kind of signal. The hissing continued to sputter on, refusing to coalesce into anything meaningful. Adda wasn't even surprised to find that the radio refused to work. After all, in this place that held an endless road and vanishing towns, it would have been stranger to hear anything other than static.

The hissing went on until, with a *click*, she turned the radio back off. Once again, she was plunged beneath the blanket of silence that muffled the world like a heavy coat of snow. Adda sat in the silence, staring ahead, falling back into the rhythm of the road. With nothing else to do, the woman kept on driving. The road had to lead somewhere and she was determined to see it to its end.

The road rolled away before her, and without meaning to, Adda's mind began to wander back over her life. She thought of the people she had met and the places she had been. Adda found herself struck by an intense feeling of nostalgia and melancholy. Was everyone else who had been evacuated experiencing a similar thing? Had they actually gotten somewhere and were doing ok? All the faces she had become so familiar with in her life rolled through her mind. On them were cast looks of fear and rage, the way that she had last seen them in their mad dash to escape home.

Bethany and her parents popped into Adda's mind and her heart constricted a little bit. Fear welled inside of her as a sudden rush of twisted images plagued her. Images of loss, and death, and pain all tumbling together. They began to magnify, growing larger than life behind Adda's eyes. They nearly overwhelmed her as she saw the young girl succumb to all manner of horror.

While these thoughts tumbled around Adda's mind, something changed.

The light outside her car flickered, causing the world to darken slightly. The colors all around lost some of their luster, the blue sky turned gray and the green grass became pale. It was as if an invisible cloud had suddenly appeared in the sky, warping the world below.

The strange moment didn't last long as the scenery reverted almost instantly back to normalcy. It was so quick that Adda hadn't even really noticed the change, yet during the event, she had seen something.

In the midst of it all, a shadow flickered on a hilltop up ahead.

It was only there for the briefest of moments, there one second and gone the next. It would have most certainly gone unnoticed on a normal day. Adda's eyes would have been glued to the road or glancing at a passing farm. Maybe there would have been a friendly passerby waving a hand or a wild animal creeping about to distract her. On a normal day, there were a million things that would occupy anyone's attention. If this movement had occurred on such a day, it would have been so slight in the grand tapestry of a moment that it would have slipped away into the nothingness.

But this was not a normal day.

This was a day where all movement and all sound had come to a complete stop. If all of life was a lake in a rainstorm where ripples collapsed upon ripples to create an endless picture of motion, then this was a day without rain. Without its constant presence even the smallest of rocks dropped through the lake's surface would create a break impossible to go unnoticed.

In this place, wherever it was, Adda was starved for anything to create that break. It was for this reason, and this reason only, that her hungry eyes snapped with laser focus to the brief motion. Though it passed as quickly as it came, Adda saw something that made goosebumps race down her body.

The shadow had the form of a person.

Adda slammed a foot onto the brakes with too much force, causing the car to cry out as it was pulled to a shrieking halt for the second time. The sudden stop caused Adda to lurch forward, ripping her focus from the hill as her head nearly slammed into the steering wheel. She braced herself at the last second, managing to avoid an injury as the car settled from its momentum.

Snapping her head back up, she looked about wildly, trying to determine where the figure was. To her disappointment, whoever had been there was now gone. Part of her wondered if perhaps she had imagined the whole thing. It wasn't uncommon for someone's mind to play tricks on them in situations of high stress.

But Adda dismissed the thought. She knew what she saw.

With a determined motion, she switched off the car, unbuckled the seat belt and swung open the door, scanning the hilltops with intense scrutiny as she stepped out. If there was a person up there, perhaps they could help her understand what was happening or if they were in the same position as her, maybe they could help each other navigate this strange existence that had sprung upon them. Her eyes saw nothing but grass and sky.

With hasty steps, Adda crossed the road, looking both ways before doing so even though there hadn't been another car in sight for hours. It was hard to break a habit so ingrained into someone. The eerie silence hung thicker with the car no longer running. It crowded around her, pushing against her on all sides. It seemed angered by the intrusion of her shoes clattering against the asphalt. Yet, try as she may to walk with a quieter step, it was impossible to mask her progress in a world so devoid of sound.

Upon crossing the street, it suddenly occurred to Adda that she had accidentally left her keys in the ignition. Knowing there had been a person some miles away, it dawned on her it would be good to keep her transportation in her control. If someone were to come along and find her car, they could easily steal it with no way for her to get it back.

With that thought, she turned around, heading back with haste toward her car. Even as she moved across the road once again, a rising sense of wrongness welled up within her. It was the same wrongness that she had felt when passing the farmhouse by. This time, however, the twisted feeling was given an answer. An answer that made Adda falter in her steps, her mouth hanging open in shock.

The car that now sat where she had parked just moments before couldn't possibly be the same vehicle- and yet, it was. It was the same make, it was the same color, and inside she could see the sunflower necklace she had hung on the rear-view mirror years ago spinning lazily around. All these things indicated it was her vehicle, yet it couldn't be the same car, it was impossible.

This car, the one that should have been her own, looked as though it were at least a hundred years old.

Instead of a well-loved vehicle that had shown only the smallest signs of use was the broken remains of a skeleton fallen victim to time and negligence. Its tires had all melted away, leaving behind naked wheels that had bent into themselves. The windows were shattered as the collapsing roof had forced them out decades ago. Rust spread like a disease across the body of the car, eating away at the metal beneath like termites on a tree.

Where the rust hadn't yet claimed, the paint had faded from decades of abuse beneath the harsh rays of the sun. It was peeling off in most places now, littering the ground around it in a shower of metallic flakes. Grass and other foliage had already begun to reclaim the skeleton. They sprouted up on the inside of the vehicle, forcing their way through every available opening. Adda got the impression that the earth itself was reaching up tendrils of green to choke and crush the car before dragging its battered corpse back into the depths.

She stared at the broken body of her sole companion that had been at her side throughout the journey. Part of her thought if she looked long enough, maybe the car would revert to its original state, ready to continue up the winding road. The other part thought that she might catch it in the act of decay and discover some natural reason of how this might have happened. Creeping beneath it all was an understanding that slowly welled to the surface.

"The farmhouse," Adda whispered, "and the town-"

It didn't make any sense, but the evidence was in front of her. Was this what had happened? Had this strange decay claimed everything in its path, wasting it away until nothing remained?

Why didn't anyone notice? Adda wondered.

A sickening thought punched her in the gut, making Adda take a cautious step away from the broken collection of metal. Was this also happening to people? If so, how long did she have?

The notion sent a chill down her spine and she wrapped her hands tightly around her arms in an attempt to ward it off. A darkness began to skulk around the corners of her mind. It whispered all manner of horrible things, projecting images of decay and death before her eyes. While she had been driving, she had had something to focus on. Now, with nothing to occupy her attention, all the pent up horrors that had been stewing in the back of her mind were suddenly unleashed.

They struck with such overwhelming force it made Adda kneel to the ground beneath their onslaught. Her breath came in gruff pants as her heart began to pound rapidly with panic. Adda raised her hands up, gripping the sides of her head as she tried to force back the attack. Her nails dug into the skin around her ears as if prepared to rip the offending articles out in an attempt to save her from those howling voices. Adda squeezed her eyes shut, the tears gathered there now rolling down her face.

Nothing made sense. Nothing was right anymore. It was all wrong, so impossibly wrong.

It was too much, it was all just too much.

Just as it seemed the last bits of hope were to be wiped from Adda's heart, a slight sound came. It was like the soft whisper of wind slipping through the trees. Even in the silence, it was nearly imperceptible. Still, Adda jerked her head up, drawn to the noise.

There, sitting upon the old wreckage before her, was a small, white dove. The dove was so pure that it seemed to nearly glow beneath the sunlight. It had its head turned to one side to get a better view of her. Adda froze as she stared at the small animal, the first real sign of life she had seen in hours.

Its little eyes peered unflinchingly toward her. They weren't eyes that were nervous or curious, they were not ones controlled by instinct. Rather, there was a will there, a purpose, and it almost seemed as though the small bird was trying to communicate something with her.

In that moment, the Certainty suddenly leapt within Adda's chest, igniting her heart with a strength she didn't know she had. Like the sun suddenly breaching through thundering clouds, a warmth spread through her whole body. The fear roiled, fighting to keep its purchase.

Closing her eyes, Adda pushed against the fear that twisted around inside of her. It fought back like something living, hissing and biting at her even as it retreated. She took in a deep, steady breath, and began to count down from ten. Adda let herself feel the fear, to recognize it, and then she let it go. As she finished counting, she let out her breath and allowed the growing warmth to chase the small dregs of fear from her.

The battle was over and Adda found herself at peace. Comforted by this, the woman took in another breath before opening her eyes.

The dove was gone, having left as silently as it had come. Adda rose to her feet and stepped up to the car, looking through the empty hole that had once held a window. There, on the passenger seat, still lay her purse.

Unlike the dusty seat which had all manner of plant life bursting from between its seams, the purse looked like it hadn't changed at all. It was still gray with a silver zipper and the design of a purple flower sewed onto the side. Not a piece of dust or grime marred its surface. Whatever had aged the rest of the car had chosen to pass over the article.

Adda could even see the outline of the small box pressing against the sides of the purse. The small package pulled on her with a force that felt magnetic. It called out to her and so she answered. She attempted to open the door but found it had rusted shut and refused to budge. After that had failed to work, she instead carefully leaned in through the window. She felt needles of glass bite into her side as she rested her weight against its frame. The woman felt momentarily irritated at herself for being so careless, but the call of the box overwhelmed those thoughts. With a deft motion, she snatched up the purse and pulled it to her. Drawing out of the car, Adda looked at the purse, feeling the weight of the box within.

Adda took a moment to assess the damage she had dealt to her side, searching for the puncture holes left by the jagged glass. To her surprise, not only did she not feel any pain, but she couldn't find even a tear in her clothing to indicate where an injury might have been. She lifted up her shirt, feeling with a hand to see if she could locate any evidence of a wound. To her amazement, there was nothing to be found, not even a drop of blood. It was as if the event had never happened.

Under normal circumstances, this discovery might have made Adda feel uneasy. It might have made her feel as though she were going mad. Yet, those thoughts were far from her mind as the weight of the box fell against her unblemished side. Confidence bubbled up within her, setting her mind toward seeking out answers.

With these things held in her heart, Adda turned, emboldened, toward the hilltop on the other side of the road. The Certainty tugged at her, calling her to traverse the grassy landscape before her. Without a second thought, she moved forward.

Adda didn't need to look back as she mounted the hill and pressed on down the other side. She knew in her heart what she would have seen if she had looked back. The car was no more, whether it was pulled into the earth, or had disintegrated into nothing, it didn't matter as the effect was the same.

It was gone.

There was not even a scrap of evidence the car had even ever existed. No tire marks revealing the sudden halt, no flecks of paint nor splattering of rust. In fact, even the road was no more, replaced instead by divots between the hills filled with ordinary grass. All the inventions of man were simply gone, the last of them snatched away as if they had never been. Even though it was something Adda didn't understand, she somehow knew this had all occurred in a fraction of a second. So the woman walked on, feeling a call to move further up and further in.

8

The hills rose in front of Adda, spreading out for what appeared to be an eternity in every direction. The only evidence of any kind of life was the grass that grew short and soft beneath her feet. Not a tree, flower, bird, or anything else appeared to exist here, just hills and grass beneath the light blue of a midsummer sky. Clouds would roll by from time to time, fluffy and white like cotton candy at the fair. They would vanish as quickly as they came, always moving in such a fashion as to not cross over the burning halo of the sun.

The scene seemed like it was ripped straight out of a painting, the colors almost too vibrant, and the details almost too fine. It was breathtaking to behold. Along with it, the picture carried something else, a feeling that rooted itself deep within her heart. There was this strange, nostalgic familiarity within this picturesque place, one that invoked feelings of peace and calm. Though she knew she had never physically been here, her very soul ached with memories she didn't have. It was like the feeling of driving down an empty road at night, or watching rain patter onto a windowpane, or like stepping into an old home that showed evidence of generation after generation living within its walls. But even then, those feelings didn't quite match exactly how Adda felt. Rather than a profound longing for something beyond words, this feeling invoked a deep sense of belonging.

Try as she may, Adda couldn't shake the feeling that she had been here before. That was impossible, of course, such a place would be easy to remember. Yet, still the feeling persisted, nagging at the back of her mind like an intrusive thought. The woman tried to remind herself that, despite whatever this sense was, she was in alien territory. It was best not to get too comfortable until she had a better understanding of the world around her. Even for all that, Adda found herself over and over being swept away by the feeling, and so after some time, she simply accepted it as her traveling companion and continued moving forward.

The going was surprisingly easy, each rising hill falling behind her in a monotonous rhythm. Up one side, down the other, and then she would do it again. Onward she marched at a steady pace, not turning to one side or the other, but moving in a straight line toward whatever lay ahead. Her legs did not tire and the breath in her lungs did not falter. Even the glaring sun didn't pull sweat to her brow. Wherever she had found herself, Adda's body apparently thrived in such conditions, acclimating impossibly fast. With each conquered summit, a new burst of energy would propel her further. Never in her life had Adda felt so good, it made her want to push on and on forever.

Adda had always loved going for long walks. They would guide her mind to quieter shores beyond the chaos of thoughts that occupied a typical day. The repetitive motion of feeling the world turn beneath each step was therapeutic, and so it was Adda's favorite activity when she needed to reflect and collect herself. The woman went to that hushed place now, letting all the worries and stress of the day roll off her shoulders. It was there that she could truly hear that inner-voice, that Certainty that walked alongside her.

Adda reflected on the past twenty-four hours, though at this point, she wasn't even sure how much time had actually passed. Had it truly been mere hours? Part of her was sure that she had left her home only that morning, but the other was not so convinced. The metallic water, the pounding headache, the suited figures urging people to evacuate; it all felt like a lifetime ago. It seemed impossible that more than a day could have passed, yet after watching her car collapse into nothingness, she was no longer confident in her ability to determine what was possible or not.

She puzzled over the events for a while, but her mind soon wandered to other territory when she couldn't make heads or tails of it all. She thought of the unfinished painting that was sitting abandoned in her home. Sorrow dug deep as thoughts of dust layering upon the brilliant canvas plagued her. How sad that such a mysterious painting would never know completion. Outside the one that she had worked on with Bethany, the painting from the cliffs had been her final project.

The thought of Bethany caught her mind, and drew her away from her melancholy thinking into happier territory.

Bethany was an unsuspecting answer to a longing in Adda's heart. Adda had been blessed to have known Bethany for the girl's whole life, getting to see her go from babbling baby, to trouble-making child, into an inquisitive teen. It was a thing that Adda would cherish always and was thankful to be a part of. The thoughts of Bethany brought warmth to Adda's heart, and though she worried, Adda didn't let that fear take hold again. Bethany did have her parents and they were good people who would do anything for their daughter.

With thoughts of Bethany, other people from home began to parade around her mind. Stray thoughts wandered to Keith, that awkward man who believed puns were the peak of all humor, and who worried a little too much about things that needn't be his concern. Candace's face came next, followed by her army of children, and all the noise that hung about them like a perpetual cloud. Had they all made it out or were they stuck wandering the hills with her?

These thoughts lead her back to her home, sitting like sunlight on a dreary day, and to the little shed of memories that waited for her out back. Those memories had once haunted her, but as she grew, and struggled, and fought, she had learned to let it go. Whereas, it had once held a great deal of pain, the shed had become a source of comfort. It had become her sanctuary when life had become difficult. Her hand strayed down to the purse, slipping it in to caress the box within. Now, she carried that comfort with her.

These reflections and many more carried Adda over the crest of the next hill, and that is where her musings were interrupted.

For a moment, she could not fully comprehend what she was seeing. She reached up and rubbed up her eyes as if to clear the image like it was an irritant. Looking again, she was forced to realize that she was indeed seeing what was before her.

Down below, cradled in a small valley, was what appeared to be a series of primitive, wooden structures. They were haphazardly placed, a chaotic layout that gave no indication of pattern or reasoning. They were dark, appearing to be empty from her vantage point. By their squat, ugly look, they were obviously built for function rather than beauty.

Like thorns on a rose, they stuck out against the shades of green surrounding them. Unlike thorns, which were to be expected on the stem of a rose, these structures were *wrong*, an affront to the world around them. The wrongness settled into Adda's gut, and sat there like a lead weight.

Her senses told her to turn around and walk in a different direction, but she felt that familiar Certainty hum within her, telling her that this was the way to go. She remained unerring in her travels thus far, and she had no intention of changing now. With a quick pat on her purse, the woman walked steadily down the hill, her head swiveling back and forth as she took in the scene.

As she approached, the buildings took on an even more sinister shade. Around the perimeter of the encampment were large posts, carved with all manner of horrific scenes and splashed with garish-red paint. They were cut with a crude hand that left the images disjointed and bulky. Though, for the lack of precision, there was little doubt what the horrific pieces of art depicted; everywhere she looked, Adda saw images of famine, disease, war, and acts of the darkest manner. Adda couldn't figure out if they were a warning, a monument to a dark triumph, or both.

Moving beyond them, Adda found that the buildings within were constructed with a dark wood, lashed together with thick cords, and sealed with a sticky substance that glistened black in the daylight. The tips of the wood that came together to make the roofs had been sharpened into piercing points, looking more like a collection of massive spears than homes. A skin of some kind of animal was tacked over every entryway, concealing whatever lay beyond. The thing that made Adda's blood run cold, however, were the darker contraptions scattered about.

To one side of the makeshift hamlet, was a large cage constructed of the same wood, and sharpened needlessly at the ends into cruel spikes. Large posts were erected in small clusters around the township. Each bore wicked, spiked chains that ended in tight, metal bands designed to lift unfortunate victims clear of the ground. The list went on and on until it seemed that the town held more tools of cruelty rather than homes. Every so often, Adda would catch a glimpse of sun bleached white glinting ominously in the light. Whenever Adda would try to focus on the thing, it would suddenly disappear, whisked away as quickly as it would appear.

It should be expected for someone caught in such a place to become sick with fear, yet, for reasons beyond her understanding, Adda found she wasn't truly afraid. Sure, her hair stood on end, and goosebumps sprung up on her arms, but deep within her, she was calm. It was as though her body was trying in vain to convince her she was in deep peril, yet her heart was certain that there was nothing to truly fear. As Adda walked through the horrible place, she began to slowly realize that there was something strange about it that ran deeper than its instruments of horror or its wicked architectural design.

It dawned on her that the valley seemed to never end. She had certainly walked its entire length a few times at least, yet the hills up ahead drew no closer. Like everything else so far, this dark place refused to conform to the nature of what was considered normal, rather, it chose to play by its own rules. In the instant she became aware of this phenomenon, Adda abruptly saw that no matter which direction she looked, more and more houses sprung up. Though the hill remained precisely where it had started, Adda found that she was suddenly in the middle of a great maze composed of dark wood and cruel points.

Adda stopped then, puzzling over her current predicament. A voice screamed in her mind to run as fast as she could, to escape before the occupants decided to come home. Ignoring such advice, Adda approached one of the buildings, deciding to take a closer look at the place that currently trapped her. There was something definitively off about the structures surrounding her. Her mind slowly turned as she stared at the wall, trying to decipher what it was that bothered her so.

Standing so close to the wall, Adda realized that the dark wood had a green tint to it. It was not a natural coloring as it did not appear the green was part of the structure at all. It was more like the wall had been superimposed over a backdrop, shading but not obstructing the color just beyond. Adda was struck then that she could actually see *through* the building. The wall of green she was seeing was in fact the soft, endless grass growing just on the other side.

This information caused her mind to stutter in place. This couldn't be possible, yet she couldn't deny what she was seeing. The building was clearly see-through as though it were a mirage dancing in the desert. The longer she stared, the more undeniable it became.

Setting aside reason and all the ways her mind was trying to make sense of such a phenomenon, Adda closed her eyes and reached out a hand. She reached and reached, her fingers stretching outward, expecting at any moment to feel the coarse wood beneath her hand.

The feeling never came, as she truly knew it wouldn't. Instead, stooping over at the hip with an arm fully extended, Adda found her fingers curling around the soft grass that should have been impossible to touch from where she was standing. And yet, the plants tickled the inside of her palm, warm from the sun up above.

Opening her eyes and stepping back, Adda saw that the wooden planks that had once been so distinct had become nearly invisible. She could still make out the outline and some of the details of the building, but like smoke from a sputtering fire, the wind stole more of it away with every passing moment. Her mind could not make sense of what she was witnessing, yet she remained strangely calm.

Perhaps she was going mad.

No, Adda thought to herself, *this has to be something else.*

She wasn't sure why she was so adamant on that point, but there was something about this place that seemed to shrug off the idea of madness. It somehow felt more real than anything Adda had ever known even though it played upon impossibility at every turn.

Adda took a long, steadying breath. She closed her eyes again, feeling her lungs swell with the sweet, summer air. She felt the sun's rays gently kissing her skin, warming her with its presence. Through her shoes she could feel the soft grass cushioning her feet. Adda let out the breath and opened her eyes. There was no way to explain where she was yet, but Adda knew that it was somehow real.

Deciding that she had taken enough of her time standing in this strange village that was unsure if it wanted to exist or not, Adda struck out again, marching toward the end of the homes. She was once again impressed by her own fortitude. Had it only been yesterday that she had struggled with the simple walk from her home to the bluffs overlooking the ocean? That hike was nothing compared to the amount of steps she had put in today, yet sweat did not adorn her brow nor did her muscles ache from an otherwise arduous journey. Straight on she went like an arrow released from its bow, honing with deadly accuracy toward its target; though what that target was remained a mystery. Adda knew in her bones that she was on the right path, all it would take was one foot after another.

In a matter of moments, Adda crossed beyond the threshold of the township. Whatever power had held her there had lost its grip, no longer able to impede her journey. Adda paused, turning about to look back over the ghost town. The buildings were hardly even shadows now as they continued to dissipate. With a satisfied nod, Adda turned and pressed on up the hill, putting the bump in the road behind her.

It was there, crossing the threshold of that last hill where Adda was struck by a new awareness. It was as if her eyes had been sealed shut– and only just then had been thrown wide to see the world. In between the passing of moments, the rolling hills before her vanished, becoming replaced by a whole, new scenery.

Towering like a lone giant over its kingdom, a lone mountain peek suddenly materialized before Adda.

Upon seeing it, Adda instantly knew that it somehow had always been there, dominating the skyline, waiting to be noticed. How was it possible that she hadn't seen it until just now? Such a question was added to the growing pile in the back of her mind. It was as surreal as anything she had experienced thus far, but it still made her take a step back and gasp. For such an incredible sight to suddenly spring into her awareness was a jarring experience.

The mountain stood beyond the scope of anything she had ever seen in her life. Adda was not a well-traveled person, yet she had never even imagined a peak so tall and slender. It looked like a knife slicing open the sky.

It looked like nothing Adda have ever seen in her life. Every mighty range she had seen was made of peaks and saddles that spanned hundreds of miles on wide bases. This mountain appeared more like a tree raised up on a powerful trunk of stone to pierce the sky above. Though it was narrow, nothing about its spindly frame spoke of weakness. This mountain held its own kind of monolithic power.

It rose jagged and grey and beyond such a term as "tall." Adda's neck ached from craning it back so far as she searched in an effort for its pinnacle. It was to no avail as the top of the mountain lay hidden behind a wall of rolling clouds that seemed to be produced by the peak itself.

Down the sides of the powerful monolith, the clouds roiled. Each rolling head ejected forth a spectacular display of flashing lightning whose forked tongues bit at the air, letting loose low booms of thunder. The way they pooled and tumbled looked like ash racing down the side of a volcano, moving with a deadly momentum. The clouds soon left their creator, leaping greedily across the sky, holding the world beneath in perpetual gray. Adda watched a fresh storm come barreling toward her, growling ominously in its approach.

Still a ways off, the clouds suddenly came to a screeching halt and pooled out away from her as if bouncing off an unseen barrier. They rolled about, appearing to test the limits of the invisible wall before falling away, their energy spent. Adda watched as the same drama was being played out in a wide circle surrounding the mountain. She saw the storm strike the barrier time and time again, seeking to break through it to the untouched blue skies that sat just out of reach. The wind moaned in despair with every failed attempt. It would draw the clouds away a short distance before bolstering back up and lashing out in fury once more.

Despite that, the invisible force wouldn't balk, refuting the storm's every attempt.

The sight was mesmerizing, so much so Adda hadn't noticed at first that the mountain was suddenly closer to her. She blinked her eyes a few times as if she were waking up from a long slumber. Adda didn't remember walking toward the mountain, yet she had somehow been drawn just outside the barrier that separated her pleasant summer day and the roaring chaos that wove itself endlessly above her. It would have taken only a few dozen or so steps to cross into the territory of the storm. She stopped moving then, tearing her gaze from the distant monolith as she tried to assess the situation.

She wasn't sure how far she had walked in her trance, but it had to have been at least a couple of miles. Adda found the thought mildly unnerving and contemplated turning back. That idea was quickly put to rest. Not only was there nothing but an eternity of hills behind her, Adda felt that now that she was aware of the mountain, she would always find herself in its shadow no matter how far she walked. Her path had carried her here, and so there was only one way for her to go. With a steadying breath, Adda passed a hand over her wooden box, feeling the indented symbol and stepped forward.

"Adda?"

This voice, coming directly from her right, was deafening in a world that had been so silent. The noise made her flinch in surprise as she whipped around to see who had crept up on her. She was shocked when she found herself looking upon a familiar face.

It was Jason Everett, the cashier from The Grocery Store, looking back at her in bewilderment.

Adda took him in, shocked at his appearance.

His shirt was riddled with tiny holes and bore a large, dark stain of a disquieting color. His black jacket hung in near tatters round his bony shoulders with haphazard patches sewn on in an attempt to keep the battered piece of cloth together. His pants were torn and ripped, coupled with stains and a worn hem. Everett's shoes were in similar disarray, with holes wide enough to reveal his dirt caked big toes sticking out like pudgy worms from the mud.

His clothing was not the only thing that had seen better days, Everett himself appeared to have gone through a similar treatment, with his hair caked in mud and grime. Along his narrow jaw and sunken cheeks, a shaggy, unkempt beard clung unceremoniously like a bedraggled creature. Settled deep into his sickly face were sunken eyes that sported heavy bags. They revealed countless, sleepless nights. His entire posture was defensive and weakened as though he had gone a long time without real food.

How odd Adda must have appeared to him in her current state. The comparisons her mind made between them were quite alarming. She had walked miles, yet her shoes held together as if new, her clothing had not so much a grass stain on them, and she had not even begun to feel the pangs of thirst or hunger. He, on the other hand, looked less like a man, and more like a pitiful shadow that had long suffered all manner of abuse.

"Everett?" Adda finally croaked out.

"Yeah!" He replied. His shoulders relaxed and he grinned broadly to reveal a mouthful of yellowed teeth. "How are you here? It's been so long!"

"I-" Adda trailed off, still in shock with his appearance. It took her a moment to process what he had said, and once she had, she found herself even more confused.

"What do you mean it's been so long? I saw you yesterday at the store."

"Yesterday?" Everett asked, "Adda, that was forever ago."

"No it wasn't, I told you I was going to bring you the guitar. Remember?" Adda replied.

This prompted further confusion on the young man's face, but before he could continue, Everett froze, his eyes suddenly growing large in fear.

His entire body tensed, every muscle quivering as if ready to leap into action. His jaw was clenched so tight, Adda worried that he would break his teeth. Everett looked like a rabbit who had just seen the shadow of a hawk and was now debating whether to lie low or to make a run for it.

"What-" Adda began to ask, looking about, trying to find the source of Everett's powerful and abrupt response.

"Ssh!" He hissed, spittle spraying from his lips as he looked around wildly, appearing more like an animal than a man. "They're here. W-we've gotta go right now!"

Without waiting for her to respond, Everett suddenly lashed out and grabbed Adda tightly by the wrist. Perhaps it was the terror in his eyes, or the intense urgency in his grip, but Adda didn't resist as he led her quickly along. He pulled her behind him, his neck hunched down between his shoulders as he more scuttled than ran as if he were some kind of strange insect. His head bobbed back and forth as he weaved in between the hills, his eyes constantly scanning the world above them. Adda attempted to look where he was looking, but whatever it was that had spooked Everett remained hidden from her eyes. Their seemingly random path allowed them to skirt the barrier that led into the territory of the mountain. Without meaning to, Adda found herself turning her focus toward the storms and the monolith beyond.

Adda noticed as they went that no matter how far they walked, she could never perceive a new angle of the mountain. It was as though the mountain was rotating with their movement, constantly showing the same face toward her in order to hide whatever was beyond. The idea of a living mountain, conscious of something as small as her observing it was a distinctly unsettling thought and Adda knew it would do her no good to dwell on it. She slipped the thought away, instead focusing on trying to make sense of Everett's nonsensical wandering.

Adda found that she was getting annoyed with him. He moved like a frightened child who was sure that some kind of monster was going to snatch him up as he tried to sneak to the bathroom in the middle of the night. Try as she may, she could make no sense of his fear. He would stop suddenly, look around, move in a direction, then crouch low to freeze like a deer sizing up an approaching figure.

What happened to you? Adda thought.

She desperately wanted answers, to even just hear someone else's voice, but Everett seemed far from a place to casually talk. So, instead she just wandered along with the unhinged man, growing more and more irritated with all the looming questions that were simmering in her mind, begging to be appeased.

It was perhaps an hour later (but it could have been longer, it was hard to tell with the sun remaining motionless above) that Everett began to visibly relax. His aberrant behavior melted away with every step, and though he still moved like prey on edge, the tension had left him. After a moment he even let out a breathy laugh.

"Can't believe we managed to sneak by them! I mean, that was pretty close."

"Everett, what are you talking about?" Adda snapped, her frustration bleeding out into her voice, "Who's *them?*"

Everett flinched back at her tone, his face one of surprise. He studied her, unsure of how to respond to her questions.

"I mean, are you being serious right now?" He finally said.

"Yes!" Adda took in a steadying breath, "I just need you to tell me what's going on."

"Wait, you really don't know?"

"Everett, please."

The young man shook his head as if still in disbelief. "That's wild. I don't even know where to start. I think you should probably talk to Mr. Baker back in town, he's calling himself the mayor these days."

Town? Mr. Baker, as in Keith Baker? Adda paused, digesting Everett's words.

Once again, she wondered if perhaps she was going mad.

Did they really manage to build a town in only a few hours? Adda thought. Something else then struck her, chilling her to the bone.

Had it really been only hours?

"Keith? He's here, too?" Adda asked, choosing to go with an easier question since Everett seemed reluctant to say much else.

"Well Yeah. I mean, pretty much everyone from home was here for a while."

At the word *home* Everett's eyes misted up and he got a far away look about him. His entire appearance had become wistful as though he were remembering the good ol' days from long ago. Between the battered image he cut and the way he spoke of home, Adda began to form a thought in her head that she found disquieting. Everett shook his head, casting off the memory before turning about and loping away at an impressive pace. Adda hustled after him.

"At first it was pretty much everyone, but people either got snatched or went into the valley, so there's probably only like, a hundred of us left now. We've been talking about going to the valley, but Mr. Baker thinks we should stay here and make the best of it. I mean, we've gotten pretty good at not getting snatched anymore. Plus, we have crops and stuff, so honestly leaving now seems like a bad idea. Ya' know?"

Adda really didn't know. She didn't know at all what these people had experienced in the time between the exodus from town and now. Whatever it was, it had to have been brutal beyond her scope of understanding. One thing was becoming crystal clear, however. It was hard for her to really wrap her mind around it, but it was impossible to deny the facts laid before her.

Everett, and apparently everyone else, had been out here for a long time.

Adda could still remember waking up that very morning with absolute clarity. She could remember the pounding headache, the man at her door, the chaos that ensued after. Yet, she couldn't deny what she was seeing. What had been only a day for her had been months, if not years, for Everett. Just looking at the man revealed the harrowing weight of extended survival. It rested on his bony shoulders like a shroud.

Everett was now prattling on about something to do with his avoidance technique that had helped keep him alive for so long. Adda just nodded as she followed him, wondering once again about this reality they had found themselves in. It was obvious that they were no longer on their planet, the impossible nature of this place made that quite clear. What had happened that had caused them to all share this experience?

Is this happening everywhere in the world? Adda thought to herself, imagining the earth going silent as its largest occupants all vanished in an instant. *Or is it just us?*

Her thoughts were cut off as Everett once again abruptly stopped.

From atop the hill, Adda could see before them a plateau. It stretched a short distance before suddenly dropping off to become a long line of sheer cliffs. It looked as though someone had taken a massive sword and had cleaved the land down the middle to make way for the impressive precipice. Aside from the looming mountain, this was the first big change she had seen in this sea of eternal hills. It reminded her of home, and, for a moment, she imagined she could smell the ocean dancing on the wind. The sensation hurried away, leaving her feeling nostalgic in its wake.

Encompassing the greater part of the plateau was a large wall made of erect, wooden posts that stood like silent sentinels. At their base, bristling like thorns from a rose, were a plethora of sharpened sticks that promised certain pain to anyone foolish enough to charge the settlement. The wood appeared to be the same kind that had composed the village Adda had wandered through some hours before, yet these pieces of wood did not hold the ghostlike quality she had witnessed in the other place. They were solid, very much so, and gave no hint as to what lay beyond their intimidating visage.

Everett guided them down, cutting off to the right, away from the cliff. They followed the face of the wall, giving the sharpened sticks a wide berth. They rounded a corner to reveal a large gate that interrupted the otherwise impenetrable palisade. Flanking the entrance were a pair of guards.

Both of them were people she was sure she once knew, but their time here had not been kind to them. Grime covered the pair like a second skin and they wore exhaustion like it was their garb. Wary eyes peeked out from underneath hoods drawn low, and in their hands they clutched make-shift weapons with white knuckles. One of them held a metal baseball bat. It was filled with dents and bore a dark stain on one side of it. Whatever team name had once been printed on it had long since faded from excessive use.

Those details were lost in the shadow of the other guard. This man was far taller than the other, looking to be upward of seven feet. His frame was massive with muscles that grew out to a great, unnatural bulk. Alongside the grime and stains, he looked more like a monster than a man.

Though he clearly didn't need a weapon to deliver devastating damage, the hulking guard still clutched a fire-hardened stick in a meaty hand. The long implement ended in a pair of knives that had been lashed, and then sealed with a dark substance onto the end. On his belt was a monkey wrench that was laughably small in comparison to the man who wielded it. The tool was as dented as the baseball bat, revealing that it was also used for more than just fixing things.

Upon spotting them approaching, the guards oriented themselves toward them, eyes full of suspicion.

"Everett!" The big man bellowed, his voice deep and booming. "How do you go foraging and bring back a person? What is this, a Snatcher trick? Someone from the valley?"

Adda knew she recognized the man, but couldn't place him. It was hard to look past the more monstrous parts of his visage. The grime certainly didn't help.

"Jeez, ease up." Everett replied in a defensive and whiny tone. "It's Adda Reinhoff. Ya' know, the art teacher?"

The guards exchanged a look. "Adda? That's not possible."

"I dunno. I mean, I just found her wandering around in *their* territory."

"I'd like to speak to Keith." Adda chimed in, putting her hands up with palms out in an attempt to show she wasn't a threat.

The two men once again glanced at each other. The smaller one just shrugged.

"If she *is* with the Snatchers, we could handle her, easy." He said, looking to the bigger for confirmation.

Snatchers? Was this what Everett had been so afraid of? Adda thought.

"Let them in." The big one grunted, sizing Adda up. "Keith will want to see her."

The command was given and the smaller turned about to knock a heavy fist upon the gate, calling out loudly to whoever was on the other side. The gate began to creak open, slowly allowing a gap to form in the barricade. The large guard then approached them, offering his empty hand out to Adda.

"Sorry about all this, Mrs. Reinhoff, it's been so long I hardly recognized you." The man's voice was suddenly filled with warmth, yet the warmth did not fully reach his eyes. They still glinted with suspicion, and something darker. He studied her as if trying to determine if she were an actual threat or a prize to be taken. When she didn't immediately offer her own recognition, the man reintroduced himself.

"It's me, Scott."

The image of a man slamming his fist angrily against his steering wheel while his wife and children cried suddenly sprang into her mind. He had struck the wheel with such force that Adda could almost feel the bruises biting against her own hand. The inside of the van must have been so loud, so tense. Adda's ears began to ring as if the image had been more than just a stray thought. She clenched her fist as an aching sensation passed through the hand. The feeling passed as quickly as it had come, leaving her to stand before Scott who waited on her response.

The man somehow appeared even more battered than Everett, which would have made him hard to recognize even without his added bulk. His beard had become wild and unkempt, a nest of twisted knots that grew thick down his chest in a crimson wave. Scars that had not been there before criss-crossed his face set by a wicked edge. They glinted in the sunlight like badges pinned upon a swollen chest, eagerly presenting their every conquest cast in gold and ribbon. Scott's face was also hollowed, appearing as though he had not slept or eaten well in some time, yet his great mass was the polar-opposite of the wisp that was Everett.

The contrast was unnatural to see, it immediately made Adda feel on edge. Scott hadn't been like this when she had known him. She used to be nearly as tall as him, and whereas he had always been strong, this new mass of muscles didn't seem physically possible. The longer she stood in his presence, the more she was sure that his change had to be aberrant.

Adda gazed into the eyes of the man she once knew, searching for any sign of the old Scott. Instead, she was received by the chilling gaze of a predator, shining black like a shark that could smell blood in the water.

"I could say the same about you, Scott." Adda replied, "You look-different than I remember."

"Well, some things change for the better." He chuckled, revealing a toothy grin of sharpened teeth.

Their eyes remained locked and Adda was overwhelmed with the feeling that she was being sized up. A wolf staring down a deer, waiting for its prey to make the first move. The smile was still there, the hand still hovered in its unaccepted greeting, but those deep holes revealed his true intent.

For a moment, Adda felt a temptation to break the contact, allowing her eyes to fall to the soft grass below. His eyes were like black pits, gateways to a darkness that was once hidden, but was now put proudly on display; they were suffocating. All at once, she was aware that she was in some kind of unspoken contest. It was her will versus his, and he was testing her defenses, wondering how hard he had to push.

It would be better to let him win a voice hissed in her head, a thought that weakened her resolve as she stared down this man.

Just let him have this, keep a low profile, it whispered again, and Adda was sorely tempted to listen.

His eyes were swallowing, encompassing, hollow, demanding of her submission. But Adda stood her ground, her jaw clenched as she pushed against her instinct's babbling voice telling her to give in.

She would not submit.

The two of them stood, almost trance-like as this quiet competition of wills played out. The other guard and Everett shifted uncomfortably in the prolonged silence, yet neither of them moved to break-up what was at play. All at once, Scott glanced down, tearing himself away from Adda's own intense glare. Adda let out a breath she wasn't aware she had been holding.

"Well, it's good to see you again. Move along now, we gotta get this gate closed up." He smiled again, the offered hand dropping to his side in a way that seemed too casual.

Adda could tell he was shaken, which she found odd considering how powerful a frame he held in comparison to her own. His eyes darted around her face, but it was clear that he was trying to avoid making eye contact again. Whatever strange battle he had initiated with her was over, and she had somehow gained victory.

"Thank you, Scott." Adda said, her voice even and calm, a tone that made Scott shift back uncomfortably, trying to put more space between the two of them.

At this point, the gate lay fully open. Tugging on Everett's jacket sleeve, Adda led them forward. They brushed past the guards, and moved to stand in the gateway. Adda hesitated in the threshold, turning around to, once again, regard Scott, a question plaguing her mind.

"Scott? How are Lily and the kids?"

A shrug, "Dead."

"Oh," Adda said, the shock of his nonchalance taking her aback, "I'm so sorry."

It was then that Scott found the strength to once again make eye contact with her. They locked vision, and though it was clear that she still reigned champion, Scott deemed it necessary to usher the following line while looking her square on.

"I'm not."

Then, he turned his back on her and Adda walked away, unsure of what else to say.

9

"How did you do that?" Everett asked, his voice a low whisper.

"Do what?"

"You know, back there, with Scott? I mean, I've never seen him look so uncomfortable." There was a tinge of awe in the young man's voice.

"I didn't *do* anything." Adda retorted.

"Yeah, whatever. It was pretty awesome." Everett paused as he considered something. "He's probably gonna be pissed at me because I brought you here, but man, that was cool."

The two of them had crossed the threshold, walking past the gate and into the sanctum beyond. Adda's shoulders drooped as her eyes fell upon a depressing sight. Before her a misshapen township of a dismally small population sprawled out before her.

The buildings were clearly made of the same wood as the village from between the hills, but they lacked the crude mastery that the other place had held. Whereas the violent dwellings she had seen previously were clearly crafted by a hand intent with design and function, these buildings were thrown together haphazardly. The black substance that acted like glue was smeared with little thought across the walls and roof of the buildings, barely keeping the bundles of planks in a cohesive form. The structures leaned heavily in on themselves, propped up only by the other walls that formed a teepee-like appearance in most of the buildings. The entrances didn't even have proper doors, rather they had boards of wood sealed together and leaned across the openings to keep out prying eyes.

Between the depressing homes, the grass had been torn up or stamped out, leaving only muddy pathways behind. Though Adda hadn't seen any kind of rain come out this far, it appeared as though they recently had quite the downpour. It was a thick, viscous mud that tried to steal shoes from feet.

The people who meandered about were in similar condition to their houses and their roads. They limped or scurried, eyes glued to the ground, making no effort to greet one another as they passed. Some were gathered around low fires, attempting to capture some of its heat into their blackened, dirty hands even though the day was still warm. Somehow, many appeared even more hollow, exhausted, and starving than Everett.

The buildings were built close together, some hundred feet from the walls, clustered with no regard to any kind of system. Off to one side, closer to the sheer drop off that lay just on the other side of their clearing, were rows upon rows of frail crops that struggled to grow. They were pitiful looking things, a small gust of wind would be strong enough to snap them off their fragile stalks. Adda wasn't sure what kind of crop they were, but they looked like some blighted version of corn.

There were, perhaps, a dozen men and women working in the field. Most of them were constructing what looked to be an irrigation system. Where they planned on getting their water, Adda wasn't sure. She could see the sweat on their brows, the bend in their backs, and the tremors in their hands. The whole scene exuded an atmosphere of exhaustion. Survival was taking its toll on these people, grinding them down to the bone. Despite that, they continued to work, burning themselves away moment by moment.

What choice did they have?

Adda felt as though she had stumbled into a sad shadow of the place she had once called home. There was a strange familiarity about it all, yet every negative aspect of the life she knew before had been brought to the forefront. It was in the slumped shoulders, ramshackle buildings, and worn out demeanors of those she knew, instead of dwelling in the background like rot eating away at a home.

The more Adda looked, the more everything paralleled their old home, even the cliff was all too familiar. She wondered if she looked over the edge if she would see a dark ocean stretching away far below; a perfect reflection to a life left behind.

Was this how we always were? Adda thought to herself, unable to shake the feeling that this scene wasn't all that different from the one she had gotten to know so well.

Of course, times were strange, and it was perhaps too harsh to think such thoughts about a people clearly struggling on the brink of utter destruction.

Yet, the feeling would not shake. It felt as though this place on this cliff had always been the real one and her home was simply the shadow it cast. Back in the shadow, they could go about their day, pretending to strive for something better, but inevitably giving into that quiet apathy.

Here, that apathy was no longer quiet.

Adda shook herself from her reverie, finding her thoughts had meandered away down a trail that led nowhere good. She instead kept her eyes glued to Everett's back as he guided her through the haphazard maze of structures. If she let herself keep looking, she was sure the crippling sadness that saturated the town would leak into her heart.

As Everett and Adda weaved through the buildings, she noticed they were gathering more than a few stares. She'd catch them on her peripherals, their heads swiveling about to get a better look at her. Adda was once again struck with how much she stuck out amongst these people. Like a flower bursting through concrete, she was impossible to miss in a world of muted grays. That brought her more attention than she would have liked.

As they moved through an alley, Adda passed by a couple that sat upon makeshift stools in front of their house. The man was staring vacantly into the sky, casting his mind somewhere far away. The woman had a long stick she used to methodically poke holes into the ground in between her feet. There was a kind of rhythm to her motion, as if moving to a song only she could hear. The action pulled Adda's attention away from her guide for a moment, where she glanced first at the stick, and then to the face of the woman holding it.

Adda was immediately assaulted by waves of nostalgia as she took in the couple. She had seen those faces thousands of times in her life. Sitting across from them as they all laughed playing some game, standing in a large yard while the smell of grilling patties filled the air, holding a small, cooing bundle swaddled in a pink blanket. They weren't just a passing familiar, and despite the wear of this world, Adda immediately recognized them. They were her friends.

They were Bethany's parents.

Images of the young girl once again popped into Adda's mind as she stopped to stare. Scott's dismissive tone about the demise of his family spun around in her head, causing her heart to leap in her chest for a moment. Breaking away from Everett, Adda approached the two who greeted her with blank looks and empty faces. If they recognized her, they didn't show it.

"Dave! Lisa! It's so nice to see you again!" Adda said, her voice filled with joy.

She reached out to embrace her two friends, but neither of them moved to return her greeting. They simply sat and stared at her.

Adda was taken aback by this reaction. She had spent so much time with them and their daughter that they had almost seemed like family. How many game nights had they had? How many days down at the beach? How many painting lessons had she taught to their child? Had this world taken such a price that they couldn't remember who Adda was?

Craning her neck, Adda looked past the couple and into the gloom of their home. There were no other shapes in there other than a bundle of cloth on the floor that looked like a nest for rats.

"Where's Bethany?"

Her question broke the spell causing Lisa to gasp and turn her head away from Adda. Dave's jaw clenched and his eyes hardened, transforming from an endless void into a hotbed of repressed rage.

"Leave us alone." He growled.

Adda's heart sank into her stomach and soured there, making her feel sick. It wasn't the hostility in the man's voice that caused this sensation, the anger certainly did take her aback, but it was the emotion behind the anger that slammed into her gut like a fist.

It was the feeling of profound, life-altering loss.

"Dave." Adda spoke again, her mouth dry as she forced the words out again. "Where's Bethany?"

"The Snatchers got her." Lisa whispered before her husband could respond.

The woman let out a wretched sound, turning into the other for comfort. Dave sat still, not responding at all to her racking sobs as he tried to master his own emotions.

There was that word again, *snatch*. It hung over them like a cloud thundering ominously. Horrid images paraded through Adda's mind once again concerning the young girl and her fate. This time, it felt different. It wasn't as though a passing thought had sprung up to try and occupy her mind, this time, it felt more like she was witnessing the atrocities first hand.

Shadowy images darted before Adda, whispering and hissing in low voices as they whipped around her in a frenzy. Their tiny claws anchored into her, pulling against her as if to drag her into the ground. She felt her breath coming in heaves as sweat beaded for the first time on her brow. This only seemed to entice the shadows all the more, causing them to crowd in, forcing her eyes to see horror after horror.

Adda closed her eyes, took a deep breath, and counted down in her mind.

Three, two, one.

She let out the breath slowly, surrendering herself and her fears as she did so. The Certainty beat in her chest like her own heart, warming her up from the inside. Adda opened her eyes, and the shadows were gone. Had they even been there?

Putting the moment behind her, Adda spoke to Lisa. "Please, help me understand."

"Leave us alone." Dave said, his anger suddenly gone, replaced instead by a great exhaustion. "Just- go. Please."

Adda opened her mouth, but no words would come. Her heart felt the weight of their loss and she wasn't sure what to say. Her mind denied the possibility that Bethany was just gone. She had to be out there somewhere.

Before Adda could do anything else, a voice abruptly wheezed from behind Adda. The speaker was so close that she could feel their breath on her neck.

"What is this wicked thing?"

Adda turned around, startled by the proximity of the other who's face hovered only a few inches from her own. The figure was a woman, but she was beyond recognition in her current state.

Her skin was grey and so tight against her bones that she looked more like a corpse than a person. Her hair was a matted nest that branched out in every direction like some kind of grotesque flower. Her hands folded in on themselves like talons, clenching painfully against their respective palms. Her entire form looked emaciated and gaunt, her tattered clothing hanging like sack cloth to hide the rest of her frail form. Only her eyes gave away that she was still among the living, though even they revealed the suffering this woman had endured. They were wide, and wild, and most disturbingly, insane.

"Leave us, witch." The woman muttered, grinding her teeth together with such force that Adda could hear it. "You make the Snatchers angry- they're so angry!"

"Oh, shut up." Everett spat with venom in his voice. He reached out to Adda, beckoning her to follow him. "Come on, let's get out of here."

Adda glanced back over to where Dave and Lisa had been sitting, but was dismayed to see they were no longer there. Wooden planks had been placed over the entryway, barring access to the room beyond. They had made it clear that they had no interest in talking to her anymore. Reluctantly, Adda broke away from the home, following Everett as he moved away.

The woman hurried after them, her voice nipping at their heels like dogs on a hunt.

"Why did you bring her here?" The woman moaned, "She has to go, she's too clean. A witch unburned will burn us all."

The woman fell into an unintelligible babble that rose and fell as though it were a discordant song. The sound of it sent chills down Adda's spine, but she maintained her course, trying her best to ignore the disturbed woman.

The commotion drew even more attention to the small parade. Everywhere Adda looked, she saw crossed arms and suspicious eyes following her. Whenever Adda would make eye contact with anyone, they would abruptly look away, suddenly consumed with whatever menial task was before them. The moment Adda turned to look elsewhere, their focus would fall on her once again.

"The Snatchers will punish us!" The woman wailed, clutching herself with her claw-like hands. "Doomed! She will doom us all!"

Everett suddenly spun around, his arm slamming out and shoving the woman hard. The motion sent her sprawling, falling to the ground where she shrieked and writhed, crying pitifully.

"I said- Shut. Up." Everett hissed, his eyes flat and hard, his hands balled into fists with his chest puffed out.

He looked absolutely ridiculous, like a goofy cartoon character attempting to be intimidating. Adda would have laughed if it hadn't been for the man's sudden violent outburst.

"Everett!" Adda cried out as she knelt down next to the other woman. "What's wrong with you?"

"I told her to-" Everett began, he faltered however, as Adda's gaze leveled at him.

The force behind her eyes caused Everett to deflate and look away. He wilted like a flower caught in an unexpected heatwave. His stance of dominance melted to one of compliance as he stammered out his excuses.

"I mean, I just told her to be quiet already," his voice becoming high-pitched as he whined, "I was just trying to protect you."

Adda turned away, not honoring him with a response. Everett sulked away, muttering under his breath as he waited for his charge to come after him. Ignoring him, Adda shifted her focus back to the woman who was making mewling noises as she rolled in the mud.

Adda tried to place the pale, stretched face with one that she had once known. The woman was so changed that Adda found herself at a loss as to who she was. Like with Scott at the gate, this place had done something to this poor creature.

The woman shrieked again as she became aware of Adda's hand creeping up on her. Limbs flailing awkwardly, she retreated away, kicking up mud in an effort to create distance. The mud splattered across Adda's shirt and pants, but she hardly noticed as she tried to calm the woman as though she were a wild beast.

"Hey, it's ok. I'm not going to hurt you. Why don't we get you up out of the mud?"

"No, no, no." The other muttered, "You won't have my name, you'll whisper it to the Snatchers and then they'll come get me." Her eyes went wide with horror. "They'll get me, they'll get me, they'll get me!"

She wrapped her arms around herself tightly as she curled up into a ball and rocked back and forth. Over and over she spoke the same words as if chanting them could ward off the monsters that had plagued them so. Adda sat there at a complete loss, staring at this broken thing before her, wondering what had happened to the world. This poor woman was clearly unstable, fragmented beyond Adda's ability to reach her.

"I'm your friend, it's going to be ok." Adda tried again, though this time she kept her hands to herself.

"Leave her." A familiar voice spoke as a heavy hand suddenly came to rest on Adda's shoulder.

Adda turned around, staring square into the face of Keith Baker.

Though she immediately recognized his face, for that had hardly changed, Adda was caught off guard with the rest of his twisted appearance. Like everyone else, his eyes were sunken and heavy, weighed down by a great exhaustion. His eyes were the only thing that ran parallel to everyone else.

Instead of looking emaciated, he appeared swollen, like a balloon ready to burst. His clothing strained to keep his swelling form hidden beneath its hodgepodge of stitches. He had always been a little overweight, but the image he cut before her was of a man who had given to plenty. He had also gained nearly an extra foot in height, causing him to tower over the other residents of this town.

In contrast to his girth, the man's arms were not bloated, but rather were thick and toned with powerful muscles. They looked as though they had been taken from an olympian god and glued onto the sides of a tick that had just finished its latest meal.

All this bulk was placed upon a pair of spindly legs that looked much too weak to actually support him. They sprouted out like an insect's, somehow managing to keep the rest of his form aloft.

The longer Adda looked at the man, the more unnatural he appeared. He looked *wrong*. His appearance was disturbing and Adda had to resist the urge of pulling away from him. She focused back onto his eyes, using his familiar face to ignore the ogre-like body that now housed the man. But even these had been changed. Those eyes that had once held anxiety, innocence, and pity had become something more predatory. They were sharp, like a wolf's, and glinted with cunning that zeroed in on any hint of weakness.

"I'm sorry you had such a poor welcome back to our community. This is not how I envisioned our reunion." Keith rumbled, his voice far deeper than it once had been.

Adda decided she didn't particularly like the way he said the word *reunion*. There was a hunger in his tone that set her one edge. It was becoming more and more obvious that Adda no longer belonged here among her old friends.

Did you ever belong? A voice whispered in her mind.

"Please forgive Mrs. Dunton," Keith continued, "she hasn't been herself of late."

Dunton. The name nearly brought her to tears as Adda glanced back at the woman who continued to wallow in the filth.

Mrs. Dunton was the dear, old retired woman who volunteered her time at the tiny library that doubled as a meager community center. She was quite protective of her books, but was equally as kind, always keeping a jar of assorted candies to give to children who took the time to read. Her books and the library were her whole life after her kids had all moved away. Everytime Adda had walked into the building, she had found the old woman there, pressing her into conversations about books and art that would sometimes go on for hours.

Adda had always been able to feel the deep loneliness that hugged Mrs. Dunton like a shroud. It weighed the poor woman down as she went about her days, dusting books and telling the same stories again and again. Adda's heart broke for her and she would often purposefully stop at the library just to give the librarian someone to talk to.

To see the kind woman reduced to the babbling mass that now rolled around in the mud like a pig was wrong. The more sickening thing was how no one moved to help her. It was as though the librarian existed beneath their attention, unworthy to garner a response from anyone. Instead, they continued to stare at Adda, ignoring the floundering woman.

The scene made Adda want to scream in frustration. She didn't though, having a feeling that it would just make the situation worse. It was time to get the lay of the land, to start getting some answers to her questions.

"Keith?" Adda asked, leaning toward Keith, "What is going on?"

The man glanced around, his eyes swept across the gathered crowd in a single motion. The look was lazy, almost nonchalant, his body relaxed as one who was in complete control. Adda swore that the people even shifted back as his gaze passed over them, bowing their heads to avoid being noticed. He was a wolf living among sheep, an image that did not sit well with Adda.

"Let's not talk here." Keith replied, waving his hand in a gesture that would suggest she ought to take it. "You probably have a lot of questions."

Against her better judgment, Adda took the hand, letting herself be lifted up by the large man. She was surprised to find the hand to be thick and harsh against her own. At first she thought they were covered in heavy calluses, as they had a quality similar to that of someone who had spent much of their life working with their hands. But the notion passed as the crushing embrace pulled her to her feet, his skin scraping against her own in a way that wasn't natural. It felt like she was gripping the hand of a stone statue, rather than that of another living human.

The shock of such aberrant things were hitting with less and less power as the day spiraled on. Adda had had her fill of bizarre phenomena, and found she was adapting faster with every passing moment. The drawback of the startling shock wearing off was the dawning realization of the situation that she was in. Adda was in a strange place surrounded by strange people that she couldn't rightly say she even knew anymore. She was an alien among them, and they resented her for that.

Adda made up her mind right then and there that she wouldn't stay. Whatever things the mountain brought would be better than hanging around here to become like these people. She wouldn't let herself be at their mercy.

Keith tugged her gently away, holding onto her hand in a possessive manner. It was subtle, but she had unknowingly become accustomed to picking up on the slightest movements. The body speaks a thousand words in a single moment, and she had spent much of her life learning how to watch for them. One thing was certain above everything else, these people were no longer her friends.

Keith led Adda through the eclectic passageways of homes, each looking pitiful and completely unsuitable to live in. As they made their journey, heads would poke out of doorways or around corners to stare with heavy, dead eyes at her. They wouldn't say anything, they wouldn't even move except to keep their focus clearly laid on her. She glanced back once to see that a small crowd had gathered and were following them at a safe distance. The people walked in a strange, hunched way, much like how Everett had moved when he had sworn their enemies were nearby. They darted about, moving silently across the muddy passageways. The fear in their bodies seemed to not fully reach their eyes, however, as their eyes remained lifeless and blank. She briefly looked about to see what had happened to her previous guide, but Everett was nowhere to be found. Perhaps he decided it would be better to disassociate himself with this strange woman that had disrupted their way of life.

Around a corner, Adda found that they were walking toward a far larger building that dwarfed the homes around it. Much like with the mountain, Adda instantly knew the building had been there the whole time, and yet somehow had remained unnoticed to her until that very moment. It wasn't like the other homes, but calling it a 'home' was a bit of a misnomer. This building was more like a castle that had withstood the march of time, rather than a space that anyone actually lived in.

The castle was made of stone instead of wood, its drab, grey color standing out amidst the blackened wood of the surrounding houses. The stone was expertly placed together and sealed with the dark liquid that glinted in the sunlight. The building rose a couple of stories high, which wasn't very impressive by modern standards, but it was big enough to make the shacks below feel small and insignificant. Throughout the walls were carved rough holes at random intervals. They acted as windows, but the building within appeared so dark that Adda couldn't see anything through them.

As they drew near, Adda saw a white vine, reminiscent of ivy, clawing its way up the walls. The coloration had a bone-like quality to it, aged after centuries in the dirt only to burst free from the soil to climb desperately out of its grave. The vines found the grooves and cubbies, pulling itself higher and higher up the walls, encompassing much of the lower half of the castle in its grasp. The heaviest concentration of the vines were clustered at the base of a single tower that rose above the roof of the castle another thirty feet or so.

A large gash was torn into one side of the tower, leaving a hole so large that Adda could actually make out the room that lay within. Just within the darkness, she could make out what appeared to be a tall, skinny figure.

In the blink of an eye, it was gone, vanishing so quickly Adda wondered if it had just been a trick of the light. With a shudder, she pulled herself away from the broken tower.

As they approached the entrance, Adda was surprised to find that the door wasn't sealed by an impressive gate but rather covered by a simple animal skin. It fluttered in the wind, showing a wide tunnel just beyond. It felt out of place when compared to the rest of the building. For a monument that boasted such strength and power, it was remarkably easy to gain access to it.

Keith pushed the skin away, waving Adda to enter into the depths. She stared for a moment, hesitating in the threshold as her eyes adjusted to the darkness within. Adda had the unsettling feeling she was being led into the belly of some great beast.

Well there's no going back now, Adda thought to herself, painfully aware of the crowd gathered just behind her.

Adda slipped a hand into her purse, brushing her fingers over the symbol on the box. The small indentation brought up a surge of confidence as she faced down the unknown. She had to keep moving forward, she had to understand what had happened to her.

To all of them.

With that, Adda stepped past the curtain and into the darkness beyond, ready to face whatever was waiting for her.

10

The first thing Adda noticed as she moved into the castle was the bone chilling cold that permeated the air. It oozed out of the walls, creating pools of icy vapor that spun around her feet. Instinctively, Adda wrapped her arms around herself to stave off the biting cold, but came to a startling realization. Her mind recognized the cold, and had even reacted to it, yet her body seemed to be blissfully unaware of the change. She didn't shiver, her teeth didn't chatter, and her skin felt warm to her touch.

One more thing to the list of weirdness. Adda thought, taking in her surroundings.

Looking about, Adda was surprised by the fact that she could see despite the lack of any discernible light source. From the outside, the castle's interior had appeared to be as black as a moonless night. Now inside, the air was filled with a sickly, green light that glowed eerily across the grey stones. This green light made focusing her eyes on anything difficult, causing weird shadows to dance across the walls.

Despite this, Adda could clearly see that they were on one end of a long hallway that ended in a 'T' shaped passageway. Between the left and right turn, an imposing staircase sprung from the ground to take travelers up into the castle.

The hall itself looked like Hollywood's interpretation of a medieval crypt with its low ceiling and drab atmosphere. All the place needed was a couple of guttering torches and the image would be complete. Adda half expected some kind of undead creature to start clawing out of the walls in an effort to attack the trespassers.

Keith motioned for her to follow deeper in, and against her better judgement, Adda fell in line. Their footsteps echoed around them as they walked, disrupting the heavy silence. The sound reverberated down the corridor, making their four feet sound like dozens. Occasionally, Adda would glance over her shoulder, feeling that there was another set of foot falls hiding in the cacophony. To her relief, there was never anyone behind her except for twisting shadows.

They reached the end of the hall and Keith eagerly mounted the stairs. He seemed giddy as he leaned his bulk against the stair's railing and hauled himself up. Adda paused briefly at the bottom, glancing to the left and right.

The conjoining hall stretched out in either direction for what appeared to be an eternity. In fact, it honestly may have been an eternity as her eyes strained to see the end but could not. The passage shrank away from her, growing smaller and smaller as the impossible distance became nothing but a murky, green speck. There was no horizon to steal away the view, and so Adda gazed into a truly endless depth that would make the ocean seem like a puddle. The sight was maddening, hypnotic, and it tempted her to walk down its cold infinity to see if there truly was an end.

She shook her head, clearing it of the sudden, muddled thoughts that fell like a fog onto her mind. With a quick turn, she followed Keith up the stairs, trying to ignore the looming void she had left behind.

They walked up the stairs, Keith leading the way with a confident stride.

Though it was good to see him so comfortable in himself, it also sparked a worry in Adda's heart. There was something unsettling about even the way he moved, though she couldn't quite put her finger on it.

Is this actually Keith? Adda wondered to herself.

Perhaps this hardened, new life had caused him to become someone else in order to survive, or an even more chilling thought, perhaps the man had always been this way deep below the surface, waiting for his chance to take control. She had seen the way his eyes had caused those deadpanned faces to turn away, as if holding the weight of his attention was too much to bear. He had become something not to be trifled with in this new world.

Where others struggled to survive, this man was thriving.

All these thoughts and more flew around Adda's mind as she followed this hulking figure through his castle. The stairs had given way to hallways that lead to animal skins that lead to more hallways. There were no ornaments on the walls, nothing to interrupt the interlocked, grey stones bathed in the green light. There wasn't anything to be used as a reference point, causing Adda to feel discombobulated. Every curtain led to more hallways, turning the castle from a home into a labyrinth.

The muted grey all around her melted together until she was no longer walking on stone, but rather was slipping through an eternal void lit only by sickly ghost light. It crossed her mind that some predators employed traps to capture and confuse their victims, causing her to eye Keith's back suspiciously. Adda was quite certain that Keith alone was able to navigate this maze, so if he decided to leave her here she very much doubted she'd be able to find her way out again. The thought sent a chill racing down her spine, and for a moment, she felt the cold bite of the air pressing in around her.

Without even really considering the motion, Adda let her fingers drift down to brush against the box again. The dimpled symbol pushed against her thumb and she was surprised to find that the wood was actually warm to her touch as if it had been left out in the sun all day. The warmth seeped into her skin and crawled up her arm, racing through her veins until it reached her heart. It collected there before spreading out into her whole body causing her to let out a quiet sigh of relief.

Keith's head snapped in her direction, though he didn't look directly at her nor did he stop moving forward. He just regarded her out of the corner of his eye before slowly rotating his neck until he faced away from her again. She wondered if he had felt the warmth too or had reacted to the sound she made in the suffocating air. Either way, she noticed that the man's pace had picked up and his hands had tightened into fists. Yet, even with this image before her, whatever fear had been gathering in her was dissipated once again.

The Certainty had led her here and it would lead her out just the same.

Up ahead, Keith pulled open another curtain, disappearing behind it without making sure she followed. With nowhere else to go, Adda hurried after him. She pushed through the animal skin to see another staircase, this one spiraling upward on a central pillar. The make and proximity of the wall to the stairs suggested that this was the access point to the lone tower she had seen when approaching the place.

At her feet, Adda saw a massive web of white vines covering both the stairs and the walls. It crept in like rot, forcing its way between the stones until the castle had surrendered and allowed the invaders access where it blemished the once endless grey with its pale, white fingers. A sickly, sweet smell permeated the air around the vines, making it difficult to breathe. It assaulted Adda's nose and lungs with such force that she felt she would vomit. Fortunately, she mastered the instinct and placed a hand over her mouth to block out the odor.

There was something deeply unsettling about the vines, and so Adda tried her best to climb the stairs without stepping on them. She placed every step with care, sometimes walking on tip-toes to keep her feet only on the grey of the stone. Keith didn't share her caution, placing his heavy feet wherever he pleased as he squeezed his great bulk up the narrow stairs. The plant made a cracking sound as the man's massive weight pressed against them, being turned into ash beneath his grinding heel. Adda hurried along after him, watching where she stepped in order to keep the ashy substance from her feet.

Up and up they went around the pillar as they ascended to the top of the castle. There were no windows in the gloomy place, making it impossible to tell how high they had climbed. Keith's breath came out in laborious heaves as though he found it harder and harder to maintain his course. Each step had become a struggle, yet the man continued to push forward just the same.

As they climbed, the twisting vines became thicker, covering every surface until it appeared like a carpet. Adda could no longer pick around the vines and was forced to walk across them. She shivered as she felt them give way to powder beneath her. The solid *crunch* was an uncomfortable sound that echoed louder than it should have. Fortunately, the vines had no effect on the green light, allowing Adda to still be able to see where she was going. The idea of tripping in the dark only to fall into the brittle embrace of this other-worldly plant was one that would send a shiver down anyone's spine.

Finally, they reached the top of the tower where yet another animal skin hung across a frame to hide what lay beyond. Keith pulled aside the curtain, politely waving Adda in. She saw that there was a heavy amount of sweat on his brow and his chest heaved as he tried to catch his breath. The climb in and of itself was not exactly easy, but Adda felt that his reaction wasn't purely from the physical exertion. No, approaching the peak of the castle seemed to make the man ill, his skin a shade paler than it had been outside when she had first been reacquainted. Adda moved past the man, trying not to brush against his feverish arm that hovered just beside her.

Hugging the wall, she was then met by the tower beyond.

The first thing Adda saw was the wide hole that she had spotted from the ground below. It boasted a grand view of both the hamlet and the mountain. The makeshift window seemed unintentional, by all appearances it was as though whoever constructed this castle had forgotten to finish this wall and had just continued right along to place the roof overhead. Though the hole was quite big, it was surprising how little natural light flooded in. The sickly light of the castle pushed back against the golden sunshine, forcing it to stay out. Adda could see the daylight just at the threshold of the castle, but it could not break through the gloom.

Tearing herself away, Adda turned her head to the rest of the room.

Hanging from the ceiling were long strips of rope that held drying animal skins similar to the ones used to cover the doorways. They twisted lazily in the breeze that trickled in, casting contorting shadows on the wall behind them. Each cord was adorned with feathers and beads that whispered and clicked with every passing breeze.

The walls around them were covered in exotic looking furs from all manner of animals. Some Adda recognized, but others were completely alien to her, boasting colors and compositions that she hadn't even seen in a book. They were sealed to the walls, presumably with the substance that was used to lash the villagers' homes together. The furs were so thick that they caused the room to become muted as the insulation effectively swallowed up any escaping sound. It made the room feel heavier, like the air itself was thicker here than anywhere else.

In the center of the room was a large, wooden table with a chair on either side. Strewn across it were bits of ancient looking parchments that had been written upon with a dark liquid.

Keith stepped past her, sweeping the papers into an orderly stack and laying them face down with a blank one tactfully placed on top.

He clearly didn't trust her to see whatever secrets were written there, but she had little time to care as he pulled out one of the chairs politely, inviting her to sit. She obliged, giving a wane smile before settling into her chair. Once she had done so, Keith sat down across from her, placing his arms on the table and interlacing his fingers.

They sat there for a minute in silence as they regarded one another. It was hard to read Keith's expression, as most of his face was clouded by the low-light that clung to this place like a shroud. She pondered what he might be thinking, wondering if perhaps he was waiting on her to speak. Unsure of the territory she had found herself in, she felt it was in her best interest to allow this strange man to make the first move.

So the silence stretched as each tried to decipher the other's inner-workings. Keith seemed to have as many questions as she did as his dark eyes searched her own. Yet, even then, he made no attempt to speak, letting the quiet grow heavy. Adda didn't like the way he was looking at her and found herself growing increasingly more uncomfortable with every second that passed them by.

Don't. Squirm. Adda thought to herself as she stared unerringly back at Keith.

Then, just as the silence was becoming unbearable, Keith let out a chuckle and relaxed back into his chair. He settled in, crossing his arms where he began tapping his fingers against his bicep. *Duh duh duh duh* from pinky to pointer they rolled, sounding as though they were knocking against stone rather than skin.

"Still the same Adda." He said wryly, shaking his head in disbelief. "It's amazing, you look exactly the way I remember you. Better, even."

Adda didn't respond. She tilted her head to one side and continued to stare at the man.

"As strong as ever, too." Keith laughed.

He suddenly leaned forward, his mass looming over her like a mountain. His drumming fingers snaked out and found purchase on her arm. Keith folded the stoney hand around her, giving her a comforting squeeze.

"I'm so glad you made it here. It's dangerous out in the hills beyond our walls. You're lucky you made it this far." He smiled at her, his voice becoming tender. "You don't have to be strong anymore Adda, let me- us take care of you. You're finally home."

Adda cleared her throat and politely pulled her arm away from his insistent grip, folding her hands neatly in her lap beneath the table. Keith's eyes remained blank and passive, the only thing giving away that he had even noticed her pull away were his pupils briefly darting down toward where his own hand lay. Now empty, Keith drew back his hand, but remained hovering over Adda as he continued to address her.

"If you hadn't noticed, the world has changed. It's up to us to stick together, to build a new life." Keith said.

"I noticed, thank you." Adda replied dryly. "I was hoping you might have some answers."

"You really don't know?" Keith asked, eyes narrowed. "You're lucky you made it this far on your own."

Adda didn't say anything, just cocked an eyebrow.

"I will make time to answer your questions, but it will have to wait. Now that we can protect you, we-"

"Keith, stop it." Adda sighed, interrupting the man.

"What?" Keith asked, taken aback.

"Stop trying to scare me," Adda clarified, "I just want some answers. So let's stop playing games and get into it. Yeah?"

Keith blinked in surprise, clearly not expecting the kind of response he had been given. Though the man had spoken to Adda's strength, it was obvious that he didn't actually believe those things. Keith had always assumed that her behavior was a front that hid a softer more feminine core. It was clear that in his mind, she would throw away this facade of confidence to be at his powerful mercy. Well now, he was in for a rude awakening.

"Well, uh, yes, right, you're right." He flustered, struggling to regain his composure. "I suppose I should just start at the beginning then?"

A fleeting glimpse of the Keith she once knew revealed himself, looking to her for permission to continue. Adda gave an expectant nod, relieved to find something familiar in the unrecognizable man.

"Well, ok, probably around a year ago the military showed up-"

A whole year? More questions buzzed, but Adda pushed them aside, not wanting to miss any details.

"-just kept driving until the road finally just vanished, we tried to push on but all our vehicles started to rust and fall apart-"

That sounded familiar. Her own car had done that very thing.

"-only some of our possessions stuck around so we gathered what we could and started hiking, trying to figure out where we were." Here Keith paused, glancing out the window. "That's when the Snatchers first showed up."

146

He took in a long breath before continuing.

"At first, only the kids could see them, saying that there were shadows following us over the hills. It put us all on edge but we tried our best to assure them that nothing was wrong. We attempted to make camp that night, but as soon as the sun set, people started to scream."

Night? Adda had never seen the sun even budge here, always stuck at its height.

"They came running out of the dark wearing nothing but animal skins and bones." Adda saw fear flicker in his eyes as he fell into his story, remembering in vivid detail a night that would haunt him forever. "They were twice our size, like giants! They had grey skin that looked like ash, and they moved faster than anything I've ever seen. They hunted us down, capturing us a few at a time only to disappear back into the hills."

Keith adjusted in his chair, bringing his elbows in close on the table and putting his hands to his face. As he sat there, rubbing his palms against his eyes, it became apparent that Keith was just as spent as everyone else. The heavy exhaustion made the great man look smaller, shrinking beneath the weight of their struggles.

"This went on for weeks. We never knew when the next raid would come, it was like they'd just appear out of thin air. We needed somewhere we could protect ourselves, set up a base to fight off the Snatchers." Keith's voice cracked as he was momentarily overwhelmed by emotion.

"I can't do this anymore, Adda. I need help." He then removed his hands from his eyes, gazing at Adda with the expression of a truly broken man. "I need *your* help."

Adda kept her expression blank, trying to keep her emotions in check. Part of her felt for the man and wanted to reach across the table to comfort him. She was an artist who had an eye for the potential of broken things. For years she had wandered about her hometown, taking on projects to help breathe life into the buildings and their residences. It was this part of her that almost convinced her that she could fix this poor man.

Almost.

The other part of her, the one that had been refined through the crucible of life, told her to sit still, be quiet, and to listen rather than act. This part of her hummed with the Certainty, affirming in Adda's heart what she sensed but didn't fully understand. Adda stared blankly at Keith, adopting the same look that the villagers had held, giving nothing away to the man.

His eyes searched her own, looking for some kind of reaction. Finding none, his glistening pupils suddenly hardened, banishing away the moment of vulnerability as if it had never been. Keith sat tall to overshadow Adda once again. He looked down his nose at her, his entire form adopting a predatory stance. Muscles twitched, hands flexed, and his feet pressed with intense force against the ground as if he was about to lunge at her. He once again sized her up, looking for a chink in her armor he could abuse.

She had been right earlier. The man was a predator, ready to lay traps for unsuspecting victims.

Be careful, Adda, the woman thought to herself.

"And then what happened?" Adda asked evenly, acting as though the moment hadn't happened.

Keith relaxed his body, but his jaw was still clenched as if biting back some response. He was unsure of what to do with her and that made him angry. Making a scoffing sound and giving a shake of his head, the man continued his story.

"We walked for a while before finally coming across the cliffs. This was the only flat space we've been able to find that wasn't occupied by the Snatchers. Scott and some others went on a couple of scouting missions when they discovered the forest that the Snatchers get their wood from."

"There's a forest out here?" Adda asked.

"Yeah, the Snatchers go there a few times a day. They always cut more wood than they need, so we would wait for them to leave and just take whatever was left over. It took us a while, but we managed to get the wall put together." Keith glanced to one side. "Since then, they've mostly left us alone, only snatching people who travel too far from our sanctuary."

Adda took into account everything Keith had just told her, letting it take shape in her mind. It didn't answer very many of her questions, but there was certainly plenty to mull over. There were a few things that didn't quite line up with what she had seen so far. For starters, the sun had yet to move from its suspended place in the sky, making the night aspect of Keith's story impossible.

Then there was the fact that she had passed through what she assumed to be a Snatcher village earlier that day. Only the huts she had seen were not big enough to house giants. Maybe it was trauma and fear working together to make these beings seem bigger than they actually were. After all, the mind was a tricky thing, prone to

149

fabricating details in times of crisis.

There was also one other detail missing from his tale that Adda felt the need to bring up. Finding enough wood to build their town and the wall in just a year was impressive, but not necessarily inconceivable. However, constructing the very castle they sat in without modern equipment by unskilled builders within that same time frame strayed into the realm of impossibility.

"You forgot to mention the castle." Adda said, broaching the topic.

"Come again?" Keith asked, his brow crinkling in confusion as though she had spoken a different language.

"You forgot to mention the castle." Adda repeated slowly. "How did you manage to build it?"

"Oh, we didn't." Keith replied, settling back in his chair and appearing satisfied with his answer.

Adda waited, thinking he would elaborate.

"Then- who did?" She said when it became apparent the man was done talking.

"I woke up one day and it was here." Keith said matter-of-factly. "I realized these people needed a solid leader and so I claimed this place as mine."

"And you don't think that's odd?"

Keith's expression suddenly turned darkened, a look that Adda decided she most definitely didn't like. The man stood, moving around to the back of his chair and laying his hands upon the backrest. He leaned forward then, causing the piece of furniture to groan beneath his bulk. Adda wasn't sure if it was her mind playing tricks on her, but she could have sworn that Keith looked bigger than before.

"No, Adda, what I think is odd is that after an entire year, you come waltzing in here without a hair out of place and ignorant to the monsters that stalk us everyday."

Keith's voice took on a harder edge becoming rough and angry. His eyes narrowed into slits as he continued.

"What I think is odd is that when I pulled you up out of the mud not a drop of it stained your clothes." He leaned toward her, looming like a storm cloud ready to burst. "It's my turn to ask the questions."

Adda didn't interject even as Keith brought his face down inches from her own. His eyes were brimming with mistrust and rage as they searched her own, trying to decipher whatever secrets she had hidden there.

"Adda, what are you?"

He was right on those accounts. She didn't have mud stains on her clothing though she sat with Mrs. Dunton and she had arrived far later than anyone else by a wide margin. Those things were curiosities to even herself. Though his question was perfectly valid, it made Adda nearly laugh. The fact that someone as changed as Keith could ask such a thing unironically was almost humorous.

The more Adda spent time with him, the more the changes to the man were obviously unnatural. Instead of looking as though he was just a big man, he actually appeared as though more than one person had come together to fuse into this entity. Though his story was filled with stone-skinned giants, to Adda, Keith looked like the real monster. She looked into his face, still so close to her own, taking in the finer details that she hadn't made out before.

The man's face was hollow, shrunken, and dry. It was like an ancient riverbed that had succumbed to generations of drought, forgetting the feeling of rain upon its cracked form. His skin was like scales, painfully flecking off with every tumbling breeze. Adda noticed that his face was also too small for the head it was attached to, making it look like someone had thrown Keith's likeness on a disturbing sculpture as an afterthought. The contrast between face and body was both bizarre and pitiful.

Yet, Adda didn't feel any pity.

No, Adda felt anger.

Anger that this man would attempt to manipulate her, intimidate her, and control her. She had once been his friend, yet he treated her like an aberration.

A stranger.

A threat.

The anger boiled louder than whatever survival instinct warned her to sit down and shut up. Adda also rose to her feet, staring down the other all the while. She would not be cowed, especially by the likes of Keith Baker.

"My name is Adda Reinhoff, I am no more and no less than that." Her voice came out smooth and deadly, slipping from her mouth like a blade, "I don't know what has gotten into you, but I will not be bullied into getting what you want."

Keith stood still, and once again Adda felt an unspoken challenge come to a head, warping the atmosphere with intense energy. But unlike Scott who had quickly turned away, Keith didn't back down. Instead, he moved closer, his eyes burning with something deep and dark, like a river cutting through stone far beneath the ground. It was building in force and racing to the surface, causing the man's eyes to turn into black pits.

"My poor, sweet Adda." Keith hissed. "Do you want to know why everyone down below falls into line?"

The air chilled all the more, allowing tendrils of frost to begin forming on the table beneath the giant's hands. They spread like spiderwebs, reaching across the table toward where Adda took her stand.

"I have no idea where we are, and honestly, I don't care anymore. Because back there, in our forgotten, pathetic corner of the world, I was no one." Keith continued, spitting bitterly.

Darkness oozed from every corner, swallowing up the room like a thick fog. It gobbled up the sickly light, leaving behind only the barest amount to see by. The blanketing gloom settled upon Keith like a heavy cloak, making him appear like a writhing mass of shadows.

"But here? I'm a god."

No sooner had the words left Keith's mouth when Adda felt something strike against her. It had no physical force, instead it slammed into her mind like a meaty fist. The great blow twisted around her brain, creating waves of mounting pressure. It squeezed at her from every direction, trying to snap her will. The fist was powerful, holding a strength against her like nothing she had ever known.

No, it wasn't a fist. Such a strike was too precise to be compared to something so weighty as the human hand. It was more like a great serpent, elegant in its deadliness. Now that it had struck its prey, the snake's scaled sides had begun looping themselves around her very being. The noose was closing and it threatened to squeeze her until she collapsed unconscious.

Adda stood still, unsure of what was happening to her. There wasn't even anything she could compare this feeling to, leaving her at a total loss as the coils pulled in tighter. The pressure weighed against her, attempting to drag her to her knees.

"Aren't you tired?" Keith said, his voice reflected as a whisper that rustled like leaves from all around. "Don't you just want to give someone else control?"

Adda didn't respond as she stared back at Keith. The snake pulled closer, but Adda hardly noticed as something else had caught her attention.

Was it getting lighter in the room?

"It's pointless to resist." Keith continued. "I know what it is you really want. I can take care of you."

It *was* getting lighter in the room. It was a subtle difference, hardly noticeable at first, but it had now become undeniable. A few moments ago, Adda could hardly make out the man before her, but now she could once again see the fur-ridden wall just beyond Keith.

And there, cast upon the wall, Adda saw a strange sight.

Just beyond Keith's shoulder, Adda could make out a second shadow that spilled out of the man like pooling water.

Is it a trick of the light? Adda thought to herself, so fascinated by the thing she had nearly forgotten about the power that brushed against her mind.

Adda could tell that this was no trick, however, taking in what lay plainly before her. Keith's own shadow hung upon the wall like a great, looming mountain. It spread its mass outward, covering most of the wall in its monstrous girth. The other shadow looked almost the exact opposite.

Instead of flesh and muscle that bulged out almost comically, this shadow looked as though it were made of nothing but ragged skin and brittle bones. It was skinnier than anything should be, its skeletal form dancing along with Keith's every move.

Another puzzle piece clicked in the back of Adda's mind as she stared at the shadow and it leered back.

She turned her attention back to Keith, surprised to find that he was still talking. He continued to whisper in a coaxing tone about all the good he could bring to her, ignorant of the light that was steadily growing around him. Adda found her eyes slipping past the man's form, piercing through his flesh and bone to see what hid beneath.

Within this man that had once been Keith, Adda saw hunger, rage, and fear. She witnessed a man who desperately wanted an ounce of power, but always came up wanting. She saw a man who had finally been given a chance and had seized it no matter the consequence.

The snake suddenly slipped from her mind, finding no purchase to hold onto. It recoiled away from her, racing back to Keith to lick its wounds. The man blinked in surprise as he became aware that Adda seemed undisturbed.

As the snake retreated, the brilliant light faded, leaving only the green pallor to infect the inside of the tower once more. Even if Keith had noticed the sudden intruder that had banished the shadows, he seemed far more engrossed with the woman before him.

Fear floated like a ghost across his face as he sized her up. He shifted his weight uncomfortably, making it obvious that this hadn't happened to him before.

The man leaned forward again and Adda felt the snake pounce on her, trying to catch her off guard. This time it could not even begin to coil before it slid past, falling away into the void. With its failure, Keith took a full step back, appearing to become agitated.

The third time that the snake came hurtling at her, Adda was now sure it was Keith's doing. How it was possible would be a question for later. For now, Adda waved off the clutching energy as though it were merely a bothersome odor. She fixed the man with her hardest stare as she leaned further over the table.

"Stop that." Adda said firmly.

"H-how are you doing that?" Keith asked, shrinking away from her, unable to hide his terror. "What are you?"

"As I said before, I'm just Adda." The woman replied curtly, sitting down and running her hands along her pants to smooth them out. "Now, I have a few more questions and then I'll let you get back to-well- whatever it is you were doing."

Keith nodded numbly, also retaking his seat. This time he looked down at the table, avoiding eye contact with her. With his bluster snatched away, Adda could clearly see the man she had known for much of her life. The body he wore could no longer hide that truth from her.

"Ok. On my way here I saw this great, big mountain surrounded by storming clouds." Adda began. "Would you happen to know what's on the other side?"

Keith dragged his eyes away from the fascinating grain of the table to fix Adda with a long look.

"Do you feel it, too?"

"Feel what, exactly?"

"The dread." Keith said sullenly.

Adda thought back to when she first saw the mountain. It had occupied her attention so fully that everything else had faded away. She had been drawn to it like a moth to a flame, so consumed that she hadn't even noticed her feet moving her closer to it. There was certainly something unsettling about it, but Adda wouldn't classify that as dread.

"I don't think I know what you mean." Adda said hesitantly. "Could you describe it to me?"

"How do you not feel it?"

"Keith, please."

The man let out a sigh and grimaced. He turned his head to look out the gaping hole in his tower, looking out across his community.

"It's hard to put into words." Keith started slowly. "It's like the mountain is alive somehow, and it sees us, and it judges us. Looking at it too long is sickening and so we try to ignore it as much as we can."

The haunted, exhausted looks on the faces of the townsfolk sprang to Adda's mind. Was this why they appeared so broken and spent?

"If that's the case, why haven't you left and found a spot further away?"

"Because," Keith said, his voice becoming distant and hungry, "this is the only place we can see the lights of the city."

The city.

The words caused her mind to flash back to just a few days prior.

She saw herself sitting on the lip of a cliff, brush in one hand as she brought life to a canvas. There, sitting on a hill to one side, she had painted a golden radiance that emanated from a blank spot. Suddenly, in her mind, the blank spot was filled in with a city made of pearl and gold, humming with energy and life.

The thought sent a shiver down her spine.

That can't be right. Adda thought to herself. *That's impossible!*

Yet the image wouldn't shake. She filed away the thought, letting it stew in the back of her mind as she looked to Keith, determined to know as much as she could.

"There's a city over there? How do you know?" Adda asked, curious.

"For a long time, we saw lights glowing from around the sides of the mountain, lighting up the night like a small sun. We never knew what it was until one day, a traveler passed through. He claimed the lights belonged to a city and that he aimed to get there." Keith hesitated and began to drum his fingers on the table. "As much as the mountain terrorizes us, it's the golden lights beyond that keep us from giving up."

A traveler?

The way Keith had said it made Adda think that this traveler had been a stranger, someone not from her hometown. The thought was an intriguing one and created many more questions. At the very least it did answer one thing. Whatever had happened to her small corner of the world was, in fact, happening to others as well.

"Well then, why are you still here?" Adda asked. "If there is a city over there, it means there's structure, industry, homes! At the very least they could probably help with your Snatchers."

"It's not as simple as that. For one thing, as much as the lights bring us life, there's no assurance that we can trust the people in the city." He paused. "And- there is another reason. Here, let me show you."

Keith stepped from the table, walking over to the gaping hole in the wall and waved Adda over. She rose and joined him there, blinking as the light outside was far clearer in the opening than it had been in the room.

Standing there, Adda couldn't help but feel somewhat like a ruler overseeing her kingdom. It gave a great vantage point of the town below where the people milled about their various tasks. The feeling grew, twisting around her as it materialized visions of what could be.

In her mind, she imagined what it would be like to stay here and take Keith's place. But instead of being a mayor, she would be a queen whose rule would be without rival. She would organize these pathetic scraps of humanity, pull them together and wipe out these Snatchers, reclaiming the people that belonged to her. They would take their jewelry and riches, and adorn her with them as their rightful ruler. Then they would no longer look at her in pity, then they would look at her in awe, and love, and fear.

Adda shook her head, banishing the alien thoughts as quickly as they had come. She had never been one to desire power or control, yet the sudden onslaught of emotions had tried to convince her otherwise. She was shocked that she had actually considered it for a moment, the temptation tasting sour in her mouth. There was something very wrong with this place and staying here too long was dangerous. Adda knew she had to leave quickly, but not until she knew what Keith knew.

Ripping her gaze from the town, she turned to look out to the left, beyond the cliffs to the mighty mountain beyond. A fresh batch of midnight clouds rumbled down its face, growling and hissing with storms. From this vantage, Adda could better see the great valley that surrounded its one peak, separating the crags and hills from their great mountain.

Keeping her eyes from the mountain for worry that it would draw her feet forward from the precipice of the tower, Adda found herself drawn to the land around it. It was more beautiful than anything that Adda had ever seen. She gasped as everything else seemed to pale around her and her vision was dominated with what lay before her. It was hard to focus on a single thing as the valley was host to so many incredible sights.

To one side, a massive lake sparkled and glinted like the bluest sapphires. Adda imagined dipping herself into the cold waters of the mountain-fed lake, audibly sighing with relief as she was taken by the daydream. A river snaked free from one side, creating a lazy path that meandered around to the other side of the mountain. Adda saw herself floating along the river, letting its currents take her wherever it pleased rather than having to worry about what choice she needed to make next. There were a number of forests that stood tall and thick along the banks of the river, swallowing up the waters into their midst, only to release it to the other side. Amongst the trunks, Adda knew she could be whoever she wanted as the trees would hide her from the judgement of others. Further along, she could somehow make out miles of thick bushes that bent under the heavy load of juicy berries of all manner and kind. Adda could taste their sweet fruit bursting against her tongue, the sticky juice rolling down her cheeks as she gorged herself upon the delicious flesh. She felt herself become intoxicated with the scene, her head heavy with images of bliss and desire.

Forget the city. Adda wondered why the people hadn't even tried to go to this valley that sat nearly in their backyard. It was a paradise unrivaled by anything earth could ever muster. To stay here, struggling to survive was insanity.

Breaking her eyes away from the scene to look at Keith snapped her from the magnetic pull. All at once, Adda felt dizzy, overwhelmed by the longing to turn back to the valley and the guilt of wanting to do so. Just like the mountain, the valley pulled on her attention, making it hard to focus on anything else.

"Why are you still up here?" Adda asked in a daze, aware that her words were coming out slurred as if from too much drink. "The valley could provide everything you need."

Keith turned his frame away from her, leveling his gaze now at the wide depression beyond. Adda saw his face go slack as he too was taken in by the view of it, leaning forward as if the valley would draw him straight out the side of the tower. The images that had swirled around Adda's mind played themselves across Keith's face. There was hunger, desire, longing, and bliss, things that demanded to be satisfied.

Yet, the man stood rooted.

"There are strangers living in the valley." Keith muttered, still looking down.

As he uttered the words, Adda saw the man's face harden, as if such a thing displeased him. His jaw clenched, his eyes narrowed, and his fists grasped against the air as if looking for something to strangle.

"They'll come up every so often to try and bring us back with them. They'll say whatever they need to trick us into leaving." Keith said, "We may be struggling to survive up here, but at least we are the ones in control."

Adda looked back to the valley, staring with fascination at the beauty encircling around the mountain.

"I sent out a small band to find a path around the mountain so that we could travel to the city beyond." Keith spoke again, "They went into the valley, but only a few returned. They reported that the moment the rest of the party had touched the border of the valley, they had abandoned their mission. They said it was like they had been taken by some kind of magic."

Keith turned to her, his jaw clenched tight, "We will not give ourselves over to the people of the valley, just as we won't give ourselves to the Snatchers."

Adda saw what this was about then, whether it was the valley or about this city beyond, they both shared a common thread. It gave others opportunity to impress themselves upon *his* people. This was about power. It was about Keith maintaining his grip over his tiny hamlet and the lives within. He not only had physical control, but also some kind of mystical one as well, ensuring his ownership of their home. The man wouldn't risk losing what he had gained. He would no doubt make small shows of trying to do what's best for everyone, but in the end, he would always devise some excuse to ensure that they would never leave.

Using fear as an instrument, Keith would convince this people that the dangers outweighed the gain. In that fear, they would stay, crushed underneath the weight of his power.

What a silly thing. The thought appeared in Adda's mind.

From her perspective it seemed foolish to slowly die out here when an answer sat so close to them. Even if there were dangers in the valley, at least it came paired with food, water, and shelter. If she had been living under the threat of these Snatchers for so long with the knowledge that there was a better option in her backyard, she would have left without hesitation.

As such things floated in her mind, Adda started to slowly become aware of the weight of Keith's attention. Even with the stupor of the valley heavy on her mind, she could see Keith looking her up and down from the corner of her eye. His gaze was hungry and wanting, taking in her form with careful consideration. The man had seized an opportunity, believing that she was too engrossed with the world outside to pay attention to him. The look was uncomfortable enough to make Adda shoot the man a sharp glare. Keith immediately bowed his head, sheepish for being caught.

"And- uh- before you ask," Keith said, trying to pretend the moment hadn't happened, "we've tried to go around the valley, but that doesn't seem to work. No matter how far we walk, this side of the mountain always faces us. It seems the only way out is through."

"Well, I guess it's impossible to get to the city then." Adda replied, this time keeping her focus on the man, daring him to look again. "If you walk in the valley, it takes you, and the mountain won't let you get around it. Unless there's something else?"

Keith pointed toward one side of the valley, off to the left and a little down. She looked where he indicated and saw a white mark that trailed right through the center of it all. It was nearly invisible amidst the lush colors that sprang up all around it.

"There is a path that you can walk that keeps your feet from the valley floor. It's the only way we've found that leads you to the mountain. But, Adda-" He paused, asking for her full attention, "Only a handful of people even make it across the entire valley, and all of them have turned back, unable to bear walking into the mountain. Please, I know you want answers, but there's no guarantees that you'll find them out there. Just stay here, with us. It's safe and we could use someone like you."

Adda took this all in, mulling it over as thoughts began to take shape in her mind. A city meant more people, but there was no way of knowing that they would be better off than those that had settled here. On top of that, with all this talk of dread, being snatched, and the valley enchanting those who walked it, it was almost enough to make one decide against such a journey.

Almost.

Whether it was just the image of the golden radiance from her painting parading through her mind or something else, the very idea of the city pulled on her like a magnet. It called her to move further up and further in. Even though she had just learned of its existence, she now understood that it had been drawing her forward ever since she had first left her car by the roadside. That is where her journey was to end, she was sure of it.

"No, I can't stay here. I have to get to the city."

"But Adda-" His voice was suddenly soft, and imploring, laying one of his stoney hands on the small of her back. It was an intimate touch, one that Adda bristled at. "-stay with me, imagine what we could do!"

He hesitated for a moment, and then rushed through his next words, getting them out before his will faltered. "If you stayed, you could be my wife and then you would have anything you ever dreamed of!"

Now that the words were out there, it brought that new, dark confidence back to the surface. His stance widened and he nearly pressed himself against her as his eyes grew distant as he envisioned their future.

"You would never have to hide who you really are again! You could do whatever you want, whenever you want! We could rule these people and lead them into a new age!"

"Keith," Adda said, crossing her arms defiantly. Her voice came out as a whisper, but it was as sharp as a blade and as hard as steel. "No."

Keith stared down at her in disbelief, a stupid grin still plastered across his face. Adda could see the gears turning in his head as he tried to process her rejection. A shadow passed over the man's face, casting him in a dark pallor. His eyes darkened and his hand pressed harder into Adda's back. It was clear that he was displeased with the answer.

"But, I love you." Keith hissed. "And I've been so good to you."

As if that meant she owed him anything at all. Anger flared like a match meeting tinder in her heart.

"I said no."

The man actually had the audacity to once again try to influence her, the snake trying desperately to find something to cling to. It came in howling with every ounce of his rage, yet it still could find no purchase, falling away more easily this time than ever before. Adda leveled her gaze at him, feeling something surging inside her as well.

Keith removed his hand and stumbled back as if he had been struck, his jaw slack and his eyes wild from the blow. He looked once more upon Adda before bowing backward away from her, trying to make himself appear smaller to show he had accepted his defeat. Adda didn't trust it, if she were to stay, she knew that the man would keep trying and trying to whittle her down.

That was his way.

Without another word, she marched across the room and pulled back the curtain, stopping only to look back once. Keith stood in that pale light, looking pitiful and weak, a thick sheen of sweat clinging to his brow. Despite his bulk, she realized how frail he actually was beneath his illusion of power. Her focus shifted from him to the wall immediately behind him, barely making out the second shadow still standing with its feet attached to his own.

It looked back at her.

"One last thing, Keith and I'm only saying this because we used to be friends." He looked up at her, a twisted hope flickering across his face. "You said earlier that this castle belonged to you."

He nodded, waiting for her to continue.

"I don't think it does."

11

The curtain fell back into place, swinging down like a blade that cut Adda from the room. She was suddenly hit with a wave of exhaustion, though not the kind that was physical. Miraculously, her body still felt in top shape as if she had just awoken from a rejuvenating rest not moments before. It was in her emotions that Adda felt the drain on her spirit.

Upon first seeing Everett, a small seed of hope had been planted. It had secretly whispered to her thoughts of sanctuary and rest, a place that was familiar amongst the alien. Yet between passing through the town and meeting with Keith, that hope had been snapped up. Such a loss weighed heavily on Adda, it brought forth temptations of staying to rest and recover.

Maybe just a night? Her mind bargained.

She put such desires away. Adda already felt that she had overstayed her welcome. Any extra time spent in this worn out town might have unforeseen consequences. It was best to leave immediately while she still had the strength to do so.

Besides, she had a mountain to climb.

Adda wandered down the stairs with heavy feet, this time ignoring the white plants that crunched beneath her heel. They made a soft sound as she moved along, almost like a whisper that tickled at her ear. In fact, it did sound like there were words being formed within the murmur as it faded into a quiet echo. As much as Adda strained to listen however, the whisper was snatched away before any sense could be made of it.

Best not to dwell on it. Adda thought to herself.

She had only walked a full circle around the stairs twice when she suddenly found herself standing at the bottom of the tower. Adda stopped, surprised to find herself there so quickly. The journey up had felt like it had taken a small eternity, yet coming back down it had been nearly instantaneous. Believing it to be a trick of the mind, Adda pushed past the next curtain, pausing once again in disbelief as she gazed down the hallway beyond.

Adda had wondered at how she would possibly find her way back out from the place without Keith as a guide. Yet instead of halls connected to doorways connected to more halls there was just a straight corridor that didn't twist or turn. It ran as straight and true as an arrow revealing no other path save one.

Against all possibilities, the hall that stretched only a dozen or so feet beyond her ended in a final, heavy curtain through which sunlight peeked around the edges. There had definitely been at least one other set of stairs that they had climbed, yet all that was gone now.

Confused, Adda cast a glance backward to find that there was now a wall where the stairs had just been. She was no longer welcome here, and somehow, the castle itself was showing her the way out. Adda was glad the building was just as keen to her leaving as she was.

Striding forward, Adda clutched the curtain and pulled it away. It eagerly swung wide to her touch, letting daylight once again fall upon her face. The woman paused there, basking in it, feeling its warmth banish away the darkness that tried to crowd in her mind. Adda then stepped forward, her feet settling into the mixture of mud and grass. No sooner had she moved beyond the castle did the entryway vanish with a low, grating sound.

Adda cast a look at it, eyeing the now seamless wall that denied her access back inside.

"Good riddance to you, too." Adda snipped at the somber building.

She let out a sigh, once again relishing the warmth of the sun. Though her body hadn't felt the full chill of the depressing corridors, it was good to once again stand in the presence of the glorious light.

Already the dank feeling of the castle and the gloominess of its occupant were fast fading from her mind as the next task loomed at her side. Adda looked to the mountain, watching the clouds gather once again for their assault on the blue skies above her. They still couldn't break through, but Adda knew that it soon wouldn't matter to her.

Soon she'd be in the valley beneath their wrath.

"You're back already?" Everett spoke as he materialized from between two buildings.

He approached her cautiously as if she were some kind of wild animal. It was as though he expected she would suddenly turn on him and snap him up in steely jaws. As he got closer, Adda could see him visibly relax upon finding she appeared normal.

Was he expecting something different? Adda thought.

"Kind of figured he'd have you up there longer." Everett went on.

"I'm sure he would have liked that." Adda said in a snide tone as she brushed past the other. "Unfortunately, I have places I need to be."

Everett turned to stare after her, his brow wrinkled in confusion as he processed her words. Realizing she was moving quickly away, Everett decided to jog after her, his curiosity brimming.

"Wait!" Everett called as he fell into step next to her. "What exactly happened up there?"

"Nothing at all." Adda said, trying not to think of Keith's advances. "We shared some stories, and in that, Keith told me about the city. After everything that's happened to all of us, I figured it's as good a place as any to go."

Adda omitted the part where she suspected that she had almost painted this mystical city days prior. She had already attracted too much attention as it was.

"He's letting you go to the city?" Everett wrinkled his nose at this, his voice tinged with disbelief.

"He's not *letting* me do anything. I'm making the choice to leave." Adda replied to him, feeling irritation rile up within her.

"I mean, Keith would never allow you to go." The young man argued.

"Well, I guess it's a good thing that I don't really care what he would allow." Adda said wryly, trying not to snap. "You should try it out sometime, it's quite liberating."

"But-" Everett's eyes went round and his mouth came agape as a realization sprang into his mind. He brought his voice down to a conspiratorial hiss as he moved closer to her.

"You *resisted* him? How did you do that?"

"I'm not really sure," Adda confessed. "Whatever he was trying to do just didn't seem to stick."

They had now moved into the heart of the township and had begun to gather up the attention of the villagers again. Their faces were as blank and as exhausted as before, yet such a visage could not hide the interest that was sparked by the duo. The people who caught sight of them left their tasks behind and began to follow at a safe distance.

"Honestly, nothing out here makes sense," Adda continued, "so, I'm going to do the only thing I know how and that's to keep moving forward. I can't quite explain it, but I know the city is where I have to go."

As she said it, the Certainty fluttered in her chest, affirming what she already knew. The valley was beautiful, the mountain was majestic, but her feet were pointed toward one thing and one thing only. She would cross through or over any obstacle to reach her destination.

To have such purpose filled Adda with determination. Although she had never felt lost or hopeless wandering through the hills previously, it had been a bit directionless. She had followed only the sense that beat alongside her heart with no name behind it to encourage her progress. Now, she knew where she was headed.

"Can I come with you?" Everett asked, his voice shaky with fear and excitement.

Adda was surprised, casting a sidelong glance at the young man.

She hadn't expected anyone to be interested in leaving and hadn't even thought to ask. She had assumed that everyone here just wanted her gone, a sentiment Adda was keen to oblige. Looking at Everett now, Adda could almost see life breathe itself once again into the man's battered frame. He still looked just south of awful, but there was a spark now that hadn't been there before.

"Are you sure Keith would allow it?" Adda asked, her voice ripe with sarcasm.

Everett nodded enthusiastically, the sarcasm apparently lost on him. "I mean, no one else has been able to resist him! Wherever you go, that's where I wanna be!"

"Stop her!"

Keith's voice boomed from behind them. The words were a command steeped with dark power. That power slithered past Adda, knowing better than to try and ensnare her again. Instead, the snake fell upon prey it knew were no match. No one even tried to fight it off as the power settled into its victims' minds, subjecting them to its awful grip. With eyes suddenly hardened, the townsfolk began to march forward with ominous intent.

Adda turned to Everett who now stood as still as a statue, his eyes wide and wild. Sweat poured like a river down his face, his forehead kneaded together in intense concentration. His entire body trembled with effort as if trying to resist. It was hard to gauge whether he was winning or losing, but the fact that he hadn't moved to grab Adda was encouraging.

The villagers surrounded them then, coming to a stop as they encircled the duo with no gaps for escape. Adda took in the faces all around her, all familiar, all broken, and all controlled.

Keith broke through one side of the circle, his frame creaking beneath the weight of his movement. Adda kicked herself for not leaving sooner. She should have known that he was not finished with her yet, he had never taken no for an answer. He had just never been strong enough to do anything about it.

"We can't let her leave." His voice rumbled like a storm, "Look at her, there's something different about her. Something- wrong."

He began to stalk the human barrier, addressing the crowd as he weaved his spell deeper within them. With each word, Adda saw the people harden a bit more, giving into the man's power.

"Think about it." He said. "How could she be missing for all these long months only to show up so strong and healthy? How could she travel so far through enemy territory without being taken?"

"She's a Snatcher!" A voice cried from somewhere in the crowd.

Everyone began to murmur in fear and anger at the thought, taken by the idea.

"She's a Snatcher." Keith repeated, his voice now coming out in an accusing hiss. "Yeah, she must be. You know what I say to that?"

The man lifted his arms up like a ringmaster at a circus. With impassioned words he implored his enraptured audience with a roaring voice.

"I say we give her a taste of her own medicine!"

The crowd cheered.

"I say we snatch her!"

The crowd cheered again, their shouts echoing louder, angrier.

"I say we throw her in the dungeon where she can rot forever!"

The crowd went berserk, chanting and spitting as the spell played upon their fears. They caved beneath him, allowing his complete control to dominate them. Keith turned to her then, a triumphant smirk on his face.

"I gave you an opportunity, Adda, you could have been my queen." He shook his head then. "Either way, I will make you mine."

Adda looked around at the yelling, screaming mob and felt for them what had once reflected in their eyes toward her.

Pity.

She pitied their sad state, knowing that no power was even necessary to control them, fear had done that all by its own might. Her eyes welled for a moment with tears, struck with a deep sadness to find these people so broken. Keith saw the emotion in her face and his smile broadened. Thinking he understood the meaning behind her misty eyes, the monstrous man drew in close to her. He brought his lips down to her ear so that he could address her without anyone else hearing.

"No need to cry, my dear, I promise that I will be good to you. You'll see." He whispered in a tone that was mockingly apologetic.

With a swipe of her arm, Adda swiftly wiped away the liquid in her eyes, letting out a dry chuckle at the same time.

"Keith." She looked up at him, "I am not afraid of you."

And just like that, she was done with him.

"Everett and I were just leaving." She continued as she patted Everett on the shoulder, "Come on, we've got places to be."

In response, Everett slowly turned and began to painfully walk alongside her, his body trembling with the effort. Yet even as his body shook, there was a triumph in his movement.

"There you go, you're doing it!" Adda whispered encouragingly as she leaned in close to him.

"Everett!" Keith's voice commanded, sending his serpent after them. "You *will* stop this instant!"

"Ignore him, he doesn't own you." Adda said.

"No! Stop them!" Keith yelled, his voice panicking, though he himself made no attempt to come after them.

Adda looped her arm through Everett's, letting him lean on her as they made their slow escape. Even with these ghosts glowering with murder from all around, Adda felt no panic as she pulled them along. She could feel that Everett's every move was one of great struggle as he combated the insidious thing Keith had planted in him. Each step was agonizingly small, but with every one completed, Everett stepped with a little more confidence than before.

They reached the barricade of people and Adda fixed the seething crowd with a hard look, her mouth pressed in a thin line.

"Move."

It was the only word she spoke, but its effect was immediate. Though their expression did not change, the crowd parted like water before her. They leered and grumbled from all sides as Adda and Everett passed through their midst, but none moved to apprehend them.

Keith trailed after the pair, seething as he did.

"You simple-minded idiots! I said 'stop them!'" Keith bellowed, but again, no one complied.

He cast about wildly, looking for any sign of obedience but found

175

none. Keith felt exposed before his people by this woman's defiance, feeling their attention turn from Adda to rest on him. The dynamic was shifting and Keith started to panic.

Finally, his eyes found an ally. He saw Scott wandering in from outside the gate, curious about all the commotion from within. Keith called out to the other man.

"Scott, grab her!"

The giant thug cocked his head to the side as he watched Adda approaching, her face set on the gate just behind him. His eyes lit with an inner fire as a manic smile cut through his face. The man swaggered up to her, his chest pumped up and his shoulders thrown back.

"Well well, if it isn't little Adda thinking she can come and go as she pleases." He reached a meaty paw toward her. "We're gonna teach you how it's done around here."

In the instant Scott's hand latched onto Adda's arm, the air was filled with the smell of burning flesh. Suddenly, a scream of intense pain exploded across the rooftops. It echoed continuously out, rending at the sky with claws of agony. It took a moment for Adda to realize that the sound was coming from Scott.

He was shaking as pain racked his body, his head thrown back and his jaw hung wide to let loose a never ending cry. The veins on his neck bulged and his eyes rolled back in his head as he shook as though he were having a seizure. All the while a steady stream of smoke billowed from beneath his hand where he held her.

His grip then loosened and he stumbled away, his hand shaking violently. Scott fell down onto his knees as he pulled the limb close to his chest. He gingerly held it there, nursing it as large tears rolled down his cheeks.

In the moments of him stumbling back Adda had seen that the palm of the man's right hand had become a mess of mutilated red and black as though having been exposed to extreme heat. Blisters had already begun to spring forth, bubbling like froth on his skin. The sight was as sickening as it was confusing. The crowd had fallen silent as they stared in terror at their champion who had been brought low without a single blow.

"Witch." A voice hissed. "She's a witch."

The crowd murmured with this revelation and they collectively took a step back, the fear in the air palpable.

"No! She's just some woman!" Keith yelled, his voice becoming strained. "What are you idiots doing? *Stop her*!"

This had become less about securing Adda and had become more about his tenuous hold on his power here. But no one made any move to come after her, rather they stood still, watching to see what she would do next. They waited, tense, unsure what kind of catastrophe she would bring upon them in retribution. A breath was collectively released as she did what none of them had expected, but all had willed her to do.

She, with Everett at her side, left.

12

With every step they took beyond the gate, Keith's hold on Everett dwindled more and more. The dark power that once had dominated the young man was burning away like morning mist before the rising sun. Everett even started to look healthier, his back straightening, his shoulders relaxing, and an easy smile coming back to his face. The weight that had loomed above him was suddenly removed, the act returning to him some of his lost humanity. He was rising on the high of victory in the face of great tribulation.

Though Adda was grateful to see him in better spirits, she wondered how long this new found strength would last. Had he forgotten why he hid behind the walls in the first place?

"So, what's the plan?" Everett was asking, practically skipping with joy. "Are we gonna go raid a camp for supplies or were you thinking we could try out hunting? I mean, I've never been hunting but I've always figured I'd be a natural at it!"

"The only plan I have is to cross over the mountain. Anything else is a distraction." Adda responded, already turning them back toward their destination now that they had given the walls of the town a wide berth.

Everett shook his head, "You must be joking."

"I like to think I'm pretty good with jokes, but no, this time I'm being serious."

"But we're not prepared to go that far! Like, we're gonna need food and water at some point!"

Adda cocked an eyebrow, "Will we?"

Everett looked at her like she had lost her mind. "Well, I mean, Yeah."

"I don't think that's how this- place works." Adda started, Everett took a breath as if he were about to interject, but Adda raised her voice to state that she wasn't finished speaking. "Look, I've been walking through these hills for hours on end and not once have I felt hungry or thirsty. I haven't even needed to rest once!"

"Ok, but *I* get hungry and thirsty, so- I dunno- maybe you're just different?"

"What do you mean by different?" Adda asked.

"Different like Keith is, you have your own powers or whatever."

Adda shook her head, thinking about the shadow standing over Keith, "I don't think either of us have any kind of superpowers. It seemed to me that Keith was borrowing his ability from something else."

"So you're not hungry 'cause something else is giving you powers?" Everett asked dryly. "Like a spirit guide?"

"Stop calling them powers." Adda replied. "And no, I don't have any secret abilities. I just think this world plays by its own set of rules."

"Yeah, but why would that even matter?," Everett argued, but it was clear he was thoroughly enjoying the conversation. "Let's say that, I dunno, we got teleported to some other world. The Snatcher World or whatever. Well, no matter how this world works, we still have the same bodies. That means we still have to take care of them from time to time. Ya' know?"

"Well, are they the same bodies?" Adda asked rhetorically. "Most of you don't look too different from how you did back home, but both Keith and Scott were very different. I could tell who they were, but there were some major physical changes."

"Sure, but that's only 'cause of the castle."

Adda regarded Everett, her interest piqued.

"What do you mean by that?"

"Keith didn't tell you?" Everett asked.

Adda shook her head, waiting for him to go on.

"Oh- Well, ok. So we just woke up one day and there was suddenly this big castle that had appeared out of nowhere. Everyone was pretty freaked out, but Keith kept saying not to panic 'cause it was his or some nonsense." Everett grumbled, clearly holding no love for the man. "He went in there for a really long time, but when he came out, he could *do* things. Like, he would just start talking and you'd want to do what he said. After a while he got together a little band of his most trusted. He took them all into the castle and when they came out they were all big and bad too, though none of them could do what Keith did."

"Was Scott one of them?"

Everett's eyes hardened. "Yeah, he was."

"Could he do- anything weird?"

"No weirdness. But, I mean, he did get freakishly strong, like, strong enough to fight Snatchers." Everett shook his head. "He got way more violent too. If it wasn't for Keith keeping him in line, I think he would have probably started killing the rest of us."

The thought of that ogre ripping through the hamlet chilled Adda. "What about the others?" She asked, moving the conversation on.

"Oh, they disappeared after a while. Most of them were part of the groups that went down to the valley to explore. The few that came back were- different. They got really strange, like talking to themselves or just standing on the cliff staring at the valley for hours. Eventually, part of them left for the valley and the others disappeared into the castle. Either way, none of them were ever seen again."

Adda thought about those confusing hallways that seemed to branch off into eternity in all directions. It would be easy to become lost in such a place. She shuddered at the thought of being trapped in a labyrinth like that. It was perhaps better to not think about what fate had befallen the unfortunate souls.

"For the record, I think this is a different dimension." Everett said, as he steered the conversation back to where they had started.

It was clear that he didn't like dwelling on the castle, or the things that it had done to people he had once known.

"Why's that?"

"Well, I mean, think about it! The water started tasting weird, then all those military guys showed up, then the world just started falling apart until everything kinda turned to dust. We're like, part of an experiment, or something!" Everett let out a sigh. "I mean, I missed out on most of it so I've had to ask other people what happened."

"You missed out?" Adda asked, "How do you mean?"

"I- uh- slept through the evacuation." Everett said somewhat sheepishly. "I also hadn't really been drinking water so I didn't really know much about that either. I woke up in my apartment to see my walls melting!"

Adda tried to imagine what that must have been like. The poor guy was probably scared out of his mind watching his world collapse around him. This tidbit did add another piece to the puzzle. Whatever happened that day effected both those who escaped and those who had been left behind.

What that meant was still lost on Adda, but she filed it away anyway, hoping that soon it would all just click together.

"I think they were testing some kind of portal technology. Or like, something to do with time travel?" Everett went on. "Probably both. Either way, obviously things went super wrong and got us stranded in some messed up hell dimension."

Adda eyed Everett, cocking an eyebrow. "I think you watch too much tv."

"Well I think it's better than what some of the others believe." Everett sulked, deflating beneath her gaze.

"What does Keith think happened?"

"Aliens."

This pulled a laugh free from Adda. It had been stated in such a matter-of-fact kind of way and it was certainly not something that she had expected. Everett chuckled too, but was more reserved. Though the town was slowly vanishing behind them, it seemed that Everett was still afraid of the older man. Adda caught Everett glancing over his shoulder as if he expected to find Keith standing over him. Not wanting to stress out her companion more, Adda cut off her laughter, to let the quiet settle over them.

They walked in silence for a while longer before there was an abrupt gurgling sound. Everett clutched his stomach and made a face.

"Ok, so are we gonna go get some food or nah?"

For a moment Adda entertained the idea of letting them get sidetracked to hunt down food; it was a reasonable request after all. But the Certainty came back and it seemed to oppose the idea as it whispered some shapeless warning into her heart. They couldn't afford the price of going for food. Even though she had no idea what events would transpire should they deviate from their path, she knew that she should trust the Certainty. It had gotten her this far, and after everything she had experienced, she was loath to ignore it.

Adda shook her head then, "No, we have to go."

He hesitated, pausing as doubts spun about just below the surface, each attempting to breach into some kind of protest. The words didn't come, instead, he shook his head and let out a long sigh.

"Ok, fine. Just- promise me you won't make me regret this."

This extension of trust surprised Adda, she had expected to have to fight him a bit more on the topic. Apparently, she had made more of an impression on him than she thought.

"I can't make any promises," Adda responded, "we're just going to take this one step at a time."

Onward they marched, moving steadily down the hills toward the great valley below. Adda held them on a course that would lead them closer to the trail that Keith had pointed out from the tower. It was incredible that as far away as the path was, now that she was aware of it she could see it clear as day, cutting a straight path to the lone peak.

The other thing she noticed was that although the valley seemed to rotate with them, never allowing a different perspective on any of the many details held within, they still somehow managed to slowly draw closer to the path. It was like they weren't moving at all, instead just standing frozen in place while the path itself was the one walking toward them. It was a surreal thing to observe, and it fascinated Adda to watch it draw closer.

She was thankful for the fascination as it allowed her to fixate on the narrow, white strip instead of the land all around it. Adda found that any time she allowed her gaze to drift into the valley itself her feet would turn and have her walk directly toward its lush borders. The motion was purely involuntary, but her mind would fight with her to try and correct their path.

The paradise of the valley sang like a siren, coaxing her like a heavy drink into the embrace of sleep. It was disconcerting how powerful the pull had become since seeing it all from atop the tower. Before she had arrived in the village, all this had been dwarfed by the magnificence of the mountain, but now that she was aware of the enchanting valley, it had suddenly become easy to forget that the mountain was even there.

The water seemed so soothing, the forests so quiet, the berries so plump and so filling. Her stomach had still not delivered any pangs of hunger, yet any time her eyes settled on the fruit, it would growl with anticipation while her mouth filled with saliva. Though many things were miles away, it was amazing how much of it Adda could easily see. There were times she could have sworn she would suddenly be right in front of any of the wonders down below. It was all so close. All she had to do was take one more step-

Adda would have to shake herself from her reverie during these moments, unsettled by how overwhelming it all was even from a distance.

She only had to be distracted by the valley a handful of times before she found that focusing on the path helped lay the temptations to bed. So Adda locked herself squarely onto that sliver of a path, refusing the call of anything else.

Out of nowhere, Everett suddenly reached out an arm and wrapped his skeletal fingers in the folds of her sleeve. He gave an incessant tug, moving himself and Adda low to the ground. Adda obliged him, noting the fear that had crept into his form. The young man crouched there, a tangle of rigid limbs and whitened joints, his pale face drawn even tighter as his eyes shifted around the hills. She too looked, but whatever had spooked him was beyond her.

"Everett-" Adda began to say, but was immediately cut off with a sharp hiss from Everett as he motioned her to be quiet.

Complying, Adda fell silent, though she felt utterly ridiculous sitting so exposed in the short grass. If they were genuinely attempting to hide from something, they were doing a poor job of it.

In time, Everett relaxed his grip and he let out a sigh, though the action did not drain the tautness that held his body like a rubber band ready to snap. The victory from resisting Keith had been sucked from his bones, leaving the poor man a trembling shell that housed only icy fear.

"You need to be more careful!" Everett snapped in a harsh whisper, his voice conveying a surprising amount of anger.

"Of what?" Adda asked, indignant.

Not wasting a moment, she brushed herself off as she stood, only to discover that there was no grass or dirt to rid her pants of.

Maybe I do have powers. Adda thought wryly.

She began to move away when Everett once again grabbed her. A stab of anger shot through her as she turned around to look at him.

"Goodness Everett, what is it now?"

"Are you insane!?" He hissed again, still keeping low.

He tugged at her, but this time she didn't fall to the ground next to him.

"The Snatcher literally just went in that direction! If we go that way, we're dead!"

Adda set her shoulders and shook her head, "Snatcher? Everett, nothing was there."

"But-"

"We *have* to go this way. Are you with me or not?" Adda asked, feeling the Certainty in her chest.

They regarded each other in the daylight, Everett's eyes searching hers in bewilderment, and a glint of something else- Hope? He slowly rose to his feet, his eyes never leaving hers as she could see questions boil beneath the surface.

"Have you ever seen a Snatcher?" He asked.

Adda shook her head, "No, I haven't. Now let's walk and talk, we have a lot of ground to cover!"

"But, I mean, there was literally one just in front of us a minute ago!" He refused to move. "You were gonna walk right into it if I hadn't stopped you!"

"Walk and talk." Adda insisted with finality before turning on her heel to march away.

"Doesn't that make you scared? Not being able to see them?" Everett asked as he fell into step behind her, his neck swiveling back-and-forth to ensure that they weren't being followed.

Adda mulled this over in her head, processing everything she'd experienced thus far. She certainly believed that there was more to life than what could be seen, and she even believed that these monsters were really there despite never having physically witnessed one. Yet, in that Certainty, she knew that there was nothing to fear from them even if she couldn't exactly explain why.

"I think that this place is more than anything we've ever imagined." She started slowly as her thoughts collected into a rough image. "It's life, but in a way we haven't experienced. The rules here are different from what we understand as normal, and we all have to play by them, including these Snatchers of yours. I think that they have some limitation that makes it so I can't see them or be touched by them. I'm pretty sure I even walked through one of their villages and it faded into nothing around me."

Something else clicked. Thinking back to when she first arrived, and being nearly overwhelmed by the feeling of nostalgia. The feeling of coming home.

"I think we actually belong to this place as much as the Snatchers do, maybe even more so."

"What does that even mean?" Everett asked, his brow furrowed.

It was already difficult to believe that this newcomer was incapable of seeing or interacting with the Snatchers; it was even harder to accept this wild theory of "belonging" in a place that was home to a people bent on eradicating trespassers. And yet, he still followed her, one foot after another, remembering that not only had she resisted Keith's power, she had inspired him to do the same.

"I'm still trying to figure it out." Adda said. "I just know there's more going on here than we realize. I'm certain of it."

She stopped then, surprised to find that they had arrived. She had been sure that a few moments ago the path had still been miles away and yet, now it was right before them. It nestled neatly between the hills and descended into the valley below.

The path was composed of a white gravel, insinuating that it had been made rather than naturally formed. From where she stood, she could see that the path shot straight through the valley and up into the mountain which rumbled ominously in the distance. Adda stepped onto the path and felt the gravel shift and grind under her shoe. The first part of the journey had been completed, yet Adda felt that the real challenge was about to begin.

"Are you ready?" Adda asked Everett.

He hesitated a moment on the side of the path, casting a look over his shoulder to where they had come from. Behind them was the familiar, the routine, it offered a level of safety in its predictability. Ahead was the unknown, and the unknown wasn't something you could control.

Adda thought she had lost him there, that this was the moment that Everett would turn tail and run home. But to her pleasant surprise, he didn't. The young man took in a deep breath before turning his back on everything that he had come to know and joined Adda on the path. He gave her an affirming nod, and then side-by-side, they set off into the valley.

Part 2

1

In the hills they had left behind, the weather had been mild and warm. It was the perfect kind of thing for being outdoors, taking in the sunny rays sent down from up above. There was even a gentle breeze to push back the more brutal aspects of a summer day making for an all-round pleasant experience.

The valley was far different.

As if the two had stepped through some kind of invisible wall, the atmosphere was suddenly completely different. Gone was the temperate paradise they had enjoyed, now they were standing in a heat that made Adda think of an overgrown jungle. It was hot and humid, the air so thick that it was difficult to breathe. The transition was so sudden that her body had no time to acclimate, and unlike the freezing temperatures of the castle, the woman was surprised that she actually felt the change in the air.

Adda reached an arm up to wipe her brow, banishing the sweat that was forming there. She stopped, realizing that this was the first time this world had any kind of effect on her. Glancing back at her companion, she saw that though she was sweating, it was far worse for her friend.

Everett's clothing was already soaked through as his body tried to cool him down. Try as his natural systems may, the heat seemed to have sapped ten years of his life, aging him instantly beneath its hand. He didn't notice her looking at him as he was more occupied with wiping the gathering sweat from his own brow.

Turning from her companion, Adda looked up to the sky.

Seeing the eternal storm from the hills had made it appear tame, trapped behind a wall. Now standing beneath it, it had taken on a whole other dimension. One of raw, destructive power.

Above their heads thick clouds the color of pitch rolled and growled, hidden bolts of lightning flickering deep within their ever-changing form. They almost looked- alive in the way they clawed across the sky with a clear direction in mind. Though the clouds thundered terribly, not a drop of rain escaped their heavy head as something kept their full fury in check.

Adda and Everett now stood directly beneath them and she could see where the invisible barrier separated the storm from the hills beyond. She watched in silence for a moment, observing how the clouds would slam into the wall and pool there, like smoke against glass, before dissipating from view. The process repeated over and over again, yet not even a single wisp of cloud managed to break through.

That barrier apparently also kept the oppressive humidity in check, only allowing travelers to experience it once they had stepped beyond its protection. Adda didn't like that thought, entertaining the idea of simply turning back and letting the mountain keep its secrets.

The Certainty thrummed in her chest, tugging gently against her, pulling her like a magnet toward the mountain.

This was the way.

"Adda, look!" Everett breathed, breaking her from her thoughts.

She turned at his request, letting her eyes fall upon the valley before them, and in doing so, immediately forgot about the clouds up above and the humidity that crushed against them. Seeing the valley from atop the tower or from within the hills had done the place an injustice. Now, standing at its edge, its beauty had increased ten fold.

Grass rolled out in every direction much like it had back in the hills, yet it was unfair to compare the two together. The hills now appeared dull and lifeless, invaded by a stiff and unruly weed. This grass was thick, long, and inviting. It was colored a green so deep it was impossible to describe. It somehow managed to look like the most comfortable thing that Adda had ever laid eyes on. Every blade sighed as they brushed against one another, creating a backdrop of white noise that caused Adda to desire nothing more than to lay down and fall asleep.

Popping up here and there in frequent intervals were large bushes of every kind whose branches bowed under the weight of their great bounty. Their berries sat plump and juicy, ripe for the picking. They waved about, inviting hungry travelers to stop a moment and partake of their fruits. The branches held no thorns and even the leaves seemed to move out of the way so that grabbing each handful of berries could be done unimpeded.

In the distance, Adda could make out large trees that swayed gently in the breeze. Their leaves whispered soothingly with the motion, beckoning Adda and Everett to come rest their heads in the cool shade. It was in the darkness of their boughs that one could finally release the mask they'd worn for so long and relax into who they were always meant to be.

The trees wouldn't judge.

The colors, the smells, and the sounds that encompassed Adda were intoxicating, pulling at some primal instinct deep within her to stop and lay down in the grass. To approach the berries and gorge herself until she too was ready to burst. To lay her head beneath the trees and let herself take root alongside them, to drift in the peace she had always craved but the world had refused to give her.

Without meaning to, both Adda and Everett had begun to walk the path before them, being pulled into the valley by some unseen thread. With every step, the choking humidity seemed to lessen, falling into the backdrop before vanishing all together as if unable to mar this perfect picture that surrounded them. Even the rumbling clouds up above became a distant thought, passing through their minds like water through a sifter.

Adda felt herself being drawn to the valley around her. It beckoned her in a lazy way, inviting her to partake in its spoils. Though she did not hunger, thirst, or even feel weary, the simple concept of enjoying such things was almost enough to tug her free of the path. Her mind felt drunk, lifting away to lose itself in a honeyed-haze that made it difficult to compose any kind of thought.

It was only the Certainty that drew her toward the distant mountain, pushing her to ignore the dreamy landscape that surrounded her. She shook her head vigorously and turned her attention to the white gravel beneath her feet. Immediately, her mind somewhat cleared, allowing thoughts to once again form. Even still, the powerful compulsion was there on the peripherals of her awareness, constantly trying to pull her in.

Worried that she would turn around and find Everett missing, Adda reached out and took his hand in her own. She pulled him along behind her, trying to ignore the brilliant colors and sensations that whispered softly in her ear.

Every so often, she would hear Everett gasp and pull against her as he tried to reach something off the path. On such occasions, Adda would tighten her grip and give a gentle tug to pull him back to himself. If it wasn't for the tiny voice dragging her toward the mountain, Adda didn't think she would be able to stop herself or Everett from walking into the surrounding grass. Her eyes focused on the gravel, falling into the rhythm of their march.

The path itself was a simple thing in comparison to the beautiful world that it had been built to guide travelers through. It was just wide enough to allow two people to walk side-by-side, but no more than that lest it make someone have to walk on the grass. The path was also as straight as it was narrow. Unlike normal roads and streets that compensated for all sorts of natural obstacles, this path seemed to pay no heed to the environment around it.

It cut through the landscape like a knife, slicing a path through grass, river, rock, and tree alike. It cleared the way with an obvious destination in mind, and not a single object along the way could do anything to bar it.

It wasn't as though someone had built a bridge to cross the river or had knocked down a tree to clear the way. The path simply crossed over and through whatever got in its way. Adda and Everett passed over the first of many streams where she stopped briefly to marvel at the fact that the gravel seemed to simply float on the surface of the water. Yet, neither the moving liquid nor the path itself interacted in any meaningful way. The water kept flowing and the path was not swept away.

They came across a tree whose roots had clearly begun beneath the path, yet it had stretched its trunk to one side, growing at an awkward angle so as to not break through the white pathway. Adda could hardly comprehend what she was seeing and was caught in awe by the spectacle of this strange phenomenon. She had seen plants breaking through concrete and asphalt back home, forcing their way through any obstacle to stretch their leaves toward the sun. Yet, this loose gravel held it all at bay, not even allowing a blade of grass to slip through.

"Ho there, travelers!" A chipper voice called out from one side.

Everett practically leapt from his skin and Adda's own heart quickened at the unexpected voice. Keith had said there were people living down here, but the lull of it all had made such a fact slip her mind.

A cheery individual with rosy cheeks and twinkling eyes had popped up from a nearby berry bush. It was a young woman, a basket on her hip, half full with the blackberries that she had been picking. The stains around her mouth and on her hands indicated that she had also been taking the choicest berries for herself. She grinned at them with a smile that would suggest that she had never met a stranger in her entire life.

"What might be your names?"

"Oh, my name is Adda," Adda responded, a smile of her own spreading across her face. "And this is my friend, Everett!"

She seems nice. Adda thought dreamily to herself, her mind feeling warm and heavy.

Everett nodded without a word, his eyes wide and his jaw slack. A light seemed to suddenly come on as he took in the stranger before them. The young man was clearly smitten.

Adda looked from the girl to him and then back. The contrast between the two was depressing to see. Where Everett was hollow and weak, the woman was filled and strong. He was grey and tired; she was rosy and chipper. It was like he was merely a ghost pretending to go about living where this woman was actual flesh and blood. It was mind blowing to think that after seeing a people like this, the townsfolk still refused to come down into the valley. The fact that they would rather wither away than enter this land of plenty was its own special kind of insanity.

"Absolutely charmed!" The young woman exclaimed, studying the both of them with wide, brilliant eyes. "My name is Lorelei."

The woman put down her basket and clapped her hands merrily together.

"It is so good to meet new friends and you came along at the perfect time!"

She waved a hand toward the bushes, pulling their attention to an extra pair of baskets nestled snugly in the grass. They hadn't been there before, but as far as bizarre happenings went, this was relatively low on the pole of strangeness.

"You see, tonight we're having a great big feast to celebrate and I was tasked to gather up berries for all the pies we're making!" The woman thrust her hands out in an apologetic motion, showing the berry stains that covered her palms and fingers. "Alas, it does seem I've eaten one too many of them and I'm running a bit behind schedule. Would the two of you mind helping me?"

"Well Lorelei, oh that's such a pretty name," Adda said warmly, quite taken with this friendly stranger, "we would absolutely love to help you out, but you see, we need to be getting to that mountain over there as soon as possible. I'm really sorry we don't have more time."

Lorelei gave out a laugh that was as warm, and pleasant as bells playing softly on a summer day. "Now, why would you want to do something like that?"

"We're trying to get to the city beyond." Adda replied easily as though talking to an old friend.

Lorelei froze for a moment, her eyes narrowing as she took them both in. She then threw her head back and laughed again, absolutely tickled with the prospect of their mission.

"You're going to the city? Why on earth would you ever want to do that?"

"You see we-" Adda began, but the woman waved away her response dismissively as she walked up to them and placed a warm hand on Adda's own.

"I don't know what nonsense people have been feeding you, but whatever little you hope to find in the city, you will find in abundance down here." She gently tugged on Adda, "Come on, I do feel we can be such great friends and you'll want to come to the feast tonight!"

Her initial draw toward the woman had begun to wane away. It was instead replaced by a nagging sense of unease that rolled beneath the fog in her mind like an undercurrent. It was at first a quiet thing, but it was enough to cause Adda to drag her heels against the pull. Still, she could feel her feet moving unbidden toward the berry bushes, drawn by the warmth of the company and the beauty of the valley. Trying to muster all her focus, Adda pulled against Lorelei, though everything in her body screamed for her to give in.

"No, I- I can't"

"You must be tired." Lorelei whispered. "Look at how soft the grass is. Just imagine lying down for a minute, resting from your journey. You can always leave afterward."

And Adda did imagine herself lying in the grass, the cool blades licking her skin to take away the heat of the warm day. Letting herself lull into its soft embrace and have a long, dreamless slumber. Adda hadn't realized how tired she was until this moment and the ache in her bones had grown immense.

"I mean, we can take a minute." Everett suddenly spoke up, breaking free from his reverie.

His eyes combed over Lorelei, completely taken by the fetching creature. The look that Everett had given the stranger reminded Adda of how Keith had looked at her. There was a hunger there, a burning desire that unsettled her to behold. It was that look that started to force the fog back from her mind, the Certainty screaming like a distant voice to open her eyes and see.

"I'm down for whatever, I mean, as long as you're there." Everett continued, blushing slightly as he said so.

At this, Lorelei let out a little giggle, and shot Everett a coy look.

"Well aren't we bold?" The woman tightened her grip on Adda's arm, drawing her once again toward the grass. "Come on then, we don't have all day!"

Everett followed gladly, still a step behind Adda as Lorelei drew them forth.

It was then, as Adda's feet were about to leave the path that the unease blossomed into full understanding. Lorelei had reached awkwardly across the border of the path to place her arm on Adda. Looking down, Adda saw that the woman had refused to take a single step onto the white gravel. The stranger had done everything in her power to keep her own feet firmly planted on the lush grass.

Something deep within Adda clicked, pulling pieces of the puzzle together. The Snatcher village that had vanished before her paraded through her mind, reminding her that not everything was what it seemed.

Like scales falling from her eyes, Adda was suddenly acutely aware of the world around her. The storms no longer sounded distant, the humidity descended again like a cloud, and the grass- it had begun to fade. All of it fell into the background as Adda looked back to Lorelei.

She gasped as her eyes didn't lock with those of a beautiful stranger, but rather the sunken eyes of the dead.

The pieces had only taken a few moments to fall together, but it was too late.

Her foot was already off the path, stepping down toward the once lush grass. It had all but vanished, burning away to reveal something composed of nightmares. The Certainty flared up in her and Adda cried out in a panic.

"No!"

Before even a ghostly blade of grass could touch the bottom of her foot, the world exploded.

A massive gust of wind, stronger than Adda had ever felt in her life, came roaring out of nowhere. The great force physically lifted both Adda and Everett from the ground, tossing them like rag dolls back down the path. Pain lanced through Adda's back, arching to every corner of her being. The breath was driven from her lungs as she hit the ground hard, coughing and gasping in an attempt to catch back what was stolen.

It was there, laying on her back that Adda looked to the sky above. At first, she was confused at what she was seeing. There was just an infinite blackness and it somehow seemed like it was drawing closer, consuming everything until only it remained. For a moment, Adda thought that night had fallen and they just hadn't noticed.

It was the first droplet plopping against her face that pulled Adda from her daze. Lifting a finger, Adda delicately wiped away the raindrop that was sliding like a tear down her face. She gazed into the blackness up above, trying to comprehend what was happening. It was the flickering light dancing in the darkness that made Adda realize what she was seeing.

The clouds were falling.

The storm let loose a bellowing roar and unleashed its magnificent wrath. First came the rain, bearing down with a ferocity and power like nothing Adda had even known. It was like a curtain, so thick that all the world became separated from them in its assault. Like a tidal wave, it slammed into Adda's prone form, pinning her to the ground in its great deluge. In a single moment, she was drenched, the rain collecting into pools around her head. Adda struggled to stand up, but the full force of the storm pinned her down as it raged.

Then came the wind.

It whipped around, howling like a beast in the throes of a blood lust. The ground groaned as the frothing creature tore into the dirt, ripping free long canyons of debris before throwing them into the sky. These dark shapes of detritus now danced like puppets, slamming against one another with frightful force. The wind spun faster and faster, its roar piercing through Adda until she felt as though it would rip her to pieces.

Lightning began to beat against the world, every strike lashing out the moment another ended. It scarred the ground wherever it cut, blasting everything it touched into craters of ash. Thunder peeled out continually from the terrible display, slamming into the world with a force that could rival even the strongest of human weapons. Its voice was so powerful and so low that it rattled Adda's bones with every impact.

She had seen a few storms of great intensity in her life, yet not one on earth could possibly compare to the raw power that thrashed around her now. If such a storm could ever exist back home, it was one that would leave no survivors.

Everett screamed against the pain, his voice joining in with the roaring chorus that filled the air. He curled into the fetal position and wrapped his arms around his head in an attempt to fend off the storm.

Adda heard him, but could not distinguish what was human and what was storm. Instead, she lay there, trying to hold her head up away from the gathering water. Adda turned her neck, searching until she saw Lorelei's hunched form standing off to one side.

Somehow, the woman was still standing, appearing as nothing more than a shadow beneath the weight of the storm. The woman was cowering, her arms raised up as if the act could protect her from nature's fury. Around her, the valley seemed to be in a similar pose, thrashing about in an attempt to fight off the power that had fallen upon them. With every passing moment, these things shifted and changed beyond the curtain of rain. They morphed into twisted shapes that rose up from the ground, looming above them in cruel angles and jagged edges. Every which way she turned, these objects hung like pieces of shattered glass sealed together to create wicked sculptures.

It was hard to ascertain the exact nature of what she was seeing, but as one moment crashed into the next, they started to become clearer. The rain began to thin out, no longer falling with the atomic force it had initially brought. The wind slowed, no longer howling and gnashing, becoming far more gentle. Even the lightning pulled away, retreating deep within the clouds, letting out an ominous rumble that was faded and distant. As abruptly as it had come, the storm had gone.

But it had left something in its wake.

With new eyes, Adda looked on in horror, shivering as her soaked clothing clung to her body like a second skin. All around her, the valley had been transformed.

No, that was the wrong word, nothing about the valley had

changed.

Just like the buildings in the village, Adda could suddenly see beyond the ghostly shell that had enveloped the valley like a shroud. She could still see the coursing river, the blooming trees, and the heavy-laden berry bushes, but now they had a ghostly pallor to them, faded and belonging to another world entirely. Beneath their beautiful images, Adda could make out the shapes of a wasteland.

Though at first it was hard to see, the longer Adda looked, the more the paradise was swallowed by the wilderness below it. Where grass once was was instead a pale, red sand that shifted and roiled like something living. The rivers and streams had been replaced with canyons filled with glistening, black sludge that moved in a slow, methodical way.

Where the trees once stood were macabre structures built to mock their living counterparts. Their bark was dark, their branches bony with long, hooked fingers, and where leaves ought to be were instead what appeared to be claws or perhaps blades. It seemed that even laying a hand upon the side of these false trees would result in blood being drawn from flesh.

The bushes had also taken on a horrific transformation, becoming sickly, scraggly things that bore not the plump berries from before, but rather a bulbous, red fruit that swelled and sank as though it were a beating heart.

Lorelei had undergone the same treatment. Where the healthy, vibrant young woman once had been, she was replaced with a frail shadow of a person. Her once lush, golden hair had withered away into a handful of thin strands that drifted from her scalp like ghosts.

Her full form had become sickeningly skinny, with papery skin pulled so tight that it looked like it could tear at any moment. She had all the appearances of a mummy without its bandages. There was no way she could be alive, and yet there she stood, swaying softly before them.

Now by comparison, it was Everett who looked the healthy one when standing alongside this corpse acting out life. Lorelei pulled her tattered clothing around herself, smiling again to only reveal a mouth full of jagged, yellowed teeth.

"My, wasn't that a strange storm!" She wheezed, her voice struggling to find purchase in a throat that had forgotten the sensation of water. "It hasn't rained in- well- I can't quite remember how long!"

She cackled, the ghost of that charming laugh still flitted on the wind, but it was swallowed by the unpleasant sound that escaped her pair of lips. She approached them again, her eyes now vacant of any kind of life, her joints clicking and grinding painfully. Both Adda and Everett scrambled away from her as she stepped up to the side of the path. Just like before, the woman stopped on her side, not letting herself step on the white gravel.

She put out a skeletal hand, reaching toward the two of them, "Come, come! There's much to do for the feast tonight and these berries aren't going to pick themselves!"

"Stay away from me!" Everett shrieked, stumbling to his feet only to fall once again with a grunt.

Lorelei wrinkled her forehead and turned her head to the side like some kind of dusty, ashen bird. Her empty eyes flitted to-and-fro, revealing nothing but an all-encompassing void.

"Is your friend quite alright?" She asked, addressing Adda.

"Hunger can do horrible things to the mind, perhaps just a quick snack?"

Lorelei fetched her basket, reaching in to pull out one of the sickening fruits. She brought it up close to an ear where she cocked her head to one side and then to the next like she was listening for something. Unsatisfied, she put it away, only to pull out another one and repeat the process. This one seemed to meet her approval as she grinned again, holding out the fruit to them.

"Here, try this! I found the juiciest one just for you!" Lorelei crowed victoriously.

A whimper slipped out of Everett's mouth as he clutched his head, trying to shut out the world around him. Adda instead gave the woman a wane smile, trying her best to hide her disgust with the repulsive fruit. This close up, it was impossible to ignore the sickly-sweet smell that wafted off of the fruit like a fog. Inexplicably, though the thing itself was absolutely unappetizing, the smell of it triggered something in her gut, causing her to go wild with hunger. Even seeing it in this state, there was a small temptation to reach out and pluck the fruit from the withered hand.

Instead, she stood her ground.

"That's very sweet of you Lorelei, but as I said before, we must get going." Adda slid down next to Everett, helping him back to his feet. The young man positioned himself on her other side, away from Lorelei. "Thank you for your hospitality, and I hope you have fun at the feast tonight."

Lorelei froze, her eyes wide and searching. For a brief moment, Adda wondered if this broken creature was going to attack them for refusing her offer.

Instead, the woman brought the fruit back over to her own mouth, letting her yellowed teeth tear into its meat. The fruit sagged instantly as a thick, red juice popped out from where she had bit into it. Lorelei munched on the fruit, oblivious to the liquid that dribbled down her chin as she continued to regard the two travelers. Everett whimpered again, clutching tightly onto Adda like she was some kind of shield.

Lorelei then shrugged, "Fine, suit yourself."

Stooping, she scooped her own basket back up, the other two baskets now suddenly gone. She then returned to picking the fruits from the bushes, once again listening carefully to each one before deciding which was to go in the basket and which was to go in her stomach. Adda tugged on Everett, pulling the two of them away from the scene with haste.

"You'll see!" Lorelei called after the retreating forms, uninterested in following them. "You'll go up that mountain and you'll realize you should have listened to me."

With that, Lorelei vanished behind them into the wasteland of shifting sand.

2

"Maybe we should turn back." Everett was talking rapidly, his voice quivering in fear as the words tumbled out at a record pace. "I mean, last time I saw the valley people they weren't like that, we need to warn the others that it's not safe down here! I mean, what if we run into more of them? What if they decide to eat us or something? Oh man, I'd take a Snatcher any day over whatever they are. Did you see how awful she looked?"

Everett shuddered, pulling his arms tight around himself as if fending off an icy breeze. "I don't want to end up like that, Adda. We have to go back."

"You can go back if that's what you want." Adda replied, her eyes set straight ahead.

Everett made an exasperated sound. "Come on, I'm not just gonna leave you by yourself."

Adda didn't reply, instead she focused on taking one step at a time. Her mind whirled with what they had both just experienced. The woman, the storm, the desert veiled in paradise, it all had to mean something.

What is this place?

"You can't be serious?" Everett chimed in again, "Look around you, we aren't safe here!"

Adda did chance a look at his request, soaking in the hellscape before turning back to the path. This land was indeed inhospitable, and normally, Adda would be inclined to agree that it would perhaps be in their best interest to turn around.

However, these were not normal circumstances.

"Do you honestly think you're safer back there? Wasting away under Keith's thumb?" Adda replied, trying to keep the frustration from her voice, "I don't want to be rude, but have you seen yourself recently? Staying back there is taking its own toll."

"Yeah sure, I guess it isn't perfect, but at least we were building a life." Everett snapped, becoming defensive, "You don't know what it was like for us. You just walked in like nothing even happened!"

Calm down. Adda's inner voice whispered.

She took a deep breath, letting her mounting anger wash through her. There were a hundred things she wanted to say to make Everett understand why he was wrong. But she wouldn't let herself, she wouldn't feed that beast. So Adda bit her tongue instead, cutting off her mounting frustration before it was allowed to blossom.

"I mean, I know we're fighting for our survival, but we aren't like these- these- *things* down here!" Everett continued, "I don't even think they're human! They're, like, corpse people! Come on, Adda, we *have* to warn the others."

He appealed to Adda's sense of community, trying to twist the words around to guilt the woman into turning around. He had meant well by it, but it still didn't change the intention. Unfortunately for Everett, his bland attempt at manipulation only made Adda more adamant about her path.

"I'm not going to argue with you." she finally said, "You can go back if you want, but I'm going to the mountain. That's final."

They descended into silence, their feet crunching on the gravel as they continued on their way. Everett offered up no other argument as he followed Adda, the quiet thick with all the clever words he wanted to say. Despite all his attempts to get them to turn around, he trailed close behind her, his footsteps following in her own.

The two hurried on, trying to ignore the world on either side of the path. All around them the wasteland shifted constantly as though it were alive, moving in a pattern that was as chaotic as it was mesmerizing. Every so often, Adda would catch sight of brilliant green or refreshing blue weaving its way over the red sand. All it took was a second look for the tapestry to unweave itself, revealing once again the dead landscape. This place was deceptive and constantly on the prowl to lure in unsuspecting victims.

"How do you know the city is safe?" Everett asked, breaking the silence.

"I just know it is." Adda replied, searching herself for the Certainty.

It rose up to meet her, beating with the same rhythm as her heart.

"That's less than comforting."

"Everett, I said I wasn't going to argue with you." Adda sighed, "If you're so unsure, why are you coming with me?"

"Well, I can't exactly go back now," Everett grumbled, "Keith will let Scott murder me if he ever sees me again."

"That's it? That's the whole reason you're still out here?"

Everett opened his mouth to say something more, but the thought never made it out into the open air. He seemed to consider it for a minute, before choosing to lapse back into silence. It seemed that the young man wasn't entirely sure of his own motives. Yet, his feet continued to march forward, indicating that somewhere inside him, he had made his choice.

It was in this quiet that they made their journey, plodding along at a steady rate. The only thing that ever broke the veil of silence was the occasional rumble of distant thunder. It was as if the clouds up above wanted to remind them that they were there, looming over the false paradise.

After walking for what seemed hours, something caught Adda's eye. It was an object, lying just to one side of the road, sitting half-buried in the sand. It would have completely passed unnoticed by the both of them if it hadn't been something Adda was familiar with. In fact, it was one that she had looked upon hundreds of times from her front porch. She had watched it bob around the corner of her street, accompanying its precious owner home.

It was a bright, yellow backpack.

The color had faded as though the thing had been there for a long time, but otherwise, it appeared to be the exact one that she had last seen Bethany wearing before that fateful day. Rushing over to it, Adda pulled it free of the sand, staring at it with wide eyes as her mind processed it.

"What is it?" Everett asked once he had caught up to her.

Adda didn't answer. What had her parents said?

The Snatchers got her.

Now, standing there, holding the parcel, Adda was struck with a sense of relief. Hope swelled in her once again as the face of that precious teen filtered into her mind. Whatever had happened to her, she at least made it this far.

The relief was immediately chased by another feeling. Mounting horror.

Her eyes flickered up and she swept her gaze across the horizon, taking it all in. Adda searched for something, anything, that might indicate that Bethany had passed through here. She looked for footprints in the sand, maybe an article of clothing like a shoe or a hoodie left behind as a proverbial bread crumb to help guide her home. Try as she may, however, Adda saw nothing else that indicated the girl had ever been there.

Had she strayed from the path or had she managed to keep her feet pointed toward the mountain? It was difficult to say with the ever changing desert that slithered woefully around them.

Adda found herself envisioning Bethany standing on the path beside her. The girl was looking around, her eyes wide and her face slack. To Adda's horror, she watched as Bethany swayed forward, taking labored steps toward the edge of the path. Unable to do anything to stop it, Adda simply watched as the teen's feet found the grass, unaware of the hissing sand hiding below its lush exterior.

The image vanished, leaving Adda staring at the spot the girl had been only moments before.

She needs you. A voice said in her ear, *She's lost without you.*

"Adda?" Everett's voice cut into her thoughts.

Adda shook her head, forcing the voices out.

"Oh you're a tricky one." Adda muttered at the sand, her eyes narrowed and her lips pursed.

"Uh- Adda?" Everett asked again, this time more hesitant.

Adda took in a deep breath and then let the backpack slip from her hands. It felt wrong to let it go, but Adda now knew that holding onto such a thing would not only threaten her own life, but Everett's as well. It was apparent now that the valley had more than one trick up its sleeve and was actively trying to lure them into its depths.

Adda would not give it the satisfaction.

The Certainty swelled in her chest, turning her once again toward their destination. All Adda could do was hope and pray that Bethany had made it across the valley. The city would provide answers, it would provide help, and so Adda would not delay a moment longer.

"It's nothing." Adda replied, leaving the pack where it lay. "Let's go."

Everett shot her a quizzical look, but refrained from saying anything, instead falling behind her once again. Like a metronome their footsteps eventually lulled them both back into the rhythm of the road. They each retreated to their own thoughts, one looking forward toward the possibilities and the other looking back at everything they had left behind.

So the valley rolled around them, looking as impossibly big as the eternal hills they had since crossed. From time to time, Adda would see figures stumbling about in the swirling sand that clung to the horizon like a mist. What they were doing was hard to see, but it was doubtful that it was anything good. It was rare to see any of them anywhere close to white pathway. It seemed as though this was a stretch of land that was given a wide berth. Whatever spell the valley used to ensnare travelers was strong indeed and clearly had no intention of letting its prey get back to safety. Adda took that as a further sign that they were heading in the right direction.

If such broken creatures avoided the path, then it was precisely where Adda wanted to remain. Lorelei had been terrifying to see, and as much as she had tried to persuade the travelers to join her, Adda believed that the wretched thing had genuinely meant well in her invitation. They might not be so lucky if another one of those corpse people (as Everett had coined them) decided to approach them.

Yet all these things paled to the back of her mind as other things of immediate importance crowded in.

Since they had stepped into the valley, all the natural processes that had been suspended in the hills had suddenly returned with a vengeance. They now collapsed against Adda, ravaging her body with aching needs.

Her throat was beginning to feel tattered as it begged for water alongside her gut cramping from lack of food. Her knees creaked with the repetitive motion of walking, making her pay for every step. Sweat trickled in thick beads down her face, the salty liquid stinging her lips as they slipped in between the chapped cracks that had begun to form and bleed.

Though sun was still covered by the endless storm, the heat was nearly unbearable. Adda ran a hand across her head, wishing that the clouds would let loose again so that she might tilt her head back to let the rain wet her throat and cool her down.

However bad it was for Adda, it was ten times that for Everett. The poor man struggled to keep up with Adda's steady, trudging pace that neither sped up nor slowed. His feet faltered as his knees knocked, begging him to fall to the ground and rest. The sand around them swirled as pictures of soft beds of moss and grass pressed upon him from every side. His eyes had been opened to the truth, but it was getting harder and harder to ignore the intrusive images from his mind.

On more than one occasion, Everett found himself wondering if perhaps Adda was just insane or maybe she had done something to him like Keith had. Of course, she had claimed to have no abilities, but could he take her at her word?

Mistrust laid its clawing roots into his heart which caused him to eye her suspiciously. Maybe she was one of *them*. Maybe it was her job to find people outside of the valley to lure back here to get trapped forever. Everett paled as he thought that perhaps the corpse people were actually cannibals. He really did not want to wind up in someone's soup. He had always hated soup, and in his current state, he couldn't think of a worse way to die than being served up as the one meal you hate more than any other.

Hunger, thirst, and exhaustion played upon them both, sinking into their bones and rattling them from within. All around, the wastes hissed on, thrusting all manner of desires toward the pair in an attempt to lure them in. As they both grew more tired and irate, it became harder to see through the false images that were filled with so much promise. This place was whittling them down bit-by-bit, it was a master of patience, and it had long perfected the art of breaking people.

"Wait." Everett gasped, falling to his knees then. "I can't keep going."

Anger flared up in Adda's chest, the exhaustion in her attempting to override her. She felt harsh words build up behind her lips, an intense heat and vileness within them. Adda clenched her jaw and ran a hand along the box in her purse. The indented symbol whispered against her fingertips, grounding her before she allowed herself to speak.

"Everett, we can't stop." Adda said though she too was exhausted.

The longer they stayed, the greater the chance the valley would win.

Everett laughed bitterly.

"Are you being serious right now?" His voice had taken on a hard edge. "Why are you so desperate to keep moving? Huh? Just give me five minutes."

"Come on, Everett, we really have to go."

"Do we?" He growled, glaring up at her from behind locks caked in red sand. "Admit it, you don't care about anything except for getting your own way."

Standing over him, Adda could see that there was a layer of sand gathered upon Everett's head and shoulders. It clung like a fine dust upon a forgotten countertop. Regarding herself, Adda noticed that she had made new traveling companions of her own.

As if sensing her gaze, Everett ran a listless hand through his unkempt hair. A disgusted look crossed his face as the grainy irritants rubbed against his fingers. He wrenched his hand free, flinging it about to loosen the sand's grip. The image was nearly comedic, a man desperately trying to rid himself of cloying sand even though it was obvious that he hadn't properly bathed in over a year.

"I mean, you didn't even let us get food or water!" He made a *chu* sound with his mouth as he continued, "Well, I'm really glad I listened to you! It's pretty clear that we don't need anything out here! I mean, we have all the putrid fruit and black sludge we could ever want!"

Adda crossed her arms and clenched her jaw. She could feel her blood boiling in frustration at him. How could he not feel it? Everything in this world pointed in one direction. They were on a road that was a literal straight shot right across the valley that none of the corpse people seemed capable of standing on. The city was *the* destination, and waiting around seemed to have an extremely adverse effect. She wanted to yell at him, to reprimand him for acting like a spoiled child, and tell him that he needed to pull himself together and act like a man.

It was on that thought that she stopped, a feeling of conviction rolling over her.

Raging at Everett would feel good in the moment, it would let her give the pouting man a piece of her mind. It would also work as a driving force to push him to turn around and head back home. Though her journey would be easier to accomplish without him weighing her down, Adda knew that she wouldn't be able to forgive herself if she was the reason Everett gave up. For both of their sakes, she had to be better.

So, Adda took in a deep, steadying breath, letting all the anger and spiteful words pass through her like air from a balloon. With a conscious thought, Adda told her shoulders to relax, her back to stand straight, and her jaw to unclench. She did this twice more, retaking control of herself.

"Everett." She started, her voice even. "The longer we are out here, the worse things are going to get. We have to keep moving."

Everett didn't respond.

Standing over him, Adda felt in her gut that this journey was going to get a lot harder before it got easier. She wanted to help get him through this, but in the end, she also knew that it had to be his choice. Without his own convictions to draw him forward, Adda wasn't sure how long the young man would last.

Adda slid down next to the other, placing a hand on his shoulder and tried to angle her head so that she could look into his face.

"Everett, why did you decide to come with me?" Adda prompted.

"I don't know." He muttered, not making eye contact.

"Come on. Tell me."

"Why?" He snapped. "Why is it so important?"

"Because you need to understand why you're out here if you're going to make it through this valley. Because, I can drag you through anything if I have to, but I can't carry you further than you're willing to go."

"I don't need you to carry me"

"Why are you out here?" Adda pushed.

"Leave me alone!"

"Everett."

"Because I hate myself, ok?!" Everett screamed, finally looking at Adda.

In his eyes she saw shame that consumed him like a deep rot. The decay weighed on him, breaking him down until he was too weak to go on. Adda could tell just by looking at him that Everett was barely treading water in this ocean of guilt.

"I can feel myself falling apart." Everett said in a hoarse whisper, "We all are. We would find things to blame it on, like the mountain or the Snatchers, but I just knew deep down that it was something else. It's like this world is eating away at us until there's nothing left."

Everett gave a humorless laugh, shaking his head at his own words.

"I mean, that's not even the full truth. It is leaving *something* behind and it's awful." He turned to the desert, watching the sand coil and hiss. "Back home, I think most people hide all their dark bits, but this place won't let you. It just keeps poking holes in you, letting all the things you hide leak out."

Tears pricked the corners of his eyes and he let in a deep sniff.

"I thought I was gonna end up like Keith or Scott, just becoming some horrible monster, but then one day, things finally changed." He said, "*You* came along. You're different from the rest of us, and I know that a lot of people probably were freaked out about that but- but it gave me hope that maybe I don't have to be like this."

Everett waved a hand over himself, indicating his sickly frame that seemed weaker by the moment.

"I'm out here because I want what you have." Everett finally said.

Adda considered this, thinking back to when she had first met him, foraging by himself outside the walls of safety. Despite the fact he was petrified of the Snatchers, it was Everett who volunteered to wander out in the hills. Despite his town's feeling toward outsiders he had embraced her and invited her into their sanctuary. Everett had even taken it upon himself to be her guide. Adda realized that the young man was well aware that something was wrong, and so he had been searching for an escape.

He probably hadn't expected that escape to be a person.

"I wish I had the answers for you, and maybe, once we figure this world out, I will." Adda replied. "Until then, I can tell you one thing. I'm going to get to that city, and as long as you're with me, I'll do everything I can to help you get there, too."

Adda stood, reaching her hand down to the other, her palm facing up and her fingers splayed wide. She felt the hunger, the thirst, the exhaustion, but in that moment it felt- separate, as though it belonged to someone else entirely.

"You chose to walk away from Keith. Now you have to choose again." She said, "So, what will it be?"

Everett hesitated a moment, looking back toward where they had come. The hills looked inviting from here with its blue skies and gentle slopes. Adda thought that he might actually turn back but then he looked to her again.

"I choose to go with you." Everett said.

He took the offered hand, letting himself get pulled to his feet. The man wobbled there for a moment, putting a hand on one knee as he bent in the middle. The weight of his physical needs were getting to him, but still he stood. Pushing through it, Everett straightened out, pulling himself to his full height. Still trembling from the simple task of standing, he gave Adda an affirming nod. He was with her.

And the valley?

The valley did not like this.

They had not walked more than a dozen steps beyond where they had just spoken when they were pulled to a stop by the unexpected.

Off to their left and some distance away, the sand suddenly erupted like a geyser into the air. It rolled upward into the sky, mounting nearly twenty feet into the air before pluming out and then falling to the ground. Sand rained down onto both Adda and Everett with tiny grains that stuck to their skin like magnets on metal.

The two of them rose their hands up instinctively, trying to defend themselves from the discharging force. The sand was undeterred, latching eagerly onto the offered limbs. As the sand began to settle, Adda peeked over her elbow that she had thrown across her face, trying to decipher the source of their journey's interruption. Her eyes widened as she saw what had caused the disturbance.

Before them, a long, dried arm was sticking out from the sand.

The entire limb was skeletal, skin drawn tight against bone, tattered pieces of cloth fitted around its wrist and down its arm. The hand at the end creaked slowly downward toward the ground in a slow, methodical fashion. Once it found the sand, it dug its claw-like fingers in to find purchase and pushed upward.

With a great deal of effort, a mighty form was pulled free from the sand, rivulets raining from beneath skin and tattered cloth. The creature's head appeared from amidst the desert, looking as a human skull with only patches of skin remaining to cover up parts of its yellowed bone. Its hollow eyes and gaping jaw freely poured sand as it pulled itself free of its tomb. The entire body of the thing groaned and creaked on joints that hadn't been used in a long time. It had once been human, but sand and decay had been unkind to it, stripping it layer by layer until only a dried husk remained. It creaked to its full height, standing over ten feet under the stormy skies as it stared blankly to the heavens.

Everett and Adda froze, taken aback by such a dramatic appearance.

The creature turned its head toward them, and for a moment, Adda could see round, warm cheeks with large sparkling eyes that winked like sapphires. Thick curls billowed around this man's head like a sculpted cloud, obviously pieced together with great care. The man would have appeared friendly if it were not for the scowl that carved cruelly through an otherwise pleasant face. That, and of course, the fact that both the travelers could see through this ghostly image to witness the horror beyond.

"Hypocrites." He growled in the same croaking voice Lorelei had held.

The creature bent down and crawled toward them on all fours, his shoulders rotating in a way that made him appear like a large, predatory cat stalking its prey.

"Cheats. Swindlers." He continued to mutter, coming up to the threshold of the path, only to pace back-and-forth on the other side like a tiger behind glass eyeing potential meals. "Liars. You're all liars."

"Um- excuse me?" Adda asked.

She wasn't sure what else to say. The corpse person's reveal, appearance, and approach had all been so disquieting that Adda was having a hard time recovering. Everett offered up nothing, instead he stood in stunned silence.

"Liar!" He snapped, slamming one balled fist into the shifting sands beneath. "You can't pretend with me! I see right through you."

The creature rose once again, his body cracking painfully as he pulled himself to his full height. Up close, the thing easily dwarfed them, looming over like a shadow cast in candlelight. In many ways, he was nearly indistinguishable from Lorelei, yet this one was far more decayed and sunken than her.

"You come here, walking on this path, thinking that you're too good for us, that you're too good to live like us." He sneered at them.

Adda could only tell that it was a sneer because his image briefly shifted to his other face to reveal the facial change. It dissipated away like everything in this realm did, shifting back to the skeletal one.

"That's it, isn't it? You think you're better than us!" Their accuser shrieked.

"Well, I-"

"Stop! Stop stop stop stopstopstop!" He screamed, crouching down and placing hands over the holes in the sides of his head as he attempted to blot out Adda's voice.

He clawed at his skull, tugging as though he were pulling on his hair in frustration, though there was no hair to grab.

"Don't you dare lie to me, I can see it! Yeah, that better-than-thou look in your eye! You judge the way I live and think that I'm some kind of trash." He spat. "You're trash! Refuse! Garbage!"

Adda looked at Everett, her eyes wide in alarm and confusion.

Where Lorelei had appeared to be crazy, this one was utterly unhinged, broken down into a deep madness that had shattered any semblance of the man he had once been. He had yet to do anything actually aggressive, but Adda could feel how dangerous he was. Thankfully, it appeared that he'd make no effort to cross over the path, instead taking to raging and raving against them just beyond.

He scooped up sand in his taloned hands and flung it about as he continued to ramble unintelligently. There were only a few scattered words that made any manner of sense, most of it lost to muttering.

Seeing he was distracted, Adda slowly inched up the path, away from the creature, trying her best to make no sudden movements. Much to her dismay, the tiniest shift in her weight snapped his attention back onto them, causing him to once again rise up to his full height.

"So, you think that you're just going to skulk off, do you?" He growled, skittering after them like some horrid insect. "Running from your sinsss?"

He drew out the 's' sound, causing Adda to shiver uncomfortably.

"What do you want from us?" Everett cried out, eyes wide and wild.

"*What do you want from us?*" The creature said in a whiny, mocking voice before spitting out a dusty globule of some black, viscous liquid. "Pathetic."

He let out a deranged laugh that was as terrifying as it was humorless.

"I was like you once, instructed that if I just stayed on the path I'd be alright." He spoke before kicking sand at them. "This is a path of *lies*! It is only for the worst of people. The valley is good, you'll see. It's better if you just step off!"

Abruptly, his voice became almost pleading and he reached out his decrepit hand. There was a desperation in his voice as if he *needed* them to listen.

"Trust me, you can be better than this. You don't have to live this lie anymore."

The pull was immediate and magnetic, physically drawing them both a step toward him. A longing was brought with it, a longing to conform to the valley, to give up this journey. Life would be so much easier if they just gave in. All their wants and needs would be met. They wouldn't have to worry about what this world was or wasn't anymore.

They could be at peace.

In a fraction of a second, the Certainty rose up at Adda's core, granting her the strength to grind her heels into the gravel. For all the temptation the valley offered, there was a compass within her that pointed only in one direction.

The mountain awaited them.

"No, we have to get to the city." Adda said, leaning into the Certainty to give her strength.

She reached out and took hold of Everett, stopping him in his tracks as well. He blinked, shaking his head as if waking up from a deep slumber. A look of horror passed over his face as he realized what had nearly happened.

And just like that, the drawing force collapsed, unable to pull them in.

The creature watched the travelers resist his plea and this angered him. He howled out and beat his fists against his chest like an ape.

"Why? Too good to get dirty? Well, let me let you in on a little secret." He snarled, "You're just as messed up as the rest of us, you're just as broken. They aren't going to let you into the city and when you get turned away, you're going to come crawling right back to us. And when you do-"

He paused, relishing his next words.

"I'll kill you."

It was at that final comment that Adda finally recovered from her shock. For some reason she couldn't yet fathom, his threat to kill them seemed almost- childish. The weakness she had felt only a moment ago quickly drained away, allowing her to stand tall once again.

"Can't you see yourself?" Adda asked, stepping forward to the very edge of the path to stand before the creature.

The thing stopped its ramblings, freezing in place to size up its opponent. He waited for her to continue.

"We might all be damaged or broken in our own ways, but you-you're *living* in it." Adda said, "Can't you see you're destroying yourself?"

The thing that was once a man howled in anger. He spun about, swinging taloned hands through the sand, kicking up clouds of it as he raged. Clenched fists pounded the ground over and over, as black spittle burst from his gaping mouth. His wild fury caused Everett to take a step back, drawing as far away as possible, but Adda stood her ground, watching the being with passive eyes. It went on this way for some time, angry at the defiance of the travelers, but clearly unable to do anything about it.

Finally exhausted, the creature fell to the ground, exposed chest heaving from the physical exertion. He eyed them both, hatred burning from those hollow pits.

"You judge me! You think you're better than me, but you're not. You look at me as though I am something evil, when it's actually you who is evil! You expect everyone else to fall into line behind you, but you're unwilling to consider doing the same for us." He hissed, writhing around in the sand.

"Pointing fingers isn't going to make your life any better." Adda chastised him, "You made the choices that got you here, you can either own that or just let yourself waste away."

The cruel thing popped back up, eyes wild with indignation and insanity. He twitched sporadically as he glared down at this woman who had the audacity to talk back to him. His hands clamped and unclamped as though he couldn't wait to get them around her throat.

Despite this, Adda found herself growing bolder and bolder by the moment. The weight of this place had been sequestered far away from her mind, replaced instead by an unshakeable spirit. She could feel the rage boiling deep within the cavity in his chest that once housed a heart.

But what could he do to her?

An idea then sprang into her mind. Adda considered it for a moment, surprised by it before presenting it to the skeletal man.

"You should come with us." She said.

The man stared back at her, the black pits where his eyes turned to dust long ago studied her with intensity. Adda caught another glimpse of the man he had once been flickering across his visage.

He, as with Lorelei, had not come from her hometown, yet somehow had ended up here just the same. As Adda gazed at him, images began to fill her mind. They were snapshots of a life spent outside of this valley- in fact, she could see they came from a world she was once a part of.

There were pockets of beauty, and light, but also a contrast of all manner of darkness. She saw pictures of laughter, love, and family. She also saw pictures of guzzling drinks in the refrigerator light, empty words shared with the wrong person, and ultimately, the heavy burden of devastating heartbreak. He blamed one moment in time for who he was, but it was in fact a million tiny ones that destroyed him. The darkness had risen up inside of him, becoming the lens through which he saw the world. Abandonment, consequence, agony, hatred, all coiled up inside of him like a serpent prepared to strike. This tidal wave roared over every good thing in his life, driving them from his mind until only the pain remained.

The longer she looked, the more this man was laid bare before her. He had made so many damning choices in his life, yet like most people, he also bore his share of repercussions that he had no fault in.

A father who was physically there, but in no other manner. A mother that drank easily and struck easier still. Every scar, tear, and cut upon his dried, hollowed body was like a window into his past. As she looked on, somehow experiencing these things alongside him, she felt a great and overwhelming pity. Not the kind that that had long been misplaced on her shoulders. No, this one was a pity that mourned such a loss of potential, of life.

Of love.

Without thinking, Adda reached out and snatched up the stranger's hand and tugged him toward her. The creature was so startled by this that he fell before her, letting himself be pulled in.

He still stood just off the path, refusing to let even a toe cross the boundary, but he was close enough that Adda could wrap her arms around him and pull him into an embrace. Adda felt tears prick her eyes as her cheek pressed up against this poor man's papery, dried skin. She could hear his heart weakly fluttering in his chest.

Despite his outside appearance, he was still alive.

"You've already been forgiven." Adda whispered so that only she and the man could hear.

How she knew this she wasn't sure, it just came into her mind and the Certainty had prompted her to say it. The Certainty prompted her again, dropping a single word into her head. It was a name, a name to someone she had never met and yet now somehow knew.

"Thomas," She spoke his name, "you have to come with us, there is no other way."

Thomas, a creature broken for so long stood in a silent stupor, taken off guard by the embrace of this strange woman. Upon hearing his name, his body tensed, becoming rigid as a look of shock flitted across his face. He looked at her, perhaps seeing his world as it actually was for the first time. Adda hoped that this would be enough to convince him to take a step forward, to trust her and Everett.

Yet, in the blink of an eye, the man recovered.

With a guttural growl Thomas broke free of her and reeled back as if he had been struck. He stumbled a few steps away, putting enough distance from Adda that she would have to step onto the sand to reach him again.

"Witch!" He hissed between his yellowed teeth, letting his anger bury his humanity. "You think you can manipulate me with tricks and sorcery?"

He leered at her. "I should just kill you now."

"Thomas, please, we have to go." Adda said, her voice shaking with a surprising amount of emotion.

"Stop saying that name!" Thomas screamed.

"You're killing yourself!" Adda screamed back at him. "Why can't you see that?"

"Stop." Thomas said, his voice as cold as ice. "I'm done with you. We-" He spread his arms out to indicate the valley around them. "-are done with you. You think you can bully and trick us into your way of thinking? Well, you're dead wrong."

Thomas turned around and started to dig himself back into the sand. His hands worked furiously, cutting long channels in the sand to create a pit big enough for his body. The grains rolled to the side eagerly, welcoming him back into their embrace.

"Don't come back here. Ever." He said, his voice threatening.

With that, Thomas vanished underneath the sand, returning to his resting place to presumably await the next travelers who dared walk this path. Adda searched for any sign of him, but that sand had hidden him entirely, holding him somewhere deep within its clutches.

Adda fell to her knees and wept, overwhelmed with his vanishing. Somehow, she had tapped into his story, had learned every last thing about him from a mere touch, and to watch him choose death- well, it was too much for her to handle in that moment. She wept for the people from her town, she wept for the people of the valley.

She wept for Thomas.

A warm hand weighed on her shoulder, causing Adda to cast a side-long glance backward. Everett stood over her, looking worried.

"Are you ok?" He croaked, the fear in his voice as thick as the sludge from the rivers.

Adda looked back to the sand, once again trying to find any sign of Thomas. The encounter had changed her forever. It wasn't because of anything that Thomas was, it was simply that something had been shifted in Adda during their interaction. She had always considered herself an empathetic and considerate person, but in that moment, she realized she hadn't even begun to understand the meaning of the word. She thought she knew people, that she *understood* them. Now, it was painfully clear how little she truly understood.

For the briefest moments, Adda had walked in Thomas' shoes. She had seen his highs, his lows, and had suffered in silence at every one of his bad decisions. His story was slipping from her mind, it was not something for her to keep, but the impression it made would remain in her forever.

We really don't know anything at all. Adda thought to herself, staring at the shifting sands.

"Adda?" Everett said again.

This prompted the woman to turn her back on the sand. She rose to her feet and took in a deep breath, letting the burning agony go. Thomas might have buried himself again, but he had given her a new perspective. In that moment, she resolved that after she got to the city, she'd come back for her people. Adda would find a way to convince them to come back with her, to live a better life.

"I'm okay." Adda said, finally letting a smile play at her lips. "You ready to keep going?"

"I mean, I don't really wanna hang out around here." He said, glancing nervously about. "I'd rather not piss that guy off anymore than we already have."

"Yeah sure, makes sense. Let's get out of here." She said, setting her feet toward the mountain once again.

Adda hesitated, turning to the young man.

"Oh, and Everett?"

"What's up?"

"Thank you for choosing to stay."

3

"How did you know his name?" Everett asked once they had left the man far behind.

"Hm?"

"With that corpse guy. Thomas?"

"Oh. Right." Adda paused, reflecting on the interaction. "I don't know, I just started having visions of his life and then it came to me."

"Do you think it's another one of your powers?" Everett asked, his voice sounding excited at the prospect. "Like, you can just see everything about people?"

He paused then, "That's kinda freaky, actually."

"What did I say about calling them powers?" Adda replied.

"Well, what would you call them?" He retorted in kind.

Adda thought about this for a moment.

"Ok fine, I guess in a way they're powers." She said, finally relenting. "But I don't think they're unique to me or Keith or anyone else for that matter. It's hard to say though, nothing about this world is normal."

"So, do you think you could teach me?" Everett asked, sounding excited.

"Well, once I figure out how I'm even doing it, you'll be the first to know."

The answer returned a spring to Everett's step as he began to daydream of all the cool things he'd one day be able to do. It was good that he had something to occupy his mind away from their current predicament.

They chatted for a while longer about nothing in particular. There was a video game Everett had been invested in before their world had been turned upside down and he regaled her all about it. Adda listened, asking questions as they went, though she was having a hard time following a lot of what he was talking about. She was just glad that they were falling into easy conversation, rather than letting oppressive silence or heated arguments be their only other traveling companions.

And so they walked, the mountain rising before them. It slowly, but surely ate away at the sky, dwarfing all in its impossible height. With every minute it seemed to swell in stature, easily hiding the world behind. As they approached, more details had begun to appear out of its grey and black face, bringing on new dimensions of life to the monolith.

A large waterfall could be seen below the cloud line, sending up a massive spray of mist in its crashing wake. Even from this great distance, Adda could tell that it was truly massive. She could almost hear the thundering water roaring down from such great heights only to crash like cannon fire on the rocks far below. From there it transformed into a winding river that carved its way down the mountain. Somewhere along its journey, the water vanished from sight, never connecting to the valley below.

Or at least so it appeared from Adda's current perspective.

Surrounding the falls and covering much of the upper area of the mountain were thick layers of brilliant, blue ice. It formed layer upon layer in those freezing heights. The journey up there amidst all that cold would certainly be treacherous. Packed onto every remaining surface was a thick blanket of snow. It was constantly fed from the forming clouds that leapt down past it to descend upon the valley.

Adda felt it was strange to see snow falling while being suffocated in sweltering heat. She didn't know enough about weather or geography to decide whether or not this was a phenomenon of this new world or if that was common where she had come from. Regardless, the woman wished she were up in all that chilly snow. Her parched mouth groaned at the idea of finally getting to drink something, even if it would result in a brain freeze.

Ease up. Adda thought to herself, *We're not there yet.*

From the ground, the path could also be seen, though the rocks did their best to hide it at every given chance. Adda would have thought its white gravel would have blended in with the snow gathered all around, but somehow it still stood out. It glinted a silvery color as it caught daylight from a sun they couldn't see. It shone like a beacon, drawing them toward it.

All these things and more popped up everywhere Adda looked. To see these details coming together more and more clearly gave both the travelers a second wind. For all Keith's talk of the mountain delivering dread, both Adda and Everett only found hope when they gazed upon its slopes. To reach the mountain meant leaving the valley and though there would certainly be challenges ahead, it had to be better than their present troubles.

That's when Adda began to notice that something was wrong.

Though the mountain increased in size, it felt like that they weren't actually getting closer to it. It was hard to truly gauge in this twisting, changing environment that surrounded them. Adda was sure it was just an optical illusion that made the mountain feel impossibly far even as it rose above them. Perhaps it was simply too difficult for their brains to process the distance between themselves and such an incomprehensible giant such as this towering mountain.

Yet, even as the hours slogged on at its trudging pace, they drew no closer.

"Is it just me or does it feel like we're kinda stuck in place?" Everett voiced what Adda saw.

"I was thinking the same thing." She replied.

Adda stopped, staring at the mountain that now occupied nearly the entire horizon. It was somehow still impossibly far away which Adda found to be most irritating. The Certainty pointed toward the mountain, tugging at her like an insistent child. For all its pulling, the mountain refused to let them get closer, mocking them from a safe distance.

Adda crossed her arms and turned herself at the waist. She bent over and tilted her head until her crown was nearly parallel with the ground.

"What are you doing?"

"Trying to get a different look at it." Adda replied, now bending the opposite direction, hair tumbling around her shoulders. "I don't know. Maybe it will help us see something we're missing."

Wordlessly, Everett began to mimic her, turning this way and that to try to take in more perspectives. It was not a mocking thing, rather an attempt to imitate this woman that had, against all odds, still managed to make it this far relatively unscathed. Whatever she had, he wanted to understand it, to master it, to use it to overcome this new world. So what she did, he followed suit now, convinced that he had discovered some kind of angel or the like.

They stood there, bending and twisting, looking out in hopes to catch a glimpse of something new. Finally, Adda let out a sigh and sat down on the path, she drummed her fingers on her jaw as she considered this challenge.

"Why are you being this way?" Adda mused out loud, addressing the mountain.

"What? I mean, I was just doing what you were doing." Everett said, sounding defensive.

Adda had certainly not been talking to him, but she let it go, not really interested in explaining where her mind was at. While she sat, her neck began to slowly turn, bringing her attention to the wastes. Around them were holes that pocketed the landscape like the many entrances of some ground dwelling mammal. With great frequency, a gaseous, yellow substance would burst forth with tremendous force from the holes, shooting for miles into the sky before finally dissipating. They appeared to be like geysers from back home, though Adda had never actually seen one in person. Instead of water and steam, however, these ones appeared to be releasing something a bit more toxic. Adda watched them for a while, trying to decipher a pattern within their eruptions, seeking an answer there to their problem.

Of course, there was no hidden message here, leaving Adda stumped.

Everett, tired of standing, joined her. Adda noticed that he didn't complain that she had chosen to stop, taking this opportunity to finally rest his aching feet. She felt a small bite of guilt, feeling bad that she had pushed the young man so hard, griping about him taking rests, and yet she was also the one now halting their progress.

"Do you have any ideas?" Adda asked, this time directing it toward Everett.

"I dunno, it's pretty weird." Everett delivered the understatement of the century.

He shifted his weight next to her, trying to get comfortable on the biting stones. He winced, arching his back in an attempt to get it to pop. No such relief came, causing Everett to stoop forward to alleviate some of the pressure.

"It's so big, but it's like we're walking backward." He hesitated then, "You don't think we have to- ya know- actually walk backward?"

Adda let out a small chuckle at that, considering for a moment what that would look like. Two people caught in the middle of some nightmare land, surrounded by living corpses, walking backward toward a mountain they could never reach. It was a special kind of insanity that she found a small drop of humor in.

"I'm open to trying anything." Adda said with a shrug, but didn't rise.

Everett grunted, using his hands to rub the soreness from his legs. Though he had suggested it, it seemed he wasn't very eager in testing his theory. To do so meant letting this opportunity to rest his tired body go and he wasn't in any rush to do that.

They continued to mull over the problem, hoping an answer might present itself to them. It was from the back of Adda's mind that such a potential solution bubbled into her consciousness. She realized that she had been here before.

Of course, not *exactly* here, but here in the sense that she had experienced something similar not so long ago. Her thoughts fell back to the first time she had tried to leave a place that seemed bent on keeping her there. An idea began to form.

"Wait! What if we-" Adda started, her mind racing.

As if in response to the words passing her lips, the valley exploded.

Unlike with Thomas who had let loose a single geyser in his escape from the sand's clutches, this time it was as though the entirety of the desert had lifted into the air. On either side of the path, a massive wall of sand blasted upward, blocking out even the sky. Both Adda and Everett froze in its shadow like rabbits who had just spotted a circling hawk.

It hung there for a moment, the world holding its breath in anticipation.

"Adda, what's happening?" Everett whispered, eyes wide.

Then, the sand collapsed.

With a tremendous roar that sounded like the sky was being ripped in two, the sand barreled down toward them, whipping into a frenzy as it fell. The walls crumbled, bringing their full force down against the two travelers. Unlike the people who dwelled in the land, the sand had no problem pushing through the boundaries of the pathway, and so, with little ceremony, it was upon them.

With great effort, Adda pulled herself up to her feet, keeping her head down against the sudden attack. The sand bit at her arms, legs, and neck, beating against her in an attempt to knock her back to the ground. She pushed forward, her arms raised to protect her face against the peppering grains. With every step, Adda made sure that she only moved along the white stones that peaked between the rapidly mounding sand. Though there were miniature dunes popping up before them, somehow those white stones still shone through. The gravel pushed up against her feet as she measured each step before taking it, aware that any misstep could lead them far astray.

"Everett!" She called back into the howling whirlwind.

Adda immediately regretted opening her mouth. Sand swirled in causing her to gag and cough, desperately trying to keep the muck from coagulating in her throat. Still hacking, she blindly lashed out against the sand, trying to find evidence of the man that had just been behind her.

One swipe. Nothing.

Another.

Still nothing.

With a silent plea, she swung out one last time, hoping against hope that it would find something solid. To her great relief, she struck a person hidden in the sand. The hit was responded to with a surprised grunt and a hand latching onto her arm. The grip conveyed a powerful desperation, a request to be led out. Adda obliged, marching with as much speed as she dared down the path in the direction she hoped was the mountain.

The sand screamed and raged, attacking them from all sides. It buzzed and hissed, putting great force upon Adda as it tried to drive her back. It quickly robbed her of her ability to see as it bit at her eyes and its intense wailing pierced her ears until she couldn't hear anything else. She stumbled forward, blind and deaf, only able to determine where she was going by the ever-present gravel pressing against her feet. She was buffeted over and over again, but she wouldn't stop moving. If she stopped, the sand would bury her where she stood.

Never before had Adda ever felt so lonely. Even with Everett's hand pressing into her own, she felt absolutely isolated from everyone and everything. All there was, was the sand screaming into her, beating against her in a bid to break her body and her will.

It would not let her pass, it would not let her win.

There was no escape.

There was now no doubt in Adda's mind that this place was actually alive and it did not take kindly to those who dare refuse its invitation. Adda found in the pressing sand that she was starting to regret her decision to ignore the valley's invitation. How much easier it would have been to just give in and live in the lie.

It's only one, little step. A voice whispered. *No one would even notice.*

No. Adda thought resolutely back.

To stay was to succumb to the sand. Even if this assaulting power was to rob Adda of her life, she would rather pass knowing she had given it her all than let the desert win. Some fates are worse than death and this valley was the worst of them all.

So, step-by-step she pushed on, pulling Everett along behind her. Adda tried not to think about how much easier this would be if she could just let him go. His steps were hesitant and heavy, slowing Adda down as she tried to get them both to safety. Maybe it would be for the best if she just pretended to lose him, to let go and let him settle into the valley.

It would be easy. The sinister voice whispered deep inside. *Just- let go.*

Adda felt a strong conviction tear through her, making her forget for a moment the pressing sand. No, she wouldn't condemn him to be like Lorelei or Thomas. Adda could go on to pretend that she had just lost the man, but she would go the rest of her life knowing she had abandoned him. As long as Everett held on, she would drag him to the city if she had to. For better or for worse, they were in this together.

The only way out is through, the only way out is through. She thought to herself, repeating it over and over again in her mind like a mantra. *Please, help us.*

And then, she saw light.

Not the muted light that filled the whole valley beneath the permanently overcast skies. No, this light was pure and shone with such a brilliance that even behind a wall of sand, it was too bright to look at. It looked like liquid gold bubbling in the great heat of a furnace.

That was all she needed.

Adda lowered her head and charged forward, screaming against the storm as she put all of her strength into this last, desperate play for escape. The tempest howled in rage, buffeting against her with a mighty wind.

Still, she moved forward.

It threw sand at her feet, covering her shoes in thick layers as it tried to trip her.

Still, she moved forward.

It pelted her arms, legs, and eyes with such ferocity as to rip her body to pieces.

And still, she moved forward.

Try as it may, the storm had lost its grip on her. Adda denied its power and its temptations, walking through its many trials and coming out the other side. Finally, she broke free of it, stumbling before the shimmering light and into the muggy air of the valley. Adda collapsed to the ground, coughing wretchedly from where she lay.

It was over.

The sand rolled back from her, rejoining its shifting form on either side of the path until it appeared that the storm had never happened. Adda blinked her eyes, attempting to free them of the intrusive grains, but only managed to smear more irritants into place. Rising up on her elbows, she squinted up the path toward the source of the golden light. She tried to discern what had caused it, but the sand made the world blurry. Already the light was fading rapidly, vanishing as quickly as it had come.

Yet, even as it disappeared, Adda could have sworn she saw something standing in the heart of the light.

It was the image of a man looking back at her.

And then, it was gone.

4

A ragged cough woke Adda, pulling her from a dreamless sleep and back into reality. She lay still, confused as to why she was covered in a fine layer of sand. It took her a moment to gather her thoughts back together as sleep still hung around her mind like a fog. It didn't take long for it all to come crashing back together.

Adda became aware of the nightmarish landscape once again, memories of what had happened flooding back in. Her entire body ached, eliciting a long groan from her mouth as she became aware of the state she was in. Though the storm hadn't the power to kill her, it had extracted its toll, leaving behind a dull agony in its terrible wake.

Adda slowly pushed herself up, wincing as pain arched through her with each movement, every muscle protesting the effort. To make matters worse, she also discovered that there was sand everywhere, clinging to her like barnacles on a ship. It stuffed up her nose, coated her tongue, and dried out her throat so much that it hurt to swallow.

Gritting her teeth, Adda lolled her head to the side, looking toward Everett who had also begun to stir. The man gave out a horrid, hacking cough that rattled his sickly frame. It was a horrendous sound, issuing out from deep within him. It was dry and so intense that it made Everett's entire body shake with effort.

Adda brought a hand up to brush herself clean, trying to get the clinging sand free of her skin and clothing. To her surprise, the motion did not rid herself of the irritants. If anything, they seemed to crowd in closer, digging into her skin where they could find purchase. They wouldn't leave without a fight. Adda looked at the tiny invaders, wondering why they didn't roll off of her like everything else that tried to stick to her.

They stared back in silence, refusing to reveal their secrets.

Realizing that the answers weren't immediately at hand, Adda rose to her feet in a slow, methodical motion. She wasn't sure the extent of the damage that had been caused to her body and didn't want any sudden movements to make things worse. Pulling herself to her full height, Adda turned to look around still feeling dazed.

The path was unmarked, the dunes that had been forming there had retreated away, leaving the gravel clean and unblemished. It was almost as if the storm had never even happened. Adda was just thankful to see that, by some miracle, the two of them had managed to stay on the trail.

The tempest had certainly tried its best, but they had somehow made it out the other side victorious. The landscape itself hadn't changed much, still boasting its miles of red, flowing sand, and rivers of glinting, black ooze. Spying the liquid, there was a tug to go lap up what she could from the sludge. A temptation to lean into the belief that it was a cool spring that could relieve her need for a drink and a wash.

She ignored it and instead staggered over to Everett.

"Are you alright?" Her voice croaked.

"I don't know." He answered, his voice ragged as her own.

The fact that he could talk brought Adda some comfort. There was no evidence of blood or bruising on either of them which was also a good sign. He was, however, covered in a layer of the red sand much like she was.

"Adda?" Everett said, looking up at her. "Thank you- for pulling me through. I don't- It was just so confusing."

A sob escaped his lips. He rolled over onto his side, resting his forehead to Adda's leg. Ignoring the sand that was collected there, he curled up against her and began to cry.

"Why is this happening to us?" He asked in between his sobs.

"I don't know." Adda whispered.

She sat down next to Everett, pulling him against her and placing a hand on his head. The young man no longer seemed an adult, but now as a child who was trying to understand the cruelties of the world. Adda stroked his hair in a motherly way, letting him cry against her as all his pent up emotions overwhelmed him.

"We're almost there, Jason." Adda said, using Everett's first name.

It felt weird to say, but at the same time, she felt that it was needed. Everett pulled himself up, looking over at her with wide, glistening eyes. The look only lasted a moment before he turned away.

"I- I think you should leave me here." He finally said after a long pause. "I know I'm just slowing you down."

That was true, Adda did wonder how much further along she

would have been if she hadn't needed to care for him. It was like trying to swim while carrying a lead weight in one hand. The extra burden constantly tried to drag her under the hungry waves, waiting for the moment her strength would give out.

Is he really worth it? The thought turned around in her mind.

The question wasn't fair. After all, who was Adda to decide such a thing? The fact was Everett had chosen to come with her and she would respect that choice even if it came with extra cost. She pushed past the temptation to take his offer and instead rose, pulling the man up with her.

"I'm not going to leave you here. Ok?" Adda said sternly.

"Ok." Everett nodded his head and sniffed, attempting to clear his stuffy nose.

"You and I are going to get to the city." Adda said. "Do I make myself clear?"

"I'll go wherever you go." Everett responded.

Adda studied Everett, searching his eyes as they stood under the rolling clouds. She reached out and placed a hand on his cheek, trying to will him into understanding. Was this what it was like to be a parent? To see beyond a child's scope, but knowing that they had to make all the choices on their own?

"Everett, no matter what happens, you have to keep pushing through. With or without me. Do you understand?"

He didn't answer.

"Do you understand?" She asked again, emphasizing every word. "If something happens to me, you *have* to keep going."

Everett nodded his head, but Adda wasn't convinced he

understood. She worried that following her wouldn't be enough for him to make it through to the end. He relayed on her strength, he needed it to keep going. But what would happen to him if that strength ran out?

This leg of the journey had been difficult and had taxed them both. If the mountain decided to take those challenges to the next level it was entirely possible that one, or both of them, wouldn't make it. If that was the case, she didn't want Everett giving up if she was the one to fall by the wayside.

Still, there wasn't much else Adda could do. She just had to trust that Everett could wrap his head around what she had said. Besides, they had made it this far, so there was a good chance that the two of them would make it through just fine.

Now they turned once again toward the mountain, seeing its looming form still in the distance. Adda wasn't sure how far they'd walked in the storm, but it apparently hadn't brought them any closer.

"We still need to figure out how to get up there." Everett said, looking at the rising monolith.

"This world likes to play by its own rules." Adda muttered to herself and absently ran a hand along a loose coil of hair.

"What?" Everett asked, picking sand from his ears. "Did you say something?"

"Where we're from we say seeing is believing." Adda continued, again mostly to herself. "But here, nothing is what it seems."

"Uh- sorry, I can't really hear you." Everett said, "Could you speak up a little?"

She didn't respond. Instead, Adda closed her eyes, thinking back to that little, horrific hamlet that she had traveled through. That place had held her too, refusing to let her go. It wasn't until she had realized that the buildings weren't fully there that she could find a way out. The eyes were deceiving, more so here than they had ever been back home.

Could that be the answer?

Adda reached out, indicating Everett to take her hand. She felt him grip onto it, his own hand slick and grimy from sweat mixing with sand. He latched on without hesitation, ready to follow where she lead.

"Close your eyes and follow me." Adda said.

Assuming he had done as he was told, Adda began to walk, allowing the gravel that crunched beneath her feet to guide her. Her body tensed up as fear nagged in the back of her mind that she would misstep and become lost in the desert without her ability to see. It pulled at her eyes, begging her to open them back up so that they wouldn't stray. Her strength flickered in her and an uncertainty rose to match the Certainty.

Adda screwed her eyes together tighter and tighter, fending off the desire to open them up. Her mind screamed that she was making a terrible mistake, but still she ignored it. The Certainty pointed her forward as unerring as a compass. Adda had to trust it wouldn't allow her to misstep.

They walked in silence, the crunch of gravel the only thing to indicate that they still remained on the road. They had only gone maybe a dozen paces when Adda felt that there was a slight change. At first it was nearly imperceptible, but after a few more steps it became more and more obvious that something was indeed different.

Their feet no longer stepped on a level surface rather they found themselves bending to compensate for a slight grade. The air around them began to thin out as well, the harsh humidity making way for a breeze that brought a touch of cold with it.

With a long sigh, Adda's eyes fluttered open to find them met with the harsh, gray rock of the mountain. Though miles had separated them from its base, in a matter of moments they had come to stand upon its threshold. It loomed above them, even more intimidating than the valley they had just walked through.

There was no dual-image here, no false reality pinned over what was real. The mountain conformed to no image save its own. The hard stone was exactly as it appeared and Adda found that to be most relieving. On either side of them, the rolling dunes were no more as they bowed away from the power of the giant they were about to challenge. The only piece of the desert that held on were the clinging grains of sand that refused to release their victims. Despite the nuisance, Adda felt an overwhelming sense of relief wash over her.

They had finally escaped the valley.

"How did that work?" Everett asked, bewildered.

"I experienced something like it before." Adda answered. "For whatever reason, it seems this place reacts to how we perceive it. We keep trying to put it into a box of what we understand, but that's not how things work here."

"Okay, but I mean, how did closing our eyes help any?" Everett pressed into the question.

"Maybe, we just rely on our sight too much and the valley used it against us." Adda said with a shrug.

Everett scratched at this chin, mindlessly picking at the particles of sand still clinging there. "Ok, I mean, that doesn't really make sense."

"Well it worked, didn't it?" Adda replied.

Adda turned about to look over the valley. She felt her heart drop as she beheld it from afar in all its broken glory. The beauty of it still clung like a shroud, yet underneath it Adda saw its poison.

The rivers of sludge were riddled with slowly moving bodies that desperately tried to clean themselves, only for the sludge to act like glue for the sand to cake on them like a second skin. Others gathered on its bank, trying to quench their thirst by gulping down its contents only to retch it up a short while later.

Between the trees, the corpse people sought the company of others, trying to hide their actions beneath the shade of the trees. Yet, the trees cast no shadows, allowing their loneliness and shame to be put on display for the world.

Others gathered around the bushes to gorge themselves upon the fruit. They sought to put substance back into their emaciated forms. It provided no sustenance, yet they walked away with satisfied looks, tricking themselves into thinking that they had had a satisfying meal.

Even more figures gathered around the gas bellowing geysers to inhale its fumes. They would lean over the cavernous openings to take in lungfuls of each toxic blast. Then, they'd stumble away and turn to their closest neighbors. They'd yell loudly over one another their unique understanding of reality, seeing themselves as gods of their own making.

But the valley lied to them all. Adda turned from it, nearly overwhelmed with grief.

"Come on, Everett."

Everett nodded wordlessly, his speech robbed from him as his eyes roamed the valley not with deep sadness, but rather sickening horror. He pulled himself away and followed Adda into the mountain.

5

The mountain drew them up as they continued to follow the singular path that led them higher and higher. The path still went straight, never diverting from its mold, yet somehow it was riddled with bends and twists. The mountain seemed to be the culprit behind the effect, moving itself where it needed in order to keep the travelers confused and debased. It disguised where the unerring path was going, keeping the destination hidden from sight. It used this power blatantly, making no move to disguise its trickery.

Adda hadn't initially been aware of the phenomenon, but after walking directly forward for so long without taking an actual turn despite rounding both bends and walls, it became impossible to miss. At first Adda tried to make sense of it, carefully watching the mountain around her to better understand its nature. This resulted in her becoming nauseous and dizzy as this break in reality made her head spin. She learned rather quickly that it was best if she just kept her eyes centered on the path and ignore whatever strangeness was going on around her.

To make matters worse, the pathway had grown even more narrow, only allowing one person to move along it at a time. There wasn't even ground on either side that one could step off onto, which Adda supposed was both a blessing and a curse. The blessing was that a misstep wouldn't result in any devilish power taking them. The curse was that while on one side was a solid, rock wall, the other was a sheer drop off that grew taller as they climbed.

The slightest slip would spell death.

They had only been walking a short time, but already the clouds appeared to be closer than the valley they had just left. When they looked down, they could see that the valley stretched out far bigger than they had anticipated. The hills that ringed it were almost lost to the horizon, left to peek up as gray humps in the darkness beyond. Everywhere they looked below was more of the same that they had crossed. One thing was made clear from this height, there was indeed only one path. From their lofty point, they could see that the valley surrounded at least three faces of the mountain, but it was impossible to tell if it held to the other side as well.

Adda hoped not as she glanced back at Everett. He struggled on after her, his breath coming in shallow heaves as the altitude took its toll. The sandstorm had been particularly difficult for him and Adda couldn't imagine him being able to cross through that all over again.

Since then, Everett had grown progressively more quiet on their journey, once full of questions and debate he was now taken by a stoic silence. What was going on inside of his head was anyone's guess. When he noticed her looking back, he gave her a wane smile, a feeble attempt to comfort her worry.

Adda turned back to the path, a myriad of concerns running circles through her head.

After her experience with Thomas, the weight of her body had been lifted temporarily. She had forgotten about the exhaustion or the hunger and thirst. Yet, the higher they climbed into the mountain, the more and more it all returned, weighing against her shoulders like she was carrying a boulder. It frustrated her that there seemed to be no rhyme or reason behind these weighty sensations. Her mind searched for the pattern, but if there was one, it remained lost to her.

The sand from the valley certainly didn't help her disposition. It still caked them both from head to toe and it felt as though it had grown heavier. Try as she may, it refused to be cast aside, clinging stubbornly to her despite her best efforts. Every time she brushed off one area, she'd find it weighing down somewhere else.

Adda wished it would release her, but it refused to oblige. She missed walking the hills, they had been so easy to conquer, taking less than a thought to move through them. The valley, and now too the mountain, seemed to be more adamant about turning her away.

As they walked, the mountain continued to grow unabated, seeming infinite in the way it stretched out in every direction. Just like with the valley, it would be all too easy to become lost within its mighty power.

The travelers wandered through a gorge that housed wild grass, over rocky crags that bit with sharp rocks at their hands and legs, through ravines long and narrow and even over gaping chasms that seemed to have no bottom. On all sides, the mountain splayed itself out with no end. Even still, with every look back, the valley beckoned them to return to it. It offered them visions of paradise; freedom from their current struggles.

After discovering that the valley's power reached even this far, they stopped looking back.

They would still be able to see the valley until they walked beyond the veil of clouds up ahead. With every passing minute, those rolling storms grew closer and closer, threatening with its lightning and growling with its thunder. Adda sent a silent prayer that it might rain and take the sand from their bodies.

No rain came.

At least it isn't hot anymore, Adda thought to herself.

Like everywhere else, time no longer mattered. It could have been hours or days that passed them by as they trudged on in this endless, gray landscape. It was hard to gauge time's passage without nighttime to interrupt the perpetual light that leaked between clouds. The only thing that kept Adda from going insane was that quiet place in the back of her mind that offered her an escape. She was there now, mostly ignoring the world around her.

It was in this place that Adda remained, unaware that something new had appeared before them. Just up ahead the mountain had moved aside to reveal that the path now led them into the mouth of a low, dark cave. The pair was so lost in their own thoughts that they didn't register the change and nearly walked across its threshold. Adda was the first to pull up short which caused Everett to bump into her.

"What are yo-" Everett stopped mid sentence as he also became aware of the cave.

Adda glanced over her shoulder at him to see that a fresh sheen of sweat had begun to bead on his forehead. His face was also looking paler than she remembered it being.

"What's wrong?" Adda asked.

"Not this." Everett whispered, "Please, not this."

The hairs on his neck stood on end and his pupils grew so wide that his eyes appeared nearly black. His breath came in shuddering waves as his chest heaved dramatically in and out. He stumbled back a step to shake his head in protest.

"I-" He started, his voice embarrassed beneath the encompassing fear. "I don't like enclosed spaces."

Adda looked back to the cave. She studied it a moment and then turned to walk down the path a dozen or so steps away from the cave. Now that she stood a decent distance away, Adda regarded the drab gray of the mountain just above them. Try as she may, she couldn't see where the path exited the dark cave and back out under the stormy skies.

The path normally stood out brilliantly against the backdrop of either sand or stone, glistening like a vein of silver caught in a sunbeam. It was impossible to miss it once you became aware of it. Seeing nothing above them, Adda concluded that it had to be one of two things: either this cave led to the other side of the mountain or it ended up taking them somewhere above the impenetrable ceiling of clouds that felt near enough to touch.

In all honesty, going into the caves seemed like a much better bargain than attempting to navigate through lightning infested clouds. They had felt the weight of those storms before and Adda wasn't keen on the idea of walking back into its clutches. Everett's ashen face, however, had some obvious qualms with this stage of their journey.

With a sigh, Adda patted the box in her purse, marching past Everett and into the mouth of the cave.

"The only way out is through." She called back, her voice echoing away into the darkness, "If this is where the path goes, then this is where we go."

"Are you serious?" Everett called after her. "There has to be another way!"

"The path hasn't led us wrong yet. Do you really think it's a good idea to leave it now?" Adda asked over her shoulder.

When no answer was immediately given, Adda continued. "Come on, we've gotten through everything else!"

"Aren't you afraid of anything?" Everett said, a plea in his voice.

This gave the woman pause and she thought of her own fears that had come and gone through their journey. So many had attempted to raise their foul head, but time after time they had all departed her, revealing how powerless they really were.

"We live our whole lives afraid. Afraid of things, afraid of concepts, afraid of being alive, and of dying." Adda said, standing just in the darkness of the cave. "I am afraid of things, I just got tired of them controlling my life."

With a slow motion, Adda lifted her hand and slowly pushed it out into the darkness.

"Everything that has happened to us is confusing. None of it makes any sense. Yet, we're here and we have a direction to go. Sure, I'm afraid, but I can't give up because of it." Adda turned back toward Everett, extending her hand to him, fingers splayed out to be grasped by the other. "It's ok to feel fear, Everett, but then you have to move past it."

"How?" Everett asked as he trembled out of reach.

"Easy, you take my hand, and you walk." Adda said, "We escaped Keith and we beat the valley, we're going to get through this too."

With a sigh that was long-suffering, he walked to her and took her hand in his own. It was slick with sweat and trembled with anxious energy, but still he held on. Adda gave him a reassuring squeeze, taken aback by a sudden rush of emotion.

She was proud of this young man who had come so far despite all the fears he had. He had been here far longer than her, struggling to survive, yet he had walked away from his security because he knew as she did that there was only one direction to go. Who would have thought that the kid stuck at the grocery store and the woman who taught teenagers to paint would be struggling side-by-side in a mysterious realm that turned their own reality on its head?

Adda led the charge into the yawning maw that rose up to swallow them into the ground. They stepped into the darkness together and into the grasp of their next challenge.

6

The cave was like pitch cast across a canvas, eating away at any form of light until the darkness was the only thing that remained. Adda led them with one hand out and slightly up, the other clutching onto Everett's as they progressed further into the belly of the beast. Fortunately, it seemed the roof of this cavernous space extended far above them which lowered the odds of smacking a head on a low hanging piece of stone. Their footsteps echoed all around them, their breath sounding like it was coming from all directions. Somewhere deep in the distance was a constant, nagging sound of water dripping in a slow trickle. The sounds felt unnatural in a place that ought to remain silent and the loudness of their progress unsettled Adda.

To make matters worse, the sand dragged them down even harder, forcing their trudge to a steady crawl, lengthening their stay in the darkness tenfold. Wherever they were being led, it would take them a good measure of time to reach its end. It was only the sharp grinding of gravel beneath their feet that comforted Adda with the knowledge that they still walked the same path.

As they moved forward, Adda began to notice that she could make out her hand in the dark. Or rather, the after image of her hand. She would see it flicker in the darkness where it had been a moment before as though there were a delay to her eyes. For a moment she thought that maybe there was some kind of light source that was sneaking into the infinite blackness, she even hoped that maybe the caves didn't go as deep as she thought. What a relief it would be to discover the cave merely a short tunnel and not a winding catacomb.

Adda then remembered reading an article once about a tour that would take you deep beneath the earth to a place that no light reached at all. They would then make you turn off your lights and stand in absolute darkness that no human should ever experience. After a time, you would begin to notice shapes in the dark, the forms of other people, your own hands in front of you, or your feet beneath you. The guide would explain that this was simply an illusion that your brain would throw out into the world as it could not handle being in a darkness so complete. Every movement, every shape was just an image that your brain would piece together for you in order to hold onto some kind of understanding of the environment. The guide had also said that if they were to just leave the people down there, that eventually a person could be led to insanity.

Adda wondered if that last comment was even true or if the guide had just been trying to scare the tourists. Either way, it wasn't a very comforting thought to have while standing in complete darkness with literal tons of stone suspended somewhere above her.

"Adda?" Everett whispered in the darkness, pulling the woman from her morbid thoughts.

261

His hushed voice hissed around her as it echoed off into the distance, every sound becoming greatly amplified in the massive chamber.

How long have we been walking? Adda thought as she became aware of her senses.

"Adda?" Everett asked again, this time his voice laced with panic.

"What is it?" Adda asked, whispering back at him.

"I- I don't think we're alone in here."

A shudder ran down her spine.

"Just take a deep breath, you'll be ok." She assured him.

"No, Adda, I swear someone just touched my back." Everett's voice cracked and his breath came in a huff that suggested he was crying. "Can we please leave?"

"It's going to be ok." No sooner had the words left Adda's mouth then she felt something brush against her as well.

It had created no sound whatsoever and it moved so quickly that Adda had barely registered the touch before it was gone. She clutched Everett's hand tighter, suddenly feeling exposed in the impenetrable sea of black.

A sick feeling grew in Adda's gut as she remembered what Lorelei had said to them.

"You'll realize you should have listened to me!"

Suddenly the space around them burst into activity, the oppressive atmosphere coming to life with motion and sound.

From everywhere around them came the jarring noise of running feet slapping against stone. Shapes moved in the dark as they closed in on their quarry. They were clothed in this blackness, so the true nature of their forms were lost, but to Adda's horror, they were absolutely physical and held no respect for the border of the path.

They crowded in closer and closer, pressing their bodies against the travelers until they crushed them from every direction. Adda was jostled on all sides as their breath came in chuffing waves to blast against her back and her neck. Where their breath was hot like a desert wind, their bodies were cold as ice.

As cold as death.

Adda pushed back against the tidal wave of limbs that crushed against her. They tore her from one side to another and it took all of Adda's strength to cling onto Everett's hand. Even if she hadn't been holding onto him, it was doubtful that anything would have been able to separate the two as Everett's grip had become one of iron, frozen impossibly tight with pure terror.

Adda gasped, trying to keep her footing in the onslaught. Her mind reeled at the clammy flesh that pressed up against her, forcing images of pale skin and empty eyes into her mind. In her head they appeared like bodies left too long in the water, bloated and disfigured. Try as she may, this horrific picture ran circles behind her eyes becoming more awful with every rotation.

Then, as if this weren't already enough, a voice spoke from the crowd.

The bodies stopped moving then, as if the voice brought with it a command to cease their panicked rush, bringing them to stand like soft, damp statues.

"Poor woman." The voice whispered from somewhere.

The bodies, in layered voices that whispered one after another, chasing each other round and round, mimicked the statement.

Poorwomanpoorwomanpoorwoman

Adda pushed forward, following the gravel, and forced herself through the bodies that blocked her way. They had to get out of here.

"Did you hear what happened?" It spoke again, becoming more familiar.

Adda recognized the voice.

Candace Bailor? Adda thought, realizing who it was.

She hadn't seen Candace since the day before the evacuation.

What is she doing here?

"Oh, that poor woman."

It *was* her, or at least it was her voice.

Adda turned her head, shocked to see the form of the woman she used to know appear from out of the darkness. She leaned against the empty door frame that separated her kitchen from the dining room, holding a phone to her ear. She was bathed in a green light, making her appear ghoulish.

"I don't know how she's going to manage without him."

Withoutwithoutwithoutwithoutwithout

"I hear that she doesn't have a good relationship with her own family." She paused, as if listening. "Yes, no kids either. Poor thing is all alone."

The woman laughed then. "I wonder how long Keith is going to wait before making his move! He should probably do it fast though. After all, the poor woman needs *someone* to look after her, so I doubt she'll be on the market for long."

Another pause, another cruel laugh.

"Do I really need to explain it to you? I mean come on, just look at who she was married to!"

Waswaswaswaswaswaswaswaswaswaswaswaswas

Adda shut her eyes, forcing back tears that threatened to prick at her eyes. A deep, black well gaped within her, salivating as it tried to swallow her whole. Adda took in a deep breath, forcing Candace from her mind as she retook control. She had beaten this already, so let them gossip. It didn't have power over her.

When Adda opened her eyes again, she found that Candace was mercifully gone. Adda doubted that the woman had even really been there to begin with.

The bodies remained though and every so often convulsed around her.

"Please stop." Everett sobbed from behind.

The young man's voice sounded like it was coming from far away. Too far to be right behind her anymore. Adda still held his hand however, so she turned back toward him, confused about this strange auditory trick.

As she turned about and looked toward her companion her breath was snatched from her lungs. A new face formed out of the darkness, standing where Everett should have been. A man with a tight jaw, hard eyes, and an upturned nose was staring back at her with a disgusted look.

"Everything I've done for you." He seethed, his teeth barred. "Everything I've sacrificed for you and this is how you repay me?!"

The grip on her hand tightened, it was no longer the long, skinny fingers of Everett, but had been replaced by the thick calloused ones of a man she knew all too well.

"Pathetic." He snarled.

Adda cried out in pain as the grip became tighter still, crushing her hand with cruel intent.

Patheticpatheticpatheticpatheticpatheticpathetic

"Please, you're hurting me." She cried out as the world around her fell away.

Old fears rose up in her like hungry beasts, their teeth splitting horridly from blackened lips. They howled and circled, drawing closer and closer for the kill.

"I'm sorry!" Adda screamed into the dark.

"Not sorry enough."

Notenoughnotenoughnotenoughnotenoughnotenough

She was a kid again, the door was locked and she hid under her bed. Heavy footsteps came slamming up the stairs and down the hall until a shadow darkened the crack beneath her door. The handle attempted to turn then stopped as the man on the other side was taken aback by such audacity. The handle rattled aggressively and the door shook as a heavy fist slammed with painful force against it. Adda let out another scream that only seemed to anger him more. She threw her hands over her ears, trying to block out the noise of the voice that swore and roared, commanding her to unlock the door.

"I won't!" Adda whispered.

IwontIwontIwontIwontIwontIwontIwont

"Let me in!" He barked.

The door rattled, the room shook, the bodies pressed, and Adda screamed.

And screamed.

And screamed.

It was in this chaos, sitting in a room too familiar, in a memory that she had worked hard to overcome that a small tapping sound became present. It was nearly drowned out by the raging man and the whispering bodies, but somehow its presence was made known to Adda. With a face puffy from crying, rivulets of tears carving rivers down her cheeks, Adda turned to see what was causing such a noise.

Across the room, on the wall that ran parallel to her bed was the lone window that allowed moonlight to spill in like a river of ivory. Just beyond the pane of glass, tapping with a gentle rhythm, was a single white dove. The bird turned its head, considered her, seeming not at all alarmed by the scene that occupied the room around the little girl. Its tiny eyes took her in before it turned around, spread its wings, and flew up into the night sky. Adda stared with wide eyes, remembering that she wasn't actually in her childhood home, remembering that she wasn't actually a kid anymore.

The door was flung open then, and a pair of stomping boots charged in with all the rage of a hurricane. Adda looked into the face of that angry man, all intensity and violence, eyes wide and wild.

"I thought I dealt with you?" She asked it as a question, but as the words left her mouth, the truth of them had already solidified in her mind. "No, I- I've outgrown this- I've outgrown you."

He flew across the room, bellowing like a raging bull bearing down on her. He was impossibly big, larger than he had ever actually been, shadows bending and dancing around his monstrous frame. Yet, even as his heavy feet pounded against the wooden floor, shaking the house with the intensity of an earthquake, Adda stood strong, not cowering away even as he rose above her. Right before he could barrel Adda over, he pulled up short. He glared at her, but would come no closer.

They stood like this, facing off against one another, but Adda didn't flinch back. This was something long behind her. She wouldn't let him control her again.

And just like that, the man began to shrink away.

It was like a deflating balloon slowly letting out air. He simply crumpled before her, shrinking in stature until he was shriveled up on the floor, curled into a pathetic ball. Still, his eyes glinted with rage up at her, accusing and hateful. But there was something more there and the more Adda looked, the more she saw.

There was anger, yes, it screamed like a hurricane around him as it always had, but beneath it, she saw fear. He had been broken and had chosen to fester rather than heal, allowing an entire life to be snuffed out in order to protect himself. This wound had grown into an aching chasm that had consumed the man and had threatened to do the same to everyone around him. She had nearly been taken by his storm once, she wouldn't let him win this time either.

"You don't control me anymore." Adda spoke to the tiny figure laying before her. "I forgive you for not being who you should have been."

Adda then hesitated, "And I- I'm sorry, too. I'm sorry that I ever held any kind of hatred toward you. I let you go a long time ago, but I need you to know that I outgrew you. I found a home, a family, a passion. I know you'll never be proud of me, but still, I wanted you to know that I made it out."

The words fell away from her as she stared down at the small man so broken by his ways. He had caused all manner of atrocity and pain, yet seeing him as he truly was, it made her heart heavy.

"I hope someone comes for you, helps make you new." She turned then, seeing all that she could, and walked to the window.

The window stretched away from her as her feet touched onto the moonlight, the wall falling into a great distance. This distortion didn't trouble her as she moved forward, her eyes steady on the window. In time, the moonlight began to harden and then it started to crunch like cold gravel beneath her feet. With every step, the window and the room faded away, bleeding into the blackness of the cave until it had vanished back to wherever it had come from.

She was back in the dark and it seemed that whatever those bodies were, they too had vanished like smoke on the wind. She let out a long breath, feeling a great weight suddenly get drawn from her shoulders, a release of something that she hadn't been aware she'd been carrying.

Coming to her senses, Adda was relieved to feel Everett's hand still crushing her own.

"I'm worthless." His voice moaned from behind her. "Please, leave me alone."

"Everett? It's ok." Adda said, "You can beat it."

"No." He whispered. "No, I'm better off dead."

"Hang on!" Adda commanded, picking up her pace, moving forward with every bit of strength she had left while dragging Everett behind her. "We're going to get out of here."

She raced away with Everett in tow, his every step resisting her as he swam in some vision she could not see. Well actually, she couldn't see anything at all, making the full tilt charge seem like less of a good idea. Yet, the way Everett trembled made Adda cast such cautions to the wind, whatever he was facing down was pulling him apart.

Further and further into the mountain they raced, deeper into the heart of the massive beast. Adda could feel the weight of the stone above her, standing neatly on the slope of the cavern roof. Though the stone had been resting for countless ages, an intrusive thought speared into her mind of the arch giving up to allow the full brunt of the mountain's wrath upon their decidedly fragile bodies. She tried not to think about it, instead concerning herself with staying on the path.

There were times that she was aware of the walls on either side of them, pressing in close like the bodies from before, looming with sinister intent. Other times she would feel a sudden, vast openness all around them, hinting at a mighty chamber on all sides. In such areas, Adda focused all her attention onto her feet, trying to make sure that the familiar crunch of gravel wasn't replaced by the solid *thunk* of stone.

And ever as they walked, the *drip drip drip* of a distant source of water echoed all about them, slowly growing louder in the darkness up ahead. It sounded like a slow trickle of water falling into a much larger body of water. Her instinct told her to slow, fearful that she would suddenly plunge into some underground lake, but Adda shoved aside such thoughts. Everett moaned something again, causing her to hasten forward all the more.

Then from out of nowhere, there was an abrupt, sickening tug from behind. The line between Adda and Everett became taut for a single moment before their hands were ripped apart.

The release was so sudden that Adda lost her footing and stumbled to the side. She raised her hands up in front of her face to brace for impact, hoping against hope that there was something there to catch her. Fortunately a solid, stone wall caught her descent, though it was none too gentle as she bounced off of it with a painful grunt. Pain lanced up her hands and arms, settling into her back with an angry bite. The hit had her spin about and she tried desperately to stay on her feet, but to no avail.

She fell down hard.

Adda sat there, her heart hammering in her chest. *What happened?*

"Everett?" Adda called out in a hesitant voice.

She was met with silence.

Adda held her breath, closing her eyes in habit to try and listen better to her surroundings. It wasn't the things she could hear that brought her panic, but rather the things she *couldn't* hear. There was no soft sniffling or moans of despair, there wasn't even any sound of rapid breath pushing out of fearful lungs. Adda's heart dropped like a lodestone into her gut, her mind scrambling to piece together what might have happened.

Did one of those things grab him? Adda thought with a shudder.

The idea that those moist, freezing bodies had reached out and plucked Everett from her was too horrible to imagine.

Adda reopened her eyes, searching fruitlessly in the dark. The lightless cave danced shapes across her vision, but revealed nothing else to her.

Realizing she was just wasting time, Adda got on her hands and

271

knees to begin crawling forward. She ran her hands back and forth across the gravel, hoping against hope that she might bump into her friend. Maybe he just tripped and had hit his head? Adda wasn't sure that would be any better, but at least he would be with her.

After traveling back a distance that was certainly more than enough, Adda had to accept that Everett was gone.

It was as that truth settled into her that Adda began to notice a difference in the air around her. At first, it was just the vaguest insinuations of movement playing behind the veil of dark, then it grew more and more noticeable. Adda was sure it was just more hallucinations, but as it became more defined, it also became undeniable.

For the first time in who knows how long, Adda could actually see her hand.

Surprised, Adda took in her surroundings, finding that she could also see the white gravel beneath her feet and the gray walls that flanked on either side. Shocked by this, Adda looked about, trying to ascertain how the darkness was being pushed away.

And there, somewhere far off in the distance, was a small pinprick of light.

Tears welled into Adda's eyes, relief swimming through her as she rejoiced that this leg of the journey was coming to a close. There was an escape, the path hadn't misled them. Adda scrambled in the direction of her freedom, her senses overwhelmed by the desire to leave this awful place far behind.

It was only after she had fully risen to her feet and was moving with clear intent toward the exit Adda hesitated. So preoccupied with images of standing under the glorious sun Adda had nearly forgotten one crucial detail.

Everett was gone.

Scenarios played out in her mind, each trying to convince her it was in her best interest to leave now while she could. Maybe she could get help from the city. She could push on and go get the people who understood this world better than her. They'd be able to come back and find Everett. It would do neither of them any good if they both ended up being trapped inside the mountain. Going now was the logical thing to do. Adda looked back into the darkness in hopes of catching a glimpse of Everett, not wanting to have to decide what to do.

As she focused down the path which she had just come, the light from behind her grew brighter.

Adda whirled about to see that the end of the tunnel had grown closer, so close that she could see plants growing around the mouth of the cave, bending toward the sun. Its inviting warmth wafted down the tunnel to her, wrapping her in an easy embrace. The heat made her realize how cold she was, causing her to wrap her arms around herself and shudder against the chill that pushed against her back. The warmth invited her forward and the cold insisted she listen.

And Adda almost did, she almost left the cave behind to once again be beneath that glorious sun. After all, she wouldn't leave Everett here forever, she would return with help the moment she found it. This was the right thing to do, it had to be.

But as she stared at the exit from this hell, she remembered the sandstorm that had set upon them. It had been desperate to beat her down and to separate the two. She remembered the valley with all its temptations and people, trying to lure the travelers away from the road. The entire place had been alive, bent on removing those who would deny it.

It seemed that the cave was the same way but instead of playing upon desires, this place capitalized on its victims' fears. It had tried to break her, bringing forth the dark bits of her past, trying to find some ground to stand upon. Yet, it could not defeat her, so instead, it changed its game. It had brought the exit to her and had offered her a trade.

She would be granted freedom and all it would cost her was Everett.

"Better to keep one than lose both?" Adda addressed the darkness. "Is that it?"

The darkness didn't reply.

Adda slipped a hand in her purse to run her fingers over the box. It brought comfort and boldness to her once again. With a definitive nod, the woman turned her back on the inviting light to look back down the path. Its white gravel shone for only a few steps before being swallowed by the cave. Though her body screamed at her the foolishness of what she was doing, Adda could not allow herself to listen. Everett needed help, and there was no guarantee she'd ever be able to find him again.

Adda took a single step back and in response the cave stole the exit away. Like the flame of a candle being blown out, the light vanished in the passing of a moment. It was snatched back to wherever it was meant to be, a punishment for her rebellion.

And so, Adda was once again plunged into the oppressive veil of darkness.

7

Going back turned out to be far more difficult than the first foray into the cave. Whereas before the darkness was just something that hid monsters from view, it had become clear that the darkness itself was the real monster. All around her it pushed against her, forcing every step to become an act of will. It pressed in closer than the bodies had, tightening like a hand around an insect, prepared to squeeze the life from her. The only comfort that Adda took when facing it down was that if it *could* kill her, it would have already done so. After all, it wouldn't risk losing Everett to her.

From every direction, she could hear scuffling and whispering sounds, creating a ringing white noise that filled the dark with an unnatural life. The sound was hardly loud, but it managed to blot out any clues to her friend's whereabouts Adda might have been able to hear otherwise. The darkness did not want Everett found and was using every trick it had to deter her.

Every so often, an image from her past would flicker into existence. Voices that were familiar and impossible would call out to her. Each tried its own tactic in ridding itself of the marching woman. They tried to coax her with promises, to warn her of dangers, and even threatened her with all manner of agonies. Adda found that if she didn't look at them, they didn't have a chance to grow into full visions. They crumbled away, never amounting to more than simple ghosts of a past she had long moved beyond.

Adda pushed all these thoughts, fears, and what ifs away as quickly as they came, focusing on the task at hand. She worried that if she were to stop at all, to put her attention anywhere else, she wouldn't be able to get moving again.

Ever since the evacuation, the only moments of peace she had been granted were those first moments of wandering through the hills by herself. There had been a simplicity to it Adda missed. There were no other people, monsters, paths, valleys or mountains, it had just been her and her aimless thoughts. Everything had changed when she had found her way into the Snatcher village. After that point, it had been one trial after another, each encounter slowly whittling her down. Combined with the impossibly heavy sand that weighed on her, Adda was exhausted.

For both her and Everett's sake, Adda refused to let herself dwell on anything. She fell into the quiet place of her mind, letting the rhyme of her feet on the gravel become her entire world. Part of her wanted to be angry, part of her wanted to despair, part of her just wanted to fall over and finally sleep, but there was no time for such things. Not with Everett hanging in the balance.

The path back had become more of a steep incline, trying harder to dissuade Adda of her mission. Her legs cramped as she hauled herself higher and higher up, ignoring the voices that told her to give up and save herself. The man had to be somewhere back in this direction and she wasn't ready to give up yet.

Up ahead in the distance, Adda noticed a green, sickly light was peeking beyond a curve. Picking up the pace, Adda rounded the corner, moving from the darkness and into this strange, new light. She blinked rapidly as the dull aura assaulted her eyes after being unable to see for so long. Raising a hand and squinting against it between her fingers, Adda took in the room before her.

The cave was round and wide here, but had an oppressively squat roof that hung only a hand's length above her head. It was hollowed out in a way that made it look like it had been intentionally crafted rather than naturally formed. The walls and ceiling had been smoothed down until not a blemish remained. It looked like one giant, uniform stone had somehow been bent in a half-circle and then placed directly atop the path. It was unnerving to look at, so Adda let her focus go elsewhere.

Off to one side of the room, lying adjacent to the path, was a large stone the light was emanating from. It cast its glow upon the chamber, causing the room to be infected by its diseased pallor. Though Adda was relieved to find she was able to see once again, she found the green light to be unsettling. The entire time she had been within these tunnels not once had she seen any evidence of glowing stones. They'd be impossible to miss in the suffocating darkness. She wondered about it, but didn't have a chance to dwell on it as she saw what she'd been looking for.

Clutching onto the stone as if it were his last anchor to reality was

Everett.

The man was sitting on the ground, his legs folded to the side. His eyes were closed and his head rested on the stone as if it were a pillow. His arms were stretched wide around it like he was giving it a hug. The light that seeped from the stone cast a garish pallor across his skin, making his already gaunt face look dead. To Adda's horror, she saw that Everett had completely stepped free of the path.

It might mean nothing. Adda chided herself, trying to quiet her mind.

"Everett?" She attempted, moving as close as she could to him.

No response.

Is he dead?! Adda thought, her heart skipping a beat.

"Everett, please, it's Adda!" She called out again.

The man's eyes snapped open. They had a glazed look about them as they stared blankly ahead, unaware of their surroundings. Adda reached out to give him a shake, attempting to rouse him.

"Hey there." She murmured, relief flooding through her, "I thought I lost you back there."

Everett's gaze flicked up to her, for a moment not recognizing her. The moment passed and his eyes shot wide and his entire body began to tremble.

"You have to help me!" He slurred, his tongue sounding thick in his mouth. "Please, help me!"

"It's ok, I'm here now." Adda said, giving him a comforting squeeze, "Tell me how to help."

"Please, I can't move." Everett whispered, tears beginning to roll down his cheeks.

"What do you mean?"

"I- I can't move, Adda."

Everett's voice rose into a panic and he began to thrash about. He kicked his feet out, trying desperately to get his footing, but to no avail. His shoulders tensed and he pushed against the stone with his outstretched arms, trying to lift himself up. He leaned hardly an inch away when there was some kind of resistance. Veins bulged on Everett's neck as he struggled there for a moment, gasping with effort to keep his head up. Try as he may, he couldn't overcome the strength of whatever held him there. It snapped him back into place, slamming him against the stone. Everett moaned in pain, his legs churning about as he tried to writhe away from his attacker.

"Hang on. I'll help you get out of this." Adda said, pulling herself closer to try and see what had such a powerful grip on her friend. "Don't do anything to make it worse, ok?"

As she drew closer, Adda saw with great horror exactly what was keeping the man from being able to move.

Small, twisting white vines that looked more like bone than plant sprouted from beneath the stone. Sickly leaves that were the same color of the vine sprouted at regular intervals along its form. They spread out like wounded butterflies, tiny veins of blood red running along their surface. The entire network of vines were growing on one side of the rock, and it just so happened to be the side that Everett had leaned on. They had gathered beneath the man's body, growing impossibly fast to reach out to him. If that wasn't enough, Adda nearly gagged when she what the vines were doing to him.

The nasty, evil things had burrowed into his skin.

The vines had found holes in his clothes that exposed his chest, his arms, and even his neck. They had pierced into him, pulling taut in order to keep him in place so that they could go about their wicked devices without their victim's interference. Mercifully, they hadn't attempted to bite into the young man's face at all, leaving some of the more sensitive parts of the body alone. If she looked long enough, Adda could even see them slowly moving as though they were more alive than a typical plant. To her relief, small as it might be, the vines had not caused him to bleed in any way, their intrusion doing no immediate damage. Adda hoped that meant that the vines weren't attempting to kill him.

Adda crouched down, bringing herself to the same level as Everett and stared at the stone and its tiny vines. She had seen both of these things before in their journey, though last time she had laid eyes on this kind of plant, it had been far less aggressive. That one had seemed content to just exist on the stairs of the castle's tower with no need to bind people. This one was more active and clearly had some intent in mind for its victim.

Against her better judgment, she reached out a hand and grabbed onto a vine that rested partly in Everett's arm. The thing felt hard like a beetles shell, but was hollow beneath the pressure of her finger and thumb. The vine went still at her touch as if waiting to see what she would do. Adda gave a slight tug on it, gently trying to coax it free of its fleshy burrow.

It tightened in her hand and Adda realized she had made a mistake.

The vines suddenly began to writhe like a nest of vipers, brushing against one another to create that familiar whispering sound Adda had heard everywhere in the caves. It reared back as if to strike, so Adda stumbled away, falling hard on her tailbone as she scrambled to a safe distance. She had nothing to fear though, as the vines made no attempt to attack her, but rather they turned their fury on Everett.

He howled in pain as the vines burrowed deeper, growing tighter as they crushed him against the rock. The rock's light flared briefly with the attack, the frenzy exciting it before it settled back into its steady glow. The vines wouldn't let their prey go now that they had him and made it clear who would suffer the consequences if Adda interfered.

"Why did you do that?" Everett moaned in pain.

"Well, I didn't know!" Adda protested, rubbing her lower back.

She felt how defensive she had sounded and immediately regretted it. "I'm sorry, I didn't mean to snap."

"Just help me, please." Everett muttered softly.

Adda approached him again, kneeling down to look over the stone and its infestation. If there was an answer hidden there, it wasn't eager to reveal itself.

"We will get you out of this." Adda replied. "Why don't you tell me what happened and maybe we can figure it out from there?"

Silence.

"Everett?"

He let out a long, shaky sigh. "I thought I saw- someone behind us."

"Someone?" Adda asked.

"Yeah- my sister."

Adda remembered the sweet girl well. She had died when she was still very young. Her loss had devastated the community. Everett was hardly a teenager when it had happened, back when people still called him by his first name.

"She drowned." Everett continued flatly, his voice utterly devoid of emotion.

Of course, Adda knew this, but she didn't interject at all. Even with the encroaching darkness, the whispering vines, and the weighing sand, Adda got the sense that this was something Everett needed. So she sat with her mouth shut and allowed Everett the space necessary to speak.

"We were down at the beach. I was supposed to be watching her and her friends, but I didn't want to swim." He went on, "I told her that if she wanted to be a big girl, then she would have to learn to do things on her own. I didn't know about the riptide. It all happened so fast."

Adda placed her hands on Everett's shoulders, willing her strength into him. She felt him go rigid beneath her touch, the horror of his experience weighing on him. His breath wavered as he choked back tears, but they came just the same, leaking out of his eyes and onto the stone.

"I should have paid attention. I should have gone after her. But I didn't." Everett sniffled. "I'm a coward."

He looked past her, eyes fixating on something only he could see. The vines hissed and whispered, their sounds growing louder as if feeding on his torment.

"I saw her, Adda, right here in the caves. She grabbed my hand and dragged me back. She pushed me onto this stone and told me that

I should have been the one to die. She said I should trade my life for hers." His body shook with grief, the vines coiling deeper. "I've wasted my life. I mean, I live with roommates I hardly know. I still work the same job I had in high school. I've never even had a girlfriend. It's not fair that I get to live but she had to die."

He began to sob wretchedly, his tears becoming heavy pools that began to spill onto the ground. The wound that festered there for so long had grown into a gaping chasm that overwhelmed him with a deep agony that cleaved into his very soul. Everything else fell away, becoming a shadow in the periphery of this all encompassing torment.

"It's not fair." He moaned.

Notfairnotfairnotfairnotfairnotfairnotfair

Adda's head snapped up, searching the darkness outside their tiny ring of light. She could see the ghosts of movement just beyond, shifting and scuttling in their gruesome fashion. They had yet to break into the light, instead staying just beyond to hide themselves from view. They whispered and contorted as they watched from a distance. The whispers were the sound of leaves brushing against leaves, an infernal rustling that echoed ominously in the tunnel.

What are they waiting for? Adda thought, watching them with a wary eye. One thing was certain, these broken creatures wouldn't stand around forever. She needed to figure out a way out of here, and fast.

"I'm so sorry for what happened, I truly am." She said once she was sure Everett was done talking. "But you have to know your sister would never say those things to you."

Adda began moving around to the other side of the stone and feeling along its underside. To her relief, she found that it was not attached to the ground.

"You didn't see her." Everett muttered, "You didn't hear what she said."

"Whatever you saw wasn't your sister, this cave is manipulating you." Adda replied. "It's using your pain against you! We have to get out of here."

"It doesn't matter anyway, this is what I deserve." Everett said, his voice becoming distant and hollow. "Just go. I'll only slow you down."

"Don't say that." Adda said

She tested her hands against the rock, feeling the weight of it under her palms. The woman found that while it was heavy, it wasn't so much that it couldn't be lifted.

"I wish I was dead."

"Everett, stop." Adda said, her tone commanding.

The light from the rock flickered. Whatever fuel source was keeping it alight seemed to be running low. In response, the darkness began to press around them in earnest, eager to snatch up its latest victim. The pale forms twisted just on the edge of the light, ready to descend once again upon them.

"Listen, I know what it feels like." Adda said, talking fast. "You're not alone!"

"How could you possibly understand?" Everett asked, his voice cracking with bitterness.

Adda froze there, feeling a heaviness pass over her own heart. It tried to grip onto her, tried to give the darkness something to hold onto. Anger, sadness, loss, it all grappled in the back of her mind. How much easier would it be to just give in? Didn't she have a right to feel those things?

The vines must have sensed the change because suddenly a few loose tendrils turned about, slowly making their way toward Adda. She watched them come, wondering what it would be like to join the creatures in the dark. Would it be less painful?

This isn't you. The thought crossed over her mind, causing her hand to drift to her purse.

After everything she'd been through, back home and in this strange world, she couldn't let herself give in now. She had faced her trauma, she had dealt with it, and she had learned to live a good life despite the scars left behind. This place was desperate in defeating her, snatching up ghosts of her pain to try and bring her down.

Adda wouldn't let it win.

She pushed past it all, acknowledging her pain and then letting it go. The vines slowed their crawl before coming to a complete stop. They lifted up their ends as if to taste the air. They seemed confused at the loss of their prey and so they turned their attention back to the man sobbing against their stone.

Adda took a deep breath and moved down so that she could look Everett in the eye. "I understand, Everett, because I lost someone, too."

And it was then that Everett finally began to really see Adda. So consumed with his own corner of the world, so consumed with his own guilt, he had never given the art tutor a second thought. He had believed his struggle and pain so unique that he hadn't considered for a moment that there was someone out there that could possibly understand. Now, looking at Adda, Everett realized how little he actually knew her. This woman that he had always considered a weird pariah was the only reason he'd made it this far despite having to bear burdens of her own.

A mixture of guilt, sorrow, and relief ran across his face.

"I'm sorry, Adda." He said, "I shouldn't have said that."

"No, I'm glad you did." Adda replied, "It's important that we understand each other."

"So you're not mad?"

Adda glanced up, seeing that line of darkness had crept even closer. "No, I'm not. But if you want to talk about it more, I think we should probably get moving while we still can."

"But I still can't stand up!" Everett exclaimed.

He tried to push himself back up as if to prove the vines were still in him. They hissed in annoyance, pulling him back down.

"Are they in your legs?" Adda asked.

Everett moved them about, surprised to find that they were not bound. "No."

"Can you grip onto the stone with how you're holding it?"

A test of his hands later. "Yeah, I can grab it."

"Okay, then on the count of three, we're going to lift it up."

Everett tried to shake his head, hopelessness edging into his voice, "I mean, I've already tried, it's too heavy."

Tooheavytooheavytooheavytooheavy

"But this time you're not alone." Adda said, "Let me help you."

Everett stared at her, taking her in, once again surprised by the strength of this woman. Rumors had built a very different image in his mind of who she really was. He grew up thinking her to be the kooky outsider that taught kids how to paint in her free time. She was

287

supposed to be someone bent by grief and denial. To see her this way now- it made him wonder how many people he had misjudged over the course of his life. Had he ever really known anyone? He found himself nodding his head, which turned more into an awkward bobble as the vines still resisted his every movement.

"Okay then," Adda said, "on the count of three. One- two- three!"

With a considerable amount of huffing and grunting, Adda pushed up her legs with all her might, trying to lift the stone free. The going was difficult, since Everett had to lift up his end from a sitting position which required far more effort than if he had been free to move around on his own. But they pushed just the same, fighting against the great weight that had never intended on moving anywhere. Somehow, someway, the two of them rose to their feet, struggling beneath its weight. Everett's face broke into a huge grin and Adda couldn't help but smile back even as her legs trembled beneath the rock.

It was when the stone had been completely lifted from the ground that its true weight revealed itself. The world around her twisted and distorted, becoming something new.

She was no longer standing in the cave surrounded by the dark, instead she was lying on a beach, taking in the warmth of the midday sun. In her hands she held a small gaming device that she was actively playing. Her fingers danced along the buttons in a blur as she made the little sprite on the screen navigate a maze of enemies. It consumed her focus, pulling her against it as she defeated every foe that rose before her with a skill that was not her own.

There was a nagging in the back of her mind that there was something important she needed to be doing, but she pushed it away. She would deal with it after she beat this next level.

It was the piercing scream that finally broke Adda's attention from her game, pulling her eyes up to look over the beach and out over the waves. In a panic, Adda realized that she couldn't see her sister. Her eyes roved the water, until finally there, further out than the girl should be, was a little head bobbing above the water.

At first, she was irritated. Couldn't she go for one second without this little terror demanding something else? And then, the realization came that that little head was moving rapidly away. Every passing moment, the girl diminished into the distance a little more. Adda's blood froze, her eyes went wide, and she found she was paralyzed. Nothing like this had ever happened, this couldn't really be happening.

"Jason!" The voice screamed.

savemesavemesavemesavemesavemesavemesaveme

Adda was suddenly once again in the cave, surrounded by those whispering voices that closed in around her. Everett struggled on his end of the stone, shaking beneath its weight, unaware of what had just occurred to Adda. She stared over at him, her skin still feeling damp from the ocean spray.

What had just happened?

It was similar to the vision from when she had embraced Thomas, but this experience had been tenfold that. It wasn't that she had just witnessed past events, Adda had physically been there. The sand on the beach, the cool ocean breeze, the warm summer sun, each had been so real and vivid.

She had tasted the fear of that moment.

"Are you ok?" Everett asked.

Adda stared back at him, wondering what was going on in his mind. She had first-hand experienced his fear and his guilt. Even now as the sensations left her, the gaping hole of Everett's shame formed in the pit of her stomach.

What is this place? She thought.

"Yeah, I'm fine." Adda said, "Let's get out of here."

With a nod and a gathering of whatever energy they had left, the two of them began to shuffle free of the cavern, moving back down the path and hopefully toward an exit. The vines seemed unaware of their now mobile home, content to merge uninterrupted into Everett's skin. Adda wondered what they would have to do to rid him of the sickly things.

One bridge at a time, Adda thought to herself.

They moved from the mouth of the wide cavern and into the darkness beyond. The light from the rock still glowed, but seemed to buckle beneath the weight of the void outside its hole. Around them, Adda could once again see the pressing bodies that convulsed in repulsive, shuddering motions.

They dared not approach though, held at bay by some invisible barricade. Adda wasn't sure if it was because of the light or because of something else. She didn't dwell long on such thoughts though, as the rock was far more demanding of a thing to focus on. She was just thankful that they didn't have to deal with both at the same time.

It was one of the most difficult things Adda had ever done. The small burst of energy they had gained from their victory of lifting the stone had vanished quickly as the true nature of their daunting challenge rose before them. Every step was excruciating, every breath was labored, but Adda refused to let her end dip for fear that Everett might stumble with the slightest change. Her hands ached as her knuckles whitened in an attempt to find a better purchase.

They would either both make it or their journey would end here.

The vines didn't make it any easier. They seemed undisturbed by the rock being moved, but that didn't make them stop their assault either. New vines were sprouting from the underside of the travelers' burden, crawling up slowly to find their own spot on Everett's skin. They'd nose themselves around, looking for an ideal point to burrow in. After a perch had been determined, the vine would simply shove itself into Everett as seamlessly as though it were slipping into a pool of water. Though Everett wouldn't even flinch in reaction, he would slow down a little more with each additional tether that bound to him.

Come on, just keep walking, Adda thought as she watched the poor man struggle beneath his burden.

As Adda looked on, she felt leaves brush against her hand on the underside of the rock. The woman tensed as the thing probed its tip against her skin as if tasting it. The thought sent a shudder down Adda's spine. Every instinct would have her release the stone and stumble away, but she closed her eyes instead. She imagined reaching in her purse and clutching the box, she imagined the comfort it would bring her in this moment, trying to put out of her mind the image of the vine plunging effortlessly into her skin.

There was the faintest of *pops* that emanated from the underside of the rock. The vine that had been pressing itself against her suddenly retreated, pulling away as a strong, acidic smell began to permeate the air. Adda wasn't sure what exactly had transpired, but she was glad that the grotesque plant had retreated for now.

It was hard to keep her mind occupied on the vines for long as from out of the darkness the maddening whispers grew louder by the moment. It weaved around them in the air, becoming so thick that no individual word could be picked out. With the their shuddering call came more and more of those horrific figures, dancing in the dark.

They surrounded Adda and Everett as a living wall, convulsing like an ocean of flesh. The wicked shapes would melt back into the darkness anytime the travelers would draw close, keeping their forms from being captured in the light. They were as elusive as they were disturbing, but it had started to occur to Adda that they were not the true threat of this place. It had become apparent to her that they were as much victims as those who were trapped in the valley. Although these people were under the hand of a different master.

It was the dark that had claimed them.

"How much further?" Everett groaned, his limbs shaking from effort.

"Don't think about it like that." Adda gasped back at him, edging another foot slowly backward, trying to keep a stance that would help balance the stone. "Just keep telling yourself, 'one more step'"

"How will that help?"

"One step is easy, right?" Adda responded, wishing that she could conserve her energy on just walking, but feeling it important to keep him focused. "So instead of thinking about how many more steps we have to get out of here, instead think of just taking one more step, and then think about taking one more. And we keep doing that until we get out of here."

Everett grunted, unimpressed. Adda couldn't help but smile when she heard him mumble *one more step* under his breath as they moved along.

"See? It helps."

Along they went, with the distant dripping becoming like a metronome to their feet, forcing themselves to move forward at a slow, but steady pace. To make matters worse, the path once again began to angle itself upward, causing any progress to become a battle. The rock also didn't help, weighing them down nearly as much as the sand did. Though unlike the sand, Adda was partly glad for the stone as it gave them a light source to help navigate the cave. The darkness hung like an oppressive curtain, but it sulked just out of reach, circling around them like a wolf waiting for its chance to strike.

"Do you feel like it's watching us?" Everett gasped out.

"Why do you insist on talking so much?" Adda retorted.

"I dunno, it helps get me out of my mind." He answered, "I mean, I'm just kinda worried that if we're quiet I might hear- her. Ya' know?"

A fair concern, but it wasn't something Adda wanted to deal with. She wished she could find the quiet place in her mind, to retreat there to help handle the moment. That was clearly not going to happen and since Adda didn't want to risk Everett falling away again, she forced herself to interact.

"Fine. Yes, I do think it's watching us." Adda said.

"Creepy." Everett said, his chest heaving as he lifted his end, "It's kinda weird how everything in this world is alive."

"Honestly? I think I'm getting used to it." Adda replied wryly.

"None of it makes sense though, I feel like I missed something when I first got here." Everett went on, "Like, I dunno, a guide book or something."

"Did you get a guidebook on how to live on earth?" Adda asked, struggling up a particularly angled rise. "That would be pretty convenient, I guess."

The voices whispered around them, bodies pressing in as close as they dared.

"I just- I mean it just feels like everything here has so much meaning or purpose or something." Everett said. "Like, it feels like everything here is designed to trap us. Nothing is just nothing, ya' know?"

"Are you so sure that things back home weren't the same way?" Adda said, though she was only half paying attention to the conversation.

"Definitely not!" Everett replied as he shifted his weight, "I mean, I might be wrong, but I seriously doubt anyone back home would ever find themselves in this kind of situation."

"Or maybe this place is just more in your face about it." Adda grunted. "How do you have enough energy to even talk right now?"

"I always helped unload the pallets at The Grocery Store." Everett replied, "It's kinda the same thing."

Adda didn't think it was anywhere near being the same thing, but at least Everett seemed to be handling his end well enough. Hopefully this strength would last him until the end of the cave.

They lapsed into silence, or it would have been silence if it wasn't for the incessant rustling and hissing that echoed all about. The voices never got louder than a murmur, yet the canopy of their speech was beginning to feel claustrophobic. It was impossible to ignore and Adda found it becoming increasingly maddening.

Just one more step Adda thought to herself, sweat rolling down her temple as she tried to keep her legs from knocking.

How many steps more would they have to take? She tried not to focus on that, following her advice to Everett and instead paying attention to each individual step. Still, that was easier said than done and the weight of the rock was becoming harder to deal with. Her hands and back ached from the strain, feeling like they would simply crumble at any given moment. Adda wasn't sure how much longer she could carry this load.

Put it down for a second, you deserve a break. A voice whispered in her mind. *You've done so much already.*

She ignored the temptation.

This isn't your burden. The voice hissed, growing deeper. *You have no right to carry it for him!*

A chill ran down Adda's spine. These were her thoughts, she had considered them before, but there was something different about this voice. Was this her own mind trying to force her to let go or was this something else?

If he falls, you'll go down with him. The voice threatened. *Is that what you want? To be trapped down here?*

Leave us alone.

He's not worth all this.

Stop it.

He will be the death of you.

Please, Adda reached out, begging to something beyond the darkness, *get us out of here.*

And as if in response, a new light burst to life.

From up ahead the warm, welcoming embrace of pure sunlight came pouring down the corridor. It beckoned them to run and stand beneath its glory. The first of its rays pushed back the crowding forms, forcing them to retreat down the tunnel where they would not be exposed by the light. Adda sighed, feeling warmth soak into her bones, returning strength to her body.

Everett gasped and Adda looked at him. She saw tears running like rivers down his cheeks, a smile of great relief splitting his face while he gazed into the light.

"I thought I was going to die down there." He said, his voice cracking with emotion. "I thought it was never going to let me go."

"We're almost there, we just gotta keep moving." Adda reminded him, though that didn't stop a smile of her own from crossing her face.

"Thank you, Adda. If it wasn't for you-"

Everett froze mid-sentence, his hands suddenly gripping the stone with such intensity that his knuckles turned as white as the vines burrowing into him. His eyes widened and his breath began to come in ragged gasps. Adda tugged against the stone, trying to get him to move again, confused as to why they had stopped with their goal so close at hand. Then, over his shoulder, beyond the glow of the stone, Adda saw something.

There was a shape in the shadows cast by the light. It stood no taller than that of a man, but its dimensions shifted and changed so quickly that it was impossible to gather any details from its form. Its frame would bleed in and out of the darkness surrounding it, making it nearly invisible where it stood. There were moments where Adda wondered if she was perhaps seeing things in the dark, that this was just an illusion of movement put on by the lost souls that continued to follow them. Yet, one look at Everett put to bed such thoughts. It was clear he was aware of it though his back was facing its shapeless mass.

The thing made no approach, content to stand on the edge of the glow, beyond the convulsing bodies behind it. Unlike the bodies, Adda somehow knew that this thing was absolutely capable of approaching them, yet for whatever reason, chose to stay put. It lifted what Adda could only assume was a hand, reaching out toward Everett.

"No, I-I'm sorry." Everett whimpered, a wet sheen building on his forehead as he began to tremble like a leaf in the wind. "I didn't know, I swear I didn't know!"

In her hands, Adda felt the stone they were holding expand, pushing against its borders to increase its size. Its weight grew with it as well, causing Adda to strain against it, trying hard to not let it drag them both to the ground.

"It should have been me." Everett whimpered.

The stone grew again.

Adda's legs buckled beneath her, her end of the stone dipping toward the ground as her left knee slammed hard against the gravel. She grimaced as pain spiked up her leg, her arms trembling against the growing weight. Everett somehow still stood, but she wasn't sure how much longer he'd be able to deny gravity.

Looking up at him, Adda saw long, tendril-like fingers composed of night creep over Everett's shoulder. The hand slid over him in a way that was almost tender, but had a possessiveness to it that made Adda shudder. The fingers then gripped onto him with tremendous force, yet the man seemed to not notice as he continued to stare ahead, tears leaking from his eyes.

Suddenly the light behind them began to fade rapidly and Adda chanced a look back to notice that it was stretching away from them, moving at a great speed into the distance.

No, Adda realized, *we're being taken from it!*

This dark form was effortlessly dragging them along, taking them back into the depths of the mountain.

"No!" Adda cried out.

With great effort, she pulled her foot back underneath her and tightened her hands onto the stone. Then she slammed her heels into the ground, arching herself back as she pulled against it as hard as she could. Her feet began to kick up gravel as she carved gouges into the pathway.

Still it dragged them.

The stone bit against her white-knuckled grip, slicing lines into her palms. Adda gritted her teeth against a strangled cry as blood began to course down either side of the stone. The rivulets caused the stone to become slick, making it more difficult to grip. Adda dug her fingers in deeper, desperately trying to not lose her hold.

Still it dragged them.

Adda glanced backward again, finding that though her efforts had slowed their descent, the light of their escape had become nothing

298

more than a pinprick in the distance. They had been so close, just a few more steps and they would have broken back into the light of day. Adda didn't even care if the storms were still overhead, she just wanted to see the sky again.

Let go.

A voice whispered into her mind. It was the same voice from earlier, but this time it didn't try to pretend to be her own inner-thoughts. This time it spoke plainly to her, speaking from the shadows directly into her head. It coiled in a way similar to the snake that wrapped itself around Keith's poisonous tongue. Unlike with Keith, it didn't try to manipulate or control her, but rather reveal what was already in her heart.

This was not her burden, this was not her problem. She had looked her struggle in the eye and had found the strength to walk away. Would she really let herself be dragged down by this man who had fallen at every turn? He had done nothing for her except slow her down. Perhaps it would be for the best if she just- let him go. Her hands slipped a little more, the stone biting deeper into her hand to send more blood splattering against the ground. She could feel her convictions draining away as her head pounded from exhaustion.

"Everett." Adda whispered into the dark. "I need you to walk."

"No, no," He whispered, his voice distant and weak, "you go on without me. I think I'm just gonna take a rest. I'll catch up."

Let go.

Adda shook her head, shoving the snake aside. Though it might have had a point, it wasn't something she was willing to do. For better or for worse, they were in this together. She would not abandon him, no matter what.

Then again, she might not have much of a choice in the matter. The stone was getting slicker by the moment and her grip had slipped a little more. She knew she couldn't hold on forever and this time if Everett was taken, she wasn't sure she'd be able to find him again.

"You have to forgive yourself." Adda gasped, her hands in tattered anguish. "You have to let go of her."

"I can't."

"Yes- yes you can." Adda snapped back at him, her tone causing him to blink back in surprise.

His eyes focused on her, no longer empty, but filled with remorse, pain, and fear.

"It takes time, and it takes a lot of effort, but you absolutely can." Her voice cracked, the stone growing bigger and heavier, its jagged edges beating against her palms. "We can't change the past and we can't know what the future holds, but we can choose what we do with today!"

Adda understood, no matter how many times she went back for him, Everett would not be able to leave unless he chose to. This was no longer up to her, but so long as she could hold onto this rock, she would fight for him.

"You've already been forgiven, Everett. So what are you going to choose to do right now?"

The light from behind them had all but faded to black, the walls of the tunnels rose up around them, greedy to reclaim their spoils. Shadows danced gleefully on every illuminated surface and grotesque bodies whispered out haunting words from all around them. Everett closed his eyes, beaded tears racing down his face like rain on a window pane.

"I choose-" He started, his voice growing weaker even as the rock grew bigger. "I choose to take one more step."

And just like that, they stopped moving.

All around them, silence descended like a sudden fog. The world had frozen, waiting with bated breath to see what would happen next. Behind those words that Everett had spoken was a choice being made. He wouldn't feel different immediately and there would be days where he would wonder if anything had changed at all, but the cave saw it and the cave understood it.

With a low wail, the shadowy fingers suddenly snapped free of Everett, blustering back into the depths of the cave as if taken by a mighty wind. The bodies all around them fled after the darkness, bumping against one another in their mad dash to escape. The thunder of their feet shook the world around them, the cacophony of noise nearly overwhelming.

There were so many of them, all claimed on their journey through the mountain, all lost with no hope to escape the vines that had tied stones to their bodies. Adda watched them go, listening after the last of them had vanished from sight until, finally, silence had fallen once again. Even the darkness around them seemed like it had turned to a more normal state. It was still an uneasy, pressing thing, but certainly not something that was alive with will and want.

"Ready?" Adda asked, breaking the spell.

Everett nodded, and together they took a step. Both of them groaned under the weight of the burden that had swelled to nearly twice its original size. They rested for a moment and then they took another step.

And another.

And another.

And they kept moving forward, the light in the distance growing so slowly that Adda wondered if perhaps the cave was not actually done with its twisted tricks. Yet, with each step it became clear that they were indeed drawing near to the light.

She also noticed that the stone had begun to shrink. It was a slow, methodical process that one could not precisely pin when it had first started. Yet as one moment chased another, Adda found she had to keep changing her grip to keep up with the retreating surface. Everett was a bit closer to her than before, and the light from the rock was starting to fade. As the light of the blessed day reached toward them, the rock physically shuddered, retreating all the more into itself until it had shrunk to the size of Everett's fist.

The vines within the rock also reacted to the growing light, lashing and convulsing beneath Everett's skin. They appeared to be hardening, and when Everett tried for the hundredth time to readjust his head, the vines cracked, snapping as easily as the ones from the castle that Adda had tread beneath her feet. They splintered like pottery and crumbled to the ground, their hard, white exterior blending into the path beneath their feet. By the time they had reached the end of the tunnel, the vast majority of the vines had fallen away.

Everett pulled his head up, relief flooding his entire body as he was once again free to move about. Tears of happiness coursed down his face as he looked on in stunned joy, surprised to find themselves free of the cave.

"We did it!" He laughed, his entire face setting alight. "We made it!"

Adda, still cupping part of the rock in her bleeding hand, smiled in return. She turned to look at the golden sunlight that poured in over them, they had finally arrived at the exit of this accursed place. Face-to-face with the end of this part of their journey Adda wanted nothing more than to fall to the ground and weep in joy. She didn't though, she would wait to celebrate until the cave was far behind them.

"Come on, we should get out of here." Adda said, her voice shaking with exhaustion. "Let's see what this mountain has for us next."

"Hey," Everett said, bringing Adda's attention back to him.

He grinned at her like a child at a carnival, his eyes shining brighter than the sun. "One step at a time, right?"

She smiled, "Yeah, one step at a time."

And so they stepped beyond the threshold and into the light of a new day.

8

They blinked in the muted sunlight, its light made intense from the time within the gloomy clutches of the darkness behind them. It took a few moments for their eyes to readjust. Adda was surprised to find that they were still beneath a cloud cover, but this one was a slate gray as opposed to the boiling black further down. Turning about, she could see that just below them the storm continued to roll on with lightning flickering intermittently. The landscape under it was obscured from view, making the entire world appear to be only this mountain and an infinite sky.

Between the two layers of cloud, and right before the travelers, stood a rocky outcropping where the path pooled together to create something of an overlook. Short, hardy grasses grew in stubby chunks, colored in an off-green shade, caught somewhere between life and death. On one side of the small area the path continued, hugging the side of the mountain before vanishing around a corner. Again, Adda got the impression that the path itself was somehow still straight and it was the mountain that was causing it to appear bent.

A stinging in her hands drew Adda away from the phenomenon. She looked down, seeing the large gouges and tears that now marked her skin. The rock had done its damage, leaving a bloody, mangled mess in its wake. Liquid pooled in her palms from the many cuts, dripping slowly down between her fingers and onto the white gravel below. It stained the otherwise perfect path with a polka-dot pattern of red and pink. Adda clutched her hands closed, wincing at the pain.

She then turned to Everett to see how her companion was faring. The young man's victory was spent quickly, his face hollow and tired, his shoulders hanging low from bearing such a great burden. Most of the vines had hardened and subsequently shattered, leaving angry pock marks all over his neck and arms. Still, a few appendages of the plant remained, writhing like worms in what sunlight broke through the clouds, but refusing to die like their brethren. The remaining cluster clung to Everett's arm around his shoulder, their heads hiding beneath his skin. The now small rock that they were attached to sat in one of Everett's limp hands.

He too had not come out of the dark unscathed.

He was eyeing the vines with a face of passive resignation, tugging slightly against them to test their ability to survive. The vines tightened, causing him to grimace and to stop any further attempts to rid himself of them. They were attached, at least for now.

"Are you ok?" Adda asked.

"Yeah, I'm fine."

His triumph had been cheapened by his new, clinging companions. Whatever enthusiasm he had had exiting the cave was quickly drained from him as he regarded his situation. Adda looked on, feeling saddened by the dower look on his face. She walked over, and wrapped her arms around him in an embrace. She held her hands away from his body, not wanting to get blood on the back of his grimy shirt. Everett fell against her, burying his face against her shoulder.

"I miss my mom." Everett whispered. "And my dad."

"I know."

"I don't know what happened to them when everyone else got evacuated." Everett said, his voice thin. "I thought that maybe they'd show up eventually, but they never did."

He shuddered, looking back toward the cave. "You don't think-"

"Don't." Adda said, pulling away to address him. "It won't do you any good speculating on what might have happened. We have no way of knowing where they ended up, so don't torture yourself over it."

Bethany's face flickered through Adda's mind as she said it. For the briefest of moments she imagined the young girl caught up within the darkness of the cave. She saw her clutching onto a rock with its waning light, her face and arms infested with vines as the contorting bodies pressed in. Adda brushed the image away, heeding her own advice.

"I don't know how much more of this I can take." Everett said, still holding on tight to Adda. "I mean this is so much harder than I thought it was gonna be."

"You can't talk like that," Adda said, "you've come too far to give up."

Everett pulled away and looked down at the rock in his hand. "I wish I had just stayed put."

"I get that, but none of that matters now, Everett." Adda replied. "We can stand around looking back wishing things were different, but the fact is, we're here, we're still alive, and we have to keep pushing forward. The only way back is through that cave, and I think we're both better off facing whatever comes next rather than throwing ourselves at the mercy of the darkness again."

Everett didn't reply.

"What did I tell you in the cave when we were trying to get you out?"

He let the question stretch before letting out a long-suffering sigh. "Just take one more step."

"See? You get it." Adda said. "Now come on, we have a city to get to."

Everett nodded, falling into his place behind her, his footfalls matching her own as he stepped into line. They were off, following the now deceptively winding path that coursed around the side of the mountain, taking them closer to the top. On one side was the solid stone of the mighty peak, on the other was a straight drop that would leave them tumbling through the clouds below. Adda forced such images from her mind, knowing that no good would come from dwelling on such a horrific fate. The going was slow, each step had to be carefully taken, and the sand was certainly not helping, still trying to find ways to bog them down beneath their crushing weight. Adda's hands also continued to thrum in pain as a constant reminder of what had happened down below.

They were just falling into a rhythm when on the wind came the raucous sound of voices. They were light, cheery sounds, twisting about playfully in the cold, mountain air. It sounded as though some kind of gathering or party was happening just ahead.

Adda and Everett exchanged looks, unsure of what to make of such a thing. Adda crouched low on the path, moving forward along its lip until it curved around a large out-cropping. She peeked around its side to see what lay beyond.

To her surprise, she saw another small clearing of white gravel, and sitting adjacent to it, was a meadow of long, lush grass blooming with all manner of flowers. The heavy blooms sighed and waved in the dancing wind, their little faces turned to absorb what light they could. The grass was a greenish-blue and looked as soft as it was inviting. The entire meadow was nestled in the midst of a pass with the path taking up one side and the meadow the other.

Amidst the grass was a gathering of people, sitting in a circle and chatting with one another amicably. They were dressed in long, white clothing that had no mar or stain upon them. The sleeves and pants were wide and flowy, making each individual appear ethereal with every movement. Every so often one would stand to wander off, picking flowers as they went before returning back to the group and handing out their spoils to the others sitting there. The people would take the stems and heads, and, with an expert hand, weave them together to create little flower crowns that they would adorn one another with, laughing whenever they did so.

Adda tried to see beyond this moment, to try and see their drawn, corpse-like bodies, to gaze into their sparkling eyes to only find horrid, hollow pits. To see that in place of the flowers they were holding, they were instead weaving crowns from wicked thorns that pierced and ripped their unsuspecting flesh. She looked to see if perhaps the long grass was in fact more clinging sand, eager to take the travelers on in another round.

To her utmost surprise, as far as she could tell there was no layer of images here. It was as they appeared, a group of people enjoying a warm, albeit cloudy day.

In her stupor, Adda hadn't realized she had leaned out too far from behind her cover, leading the eyes of one of the young girls in the group to spy her. The girl startled for a moment, equally surprised to see someone staring back at her, but then the surprise melted away into a welcoming smile. She gestured to the rest of the group, pulling their attention to the one who was skulking beyond the outcropping.

"It appears we have a visitor." She said in a melodious voice. "Someone made it beyond the cave!"

The group turned as one, standing as they walked toward her, wide grins on their faces. They began to clap and whoop and cheer as they approached. Unlike the people in the valley, they stepped onto the path without hesitation, not even reacting to their bare feet crunching across its hard surface. Adda was in shock with the image before her and made no attempt to resist as they placed their hands gently upon her to guide her away from the edge.

"Another one!" A strong looking man cried out in joy, leading the crowd down the path to latch onto Everett as well.

Everett looked about warily, but he also allowed himself to be led away with Adda. The strong man touched Everett's arm, feeling at the vines that bit into the younger man's shoulder.

"This one still carries his rock in the open." The man spoke again, giving Everett a pitying smile, "Come now, child, the hardest part of your journey is at an end. Join us in the meadow."

Everett was left staring in surprise as he realized that all the people surrounding him had marks on their bodies from where vines had once intruded their bodies as well. Amidst the crowd there were even a handful of people who still carried their rocks with them, but they seemed to be trying to hide the evidence behind them, their eyes flashing with shame.

The two were led around the corner and toward the field. Adda snapped back into control as they approached the long grass, pulling herself to a stop, and tensing against the others' gentle tug. Most of the crowd filtered past her, but some came to a stop to regard her in confusion. Adda looked at the line that separated the path from the lush grass, then over to the side where the path continued, moving from view around yet another bend.

"Ah." The man said again, leaving Everett in the hands of the others and moving to stand beside Adda. "You're worried that if you leave the path, that you'll never be able to come back to it. Is that it?"

Adda nodded, finding it difficult to trust this grinning man. The grass was inviting, but she had come to suspect anything off of the gravel had some sinister trick up its sleeve.

"We were all like that to some degree or another." He said, placing a hand on her shoulder.

Adda threw him a look, causing him to remove the hand, lifting it up apologetically as though showing a feral dog he meant no harm.

"The valley and the caves certainly take their toll, and I don't want to force you to do anything you don't want, but you're walking among friends now. Why not just take a minute and join us? It's very relaxing."

"I can't. We have to get to the city."

"Oh, my dear." The man laughed in a condescending way that made Adda bristle. "This *is* the city!"

There were two things that immediately became clear to Adda. One: this was most certainly not the city, and two: this man absolutely believed his own lie.

She shook her head. "No, the city is beyond this mountain, not in it."

"And who told you that, hm?" The man asked, arching an eyebrow.

Adda's jaw tightened.

Seeming to notice how tense she was becoming, the man sighed. "I'm sorry, I feel as though we've gotten off on the wrong foot. My name is Leri. And yours?"

"Adda." She said her name in a flat voice, trying to keep her mistrust from coloring her tone.

There was something decidedly off about these people and whatever it was, it rubbed her the wrong way. Without much indicator as to why, Adda could feel irritation bubbling up inside of her, trying to evolve into anger.

"Adda! What a beautiful name!" Leri responded loudly, stepping out onto the grass and waving for the others to join.

Everett walked past her, letting himself be guided away. Without even hesitating, he stepped onto the grass, leaving the path behind. Though he wore shoes, Everett let out a contented sigh as though he could feel the cool plants against the sole of his foot. He closed his eyes, a look of contentment washing over him.

"Everett, get back here. Right now."

"Hey," Leri said, moving between them, "you need to let him make his own choices. Now it's clear to me that you're the reason the two of you made it this far and as such you feel a certain responsibility for his well being. Am I right?"

He didn't wait for her to answer, assuming he had assessed the situation correctly. "Feel free to do whatever you want, but that's your choice alone. Regardless, I'm telling you the truth, you're at the end of your journey! Why not join us?"

"Ok, well if this is it, then why does the path keep going that way?" Adda asked, shoving a pointed finger toward the curve.

Leri scoffed and rolled his eyes. "Oh trust me, there's nothing up there but an angry old man."

"Someone lives up there?"

"No one of consequence, that's for sure."

"Tell me about him." Adda demanded, dropping down to the path and settling in as if preparing for a story.

Leri looked down at her with a look that was the perfect meld of mild amusement and irritation. It was as though he was considering the request of a child that was beneath him to resolve. When it was clear she wouldn't rise or move until answered, Leri let out a sigh, settling down onto the grass just beside the path. He positioned his body to face her.

"First of all, this isn't like down in the valley. You can come and go off the path as much as you want." He kicked at the gravel with a foot, "It's not going anywhere. Secondly, I can see that it doesn't matter to you, so I'll go ahead and not waste any more of your time and get down to it."

Adda nodded, but her eyes were on Everett who was led to settle into the grass twenty feet or so from her. Someone had adorned him with a crown and the people were already incorporating him into a circle. A pang of sadness hit her heart as she saw how tired and bedraggled he looked sitting amidst these clean, easy-going people. He looked far worse off than when she had first ran into him those hours (days? weeks?) ago. Was he truly better off here?

"The first thing you need to understand is that no matter how much time passes, none of us ever age. Most of us have been here for a very long time, and yet the old man has been here longer. We know very little about him aside from the fact that he predates everyone here." Leri shifted to get more comfortable, falling into his story with practiced ease. "He stands somewhere up there, yelling down at us to wake up and come to him. It's *very* annoying. Sometimes someone tries to go up but they usually come running back down screaming about being unworthy or something to that effect. No one can ever remember what made them come back down, but it can't be anything good."

"You said that they *usually* come back down. What do you mean by that?" Adda asked.

"Well because, every so often, the person just doesn't return to us."

"Do you have any idea what might have happened to them?"

His eyes lit up, "No, but we certainly have our theories! Some say he's a cannibal, like the Snatchers, and he'll take you into his hut to fatten you up. Others say he lures people up there just to throw you off the side of the mountain as a sick game. There are even those who claim he's the devil himself."

"And what do you think?"

"Oh, I think he's just a kooky, old man that's been stuck in this universe for too long to remember how to be civilized. Which really just reinforces why you should stay here with us. This world is treacherous and the smallest misstep can lead to eternal consequence. This is the safest place you're going to find."

Adda considered this, then moved on, "How long have you been here for?"

"Wow, you ask a *lot* of questions." He huffed, though it seemed all for show as he clearly liked the sound of his own voice. "I've been here for what feels like an eternity and there are still others who have been here longer. After all that time, it becomes pointless trying to keep track of it. Days run into each other, new faces join us, and we get to exist in our own pocket of paradise. I hardly even remember my life back on earth before all of this, but it seems to hardly matter anymore. This is my life now, and it's perfect."

"So, do you have any theories on how we got whisked away to this place?" Adda asked, gesturing about them for emphasis.

"Aliens, definitely aliens." Leri replied so matter-of-factly that she couldn't help but laugh. "Oh yeah, scoff all you want, but the last thing I remember before getting vanished from earth was this bright light coming straight at me! Everything went black after that only for me to wake up in grassy hills surrounded by angry, inhuman natives. If that doesn't sound like an abduction, I don't know what does."

"Well ok, but what-" Adda started into another question.

"Good lord, woman, don't you ever rest?" Leri cut her off. "I've already told you that we don't age so you have untold centuries to debate and theorize to your heart's content."

He wrinkled his nose as though catching a whiff of her. "Why don't we find you a nice, warm spring to hop into and help get you adjusted. Then- *and only then*- we can start really digging into the meat of your new home."

She shook her head definitely, "Thank you for answering my questions, but I need to be going. Crazy old man or not, I've come too far to give up now. One way or another, I'm getting over this mountain."

With a grunt of effort, Adda drew herself up and raised her voice as she addressed the crowd before her. "Everett and I are going to go find the city- the *real* city. The path has led us through every difficulty so far and since it doesn't stop at your meadow, I don't believe this is where any of us are supposed to be. I intend on following the road to the end, so before we go I want to know, is there anyone here who would like to join us?"

The crowd went quiet and turned toward her as one body. They gazed upon her with expressions that Adda was all too familiar with.

Pity.

Looks were exchanged and they shook their heads at her words. Whispers hissed from behind hidden lips as they discussed this poor woman in hushed tones. No one moved to join her.

"You're wasting your time." Leri said, standing to match her. "Stop making a scene and just come with us. We have food and water and there aren't any Snatchers here. Of all the places to be, the meadow is the safest."

Adda looked him up and down. She had to admit she did feel as

315

though she were being unreasonable. There was no illusion here hiding something sinister in the shadows. There was no encroaching darkness trying to break her down with haunting images. Besides, his offer was tempting and it caused her body to quake just imagining sitting down to eat and drink and rest.

Yet, Adda hesitated unable to shake the feeling that there was something off about the meadow.

It was as she was contemplating what to do that Adda's attention was drawn to the loose clothing that the strangers were wrapped in. It flowed around them, dancing upon every slight movement to create a mesmerizing mirage that didn't settle for long. It was in these passing moments of inaction that Adda saw the sleeves had been tailored in such a way on purpose. The flurry of cloth distracted the eye and carefully disguised a strange bulge sprouting from the upper arm, just below the shoulder. The more Adda looked, the more it became obvious that every member of the meadow hid a similar anomaly.

Looking back to Leri, she saw that he too had a strange shape sprouting from beneath his sleeve. With a deft motion, Adda reached out and gripped the stray cloth. She pulled, tearing away the sleeve as easily as if it were made of paper. The seam split apart, falling away to flutter weakly in Adda's grasp. She stood there, motionless as she stared in shock at the revelation before her.

On Leri's upper arm was a green, sickly bump roughly the size of a human fist. It protruded only an inch or two from below the shoulder, appearing like a large cyst. The skin was drawn so tight that it looked like it was about to burst, ready to release whatever horror slept just below the surface. Completely encircling the infection were

316

crusts of red sand, dark with some kind of liquid that seeped slowly from the peak of the boil. The sand looked like a colony of ants, swarming over their hill.

Adda's stomach twisted at the sight and she brought a hand over her mouth to keep back a gagging sound that wanted to escape her lips.

This attack had been so quick that Leri hardly reacted at first. He stood there for a moment looking down at the torn sleeve with blank eyes. Once his mind had caught up with what had happened, Leri reeled back, his eyes wide. He placed his right hand over the infection, glancing about as if hoping no one else had noticed.

Unfortunately for the man, he wasn't so lucky. A collective gasp went up from the crowd and those nearest to Leri took a step back. Looks of disgust crossed many of the faces, while the rest just shook their heads in disappointment.

"The rocks from the cave." Adda said, her eyes wide. "Is that what's in your skin?!"

"Oh, don't act like you don't have your own stone to bear." Leri snapped, rattled by being revealed before the congregation.

Adda didn't hear him though as she had already turned to the crowd once more. Their response to Leri's revealed shame sparked anger inside of her. They turned their noses up at him even though every last one of them also hid their own diseased arms from views.

Hypocrites. An echo of Thomas' voice rattled through Adda's mind.

"You're living a lie." She muttered, then shook her head and addressed the crowd. "You're all living a lie. You have the audacity to judge one of your own for being revealed to you even though each and

317

every one of you hide the same curse?

Anger spiked in Adda's heart as she looked at them. The valley twisted people with its illusions, the cave broke them with their fears, but this meadow employed no tricks to control its victims. Its only illusion were the lies these people told themselves, its only fear was what the community hid in shame. It didn't need to do a single thing to control the inhabitants, they had gladly cast aside their mission for a false peace.

"Do you really think you can stay here without consequence?" Adda went on, her voice raising. "Look around you! Wake up! How can you pretend to not see the suffering of the people next to you? How can you be so willfully ignorant?"

"Who are you to judge us?" A woman asked, approaching, but staying out of reach lest she be Adda's next victim. "We've built a life here! After everything we've been through, don't you think we deserve a break?"

"Built a life?" Adda said, incredulous, "What life? You sit around all day making daisy chains thinking that loose clothing might hide away your shame."

In a flash of inspiration, Adda rolled up her own sleeve, revealing the skin of her upper arm. It was smooth and unblemished, showing no evidence of any kind of mark.

"Look! It doesn't have to be this way! Come with me and we'll find a way to free you from your burdens."

There was another collective gasp, though this time it was one of fear rather than revulsion.

"What magic is this?" The woman hissed, her eyes full of

suspicion.

Leri stumbled away as well, doing his best to keep his growth hidden.

"There is no magic," Adda said gently. "There's a better way, I'll help you find it."

The crowd whispered and murmured once again, exchanging looks as they began to appear more unsure. Who was this woman that she could walk through the darkness and come out nearly unscathed? She was certainly haunted by the touch of the valley as sand clung to most of her body, but for some reason she had been spared the grip of the vines. They were at a loss.

Leri shook his head, and spat at her, his eyes glinting with rage. "Liar! Tempter! Can't you all see that she's some kind of monster sent here to pull us away? She would have us go to a false city even though we are the ones who discovered it."

His eyes widened as though visited by a great revelation. "The old man sent you, didn't he? He has grown tired of his old tricks and now sends you to do his dirty work!"

"That's no-"

"We will not be fooled by your wicked ways!" Leri cried, his voice reaching a fanatic level. "We are better than you, stronger too! We have overcome everything to get here and we will not allow some temptress creature to take away all that we've built!"

Adda stared at them, pity of her own biting her heart. Sure, in many ways they were better off than anyone else she had met in her journey. They even seemed comfortable with the life they lead, but Adda also knew that even this wasn't enough. The poison, the brokenness, it was all still there, hidden just below the surface. Though their suffering was not as obvious as anyone else's, the Certainty revealed to Adda the deep ache that cut them all to the heart. They all went through the motions of joy, believing that everyone around them had mastered the secret, and if they kept following in suit that maybe, just maybe, they too could find this contentment. But they all were lying to one another, hiding away their shame and fears beneath flowing cloth, and pretending that this was enough.

Living here would surely drive one mad.

"Let's go, Everett." Adda called out to him.

He had been watching the entire exchange from his place in the grass, his fingers idly twisting flower stems that had been thrust into his hands. Though he had said nothing the whole time, he had been intently listening. Adda's words enraptured him, speaking to the parts of his heart that knew this wasn't the end of his journey. With a nod, he took up his stone and followed her back onto the path.

"You're making a huge mistake, kid." Leri yelled after him. "You're better off here."

"Maybe." He said in return. "But Adda is the only reason I'm even standing here right now. If she says we have to keep moving forward, then that's where I'm gonna go."

Leri shook his head and scoffed. "So naive."

Without favoring the shamed man with a response, the two of them departed, walking along the path and around the bend. The people of the meadow gossiped about the strange, ignorant woman for a long time, their fingers building flower crowns, and their sleeves hiding the burdens they carried.

9

The ceiling of drab clouds drew ever closer as they ascended, blocking the top of the mountain from view. It made it impossible to tell how much further they had to go. To make matters worse, the path inclined even more leading them over the very peak of the mountain, refusing to find pass or saddle in order to save the travelers from more climbing. Eventually they'd get through that cloud cover, though Adda was dreading the moment. After all, even if they breached the clouds, how much further would they have to go? Would there be more mountain, more gray clouds, more endless path riddled with numerous trials? At least in the valley the two of them had a clear destination laid before them.

Now upon the slope of the monolith, Adda felt that she was walking blind. She knew that the city was where she was going, the Certainty reminded her of that, but it was much harder to find the strength to take each step without the finish line in sight. Instead of taking determined steps toward her goal, she felt like they were meandering along with no real idea of where they were. She wanted to be able to look up and see the peak, or look past the mountain's side and see the city glowing in the distance. Anything would be better than being surrounded by the endless palette of gray tones.

Atop the depressing scenery, the sand still hung heavy, bearing down on their every step. It held onto the travelers' like a second skin, refusing to budge no matter what either of them tried. Hunger and thirst was also taking its toll, biting at their throats and stomachs in hopes to motivate them to action. It wouldn't have mattered either way though as there was no food or water to be found in this place. Instead they slogged on ahead, not knowing what else to do except to just take one more step.

They had been silent for a long time, both of them conserving their energy for the tedious climb. The need to stop and rest gnawed at them, but neither seemed inclined to slow their pace. It passed through Adda's mind that they should have stopped in the meadow for a time. Maybe they'd have been able to eat, drink, and bathe themselves.

What I wouldn't do for a hot bath. Adda daydreamed, imagining leaning back in a tub and feeling the sand peel away from her skin.

The thoughts departed though as images of straining flesh and oozing cysts invaded her fantasy. As tempting as it was to take advantage of the safe haven, Adda knew she wouldn't be able to ignore the reality of what was happening to those people. It was for the best that they keep moving forward, they couldn't risk becoming infected like the rest of them.

Adda found herself reflecting on the journey, realizing how much she had changed since abandoning her car so long ago. How long had it been since that moment? To Adda it was beginning to feel like years had stretched by her. Maybe an entire lifetime. Regardless, her destination was still the same, calling to her from somewhere out of sight.

The city.

The word brought on a myriad of emotions that were as powerful as they were confusing. It elicited feelings of excitement and adventure, to explore and see something new. It also brought out feelings of deep, rooted nostalgia as if returning home after a long season away. Originally, Adda had wanted to get to the city in order to find some answers, but so much has changed. Now, to Adda's own surprise, she had begun to think of the city as her one, true destination. Her motive for reaching it had changed from trying to find a way to escape this world into looking forward to making it her home.

It was too confusing to consider, so Adda drifted away from the thoughts. She found herself once again thinking about Bethany.

Where are you? Adda looked back down the path, past Everett as if trying to manifest the girl just behind them.

Had Bethany escaped the Snatchers only to fall victim to the valley? Perhaps the caves had claimed her, filling her skin with intrusive vines and haunting memories. Was she trapped there now, cowering in the dark before her greatest shames and most harrowing fears? Would Adda even recognize the poor girl if she came across her or would Bethany be another victim of this wicked place?

The thoughts haunted her, nipping at Adda's mind as they went round and round. She tried her best to ignore them, instead concentrating on taking one careful step at a time.

The path had narrowed again, it was now barely wide enough for a single person to walk it. Both sides of the path had become a slope steep enough that one misstep would result in a nasty tumble.

Looking down, all Adda could see was black, stormy clouds that boiled with a primordial wrath, bubbling like a pot ready to explode. It would be a long fall down if one were to slip now. The image of them sliding off the side of the mountain made her immediately regret her decision to look. She forced her attention back to the road and tried not to think about the precarious position they were both in. With every ounce of her focus, Adda took each step carefully, ignoring intrusive thoughts, shaking legs, and aching lungs that all vied for her attention.

After what seemed like days of trudging, the path curved inward, leading the both of them to a wide ravine that split the mountain in two. The ground leveled out around them and both found themselves relieved that they no longer had to walk on the edge of such a daunting drop anymore. Well, at least for now.

The path encompassed the entire area before them. Not even the smallest window of gray peeked out from the ground beneath their feet. Its white gravel ran out in every direction before coming flush with mountainous walls on their left and right. There was no possible way for them to leave the path in this place as the path was all there was.

On the far side of where they stood, Adda could see that their trail separated off in many different directions. It had carved miniature canyons into the rock, each beckoning them forward and each giving no indicator as to where they lead. It had all the appearances of the beginning of a labyrinth and it made Adda's heart sink. So far, the path had led them unerringly on its way, but now things had changed. Was there only one right choice? Was this perhaps another test, another trial?

Everett grabbed onto Adda's arm, jolting her from her thoughts. The man lifted up a shaking hand and pointed toward something that Adda hadn't yet noticed.

"Look!" His dry voice croaked with excitement, "Water!"

There, smack dab in the middle of the ravine was a large, near-perfectly round pool of crystal, clear water. Not a ripple disturbed its pristine surface, making it look like a great mirror instead. It looked so cool and refreshing that it made Adda sink to her knees as joy overwhelmed her. To think that they might have their thirst satiated and have the sand banished from their skin was almost too much bear.

Standing in between the travelers and the pool was something even more surprising. There was a sign, carefully carved from a red-tinted wood. It was the first indicator of civilization that either of them had seen since leaving Keith's town behind.

"Do you think it means we're close to the city?" Everett asked.

"I don't know." Adda said, "But I really hope so."

Across the sign's face were large, flowing letters that had been first chiseled on and then painted to better emphasize their shape. The paint hadn't chipped or worn despite being out in the open which made Adda think that it was being maintained by someone. What the words said, however, were lost on the pair as it had been written in some kind of foreign language.

Or, at least it had been when they first looked.

Adda blinked back surprise as she found that she could abruptly comprehend the message the sign was trying to convey. Though it was still written in the same strange language, it didn't stop her mind from translating it as though she had been reading it her whole life.

It simply read: Bathe.

Adda's entire body pulled against her will, begging her to launch herself into the water's cool embrace, yet she did not budge. A deep suspicion flared up in her mind, reminding her of all the close calls they'd had on their journey. She reached into her heart, searching for the Certainty to guide her as it had done so many times before. It was silent, leaving her alone to decide what to do next.

"It's actually on the path." Adda reasoned out loud, posing the insight to both herself and to Everett.

"I guess that's true." He said, his voice heavy, "Do you think we can trust it? I mean, after everything else?"

Everything else.

The words struck a chord in Adda who let her eyes slip closed. The military pounding on her door, a once lively farmhouse rotting like a corpse, a car decaying into dust, hills infested with ghosts she couldn't see, a valley of duality and corpses feigning life, a cave infested by darkness and memories, a meadow of people trapped in their own, willful ignorance, and between all of that, the monotonous motion of endless walking.

Everything else indeed.

Still, even with that all in mind, neither of them could deny the fact that they were tempted to take a moment and plunge into the welcoming waters. The mere idea of the sand being stripped from their bodies was enough to bring tears to Adda's eyes. She couldn't wait to cast them off.

"Adda?"

Adda snapped out of the momentary trance, realizing that she had begun approaching the pool without so much as a thought. The waters called to her like the mountain once had, pulling Adda toward it without her being aware that her feet had once again betrayed her. Everett stood back, resisting the pull, hesitant to approach.

Again, without meaning to move, Adda found she was suddenly closer still to the lip of the pool. Part of her reeled, fear biting at the corners of her mind as she found herself like an exhausted fish on a line, powerless to escape. Yet, this part of her seemed so distant from Adda that it may as well have belonged to someone else entirely.

The water was irresistible and so she took another step.

Am I under a spell? Adda thought, her mind heavy. *Is this it for me?*

Though those questions were important in this strange world, Adda didn't care to answer them. The water called out and she desperately wanted to answer.

"Adda, you're scaring me." Everett cried, still not moving as he clutched his rock to his chest as if it would protect him.

Her feet now teetered on the edge, the water reflecting back a perfect image of the sky above and a person that Adda knew to be herself, but she hardly recognized. This woman had the same eyes as her, but she was bent in a way that Adda had never been. Her shoulders were pulled forward, and her neck was hunched, nearly broken under the weight of the oppressive sand that could be seen covering nearly every inch of her being. Her clothing seemed to remain in one piece, but it was so weighed by the grime that it was nearly impossible to tell where the cloth ended and her skin began. Her hair hung heavy in thick knots, twisted into unintentional dreads held together by sweat and infesting grains. Even her purse had turned to the reddish-brown color of the wastes down below, its original color and texture hidden beneath layers of clinging sand. Her hands were clenched into tight fists, dried blood crusted between her fingers. The sight filled her with sadness, and though she did not carry the mark of the vines, it was clear that the journey had taken its toll on her just the same.

Looking back to Everett, Adda saw every trial they had endured together worn like a weight on his shoulders. Haggard is the word that popped into mind as she regarded him, yet there he still stood, having followed her through so much.

Turn back. A voice whispered. *You owe him that much.*

I can't. Adda thought dreamily.

Why not? Came the reply. *You've come so far, you deserve a break.*

These thoughts swirled like a tempest behind Adda's eyes as she looked at her traveling companion. Guilt built up inside of her as she thought of everything she'd put this man through. Sure, he had chosen to follow her, but had she ever really given him a choice? After all of the trials, he also deserved a rest.

If you cared about him, you'd go back. The whisper came again.

The idea began to stick. Once they got back to the meadow, Adda could prove to the people that she was one of them. Adda could even make her way into the cave and find her own rock if they wanted her to.

Maybe it's time to give up, Adda thought to herself, *maybe it's time for us to go home.*

Home.

The word settled deep within her, planting its roots into the soil of her heart.

Home.

It dug in deep, searching for something within the recesses of her being.

Home.

The roots found the Certainty, it grabbed onto it, and exploded.

The Certainty raced through her body like lightning, igniting every nerve as it passed. It overwhelmed her senses, it tore through her mind, and it caused her entire body to twitch sporadically. It brought with it a wave of visions that cascaded past her.

She saw herself overthrow Keith just to balloon into a worse version of him. She saw herself diving into a brilliant ocean, only to resurface and find that it was now black sludge pulling her back under. She saw herself running blindly through the dark, dragging her stone behind her as she was chased by voices that couldn't be. She saw herself sitting in the meadow, making daisy chains, trying not to flinch as every pass of the fabric across her blister caused it to flare with angry pain.

"There's no going back." Adda said, her voice dreamy and distant. "We have to keep going."

The visions spun around her so fast that she felt she would be sick. She shook her head, trying to rid herself of the sensation, but that only seemed to make it worse. Adda looked over to Everett, who still stood so far away. His eyes were wide and fearful, his body tensed and ready for action.

"Help me." Adda said to him.

And upon uttering the words Adda tipped over, no longer able to resist the pull of the water and plunged into its depths. The last thing she heard before the surface closed over her head was Everett's voice screaming her name and the sound of feet scrambling on gravel.

10

The water was cold; shockingly cold. It struck against Adda's body like a mighty fist, forcing the air from her lungs as she gasped in surprise at its sudden onslaught. Bubbles erupted from her mouth, racing to the surface with her stolen oxygen. She clamped her mouth back shut, but the damage had been done.

Thin, red lines began to ooze from beneath her palms. The cuts that the cave had left her with must have torn back open. They leaked at a steady rate, muddling the crystal, clear water with its presence.

Adda's heart thrummed in her ears, her blood racing in panic as she suddenly became all too aware of her situation. Her clothing was heavy now that it was drenched through, her purse pulled against her neck as it became waterlogged. The extra weight began to drag her further into the depths.

To Adda's great horror, she saw that there was no bottom to the pool or even sides to define its space. Rather, every direction she looked she was met with an eternal black of dark water. The only light in the water filtered from the tiny hole that she had just plunged through. It was as though she had fallen through ice to find herself in the middle of an ocean.

In the clutches of fear, Adda twisted about and struck out toward the surface, moving as fast as she could to escape the water's icy grip. Images of great sharks shooting toward her out of the dark made her swim all the faster. She reached out her hands, pushing with all her might to break free. Yet, none of that effort seemed to matter. The surface never seemed to get any closer to her. Trying her best to ignore her own mounting panic, Adda closed her eyes and focused as hard as she could on swimming free of this watery prison.

Stroke, push, climb.

She did this without thought, willing the motion to carry her to the surface just as she had with the village, just as she had with the mountain. All she had to do was trust that she would make it, trust that it was enough. But her hands never broke the surface and the sweet air never crowded back in around her.

Adda opened her eyes, her heart spiking as she saw that the surface wasn't any closer. Despite it all, it still lay just out of reach. She couldn't hold her breath much longer, already the darkness was crowding in around her vision. Dizziness swept through her and she had to fight against falling unconscious. In desperation, Adda reached for her purse, hoping to find the answer with her box, but found it was gone.

Her body twisted in the water, searching desperately for this sliver of salvation. In the flailing chaos of trying to escape, the purse must have slipped from her shoulder. There it was, directly below her, falling deeper into the water, faster than what Adda thought was possible. It wouldn't take longer than a moment for it to drift completely out of reach.

Adda cried out, losing what little air she had left and spun around to try and grab at it. Her arms thrust from her, her fingers stretching to their limit as she kicked downward to try and catch the descending parcel. Darkness rolled across her vision and when she blinked, the purse was suddenly a distant speck, spinning around lazily in an unseen current.

Had she just blacked out?

Regardless, the purse and the box had been claimed.

It was like a dagger to the heart. To have lost something so valuable, so important was too devastating to even describe. Adda wasted a precious second to stare after its retreating form and wondered how she could have let this happen. The squeeze on her lungs snapped her back to reality. Too much time had already been wasted and she could mourn its loss later. Right now, Adda had a more immediate problem to contend with.

Unconsciousness swirled around her, it threatened to take her at any moment. It wouldn't be much longer until she passed out. She spun around, kicking back toward the surface, her eyes searching wildly.

Through the covering fog of her dying mind, Adda saw Everett's refracted form come sliding up to the pool. He plunged an open palm into the water, splaying out his fingers as he desperately reached for her. It was a helping hand, a begging hand. Everett needed her to escape this trap for if she couldn't beat it, how could he possibly fare?

Adda cast out her own hand and kicked her legs furiously as she stretched out to her absolute length, fingers clawing toward his. It was no use. No matter how she tried, he always seemed to be a moment away from being able to help her. Adda realized that in order to pull her out, Everett would have to climb further into the water. Adda looked up, past the offered hand, toward the one who would give it.

And she knew he wouldn't do it.

Adda was the strong one. Adda was the one with the endurance, the one with the answers, and Everett had come to rely on her. So this was his moment, the moment she needed him to step up and save her. But he couldn't do what he knew he must, instead reaching from a breadth away. Everett prayed, screamed, begged that Adda would just have the strength to reach him so he could save her without going in after her. But Adda wouldn't reach him, she couldn't.

It was Everett's moment to be strong, but he didn't want it to be.

Then, as this understanding passed through Adda, she saw Everett's head snap up as if startled by something. He sat there, frozen like a deer who had heard the hunter make a wrong step in the forest beyond. His hand withdrew a little as he tried to get a better look at whatever had disturbed him. While Everett's attention went elsewhere, the cold finally sapped Adda of the last of her strength.

The black crowded in, even more absolute than the one from the caves they had left behind. It whispered and twisted around her, blurring her vision and causing her head to nod. It stole from her body every last bit of warmth and began coaxing whatever oxygen was left from her lungs. In her last moments of consciousness, Adda saw Everett look down at her once more. Despite the surface distorting his face, she could see heavy tears coursing down his cheeks. He mouthed something to her before he turned and ran from the water's edge, retreating out of sight.

The darkness closed and Adda was pleasantly surprised to find that she wasn't cold anymore, just comfortably numb from head-to-toe. She let out a sigh of relief, the last amount of air escaping her in a burst of bubbles. Water rushed in to take its place and Adda drifted away, unaware of the new set of hands bursting through the water's surface to grab her.

11

"Bethany?" A voice pierced through her mind, rousing her from a dreamless slumber.

Breaching the surface, she let out a long groan, pain exploding like fireworks behind her eyes. She rubbed her hands against her temples, eyes squeezed shut against the intrusion of light that filtered in through pink-tinted curtains. Everything was so bright, so loud, all of it painful. To make matters worse, someone was screeching her name over a raucous collection of noises that blared from all around her.

Was her dad watching a war movie or something? Irritation built up inside of her and she rolled over in her bed. She pulled a pillow over her head and squeezed it against her ears to block out the world.

Try as she may, she couldn't rid the sounds of horns blaring, engines roaring, and people barking out loud demands. It was too early to be blasting some dumb action movie, and on top of that, the poor girl felt like there was one of those creepy, cymbal-wielding monkeys slamming its instrument together inside of her head.

"Bethany!" The shrill voice called from the doorway.

This was quickly followed by hurried feet marching across thick carpet. Hands laid upon her still form and shook her aggressively in an attempt to rouse her.

"Mom!" Bethany snapped in frustration, rolling over to glare at her mother. "You can't just come barging into my room like that!"

"Bethany, get dressed, we have to go. Right now." Her mom said, ignoring the girl's attitude.

"But why?" She asked in return.

"Just- get up." The woman answered, her voice tight as if holding back emotion. "We need to leave."

Bethany opened her mouth to argue, but caught herself before the words could escape. She had just become aware of the fear that rolled off of her mother in continual waves. Though the woman tried her best to hide the unrelenting terror, Bethany could tell something was wrong. She was used to her mother worrying and fretting over all manner of things, but this- this was different. There was a depth to this fear that she had never seen before.

Something had happened, something bad.

"What's going on?"

"Please, Bethany, get dressed. We really have to go." Her mom replied.

The woman then whisked from the room. She held a hand over her mouth as she disappeared into the hall, her shoulders shaking as if she were just beginning to cry.

Bethany sat in bed for a moment, filled with a mixture of confusion and mounting dread.

Dutifully, she rose from her resting place. She didn't make it too far though as the room began to spin like a top. Her vision blurred and she felt light-headed. Reaching out, Bethany grabbed onto the side of her bed frame to try and keep her balance. She clutched her head with the other hand as a wave of vomit-inducing pain rolled over the landscape of her mind. It bit with sharp teeth and cut deep like nothing she had ever experienced before.

Taking a steadying breath, Bethany screwed her eyes shut, trying to will the pain away.

The waves began to subside, leaving behind its wake a terrible, throbbing, dull agony that chewed against the inside of her brain. It was almost too much to handle, but something within her urged her to rise up. Bethany complied, putting both her feet on the ground and stumbled across her room.

As she passed the window, a constant flicker of motion caught her eye. The blur of movement slid between the curtains, hard to understand from where she stood. Bethany walked to the window, her curiosity getting the better of her.

With apprehension building, Bethany gently pulled aside one of the curtains to take a peek outside. She squinted against the morning sunlight, the brightness taking another stab at her mind, causing her vision to swim. The pain was so great that the girl nearly threw up from its assault. Still, she didn't leave the window and as her eyes adjusted to the scene, her mouth swung open in surprise.

The street was a mess of bodies stumbling from their homes, blinking in the early light and shying away from it as though it burned. They were being ushered along by figures in hazmat suits who were systematically funneling the people from their houses and into their cars. Most of the suits held no weapons, only moving to help get people from their residences, but at the end of every street and drive, Bethany could see other suited individuals standing with evil looking rifles swung off their backs in a readied position. Behind it all, a tank was rolling up the street, moving somewhere deeper into the town. Bethany took it all in, stunned by everything she saw.

What's happening? She thought to herself.

A sudden commotion caught her eye.

There was a man charging out of his house with his family in tow. His entire stance was combative and his head snapped about, looking for a fight. Bethany heard him yell, and curse, and demand answers to this nightmare they'd all awoken to. With rough hands, he seized one of the suited figures, shaking them as he roared against their visor, his face turning bright red.

Immediately, the figures standing with weapons ready came sprinting toward the man. They bore down on the wrestling pair, intent on containing the altercation. Bethany gasped as she watched one of the figures drive the butt of their rifle into the side of the unsuspecting man's head. The blow caused him to reel backward and fall to the ground where he clutched the wound. A thin line of blood ran down the side of his face as the hit had split the skin. The figures barked commands at the dazed man, their rifles leveled at him. He shook his head at something they said before he was pulled roughly to his feet. They then ushered him and his wailing family to their van, the muzzle of a gun sticking in the man's back the whole way.

Bethany let the curtain slip from her hands, shocked at what she had just witnessed. Without a second thought, she obediently changed into more active clothing and picked out a few objects from her room. As she stood there, a question one of her friends had once posed crossed her mind.

If there was a fire and you only had time to get one thing from your house before it burned down, what would it be?

Back then, she had immediately answered without so much a second thought. After all, the likelihood of that happening seemed impossible. Now, as the world itself seemed to be burning down around her, Bethany found that she didn't have a good answer to that question.

In a daze, she looked around her room, taking in all the objects that represented her life. There where so many things in here that defined her, that had helped build her into the person she now was. Memories stacked on memories, peeking out from every corner.

What will happen here once we're gone? Will we get to come back? The questions twisted her stomach into knots.

"Bethany!" Her father yelled, his own voice tainted with the infecting fear, "Let's go!"

Snapped from her reverie, she made a decision.

Bethany strode across the room and reached up to a shelf holding all her favorite books. She thumbed through them, finding the one she was looking for and pulled it down. The girl looked at the leather bound book, gazing at its sleek form as if trying to pull some kind of understanding from it. It had been a gift from Mrs. Reinhoff awhile back and Bethany had made a habit of reading it through every year.

Or at least tried to.

She wasn't entirely sure why she had chosen this over everything else in her room, but it felt- right. Her mind made up, Bethany dropped it into her yellow backpack, zipping it shut and throwing it over a shoulder. Without stopping to add anything else to the bag, Bethany hurried downstairs, her heart pounding in her chest.

The moment the girl's foot left the last step, her mom latched onto her with a grip of iron. The woman's eyes were puffy like she had been crying and had only just managed to stop. Standing just before them was Bethany's dad and one of the figures from outside. The suit asked a question, or at least, Bethany was pretty sure he had. Instead of words, a garbled mess of noise struck her ears instead. It was like someone was trying to talk to her while she was underwater.

As if a switch had been flicked, Bethany found it hard to understand anything. Her mother said something to her, but again, it didn't come out as words but rather a convoluted mess that collapsed in on itself until it just sounded like a low, droning sound. Bethany tried to ask her mom what was going on, but found her mouth unwilling to work. Her tongue had grown so heavy, refusing to make the necessary motions for speech.

Bethany must have made some strange kind of sound though as her mom's eyes suddenly went wide in fear as she stared at her daughter. Then the world began to flicker around her.

It felt like her brain was starting to hiccup. There would be moments where she'd come to, seeing the world moving around her in slow motion, and then there would be a skip and she'd be somewhere new. Whatever was happening had become an incomprehensible blur that rushed past her.

A man in a hazmat suit running alongside them to their car. Her dad fumbling with the keys while her mother stroked her daughter's hair, shushing her though the girl was silent. The traffic all around them, noise exploding from every side, making her head scream in agony. Passing by a familiar Subaru that was, for some reason, driving the speed limit as though this were just any old day. Hills and homes rushing past the window, too fast to comprehend.

On and on it went, colors stretching and colliding until the entire world seemed to lose definition. It muddled into itself becoming a smear of bright lights that hurt to look at. In it all, Bethany lay in the back seat, clutching her backpack to her chest as though it was a life vest keeping her afloat in stormy seas. Her heart hammered with painful force, her breath came in shallow gasps, and her mind swam with agony.

And then, the blur stopped.

She snapped back into reality all at once, gasping as air rolled back into her lungs. Her mind was suddenly hers again as the heavy fog was lifted away from her. To her relief, she found that the fog had also taken all the pain with it, leaving her feeling mercifully better. To her surprise, Bethany found she didn't just feel better, but that she had never felt so good in her entire life.

Now that she had gotten her bearings, Bethany realized the panicked motion around her had also come to a halt. The car had been stopped for some reason and Bethany could see her parents outside yelling at each other. Fear thundered around the pair like an ominous cloud and Bethany was shocked that she could literally see its presence choking the air.

Must be something wrong with my brain. Bethany thought ruefully, shivering against the waves of harsh emotion.

Sitting up, she looked around to see they were surrounded on all sides by grass, and massive, rolling hills. In a dreamlike haze, Bethany grabbed her backpack from the seat next to her before opening the car door and climbing out.

First, she glanced over at her parents who were still yelling about something. They were so lost in their argument, they hadn't noticed their daughter climb from the car. Bethany turned from them to look around, taking in the environment which surrounded her. On all sides there were towering hills that Bethany was quite certain were larger than they should have been. She had lived in this area her entire life and yet she found herself looking at a land she was all but unfamiliar with.

How long was I out? Bethany thought to herself.

It was odd too that there were no other cars zipping past them as they parked by the side of the road. There wasn't even the sound of distant traffic to break the air. It was as if they'd stumbled somewhere far into the wilderness, away from any form of humanity. There were no power lines either, no indication save for the road and their car that they were still somewhere near civilization. It was deeply unsettling and it put Bethany on edge.

Her parents fighting certainly wasn't helping.

Bethany walked toward the base of one of the hills, mindless curiosity pulling her forward. It was as she reached it that a sudden shadow cast itself on her from overhead. It wasn't the passing of something moving across the sun that was there one second and then gone the next. No, this shadow *lingered* as the one it belonged to stood in place.

A shiver went down Bethany's spine, overwhelmed by the knowledge she was being watched. It was an unnerving thing that chewed at her gut, calling her to look up. She didn't want to as she was afraid of what she might see, but she was no match for her instinct. Before she could think against it, Bethany found herself arching her neck back to get a better view at what was above her now.

She froze as her eyes met the hilltop, her mind struggling to comprehend what she was seeing.

To everyone else, there wasn't much to see. If one stared long enough, they might catch a glimpse of a twisting shadow dancing against the backdrop of the blue sky. The shadows would fall away quickly under scrutiny, losing the interest of any onlooker who happened to notice them. To Bethany's eyes however, she saw something more than shadows.

There was something there. Something physical and deadly. Something great and terrible. In her eyes, there were figures upon the cusp of the hill. They gathered as a great multitude, waiting for the girl to react. Tears began to course down Bethany's face as true fear gripped her heart.

"No." She whispered.

Then, she ran.

Her feet cut grooves into the grass, kicking up clumps of dirt as she bolted away with as much speed as she could muster. Her parents called in surprise as she brushed past them, her heart hammering in her ears as she pushed herself to the limit. If they gave pursuit, Bethany didn't know. Her vision had narrowed to a single point, letting all else fall away to darkness. The entirety of her being had become about one thing and one thing only- escape.

On and on she went, running from the phantom enemy that only she was aware of, her fear a catalyst for the full tilt sprint. She would have probably run forever if her feet hadn't met an awkward patch of loose dirt that broke beneath her manic charge. The sliding dirt caused her to slip, gravity taking her to the ground.

Bethany yelped, pulling up her arms as she tumbled a few feet down the other side of a hill. Fortunately, this one was not very steep, and so she only gathered a few cuts and bruises before pulling to a stop. Dazed, she struggled back to her feet, the fear pounding in her chest begging her to hurry.

As she gained her footing, Bethany looked forward, surprised to see an abrupt change in the scenery. Before her, a mighty peak thrust up out of the midst of a great valley. It towered so high Bethany was shocked she hadn't seen it from the car.

The sight of it was dreadful and yet something about it beckoned to her. For a moment, she turned back, unsure of what to do. After all, she had left her parents behind and wherever they were was obviously not safe. She was torn as to whether she should go back for them or if she needed to keep running.

The choice became clear as she searched the endless, rolling sea of emerald green behind her. It took a fraction of a second for her to see it, but that's all she needed. There in the distance, a lone shadow was cresting a hill, moving at a steady pace straight toward her.

She was being followed.

Bethany turned back to the mountain, her breath coming in

panicked gasps. She paid no attention to the valley of plenty or the raging storm trapped above it. Bethany looked forward with a singular purpose burning into her mind. She had to escape her pursuer, she had to climb the mountain. A Certainty beat in her heart, driving her feet forward.

She shouldered her yellow bag, feeling the book Mrs. Reinhoff had given her gently bounce against her back. There were so many things she didn't understand, but she had a direction, and so she would go. Whispering a silent apology to her parents, Bethany ran.

And the shadow drew closer.

Part 3

1

"No!" Adda cried out.

The woman sat bolt upright and took in deep, gulping breaths. Sweat rolled down her shaking form, causing her clothes to stick to her body as though she were in the midst of a high fever. Her eyes were wide and she cast about, unsure of what had just happened.

One moment she had been drowning in a pool, the next she was waking up as Bethany. While she had been the teenager, there was no question in her mind as to her own identity. It was like she had literally stepped into the girl's shoes and lived in them. The experience was jarring and surreal. It had been more vivid than either the vision from Thomas or Everett. But as much as Adda wanted to lay back and mull over what had happened, it would have to wait.

There were more pressing issues.

Looking around, Adda found she was laying in a comfortable bed in an unfamiliar room. The room was dark but not impossibly so. There was a window to one side from which thick curtains hung. The curtains were drawn shut, allowing only the barest of light to come in.

Fortunately, it was just enough to allow Adda to see.

Across from the bed was a small table and chair, all made of a light wood that glowed ever-so-slightly. The table was bare, but the chair had a narrow cushion placed upon it to make sitting more comfortable. The pair was positioned perfectly under the window so that whomever sat there would be able to fully enjoy the rays of sunlight dancing on the back of their neck.

On the far wall, running parallel to the window, was a doorway covered by layers of stringed beads. This acted as a curtain, allowing the room's occupant some privacy from the rest of the building. The beads were colored white and brown, and strung in a way to create a pattern. This pattern appeared as three circles all intersecting one another. If the design had any meaning, it was lost on Adda, but she appreciated the artistry of it.

Adjacent to the door, carved with an expert hand and hung with care, was a large portrait of some kind of tree. The picture looked like it was made from one piece of wood, the image freed by someone who understood how to use a knife. There was an amazing attention to detail Adda couldn't help but marvel at.

Along the outside of its circular frame was some kind of lettering. It followed the entirety of the curve, eventually looping back into itself. The words had a runic quality to them, looking to be from some ancient culture.

Besides all that, there was just the bed that Adda was laying in and a small trunk at her feet. The trunk looked to be a storage container for extra blankets in case one were to get too cold. Though its function was simple enough, whoever had made the piece of furniture had taken extra time to make the trunk nearly as beautiful as the picture of the tree.

With her initial inspection of the room coming back with no obvious dangers, Adda went on to assess herself. She was uneasy to find herself no longer planted on the gravel and wanted to ensure that there were no tricks at hand. Adding to her paranoia, there was a nagging sensation in the back of her mind that something was missing.

And, to Adda's surprise, something was gone.

The sand that had so long weighed her down, holding her in its insidious fist, was nowhere to be found. She checked herself, but no matter where she looked on her person, there was no evidence of her burden anywhere. Not a single grain remained.

This discovery brought such a flood of joy and relief that tears began to spill unabated down her cheeks. She began to reach up a hand to wipe the tears away, but stopped as she noticed something more.

Not only had she been freed from the sand, but Adda had also been healed. Her hands, once ragged and bloody from trying to clutch to the stone, were splayed before her unblemished. Not so much as a scar remained to remind her of the battle in the dark. It was as if the event had been wiped clean.

The strange dream of Bethany and the unfamiliar place to which she had awoken were pushed momentarily from her mind. It had been so long since she had felt so put together that she didn't want to spoil it with unnecessary haste. It was like she had just stepped into the hills for the first time again, full of life and fervor, blissfully unaware of everything that would rise up against her.

After a long minute, Adda finally forced herself to take action. She was in a strange place after all and it would do no good just to lay about. It was time to get out of bed.

As Adda was about to stand up she heard the sound of feet on the hardwood floor outside her room. They padded in her direction, moving with quick, quiet steps. The moment of peaceful joy was taken away as images of corpse people, living darkness, and shadowy forms in hot pursuit came to life in Adda's mind. Panic stole at her and she looked about the room, trying to identify a way to escape.

The window might work, but she couldn't tell if there was glass on the other side and she didn't know how high off the ground this room was. Whereas it would probably be easy to break, Adda didn't want to risk a fall that might result in injury. Her hands might be healed, but she didn't want to tempt fate.

The other choice was to charge the door and hope to catch whoever was out there by surprise. This idea also came with risks of its own. After all she had no way of knowing what was on the other side of the beaded curtain. Rushing out into unfamiliar territory was a recipe for disaster.

There was only one other option Adda could think of. She had to find a weapon and hide by the doorway, using the element of surprise to her advantage. If she could catch them off guard, she might have a chance of overpowering them and making a run for the path. Adda knew she'd be safe on the white gravel- now she just had to get there. With that settled, she looked for anything that could be used as a weapon.

It was as she had made up her mind that she would bolt across the room to use the lone chair as an awkward club that the curtain slid open. Adda froze in place, her eyes wide as she watched a wizened, old man push through the beads.

He carried a small pewter tray that held a neatly folded napkin and a clay cup with some kind of steaming liquid. His eyes went from the woman who was already half out of the bed, frozen like a child caught with her hand in the cookie jar, and to the chair across the room. He furrowed his brow and nodded his head as if her entire plan had been laid out before him.

"Now there's certainly an idea." He said, his voice surprisingly strong from such a frail frame, "Although, your opportunity for surprise has certainly passed."

"You got here faster than I expected." Adda responded.

She eyed the old man cautiously but still felt somewhat guilty with having entertained the idea of bashing him with the chair. Then again, who was to say that this person was actually old? Or even a man, for that matter.

"Well, I've been known to be quite spry when called to action." He said with a wink and an easy smile.

He walked to the table and placed the tray down on it. Reaching above it, he gripped one corner of the curtain, pulling it slowly aside to let in the light from outside. Adda gasped and blinked rapidly against the sudden intrusion. She'd forgotten how bright the sun could be after having to walk beneath the heavy, ever-present clouds for so long. So taken aback by the blinding light, Adda hardly noticed the man take her by the arm and lead her over to the table, prattling on as he did so.

"Not that this is a time for action, of course, you have nothing to worry about! You're perfectly safe here! So, with that in mind, I would kindly ask you don't attempt to weaponize any of my furniture. Oh! Go ahead and drink this, but careful dear, it's very hot."

The man pulled out the chair, indicating she should sit to which Adda obliged. There was such a genuine warmth about the man that it was hard to remain suspicious of him. She looked for something, anything, that might cue her in about this stranger's true motives. There had to be some kind of trick to it, just like everything else.

Yet, there were no red flags, no gnawing suspicions that made her careful where her feet stood. Instead, he radiated peace, warmth and familiarity as though she were some dear friend or family member that had dropped by for a visit after a long time away. The man was still talking, reassuring her of this place as a sanctuary for however long she needed. Adda lifted the cup up, retaining almost none of the words spoken into her ear, instead turning her focus to the mug.

The liquid was a greenish-brown tint, with a pleasant, floral smell to it. It looked like tea and it smelled absolutely divine. Her dry throat groaned in anticipation of taking that first sip to help ease its discomfort. She certainly would have preferred something ice cold to numb the flaring pain, but either way, she found herself still hesitating.

The man must have picked up on it. "Are you afraid?"

It was an odd question to ask. She had woken up in a stranger's home after having been beaten down at every turn by a world not her own. Nothing was ever quite what it seemed, there always was a trick to everything. It should be expected that Adda was afraid on some level having learned quickly to be suspicious of anything this place tossed her way. To her own surprise though, Adda found that she was, in fact, not afraid.

"No, I guess I'm not."

"Good." He replied, "But if you are not afraid, then why do you hesitate?"

"Because I don't know you." Adda answered, "You seem really nice, but I've learned that looks can be deceiving."

"Ah, you require a test then?" His voice rose in excitement.

Adda turned to regard the man, surprised about his enthusiasm. Most people did not take to the idea of being tested, much less when that was a test of character. Such a thing often would be perceived as an insult, not an opportunity. But this man, he relished the idea. Moreover, Adda hadn't even suggested such a thing as she would've been happy to be on her way. The man had freely put this on his own shoulders.

He clapped his hands together, clearly giddy, before he walked across the room and pushed through the beads. Only when he was halfway through did he pause to turn back and look at her.

"Well, come on then!" He said with a wide smile, "Oh, and bring the tea. Once we get finished it will do you wonders."

The beads clacked together as he vanished from sight, humming a tune as he went. Adda stared after him.

What am I doing? Adda thought to herself. *This is a bad idea.*

Yet, her curiosity burned bright and there was no inner-voice that tried to sway her one way or the other. With that in mind, Adda made her decision.

With a careful hand, she scooped up the clay mug, feeling the heat of the liquid gently kiss against her skin before she hurried after the man. The beads clicked once more as she took a step into the next room and looked around.

The room was made of the same light wood from her little bedroom which caused the place to appear bigger and more breathable. It was well lit with two large windows on the right wall that allowed sunlight to flow in unabated. Cloth curtains were held aside by simple, wooden rings.

Part of the room was taken over by a wide couch that appeared well loved and quite broken in. Though the cushions were still fluffed and maintained, there were impressions that revealed many a person had whiled away the hours here in conversation. Adda imagined that it was probably as comfortable as the bed she had woken in and envisioned herself sipping tea there with a friend. The daydream warmed her.

The couch was positioned to face a table that sat in the center of the room with a pair of chairs sitting opposite. The two chairs held similar cushions that also looked well used. Clearly, this man had many a guest stop by.

On the table itself was a large game board which held a basic grid across its surface. Carefully placed on intersecting lines were rows of two different kinds of game pieces, one ebony black and the other pearl white. They were rounded in a way that made them look like pebbles pulled from a river bed. A stack of each kind of piece sat in a neat pile on either side of the board, showing the game was one meant for two people to compete in. Adda was sure she recognized it, but it wasn't one of the games she had played with Bethany's parents, so she couldn't place its name.

The thing that interested her the most was the fact there were two more of the clay mugs in this room, sitting on either side of the table. Both of them steamed, their liquid only half-drunk but clearly still very hot.

Someone else was here with the old man.

The thought, surprisingly, did not put her on edge. She still made a mental note of it, a reminder to keep her eyes open for any indicators there might be danger. If this turned out to be another trap, she would get out of it like anything else.

One step at a time. She thought.

Adda heard a sound coming from a doorway to her right, one of three in the space. They all held a curtain of beads such as the one that led back into the tiny bedroom. From the sunlight filtering through the curtain, it was clear that it lead outside. This fact relieved Adda as she didn't want to have to navigate the stranger's house should she need to escape. It was better to be out in the light of day where she could find the path rather than get stuck on someone else's turf.

Lifting up a hand, Adda parted the beads before her and passed through them. The sunlight rolled over her, unfiltered and pure as it warmed her entire body. The ache in her muscles seemed to melt away before its golden touch, causing her to relax away the burden of all the tension she carried. The sudden release made her suddenly feel extremely tired. It was a good kind of tired though, one that felt earned from laboring for so long.

This simple joy was pushed to the side as Adda took in the space surrounding her, her mind at awe with what she saw.

She found herself on the threshold of a small, quaint cabin that would probably have been featured in a rustic, vacation magazine. It was constructed from some kind of red wood with a single chimney poking up out of its roof. A lazy stream of smoke spilled out of the opening, coiling like a dream into the sky above. As beautiful as it was, it was certainly not the thing that had given the woman pause.

The cabin was situated near the peak of the mountain. In fact, it was so close Adda was sure it would take no more than a ten minute hike to complete the journey. While the top of the monolith occupied part of the view, stretching out like a majestic spear to pierce the heavens themselves, it was only a single piece of the incredible sight.

Around them, Adda saw everything.

The clouds still hung below them, covering the valley and most of the mountain in its thunderous shadow, but her eyes pierced them. Layer-by-layer the clouds thinned, allowing her to look upon what lay below. First she saw the path, glowing like a beacon in the sunlight, carving its way toward its single destination. From this distance, it appeared as though it were made of molten silver, so brilliant did it shine.

Around it, the valley spread out like a country all its own, rolling toward and consuming the horizon anywhere it could find it. The longer she looked, the larger it grew, becoming impossibly vast before her, yet her eyes did not strain to look upon anything. The valley immediately around the path was desert like, flickering between its two forms to draw people into its clutches. But Adda could see it went far beyond that, becoming darker and darker the further one strayed.

Great forests sprang up that stood as thick and dangerous as the darkest jungles. Between the black barked trees were massive vines adorned with wicked thorns. The vines slithered about like great snakes, hunting for their next meal. Adda shuddered as she saw forms writhing in the forests. There were corpse people caught in the clutches of the deadly vines whose thorns pierced and tore at them the more they fought back. They were dragged unrelentingly up into the canopy where they joined the other victims. Still others lay beneath the crushing weight of the trees' roots, pinned under the full force of the forest. The roots moved slowly, pulling anyone caught within them into the ground and out of sight.

In the other direction was a massive ocean of black, viscous liquid that gleamed darkly with every flicker of lightning. A great host of people could be seen desperately attempting to swim free, to get back to shore, yet the currents were confusing and Adda could see their attempts only drew them further away. They splashed and floundered, the thick liquid weighing them down the more they struggled. Somewhere in the dark mass, something moved. It twisted and contorted like a kind of serpent that belonged to myth, brought to life by the horrors of the world around it. It would slowly curve itself around a struggling form, pulling closer and closer until the corpse person would let loose a wretched scream before vanishing beneath the surface.

And horror upon horror, she could see that despite it all, there seemed to be an endless supply of people freely wandering into these places. Within the forests, they met with one another, pulling each other close as they whispered, ignoring the encroaching roots or reaching vines. By the ocean, they splashed about in the liquid, playing in it, drinking it. They seemed to be entirely unaware that every second they spent within the black substance, the further they were dragged away from the shore by some unseen force. They all went about their false lives, either willfully ignoring or just completely unaware of the screams echoing out around them.

Adda shuddered, already beginning to see beyond these. There was an eternal nightmare that surrounded one side of the singular peak. She pulled herself away, unable to bear it any longer. She drew her eyes up and looked further out. Somehow, she found the rolling hills that were hidden beyond the horizon line, her sight overcoming that which was physically possible.

As she swept her gaze over them, Adda was struck by a feeling of great insignificance. How small was she in the vastness of this place. The hills were absolutely eternal no matter which way she looked. She could gaze until the world turned to dust and they would still stretch on forever, a gently rolling ocean of emerald green. As with the valley, Adda found just by looking, she could see far beyond her limits, being able to pick out even the finest of details in the landscape beyond.

And, to her surprise, Adda found she could see people.

Not the people from the valley, or the caves, or even the meadow. She could see regular people. They were somewhat battered, somewhat scared, but all of them were slowly stumbling in the direction of the mountain. Adda could see some were racing over the hills, glancing back in a panic at something she could not see. Others moved at a steady, focused rate, their eyes searching the skyline but not yet seeing the mountain. There were groups who had even begun to band together to try and solve how they had arrived in such a place.

Out there in the hills were many small towns hobbled together by those too afraid to move forward. Among them, Adda found the one that had been built by her old friends. She saw them all milling about, hardly better than the corpse people in the valley just below their cliff. Their numbers slowly dwindled, yet they still refused to leave. They sought solace in their mundane tasks, searching for the strength to take on the day.

Above them all was the castle that had grown larger than it had been when Adda had first arrived. The tower had also risen further into the sky, looking structurally unsound as it stood over the town. Adda's eyes found the gaping hole in the side of the tower and saw Keith sitting in his chair. His form had grown even larger, making it impossible for him to squeeze himself through the doorway leading into the rest of the building. He stared blankly at the wall, his lips moving silently as though rehearsing a prayer.

All around him the white vines had grown thicker. Though they had once appeared so harmless, they now moved as a great mass to overtake the man. They coiled around the legs of his chair, clamoring up to find a spot in his infested skin. Slowly, from out of the recesses of the tower chamber, more tendrils slithered, intent on claiming their docile prey.

And standing above Keith was the shadow. It had also grown since last Adda had seen it. It no longer hid itself behind the massive human, rather it leaned in close, whispering dark secrets into Keith's ear. Its long, twisted hands caressed his shoulders as it worked its twisted power within the man's heart. All around them, the castle continued to glow its sickly green, casting the whole scene in a wicked light.

"Awful, isn't it?" The old man spoke, his voice tinted with despair.

Adda tore her eyes free and turned to the man who stood near her, his feet poking over the lip of a cliff. The man held an expression that spoke of one who was greatly burdened. His own gaze swept about, resting momentarily on far off figures that struggled to make it to the mountain. Adda got the impression that he had seen it all from his lofty perch, yet it had never gotten easier watching people struggle.

"What's happening to us?" Adda asked.

"Do you not already know?" The old man shot back.

The answer elicited frustration from Adda, but she didn't push the point. Instead, she looked back at the clearing that was just behind her, for the first time really taking it in. The entire area around them was a wide, open space perhaps a hundred feet in diameter. The white gravel covered its entirety, not allowing any other form of ground to show. It reminded her of the ravine where the pool was. Though instead of water, this area was occupied by the cute, red cottage.

On one side of the cottage was a small fence made of the same wood as the rest of the home. It had a gate that led to a small garden. Within the garden, a myriad of brilliant, green plants grew tall and healthy despite their roots digging into gravel instead of soil. The flourishing plants composed a tapestry of green from behind the fence. Everything about the home was small and humble, yet also absolutely beautiful to look at.

"Is it all real?"

"Dear, it's more real than anything you've ever known. For the first time in your existence, you're starting to finally see." He shook his head, turning to her. "There is much to discuss, but first we must accomplish that which we set out to do."

With a gnarled hand, he pointed to one side of his clearing, his other took from her the clay cup. He seemed unfazed that the drink had remained untouched.

"If you turn about, you will see that there is a cave similar to the one you escaped not so long ago."

Obliging the man, Adda looked and saw the cave that he was pointing at. Like so many other things, she was struck with the knowledge that it had always been there, lying beneath her perception. The novelty of such discoveries had long since worn off.

"And?" Adda asked.

"And," the man continued, "just within the threshold is a stone infested with vines. I want you to bring it to me."

Adda made a face at him and shook her head. "So the way to make me trust you is to ask me to go into a cave that I already know is inhabited with- well- something, and retrieve a stone for you? Something that, by its very nature, requires that I trust you?"

The man shrugged, unfazed by the presented paradox. "You know as much as I that the dark cannot keep you."

The dark.

It was spoken like a title as though it belonged to a singular entity rather than a general concept. It affirmed to Adda what she already knew, there was some kind of consciousness behind the shadows that flickered inside the cave. Under normal circumstances, such a revelation would be terrifying, but Adda also knew what the man said was true.

The dark could not hold her, could not contain her, and had even actively sought to help her leave if it would only rid it of her sooner. The cave, even when it had risen against her, had never had any real power over her. Even the vines had coiled away from her touch, unable to find any purchase on her. The Certainty didn't need to reassure her of these facts as they were now plain to her, but it still warmed her to know she was on the right track.

Though Adda had already made up her mind on what she was going to do, she still asked the question. "Why not go get it yourself?"

"Why indeed." The old man mused, not seeming put off in the slightest as his motives were continually questioned. "I suppose there's only two real reasons. For one, I don't have permission to enter and for two, this is your journey, I wouldn't want to rob you of the moment."

"You don't have permission?" Adda asked.

"That's not my story to tell." He replied with a shrug.

It wasn't an actual answer to Adda's question, but the man seemed unwilling to say more than that. There was a way about him that made him come across genuine and inviting, yet at the same time elusive and cryptic. Adda couldn't decide if she found it endearing or annoying.

The Certainty thrummed and Adda walked from the man toward the cave.

This cave was nearly the exact same as the last one she had gone through. It was a jagged slice of darkness that cut into the mountain's side like a wound. Freezing air oozed out of the hole, seeking to suck the warmth of the day from her bones. The veil of shadows thickened before her, anticipating the fight ahead. It swirled like a vortex, whispering and hissing at her as it dared her to try. For all its bravado and all its tricks, Adda felt no fear and so she stepped into its midst.

The dark recoiled.

The moment her foot stepped upon the gravel within the cave, the shadows receded before her. It made no effort to fight or resist, it peeled back as if Adda was the sun here to banish the night.

Even her attention seemed too much for it to bear. Anywhere her eyes roamed, the darkness would only hold a moment before shriveling up and slinking away to a different corner. It still hissed and coiled, but it was no longer the great beast that had tormented her and Everett from before. Now the truth of it was revealed: it was a tiny, weak thing that relied on the fears of others to build its strength. With nothing to feed on, it could not be a threat.

It tried to hide the stone within its shroud, but again it retreated under Adda's gaze. It wisped away to reveal her quarry, unable to stop her. Instead it pooled into the back of the cave, seething as it watched from afar. The rock now lay before Adda as plain as day.

It was roughly the size of a stool and looked no different from any other stone. To anyone else it would have hardly warranted noticing unless someone was looking for a place to sit. But Adda's eyes fixated on it, and it too seemed to shy away from her, attempting to become smaller so that it might be spared her attention. There was nothing it could have done, of course, as Adda stepped over to it, bent down, and lifted it up.

As her hand closed around it, the stone shrank rapidly in size, shriveling up like a weed on a hot day until it was no bigger than her palm. Adda pulled it up to eye level, marveling at how such a small thing had caused so many people so much suffering.

Vines thrashed about on its underside, upset about being taken from their resting place. They whispered and hissed, seeking the one who had disturbed them. The moment they became aware of Adda, they reeled back, but not to strike as they had with Everett. Instead they retreated from her, trying to create as much distance between them and her as they could. Yet, there was nowhere for them to go, so they gathered, trembling, on the far side of the stone. Like a nest of vipers they coiled into a tight ball, whispering threateningly at the woman, but making no effort to attack her.

With prize in hand, Adda left the cave.

She approached the man again who gave her a broad smile. Then he looked down, his face hardening as his gaze fell upon the rock and the vile vines. They thrashed about under the sunlight, some of them disintegrating. The others tried to seek the underside of their home, but slithered away upon sensing Adda.

"Give it to me." The man said, offering out a hand.

Adda obliged and dropped the rock into his open palm. The stone made a quiet sound as it settled into the man's hand, it even started to stretch outward seeming curious about its new wielder. The vines too reacted, pausing their trembling as they sensed a difference. They slithered about, stretching out to gingerly test their noses against the man's flesh. In the sunlight, Adda could see their tips were covered in glinting bards angled in a way that made going in easy, and getting pulled out devastating.

Without ceremony or sound, the vines suddenly pierced the man's hand, slithering into the skin with a greedy motion that sickened Adda just watching. To imagine those things burrowing beneath her skin- the thought made her shudder. But she didn't look away, she wanted to witness whatever was going to happen next.

The man grimaced at their digging, his jaw tightened as they bit into him and began coiling around his veins. They twisted this way and that, tightening their grip as they climbed deeper and deeper, their vile motion could be seen bulging from under his skin. The man clenched his fist and closed his eyes, muttering something under his breath.

An acrid smell began to assault Adda's nose as something started to burn. Smoke came drifting from the closed hand and the vines froze as if meeting some kind of resistance they didn't understand. There was a sharp *pop* which was followed by high-pitched whine that sounded like water being boiled out from burning wood.

From inside the man's fist, the rock cracked.

He brought his fingers together, tightening his grip on plant, root, and stone alike. The whining sound rose in pitch and depth, now sounding more like a scream. Adda wanted to cover her ears to blot out the horrid sound, but she found she couldn't as she stood transfixed by the sight. The vines tore at the man's hands, ripping off chunks of his flesh in the process, yet not a drop of blood came free. The rock tried to escape, changing its shape in order to slip from the crushing grasp. The man clenched his hand tighter, his face passive as it seemed the act was neither difficult or painful.

Then, the stone shattered.

In a flash of brilliant, golden light, the rock exploded into a thousand pieces. It scattered in every direction, though not one fragment touched Adda as they sailed past her. The vines let loose a final cry before they crumbled, brittle, from the man's hand. They drifted down to the ground, joining with the gravel as they shriveled and died.

The man opened his eyes, staring at what remained of the stone. With a careless motion, he tilted his palm to the side, letting the debris fall away to get snatched by the wind. To Adda's amazement, there was not a mark of injury on the man's hand despite the vine's burrowing and biting. Not a cut, scab, or scar stayed behind to mark the victory. Only a crust of ash remained as any kind of evidence.

That too was claimed by the wind, blowing away until none of it remained.

He flexed his hand, turning it over, inspecting it as if admiring his work. Then he turned his attention to her, a slight smile on his lips, and an eyebrow cocked.

"Convinced? Or perhaps another kind of test is in order?"

"How is that supposed to convince me?" Adda asked, "For all I know, you work for the darkness and just sacrifice a stone to trick people into trusting you. It was an incredible display, but how can I know if it's more than just that?"

He smiled, "Because, as it was once said, 'A kingdom divided against itself cannot stand.'"

The words struck Adda's heart like a chord, ringing with truth into the recesses of her soul. They were familiar to her, ones that she had read hundreds of times. It was with this phrase Adda knew she could trust this man, whoever he was.

Out of habit, Adda reached a hand down to try and find the box at her hip which carried the very book where those words were written. She was hit with a feeling of loss when she found that her purse was still gone, drifting somewhere down in that infinite pool that had tried to claim her. This sense of loss prompted her with another thought, one that had been nagging at her since she had awoken but had yet to address.

"Where's Everett?"

2

Everett watched Adda walk away from his check stand, unsure of whether to tell her to have a good day or to thank her for offering the guitar to him. In the end, she slipped out the door and into the day without a word escaping him. He had done as he had been trained to do, to politely decline, yet was taken aback when she had insisted.

After everything that had happened to her, how could she just give up her husband's guitar?

It had already been a stressful day with everyone clawing over one another for bottled water, yet it was not them that had now set Everett on edge. There was something with the insistence in Adda's tone that really got under his skin. He regretted even saying anything to her.

Who does she think she is? Everett complained in his mind.

By the time it came around for him to clock out and leave, Everett was in poor spirits. There was an eagerness to his step as he left his check stand, looking forward to being able to distract himself from the day's events. He walked into the back of the building, entering in his employee code in a small box that registered he was free to go and to have a *great day!* Back when Keith's dad had run the place, tracking the hours had been all put into a computer by hand. It was inefficient and Everett wondered how often employees ended up getting underpaid. Keith had helped update quite a bit of the tired, old store, though sometimes his obsessive need to be up with the times was obnoxious. The way the man would talk about his store was like it would soon be some massive, national chain rather than a mom and pop stop in a forgotten corner of the world.

I guess a guy's gotta dream. Everett thought to himself.

He waved goodbye to the handful of other employees who were milling about in the back. Some were just arriving and others were counting down their time to go home. Grabbing his backpack, he slipped out of the store, taking one of the aisles on the far side of the building, the hygiene department, to make good his escape. It would have been quicker to walk down an aisle with a more direct path, like the snack-slash-electronic one, but Everett was trying to avoid his boss.

Keith was often flitting about the middle of the store, welcoming customers and ensuring that no one was sneaking off with any of the more valuable things. Everett had once posited they move the expensive stuff further away from the door to discourage shoplifting (not that that was a huge problem to begin with) but Keith had just scoffed at the idea.

"Come back when you got your own business, kid." The man had said, shaking his head in amusement.

Everett turned the corner and internally groaned. Today was just not his day. Keith was leaning over a shelf of hair-care products, his eyes narrowed as he ran a finger along them as if testing them for dust.

Everett casually turned, trying to escape down a different path, but it was too late.

"Done already?" Keith asked, his voice chipper as he approached Everett.

When it came to everyone else, Keith was always so unsure of himself, so anxious of saying the wrong thing even though he tended to come on a little strong. When it came to his employees, however, it seemed like all those inhibitions evaporated. He would never say so, but Everett suspected the man believed all his workers owed him something since he had been gracious enough to give them a job. Which was a stupid thing since there was no way the place would be able to stay open if they all just up and quit. Sometimes Everett dreamed of unionizing just to spite the man, but that would require more effort than Everett was interested in investing.

"I mean, the schedule said it was time to go, so-" Everett slipped past the man, trying to project a sense of confidence and hurriedness to convey that he wasn't interested in standing around chatting.

The attempt didn't work as Keith moved along with him, a smile still plastered on his face.

"I suppose it did, but did you take the time to ensure that you had done everything that needed to be done before clocking out? A diligent worker understands that sometimes we need to stay after a little longer to make sure everything is in its place!"

Everett strongly disagreed. If his time to go rolled up, then there was little outside of a pretty girl coming through his line that would stop him from flicking off his light and clocking out. Sure, he would finish up whatever he was doing, but that was the extent of it. As far as

Everett was concerned, he had done his duty and had no interest in hanging around.

Of course, Everett wasn't a bold man and would never say such a thing to Keith. So instead of just walking out, he found himself once again cornered by the bigger man, listening to him go on and on about work ethic. It was clear Keith wished he had had children to impress his legacy upon, but as he had never been married, it fell to his employees to get the brunt of his lectures.

I should get paid for this. Everett thought to himself, nodding in time, and muttering "uh-huh" when the conversation called for it.

As always, Everett wanted desperately to speak his mind as he was clearly no longer a child, but it seemed like everyone insisted on talking to him like he had never grown up. Maybe if he would stand up for himself every once in a while, it would change the way people saw him. Then again, that would require a boldness he wasn't familiar with.

Keith placed a hand on Everett's shoulder, jarring him from his thoughts.

"Son," He said, his face searching. "I'm just worried that you're not living up to your full potential."

Everett furrowed his eyebrows, cocking his head to the side as he tried to decipher what the other man was trying to say.

Am I getting fired?

Everett voiced the concern, hesitating as he spoke. "I mean, are you saying I should be looking for another job?"

At the question, Keith let loose a deep, hearty laugh. He shook his head and wiped his eyes with a hand as if he had just been told the most hilarious joke ever.

"Oh Everett, don't be ridiculous! No! You've been here for too long to just let you go." That last statement made Everett bristle, he didn't like the way Keith was talking, as if he were something owned. "No, no, no, I'm talking about opportunities for promotion!"

Keith grinned broader, squeezing Everett's shoulder as if he gave him the greatest news ever.

"Uh- thanks?"

"Well, I'm not going to be promoting you right now. There's a lot you need to knuckle down on before we start talking about extra responsibilities." Keith said and finally released Everett, "Tell you what, next time you work, we'll have a little chat on areas to improve on to help make that dream a reality!"

After profusely thanking Keith for such an incredible opportunity that Everett hadn't even asked for, the young man finally managed to slip away. He glanced at the clock on his way out, feeling a needle of frustration as he saw that an extra half hour had been added onto his time being trapped in his modern prison. Walking out the doors, he kept his head ducked low, trying not to gain the attention of anyone else who wanted to waste his precious time.

He went over to the bike rack, pulling out a key to unlock the chain that kept his mode of transportation secure. After stashing the chain in the pack over his shoulder, he mounted his wheeled steed and started the journey home. Everett had never gotten a license, insisting that it made no sense paying for gas and insurance just to get around a place he could easily bike from one end to the other in only an hour or two. Whereas that was certainly sound logic, the real reason that

Everett chose to bike everywhere was that he was terrified of failing.

It was easier to logically dismiss any prying questions as to why he chose this lifestyle than have to go take the test and fail. This fear touched every part of his life, rooting him in place so that he may never know that crushing feeling of defeat. This is why he was still here when so many others had moved on, this is why he was still at the same job rather than finding something more suited to him.

In fact, Everett was actually quite a brilliant young man, brimming with all manner of incredible potential. The only thing that held him in place was the man in the mirror, too prideful to even let himself fall for fear that someone might see. It was better to never even try.

So Everett pedaled home, secretly wishing he had a car as his feet were killing him from being on them all day. The town passed him by like a dream as he fell into the rhythm of his commute, his mind casting itself far away from his current, suffocating lifestyle. What was with older people always trying to push things upon him? Adda promising a guitar that he knew he wouldn't play, Keith grooming him for a promotion he didn't want, heck, even his parents nagging at him to go to college or to turn one of his interests into a viable career. They all meant well, he was sure, but none of them seemed to understand how hard his life was.

It was these thoughts that led him back to his apartment that he split with two other people. It was only a two bedroom, so they managed to cram all of their beds into one room, turning the other into a gaming lounge. Originally, there had been many arguments over the setup as they were worried about the idea of having girls over, but that turned out not to be much of a problem. Of the three of them, only one had a girlfriend, and she seemed more inclined to have him stay at her place than the other way around. After years of living this way, they had simply accepted their lifestyle.

One room was meant for sleep, the other was for gaming, and that's the way they liked it.

Everett turned his bike into the parking lot, guiding the wheels over the speed bumps that had been built a little too big. They were obnoxious for cars, but perfect for a bike that wanted to get a little air, so Everett went out of his way to bounce over every one. Dismounting, he pushed through the main door to his building, taking the bike upstairs with him. Everett walked down the short hallway, his bike clicking softly in the space that was muffled by heavy carpet. He mumbled a greeting to a neighbor who stepped out of their adjacent home, but ignored any kind of response. He pushed through his front door, moderately irritated to find that the door was unlocked.

Neither of his roommates ever locked the door and would just roll their eyes anytime Everett would mention it. They would retort that he needed to lay off the monster movies and serial killer documentaries. After all, nothing ever happened in their little town.

Stepping into the front hall, Everett snapped home the lock and kicked off his shoes, leaving his bike sitting by the door. He could hear both of his roommates in the gaming room, they were cursing and laughing loudly in the midst of something competitive. They were supposed to be partying up and performing a raid in one of their games, but Everett getting home so late had clearly turned them to other ventures.

Taking a left, Everett walked past the two closed doors and went through the one at the end of the hallway. Fumbling in the dark beyond, Everett's hands brushed the light switch, flicking it on and flooding the space with sharp, white light to reveal a bathroom. He hated how intense the light shone, but had never gotten around to switching out the bulbs for something softer.

Fueled by habit, Everett stripped off his work clothes and, after depositing them on the floor, he clambered into the shower. With automatic motions, Everett twisted the two handles, adjusting the temperature of the water until it was at the perfect spot. He let out a long sigh, letting the stresses of the day wash away with the water that rolled down his skin. The young man was so tired he hardly noticed the metallic scent that filled the shower and didn't even consider its heavy taste on his tongue as the steam wrapped itself around him.

All anyone had talked and worried about was the water, but he had paid it little heed. His life was a loop that played out the same way everyday. Rinsed and repeated so many times that the groove he had cut became too steep to clamber out of. There would have to be a bigger scare than the water being a little funky to get Everett to change his cycle. Besides, he mostly drank sports drinks anyways, so he figured there wasn't much to worry about.

Everett ran his fingers through his hair, working the knots and sweat loose as the hot liquid poured over him. He played out the day in his mind, reflecting on it as the images rolled by. This part of his ritual came to a stop when Adda's face once again popped up, so insistent, so demanding.

When she comes in with the guitar, I'll tell her I can't take it. He thought to himself, letting the scenario play out.

He practiced the interaction in his head a few times, trying to predict what she might say and how he ought to respond. In his visualized version of the event, he was graceful, but adamant, and Adda would obviously oblige, realizing how silly it was to offer such a gift to a man who was just trying to do his job and go home. Besides, when would he even have time to practice?

Once he was satisfied with the combination of words that he would use to free himself of obligation, Everett slid to the floor with another sigh. He sat in the tub, letting the water patter on his skin. His eyes flickered shut, suddenly feeling heavy with exhaustion. A great weight had tied itself around his neck, making it hard to focus on anything. The telltale signs of an intense migraine began to build in the back of his mind, manifesting as a deep, painful throb that strobed against his skull.

I should've drank more water. Everett thought to himself, repeating the same line his mother had ingrained into his being over a lifetime.

The day had been stressful, but so had other days. On all those days he had come home, ready to game out his frustrations. It was part of his cycle, but the cycle had run against something unexpected.

A wall of exhaustion slammed into him, sapping out every ounce of energy from him. His bones felt heavy, his muscles frayed, and his mind began to fragment. It was difficult to focus on anything and his thoughts became more and more incoherent. Darkness crowded in around him, stealing away what was left of his consciousness until all that remained was a black, infinite void.

The void reached out and plucked Everett where he lay, pulling him into a deep, still slumber.

3

It was the overwhelming silence and biting chill that drove Everett to wakefulness. For a moment, nothing made sense as his thoughts couldn't get themselves in order. It was as if his inner being had been scattered with its pieces floating freely around him in a jumbled mess. With some concentration, Everett managed to reel in these loose parts, rousing himself from his stupor.

The first thing his tired mind latched onto was that he was still sitting naked in the shower. Panic shot through his head, thinking about how angry his roommates were going to be when they found out he had been showering all night long. They would probably demand he pay for the water bill next month if he was going to be so wasteful.

The next thing he noticed was that, miraculously, the shower had been shut off. Perhaps when the hot water had begun to dwindle down, he had risen sleepily to turn it off before passing back out. Convinced this is what had happened, Everett marveled about how tired he must have been to have fallen asleep in such a manner.

Another thought then occurred to him.

Their apartment only had the one bathroom, a fact that had often become a point of contention between the three of them as they often warred over who got to use the bathroom when. He was surprised neither of the other men had pounded on the door, demanding he get out so they could at least use the toilet.

Everett tried to explain away that as well, coming up with all manner of reasons as to why they hadn't woken him up. Even though he could invent perfectly reasonable explanations, he still couldn't shake the sudden chill that trickled down his spine.

Something felt out of sorts, though he still would not allow himself to admit it.

Everett grabbed a towel, but then realized he was actually dry. It was probably hours ago he had turned off the water, so it made sense he wouldn't be wet. Right?

Trying not to dwell on it, Everett clambered out and hurriedly got dressed. He kicked himself for not grabbing new clothing as he pulled on his work clothes from the day before. They hadn't quite gotten to the stage where they smelled well worn, but Everett still wished he had something cleaner to wear.

Pulling the uniform's shirt over his head and securing the belt into place through the loops in his pants, he pushed through the door into the hallway beyond.

It was dark. Unnervingly so.

Was it still the same night or did he somehow lose an entire day? Everett opened the door to their gaming room. It was well kept with posters of video game characters and logos on the walls, a collection of monitors, cpu towers, and TVs with consoles neatly arranged around the room. Everything seemed to be in order here. The door made a soft click as he closed it before he moved onto the next room.

This door he opened with more caution, trying to make as little noise as possible, not wanting to awaken his roommates if they were sleeping. The metallic handle was freezing to the touch, almost painfully so, and it sounded far too loud in the surrounding silence as he twisted it inch-by-inch. For some reason, this simple act of opening a door that had been his room for years filled him with a peculiar sense of gnawing dread. Brushing passed the feeling, Everett peeked into the room beyond, his eyes taking a moment to adjust to the dark created by the black-out curtains hanging over the rooms single window.

His breath caught as his eyes finally pierced the dark, unfolding something he couldn't simply logic away.

The beds, one of them a bunk bed, had begun to sink into themselves with great age. Black stains blemished the center of each mattress as they broke down into pits of mold. Where there was metal on the frames, they showed signs of rust, their once shiny, metallic surfaces giving way to invasive, flaking red. The wood that helped support the beds was also showing signs of impossible age as it bent and warped beneath the march of time.

The walls too had become greyed and faded as if centuries had swam by, draining every bit of color free from the paper. The posters that adorned the walls had begun to disintegrate, fading slowly into nothingness. The laundry basket that sat on the far side of the room was so filled with creeping mold it made Everett want to retch just looking at it. Without another thought, Everett slammed the door and stumbled back into the entry hall.

He tripped against something, his heels kicking into an object that nearly made him lose his balance. Everett yelped in surprise and terror as his spiraling mind offered up all kinds of horrible things that might be the source of his stumbling feet. Even after the room, however, he was not prepared for what he saw.

The bike he had ridden mere hours ago sat in a mauled, twisted mess. It was rusted and bent, leaving it nearly unrecognizable on the hallway floor. The tires sagged and looked as though they were melting away as they stretched in the hand of gravity. To Everett's mounting horror, he could actually see the bike falling apart in front of him. Rust spread like angry termites, holes widened in the tires as the whole vehicle crumbled in front of his bewildered eyes.

Having seen enough, Everett turned and stumbled toward the door, his fingers fumbling against the lock as he tried to get it open. In the few moments it took Everett to make his hastened escape, he was suddenly made aware of something else.

It was dark.

It was alive.

It was a presence in the room behind him.

He wasn't sure how he knew, but he could feel it there. Maybe it was in how still the apartment had become, waiting with bated breath. Maybe it was the faintest sounds of rustling from somewhere around the corner, like a predator sinking into the grass. Maybe it was some sixth sense that rang out like a siren in times of dire need. Regardless of the source, Everett knew *something* was there.

And that something was waiting for him.

As if the thing had become aware Everett sensed it too, there was a sudden explosion of sound. Heavy feet hammered against creaking wood, the sound so loud it had to belong to something far too big to be real. Not looking back, Everett pulled the bolt free and threw the door open. He launched himself into the long hallway beyond, turning sharply and charging away, desperate to break free of whatever nightmare he had found himself in.

The hallway too was breaking down, evidence of extreme age facing him at every turn. The carpet was turning black as it decayed away and large circles of water and mold damage plagued the walls. All around him, the building was actively falling into itself like some horrific disease was eating it from the inside out.

To make matters worse, some of the doors that Everett sprinted past not only showed the same signs of great age, but also of forced entry. Like broken teeth in a shattered smile, the doors had been splintered inward, their broken remains scattered into unnaturally darks halls as though a great force had come against them. Seeing these portals that had once secured the homes beyond so handily dismantled caused Everett to run all the faster.

He instinctively looked back, dying to know whether or not he was being pursued. Everett immediately regretted the decision.

In the brief moment before he was sailing down the stairs and into the light of day, Everett saw someone- *something*- exiting the door to his apartment. A shadow was reaching out, gripping the side of the door frame as if to pull a great host free of the tiny hall beyond. It was hard to see the exact dimensions of this entity, but it was clear the thing was big.

Too big.

And it was coming after Everett.

His feet slammed down the stairs, nearly tripping over themselves as his full-tilt escape wouldn't pause for anything. Successfully keeping his footing, Everett burst through the door to the complex. His body revolted at the soft give of its wood beneath his hands so taken by decay and the stubborn shriek of the hinges as they were forced to do a job they hadn't done in a long time. He stumbled free and scrambled across the asphalt as he launched himself away, his eyes rolling in his head as he moved without thought.

All around him the town aged and collapsed, giving way before the rapid march of time. The buildings tumbled to the ground, groaning as grass and root reached up to swallow them into the earth. Whatever process had been slowly taking them had accelerated as Everett's entire world came crashing down in an instant. Windows exploded, foundations cracked, and walls collapsed. Cars buckled, street lights twisted, and even the trees fell. In the distance, the clock tower, the pride and joy of the town, made a baleful noise before tumbling into itself. Noise of destruction echoed out in every direction, a cacophony of apocalyptic proportions.

And in a matter of moments, it was all over.

Everett hadn't even left the parking lot by the time the last of the buildings were pulled into the earth. He hardly had time to register any of this as each building became a great hill in a sea of infinite green. He was surrounded by the graves of human innovation with only the road left to lead him on his way. His mind reeled, trying to understand, but understanding didn't come.

It was heavy feet, charging on the road after him that forced all thoughts from his mind.

Everett put his head down and ran.

4

Adda fell to the ground, sitting down hard as she gasped for breath, her lungs working double time to keep up with her beating heart. Just like with Bethany, the images had been so real, so life-like, crushing in from every direction until she nearly had forgotten who she was. Gravel bit into her hands as she held herself in a seated position, trying to gain control of herself again.

"What is this?" She gasped, her mind still clouded with visions of Everett running in fear.

"Your eyes are finally seeing." The old man said, offering a hand to her.

He helped her to her feet and then continued.

"The part of you that clings to what was is letting go. The byproduct is you're finally able to look beyond yourself and see Truth." The old man turned from her, gazing back into the valley, "In your life before, it was as though you were looking at all of reality through a crack in the wall. You were miles ahead of your fellow man who insisted on playing within the confines of the room behind you, but even you could not grasp the full scope from your limited perspective the crack offered. Here, the wall has suddenly been knocked down and those who are practiced in looking can now see far more than they normally would have. In contrast, the people that have never even taken a moment to so much as glance at the wall are left lost and wandering."

"What does any of that even mean?" Adda asked, exasperated.

"Search yourself. You already know the answer." The man replied.

Sensing this direction of questions would go absolutely nowhere, Adda moved to a more pressing concern.

"Where's Everett? What happened to him?" She asked, visiting her earlier query though this time with more force.

"You could easily look and see," The old man said, jutting his chin toward the edge of the cliff, but before she could walk to its edge, he continued. "Everett ran because he was tested and found wanting."

"Are you going to give me a straight answer or are you going to keep being cryptic?"

"Even when you were in need, the very person that had carried him so far, he let fear be his master." The old man said, turning his gold eyes back to her, burning with the heat of a flaring sun.

She looked upon him, suddenly aware of how vast the man seemed. It was like looking into space and coming to the realization of just how small everything actually is. Despite his frail frame, there was an infinity that rippled below the surface, fluctuating with near immeasurable power. It would have been intimidating had the man not been so inviting.

He shook his head and ran a hand through his thinning, grey hair.

"I only came to assist you when it became clear he lacked the strength. He saw me and ran away."

Adda sized the man up again, taking in his entire form with probing eyes. There was no trick, no illusion to his form as far as she could tell. There was certainly more to this man than met the eye, but she couldn't quite put her finger on it. For all her eyes told her, he was just a liver-spotted old man living in a simple cottage on the mountain of insanity overlooking a valley of absolute destruction. Yet, as much as she wanted to mistrust him, she found that she couldn't. After all, he seemed quite comfortable staying on the gravel and he had remained untouched from the stone. He had offered other tests, but at this point Adda didn't feel like she needed anymore proof.

"So, I can see anyone from up here?" Adda asked, moving to stand beside the man.

"As I said before, your eyes are simply opening. The mountain just helps put things into focus." The old man said and looked down. "To answer your other question; Everett has joined the commune living in the meadow, he wandered in muttering words of your death. He was taken in with a warm welcome and the lie that he is finally home.

"And Bethany?"

"You've equipped her to get further than most. You will see her again." He answered cryptically.

Adda had not mentioned the young woman before, so perhaps this man had heard her cry out the girl's name upon waking up. But Adda doubted that. With how quickly and assuredly he had answered, it was clear he knew exactly who she was talking about.

He turned to meet her gaze, his own eyes seeming bemused at her examination. She stared back, unwilling to yield ground to the stranger, yet unlike the times before with other people living in this realm, this was no contest of wills. There was a look of familiarity in his eyes, a light that suggested a knowing that a stranger shouldn't have.

"Who are you?" Adda asked at last once the silence had long hung in the air.

As she gazed back, Adda was once again struck by that same familiarity and belonging that had overcome her back in the hills. It was something that had nagged at her for a long time. How could one belong to a place one had never been? She couldn't deny the overwhelming sense though and it brought about another revelation.

"You know me, don't you?"

"First; though I go by many names and titles, you can call me Mike. For the second, yes, I do know you and perhaps better than anyone you've ever known. As to how that's possible, it's not my place to say but I will tell you one thing, Adda Reinhoff, you are standing with a friend." Mike placed a comforting hand on her shoulder before turning about and walking up toward the mountain peak. "Come, there are things to show you before the next leg of your journey. Oh, and also, please drink this."

Mike offered her the cup that she had yet to take a sip of and Adda plucked it from the man's hand as she walked beside him. Whatever mistrust she had evaporated, and at long last, Adda soothed her ragged throat. She tilted back the clay cup, breathing in the drink before taking a long draft.

The taste was pure and soothing. There were floral hints around the outside of the liquid, with a sharp, pine flavor taking up the middle. It tasted like the sensation of waking up on a mountain in the early morning, just before the sun rose to burn away the fog from the night before. The world was light grey and dark blue, with large pine trees sighing pleasantly in the wind.

She took another sip, reveling in the taste before she began to speak. "It's strange. Nothing about this world really makes any sense, yet somehow I feel at home."

Mike chuckled softly, shaking his head as if she had shared some secret joke with him. "The times that I've heard those very words spoken."

"Others have come through here?"

"More than the grains of sand on all the beaches in the world and more than the stars in the heavens above have come to this world." He said. "Not very many make it this far, but you are certainly not the first."

Adda considered this, letting it take shape in her mind.

White gravel crunched beneath their feet as they rose higher and higher into the air, allowing more of the landscape to spread out around them. Everywhere she looked, the valley stretched further out, revealing more horrors that gathered on the horizon. It encompassed every side, alway remaining no matter what perspective Adda held. The sheer mass of the valley below was beyond comprehension and it left Adda dizzy trying to look at it. It seemed bigger than any continent, and perhaps, even bigger than the earth that Adda had once known. When she and Everett had initially marched across it, it had certainly felt big, but not monumentally so.

Now looking at it, Adda reviled against the idea of straying from the path. Once free of its shining aura, it would be easy to become lost forever within the ever-expanding eternity of the valley. Adda turned from it, no longer interested in being captivated by its vastness. Instead, she considered her new companion who walked just before her.

Mike moved at a pace that would be impossible for someone his age, yet he seemed unconcerned with such constraints. His slippered feet padded like a cat over the gravel, making barely a sound despite how powerful his stride was. Adda found she didn't have any trouble keeping up, however, the weight of exhaustion that had once plagued her had been stripped from her shoulders. It was as though she were back in the hills with a bottomless well of energy to draw from.

The peak loomed ahead, a short walk to finally stand upon the mountain, conquered. The white gravel stretched out wide here to create a plateau, much like the one surrounding Mike's house down below. Amidst cracks in the gravel was a thick carpet of grass and moss which flourished, though neither had any business growing at such an altitude.

On the very top of the peak in the center of the wide circle stood a lone tree.

This was the first tree Adda had seen since arriving that had any semblance of real life to it. Its trunk was wide and thick, bigger than even the redwoods Adda had once seen. Its roots sunk in deep, a tangled mess that showed this tree had no intention of being moved. Its branches raised up above it like powerful arms flexing their might far beyond its base, with leaves of brilliant green and flowers of snowy white bursting forth in beautiful life.

Amidst its mass of reaching branches, Adda could see all manner of birds gathered together. They nested and sang and preened and flew about from branch to branch in a colorful conflagration that was dizzying to behold. They adorned nearly every part of the tree like living ornaments dancing about in the firmament of leaves. The longer Adda looked, the bigger and deeper the tree appeared until she was convinced this tree was indeed as eternal as the valley or the hills beyond.

Adda gazed on in awe, aware she was looking upon something truly sacred. There was a story here, a history she knew but could barely comprehend. Such a revelation drove her to her knees, forcing her to bow her head in reverence even as her eyes desired to gaze ever on, enchanted by the infinite glory before her.

"Incredible, isn't it?" Mike asked, his own voice breathless and strained with awe and wonder.

She looked to him, seeing his own eyes were searching the branches, his expression suggesting how deep his gaze pierced into this veil of eternity. Though he had most certainly looked upon the tree countless times, it left him stricken as if seeing it for the first time.

He shook his head, turning her attention back to Adda who, in this moment, realized how small she truly was. "This tree represents the most important moments to ever happen in the entirety of all reality."

Adda's eyes slipped down the trunk, settling upon the base of the tree amidst the roots, taking in all she saw with a reverence she didn't quite understand. There, among the twisting roots, was a large pile of stones that housed tangled masses of white, brittle vines. One by one, the vines would harden and shatter, falling to take their place upon the gravel that surrounded the tree. The more she looked, the more stones appeared, coming into focus no matter where she turned her attention. She stared on, trying to make sense of the scene before her yet still missing the point. Adda looked once more to the old man, taking in his continence, his glow, and his golden eyes.

"There are so many stones here. Why?"

"In order to move beyond the mountain, one must cast off their burden. The tree gives them the power to do so." He replied matter-of-factly, his eyes entrapped by the view before them.

"It seems like everyone who goes through the caves exits with a stone attached to their arm." Adda observed, thinking back to the people of the meadow, the evidence of their hidden shame bulging against their arms. "Why was I spared?"

Mike's eyes squinted into narrow slits and he raised a hand to his brow, casting about as he looked for something. Adda tried to follow his gaze, but it was lost in the mounds of stones. Then, he pointed, his hand stretching out to stand as rigid as a sign post.

"Look there and see."

Following the indicated digit, Adda found nestled beneath a coiling root, a small mound of moss and dirt. It was impossible to actually see any part of the stone under such a thick layer of growth, yet she somehow knew in her heart this was her stone. It was clear it had been here for a very long time. So long the ground itself had reached up to claim it much like it had with her car at the beginning of this journey.

"You were not spared. You bore a great pain, one that faced

crippling tragedy and longed for vengeance and justice. These things would have grown into bitterness and would have defined your very existence. And yet, a lifetime ago, in a different form, and a different way, you approached this very tree." Mike said, his voice tinted with awe and wonder, as if such a thing were incredible to him. "You bore sand and vine and stone, all weighing you down, all trying to claim you as theirs, and despite it all, you did the thing nearly impossible. You let go."

As he spoke, memories flooded Adda's mind; of pain, loss, heartache. Of being pitied, of being looked down on, of not being allowed to grow beyond the way she was seen. Even further back, she saw the abuse, the anger, and the hatred that attempted to mold and define her. Yet, even as these things tried to take root, she had released them, mourning only until the time for mourning was done, only being angry until the time for anger was done.

"You've lived a life where people saw you as small and insignificant. You struggled with acceptance and a fear of becoming your parents." Mike continued. "But despite it all, you found a way to move forward."

She stared at the tiny lump, suddenly remembering the bite of the vines and the weight of the rock. They had once claimed her, they had once held her within their grasp. There was a moment, however, that she had dismissed them, giving over such pain to release herself from its hold.

Now, it looked so small, so inconsequential even though at the time such a decision had taken more strength than she could bear. Standing here, gazing at a thing that had ruled her for most of her life,

Adda realized how pale the valley was, how short the cave, how unsatisfying the meadow. From the town to the peak, so many things had tempted her, tried to corrupt or break her, but all of it fell away as it had no ground to walk upon. Before even arriving here, she had outgrown everything that had been cast at her.

"What was the point?" Adda asked, thinking back to the draw of the valley or the fear of the cave. "Why is it that this world is trying so hard to break me if I've already won?"

"There was- *is* a point to all of this, Adda. The first is to give you an understanding of what you're up against." Mike answered. "The second is that not all of this journey was about you."

A flashback to a chance meeting. The path, the valley, the cave, and ultimately the pool; all of those things spun around not one person, but two. Everett had hesitated at the very moment Adda needed him and had fled when he found himself too weak. So focused on herself, Adda had hardly considered Everett's role.

"But he's gone now." Adda said, "Does that mean I've failed?"

"You didn't fail, he did," Mike said, "but even in that, he learned. It is from the root of mistakes that people often grow. All we can do is wait and see what becomes of this lesson."

Mike took Adda by the arm and guided her around the tree. They passed by the trunk and Adda was nearly overwhelmed with the rich energy of life that rolled from out of it. She wanted to stop and touch it, to feel that power flow from out of its bark and into her, but she resisted the urge. Perhaps one day there would be time to linger here, but today was reserved for other things.

"But that is no longer your concern. You taught him the value of a choice, so now put him from your mind." Mike said, drawing the woman to look down the other side of the mountain. "You have overcome much, but the journey is not yet done. Go to the city and you'll find what you're looking for."

Adda looked down with him and fell to her knees for a second time as she beheld another incredible sight. The opposite side of the mountain was dramatically different from the one she had just defeated. The path still remained, carving like liquid sunlight through the mountain's face. However on this side there were no caves, no clouds, and no valley of death. Instead the path shot straight, cutting down and then out over flat, grass covered plains. It moved with unerring intent toward a single, rising hill that dominated the horizon. This hill rose from the landscape like a monolith, and though it was not the size of the mountain, it still held an incredible supremacy.

Atop it, shining like a diamond in the brilliant sun, was the city.

The city was so bright that it was difficult to look at, its spreading form glinting like a beacon to call out to all those who were lost. Even from this distance, Adda could see massive walls encompassing the entirety of its form, but unlike the town she had left far behind, this city's walls were not made of dark, tainted wood, but rather of pure pearl pulled straight from the sea. It shined every conceivable color, mesmerizing in the brilliant sun. Facing the mountain, Adda could see a massive gate swung wide, the gravel path moving directly through it, expanding wider and wider until it finally reached its destination, allowing a great host to now walk along its width. From the city, a beautiful sound could be heard dancing upon the air, a music that was so pure that it caused Adda to weep, the sound it brought inspiring a new strength to her limbs. It was a gentle sound, yet it could be heard hundreds of miles away.

It was a song of praise, of life, and of victory.

But the most awe inspiring thing about it was that Adda knew she had seen this all before. A long time ago, standing upon cliffs over a roiling ocean, she had painted this very scene.

Even though she had long suspected it, her mind still struggled to process how that was possible, that the unfinished painting she had left behind somehow was a pale reflection of what was before her now. Never in her life had she witnessed such a thing, yet her hands had foretold of this moment just the same. Looking upon all glory in front of her, Adda resolved that she would return to this place and finish that very painting.

Mike sank down next to her, nestling among the grass and moss. They sat there in silence, enjoying the view. Above their heads, birds spiraled and called, their own music mixing harmoniously with the city's' own.

"Beautiful." He breathed, a small smile cutting his face.

"Is that where you're from?" Adda asked, her voice distant.

"It's home for both of us."

Mike gripped her arm then, pulling her to her feet and called her attention away. Reluctantly, she stood with him, feeling in her The Certainty that had drawn her this far thrum like a deep chord from far within her. This was her purpose, she had been sure of it before, but now looking upon the incredible jewel below, that assuredness had grown to new heights. Since the moment she had arrived, this place had called to her and she was eager to answer it. In fact, Adda was suddenly aware she had been called by this place her entire life. It had rung in the background of every day, in the moments of pain and the moments of joy, an ever-present hum that had gotten her through the worst of it. It was the thing that had first inspired her to pick up her brush.

"I wish I could paint it." Adda said ruefully, casting another glance toward the city.

"You will." Mike assured, "But let's get you home first, yes?"

Home.

This was her home now. Deep within her, she understood why but her conscious mind still hadn't put the pieces together. It should have saddened her to think that she may never see her little house ever again, but it didn't. Instead, a profound sense of peace descended upon her shoulders and for the first time in her life, Adda felt truly free.

Mike led them back down the side of the mountain toward his little cottage. She followed along dutifully, feeling like a child walking in the footsteps of her father. The trip back down was one of contemplative silence. There were many miles left to walk, but Adda could feel a sense of finality weighing the air. This would be the last leg of her journey, a fact that made her become reflective.

They drifted into Mike's home, moving beyond the beaded doorway, and back into the main living area. Adda's gaze drifted around the house and fell once again on the small table in the middle of the room. Two cups still remained there, flanking a half-played game.

"I was meaning to ask." Adda said, "Does someone else live with you? The table looks like it was set for two."

"How observant!" Mike said, "No, I live alone, though I often have friends visit me from the city. I do make a good cup of tea, after all."

No arguments from Adda on that one.

"We didn't realize you would be up so soon, so with you waking up, he took his leave." He continued.

"Oh, I'm sorry, I didn't mean to interrupt anything."

"It's perfectly fine! You'll have to make it up to me by dropping by for a visit sometime." Mike said, flashing her a broad grin.

He seemed confident that the remainder of her journey would go off without a hitch and that confidence bolstered Adda's own. So focused she had been on getting to the city she hadn't really taken the time to consider what might be after. This journey might be coming to an end, but it most certainly didn't mean others wouldn't begin. The possibilities rolled within Adda's mind as she followed Mike deeper into his house.

They stepped through another one of the beaded curtains and into a kitchen. Within was a quaint table, small cupboards, a stone countertop, and a chest that looked to be an ice box. Opening a cupboard, Mike pulled forth a loaf of bread that steamed as though it had just come out of an oven rather than the wooden shelf within. The smell struck Adda's nose and her stomach immediately growled which pulled forth another chuckle from Mike.

"Oh my, I'm sorry that we didn't stop to eat before going up to the peak! You sound famished!"

Adda laughed, clutching her stomach in an attempt to quiet the irate gurgling that continued to emanate from it. "I guess you could say that."

Pulling a knife from a drawer, he swiftly cut slices from the bread. The crust crackled with a delightful sound as Mike carved large chunks from the loaf. After pulling a few free, he let them cool on the counter as he began to fish around in another cupboard. From there he pulled out a bottle of a reddish liquid. Wine, Adda realized, as the man uncorked it and poured it into another one of those clay cups. Gathering the bread onto a plate, he carried both bread and wine to the table, setting them down and indicating to Adda to take a seat. Following his direction, she settled in while he sat across from her.

Upon the table rested a tiny jar with a utensil's handle sticking out. Removing the lid, Mike pulled the implement forth to reveal golden honey oozing around one end of the tool. With a gentle, practiced motion, Mike drizzled the honey across the bread. It glinted in the sunlight that poured through a nearby window, its sweetened scent tangling delectably with the bread's own. Mike then offered the cup of wine and the bread to her, taking some for himself as well.

Adda bit into the bread, her body coming to life as it rolled around in her mouth, causing her tastebuds to explode in joy. It tasted like warmth, like coming home after a long time spent away. The sweetness of the honey paired perfectly with the blended grains in the bread, coming together in the most satisfying of ways. Taking the cup, Adda sipped the wine and reveled at the mild, nutty taste of the liquid. It danced along with the rest of the flavors in her mouth, a harmony of food and drink that she had never before tasted in her life.

"With this bread and this wine, you shall never know hunger or thirst again." Mike spoke over their meal, delivering a blessing as she continued to eat. "Though you will enjoy such things as you see fit, you are now forever freed from the need of them."

Mike then lifted his own cup up and toasted her. The words weren't delivered as an old man to a painter, but rather a lord's blessing upon the shoulders of his most trusted warrior.

His voice rang out, brilliant and low. "The hills are filled with shadows, the valley with death, and the caves with fear. Despite this, the pool has cleansed you, the tree has freed you, and this meal has strengthened you. You have overcome it all and so fear has departed from you. You are forever free, Adda Reinhoff."

"Thank you." Adda said, feeling the gravity of the moment.

The words washed over her like a warm wave, filling her up with determination to finish what she had set out to do. A part of her certainly wanted to stay behind, to learn of this world from Mike and live in such a warm place forever, but she knew there was more to do. From the moment she had set foot in the hills, the city had called to her, tugging on her like an invisible thread. She knew that was where she had been fated to go and so she would delay no longer. The call beckoning all the louder, Adda rose, addressing Mike.

"I'm ready now."

"You always were." Mike replied.

He also stood, moving around from his side of the table and stretched out his arms to embrace her. The man caught her up in a warm, familial hug and Adda sank into it. They stood there for a while, arms tight, before Mike broke away, giving her a broad smile.

"My child, remember, these elements that you've encountered are things you've already overcome. The valley, cave, pool, and tree.

They've all already been a part of your story long before you arrived here. I want you to remember that as you take on this final leg of your journey."

Adda searched this strange man's face, trying to decipher the hidden depths of what he might mean. Her understanding was partial, trying to bring the puzzle together so she could finally look back and see what she was missing. The pieces were all there, she just needed to figure out the shape of them so that they might finally be complete. A thousand questions ran through her mind, all of them seeking the solution she knew she already had, but couldn't yet fathom. There was much to ask, but Adda held her tongue. Whatever it was she needed to figure out, it seemed as though it was on her shoulders alone to put it together.

"I'll remember that." Adda assured the man.

His smile broadened and then he ushered them from the room.

"Wait here." He said, leaving her in the main living area and moving into the room that she had woken in.

He was gone but a moment before returning with a blue, leather satchel with tufts of white fur along its outside. It was fashioned in such a way that it would rest on her hips, putting it in easy reach if she needed it. There were a number of straps and buckles upon it which seemed to serve no obvious function.

Mike offered it to her. "I believe this belongs to you."

Giving him a quizzical look, Adda took the gift, immediately feeling the weight of an object housed within. She reached down and loosened the satchel's mouth to take a peek inside. There, nestled as the sole occupant amidst the hardened interior was the small, wooden box with that familiar indented symbol. Reaching in, she pulled the box out so that she could slide its lid free. Within the confines of the box she had taken so far was that same well-loved book. To her surprise, neither box nor book seemed to have suffered any kind of damage.

"I thought the pool took it!" Adda said in awe.

"No, the pool strips away what holds us back, it cleanses you of your trappings." Mike said, "This most certainly isn't holding you back, so the pool returned it."

"There's something I've been wondering." Adda said as she strapped the bag onto her waist before returning the box to rest within it. "If you hadn't come along, would I have drowned?"

"Oh Adda," Mike chuckled, "You already know you can't drown here."

And that was all he would say on the matter.

With that, they both pushed past the beaded doorway to the outside. It clicked and clattered pleasantly, lingering on Adda's shoulders as if to say its own farewell. Adda and Mike shared a few more words, but it was clear it was time for her to go.

After assuring one another they would see each other again, they both said their final goodbyes and then Adda broke away. She walked confidently up the trail toward the mountain's peak and the tree that dwelled there. The moment she rounded the bend, Adda found herself standing mere yards from the mountain's top even though the last time she had hiked it had taken far longer.

Adda paused on the mountain's peak, turning to look back. She allowed her gaze to be pulled far, seeing all the people that were still figuring out what kind of world they had stumbled upon. For a moment she thought to look for Everett or Bethany, but she knew if she were to divine their whereabouts, then she would turn around in an instant to go find them.

No, their journey was their own for now, she had something she needed to do.

"I'll come back for you." Adda said into the sky, her voice strong, confident, sure.

The wind swirled about her and picked up, whipping into a brief frenzy before dying out down once again. With a nod and an about-face, Adda turned to make her descent from the mountain and into whatever this world held for her next.

Far below in a meadow, Everett stirred briefly, thinking he heard a voice on the wind that sounded familiar. He tried to rise, to draw himself up the mountain toward his friend, but hands reached out and clutched at him. They gently drew him back into the grass where they thrusted daisies into his hands so he might help continue making flower crowns. Everett returned to his task, the familiar voice falling into the back of his mind.

5

The mountain bent down away from Adda, leading her on a direct path toward its base. Once again, the road went straight as an arrow with no deviation, yet this time the mountain made no effort to intervene. It stood to the side, allowing the traveler easy access. There were times the track led her down areas that were so sheer it would have been impossible for her to normally tread it. Yet the path reached up to her, and where it met her feet, she found she could easily stand despite the act being in direct violation of physics. She never tripped, never misstepped, and she never fell even as she stood almost perpendicular to the face of a wall.

It seemed no matter the obstacle, the gravel beneath her feet would not lead her astray.

Adda longed to be in the city, but she purposefully slowed her pace, allowing herself to drink in the sights around her. She had spent so much of her life in one place that she wanted to take the time to enjoy this leg of her journey. Besides, after all the threats she had overcome, Adda wanted to see what this world had to offer outside its many dangers.

She wandered past a waterfall, her own form sticking straight from the wall so the thundering water appeared like a river flowing beside her. She could almost convince herself of that fact save that Adda could see where the water separated from the mountain. It whipped past her at a pace inspired by gravity to slam with great force into the ground in the distance. Beautiful rainbows were thrown high into the sky in beautiful rings as the sunlight's rays danced in and out of the droplets to create this natural art. The colors were more brilliant than those she had ever seen, leaving her to look on in awe at the dazzling display.

Reaching the bottom of this particular cliff, Adda once again was level, standing on the edge of a pool that had formed where the waterfall had ended. She stopped there and watched the roiling water come descending down with impossible force. The spray felt cool and refreshing on her skin.

Adda leaned into the rolling mist, letting out a long sigh. She looked down into the water below her, watching the ripples spread out and begin to calm. To her joy, and surprise, she saw the sleek, grey bodies of fish slipping about the pool where the water was less chaotic.

Getting down on her hands and knees, she scooted up to the water's edge, gazing in fascination as they darted this way and that on the hunt for food. On the opposite side of the mountain, Adda had seen no evidence of any living animal outside the dove that had appeared or the birds from the infinite tree. It warmed her heart to see things were alive and going about their existence as if any kind of hardship was not a mountain away.

She watched them for a moment longer before dragging herself away, eager to see what else she could find.

Her footsteps became lighter as she moved along, so at ease with her surroundings. Everywhere she turned, she could see all manner of beauty peeking out. On top of the mountain, the city had so occupied the center of her attention she hadn't managed to look anywhere else. Now, as she progressed ever onward, details began to spill out toward her.

Immediately around Adda, all manner of wild flowers, both on stem and bush, had sprung up to encircle her. Their tiny faces were turned upward to soak in the rays of the brilliant sun far above their heads. Just like the rainbow from the waterfall, the flowers captured color in a way that felt impossible. They virtually glowed with an inner light with how deep and lush their colors were.

Crowding together, they created a natural masterpiece Adda could only dream of being able to put down onto a canvas. The reds, yellows, blues, purples, oranges, they all danced and collided against one another across patches of vibrant green. Their motion created a mesmerizing tapestry of living color.

Beyond them, scattered amidst this other valley, were genuine forests of all manner of trees, knitting together their mighty heads to create a roof of leaf, flower, and nettle. Their trunks sat wide apart, allowing sunlight to easily find its way to the low growing vegetation of the forest floor. It was a great distance away, but Adda could easily see a herd of deer weaving in and out of the tree line, leading stumbling fawns behind them as they moved boldly about the underbrush.

Further on, a lake spilled out, being fed a river that appeared from beneath the city's wall. It glinted like blue sapphire in the bright day, shapes of great fish could be seen breaching the surface before vanishing once more into the depths. The lake was massive and spread around the many forests that dotted the landscape before vanishing around the foothills of further mountains.

These mountains, unlike the lone peak that she had just summited, were a mighty range, stretching out to run perpendicular to the hill on which the city rested. Where the mountain she was leaving had inspired feelings of ominous foreboding, these frosted peaks projected might, challenge, and true adventure. The colossal wall cut an awesome swath behind the scene, occupying much of the skyline with its powerful form.

Everywhere she looked there was something more to see. This place was a true paradise, unlike the false one constructed by the valley far behind her. There were no double images and no luring temptations, everything was exactly as it was. Even the air was purer here and every breath in brought a sense of wellness and profound peace. It settled into her bones and she felt herself relax into its hold.

A sigh escaped her lips and Adda found herself to be truly content in the moment. She could spend a lifetime here, looking down over everything that sprawled out before her and never want for more.

As much as she wanted to stay, it was the hum of the city that kept her feet moving. It was the only thing that could draw her away from such an image.

Soon, her feet left the side of the mountain and began to walk across the flat expanse before her. To her delight, Adda saw that just as around the tree, the grass grew unimpeded through the gravel beneath her. On a whim, she took off her shoes, letting her feet nestle against the grass that pushed up from the ground like a thick carpet. The gravel did not bite her feet, instead it pressed warmly against her bare soles, heated by the sun. Her eyes closed and she dug her toes into the grass and stone beneath her, feeling the tiny blades tickle lightly against her skin.

Adda drank in this moment, allowing her senses to get carried away from her. A profound feeling of peace fell upon her shoulders, warming from without and within. She had experienced such a thing in her life before, but never to such an extent as it felt now. It was starting to feel as though the things she had once known were but shadows of a deeper truth. She had always believed such a thing to be true, but to experience it first hand was remarkable.

A thought stirred deep in her mind, the mystery of this world coming close to the surface of consciousness. Adda knew she was close now, there was an understanding that was finally coming together. Yet, before she had time to reach out and pull the thing up from the depths, one of her far flung senses detected something. Adda's eyes sprang open as her brain registered the sensation.

It was the smell of burning.

It had been subtle at first, slinking around the currents of the air, attempting to avoid alerting the woman to its presence. As it grew in strength, it could no longer hide its form, so a wisp of its acrid scent danced along the inside of her nose. There was nothing pleasant about the way it smelled, not like wood popping merrily in a fire. No, it was closer to the smell of melted rubber mixed with burning hair. It was appalling, a deviant in this realm of perfection.

Casting about, she quickly found the source of the smell. There, in the distance, a thin plume of wicked smoke cut through the sky, twisting like a rearing viper, ready to strike. Following the smoke down to its source, Adda could make out at the base of the hill, standing in the center of the path, was a large figure.

The figure was facing toward her, though it was hard to make out any other details. Adda tried to get her eyes to draw close to it, just as she had on the mountain, but any attempt was blotted out by a veil of smoke that billowed thicker with every moment.

With nothing else to do, Adda slipped her shoes back on and began to walk toward this next trial. There was no hesitation in her stride or second-guessing in her stance, having left those things behind in an icy pool. It didn't matter who this was or what they wanted, Adda only had one goal and there was nothing that could get in her way.

With boldness she approached her next challenge, ready for whatever was thrown at her. Her head spun as thoughts began to race through her mind with all the possibilities that could occur. Focusing her attention, she forced out the thoughts, choosing instead to let things unfurl as they came. This world was too unpredictable to try and guess what might come next, better to leave the brain power to the action.

As she approached, two things became apparent.

The first was that the figure was far bigger than she had anticipated. From the distance she had been at, the depth had held the figure's height a mystery. Now that she was approaching (and far faster than she had expected) she found the figure hulked above eight feet tall.

It was a man, though a brute of form. He stood with thick muscles that added a bulk to his already mountainous height. The man's skin was the color of stone, appearing a grey-blue that acted as a natural camouflage and was distinctly unnatural. His body was wrapped in animal skins similar to the ones she had seen back in the wicked village used to pin up over doorways. They were laced together by thick cords that hung loosely from wherever their thread ended. Adorning them was a mixture of animal and human skulls.

Looking up, the ogre's head was nearly lost beneath a helm made of another skull, this one belonging to a creature that looked like a cow's but it was far bigger than any beast she had ever seen. In a hand, he held a white, glinting knife that formed a cruel curve to its blade, wielded at the ready.

The second thing that Adda noticed was that there was, in fact, a second figure on the road. This figure was far smaller than the hulking man behind it and was being held in place by the giant's other, powerful hand. This figure stood limp, their head hanging down in a look of defeat. Their clothes were bedraggled, torn in all manner of places with a thick layer of sand clutching to every available surface. The figure stirred as she approached, looking up under a tangle of dirty hair to peek out at Adda.

The moment their eyes met, Adda's heart dropped.

It was Bethany.

6

"Stop." The giant's voice boomed like a cannon and brought the knife down to hover next to the young girl's throat.

Adda complied, trying to keep herself calm. Her heart thumped in her chest like a wild animal seeking escape. Her mind argued that this wasn't happening, that this had to be some kind of illusion sent to bar her path one final time.

But no, she knew that this was far too real.

They stood perhaps twenty feet apart, sizing one another up. Neither moved an inch as the silence stretched on between them, growing heavier by the moment. Bethany's breath came in ragged gasps as her eyes looked wildly on toward the other woman.

"Mrs. Reinhoff, please." Her voice came out thin and pleading, her body trembling against the powerful frame that stooped over her.

"Quiet." The giant growled, using his hand to jerk her head back, exposing her throat all the more to the hungry knife.

The blade glinted with vile intention, practically squirming in the giant's hand in an attempt to lunge at its victim's throat. Adda's gaze flickered to the knife and then back to the giant's own heavy eyes that rested on her. His focus was zeroed in on her as if gauging what she would do next. The giant cut a horrifying visage, but it wasn't the appearance of the cruel figure that was so jarring.

It was the monster's eyes.

One might be tempted to think the vacant eyes of the dead are the most horrendous to behold. Indeed, such a glazed, hollowed look is something all of humanity fears. It reminds us of the inevitable end, the spark of life being cruelly cut short to leave nothing but a void behind. To imagine such emptiness pooling in eyes searching a person's own seems like it would perhaps be the most awful thing anyone could ever witness. But Adda knew better now, there was something worse than facing the void of death.

This giant's eyes were filled with spark, vigor, and life, but it was a flame built in the foundry of cruelty and perfected by the hand of malice. Those eyes reflected a hatred so deep Adda instantly knew there was not a human on earth capable of such a thing. They were eyes that had committed countless atrocities and would do so again without hesitation. To those eyes, death was too gentle a punishment, they wanted to feast upon torment. They had seen plague, disease, famine, pain, and hopelessness, and it still wasn't enough.

Those eyes fell upon her now and she could feel the eternal expanse of loathing that floated within those infernal pits weighing her in utter contempt. It wasn't a hatred against her race, or gender, or upbringing, or social standing, or career, or anything she had ever said or done.

This hatred hated *her.*

It *knew* her.

It had known her her entire life, watching her grow, and change, and become, and it hated her for it. This giant knew her as assuredly as Mike knew her, but whereas the old man greeted her with open arms, this entity welcomed her with a knife.

Adda knew this was a Snatcher. It had to be. This was the thing everyone had feared so much and, finally, she could understand why. To imagine running through the hills being pursued by such creatures formed a pit in Adda's stomach.

There was a moment between the two of them, an unspoken recognition. As much as this thing knew her, Adda realized she knew it. As if reading her thoughts, the giant smiled, his yellowed teeth barred wolfishly, his brow arching up to let his eyes grow wild.

"You've come so far-"

"Let her go." Adda cut him off, her voice level even as her hands shook.

"Now, now, there's no need to be so demanding." The giant hissed, sinking grey fingers into Bethany's hair and pulling her head back further.

This elicited a whimper from Bethany but she made no further attempts to speak. The giant trailed his knife down the girl's throat, his face taking on a crazed look.

"Such a pretty neck, it would be a shame to mar it, don't you think?" He said.

A thin line of red suddenly appeared under the point of the blade, a puncture that let a ribbon of blood spring free. Tears ran down Bethany's face, her hands balled into fists at her sides as she shook like a leaf. Still, the girl didn't speak, terrified of the consequences.

"Stop." Adda commanded, her tone sharp.

The giant scowled at this, clearly irritated by her reaction. He pulled himself to his full height and glowered down at Adda. The monster pointed the blade at her, the tip red and dripping. The blood fell onto the white gravel, staining the otherwise pure path.

"You should have stayed in that little town." He smirked before letting out a barking laugh. "Hidden behind those pathetic walls, maybe we might have let you live a life there, a queen of dirt and mud."

"Do you find something amusing?"

"No, of course not, I would never laugh at the great Adda Reinhoff." The giant mocked, cocking his head to the side.

The creature's neck creaked and cracked with the motion, sounding like a great, wooden ship stuck at sea. It was a painful sound, but it appeared to not bother the thing in the slightest.

"You think so highly of yourself for one so often abandoned." He said, and when Adda didn't respond, it goaded the giant to continue. "Yes, the list of people that have left you behind is long and tiresome. If you're so special, then why is it that you're so easy to leave?"

The giant nodded, bringing the knife up to his face and tapping the flat of the blade against his cheek, as if in thought. His grip tightened on Bethany's hair, pulling another ragged sob from her.

"Your family, your friends, even the children you pretend are yours have left you. I mean, try as you may, Everett ran the very moment it fell on him to lift you up. After everything you did, after everything *you* overcame, he abandoned you the second you needed him. Doesn't that

415

make you sad? Angry?"

Adda's hands had balled into tight fists, her breath coming unevenly from her lungs. Her body wanted her to run, but she stayed in place, keenly aware of Bethany's plight. She knew physically she stood no chance against this thing, but there was something deep within her that was finally beginning to fall together, becoming a picture that would lead her to understanding.

"What do you want?" Adda finally said, her mind working in overtime.

"Very little, as it turns out." The giant looked down at the girl, his slate eyes gleaming with the temptation of inflicting agony, but he refrained.

He shifted back toward Adda.

"I'll release this poor, mewling creature into your custody if you promise to turn back and never return to this side of the mountain."

"That's it?"

He nodded, "I'm feeling generous"

"So," Adda spoke slowly, stalling for time as her mind mulled over her journey. "What you're saying is that you'll let her and me go if I just turn back, climb over the mountain, and never return?"

"Yes, that's what I said." The giant grunted, his eyes narrowing.

"And if I refuse?"

The giant's eyes went wild again, the fires of worlds burning stoked deep within as the bonfire of malice erupted. The knife hissed down faster than Adda could react, carving a clear path around toward Bethany's neck. There was a scream and the metal pulled short, hardly an inch from slicing a fatal wound into the teen's body. Bethany went limp in the giant's grasp, her body shuddering from the close call.

The girl's scream still echoed out around them as the giant spoke again. "Then her blood is on your hands."

Adda found herself to be suddenly calm. The tension left her shoulders, allowing her to breathe evenly once again, her hands unclenched, and her jaw relaxed. She knew the threat should have left her afraid; terrified of losing this young girl that she considered in many ways to be her own daughter. Yet, instead the fear began to roll free from her as that Certainty deep within her began to slowly climb its way to the surface. The fear wasn't hers, it couldn't own her anymore.

And that's when it started to click.

"Why are you holding her hostage?" Adda mumbled to herself.

"Do we have a deal?" The giant asked, his voice hardening with impatience.

"Why are you holding her hostage?" Adda asked again, this time addressing the giant.

Not waiting for an answer, Adda continued, feeling the puzzle coming together as she spoke.

"If you wanted to kill me, there's nothing I could physically do to stop you. I mean, look at you! Yet instead of coming after me, you make threats and hold a teenage girl as a bargaining chip." Another piece settled into its groove. "You're threatened by me."

The Snatcher threw back his head and laughed. The laugh boomed out around them, heavy and barking with amusement. The sound echoed out, filling the air with his mocking timber. Then he snapped forward once again, mouth set in a curve of disgust, and nostrils flaring with rage.

"You dare insult me?"

"You haven't answered my question." Adda crossed her arms, scowling back at the giant.

He looked at her, surprise momentarily gliding across his face. This was not going how he had planned. That surprise doubled back into his mounting wrath.

"You insolent piece of chaff." The giant pointed his knife at her. "I'll give you one more chance to come to your senses."

"Why are you holding her hostage?" Adda asked again, not backing down.

His knuckles tightened around his knife, eyes wide, mouth grimacing, jaw clenched, body trembling, infuriated by this woman who had the audacity to stand so boldly before him. "I'm going to kill you."

"You *can't* kill me." Adda said defiantly.

The moment those words passed her lips, realization finally dawned on her. It had all started back in her home, the one that lay so far behind her now. She remembered those last few days before the military had rolled in and evacuated them all.

The birds had abandoned town and the fish swam back from the coast. There had been the difficulty breathing, the headaches, and the metallic bite that had tainted the water. There had been the farmhouse feeling off, an entire town suddenly missing, and her car falling apart before her eyes. There had been the moment where all the physical issues Adda had been struggling with had suddenly vanished as she walked through the hills.

Then there were all those extra people from outside her town. There was Lorelei, Thomas, and Leri. There were all the other nameless bodies that were running through the hills, tempted by the valley, captured by the cave, and ignorant in the meadow. They had helped her realize that whatever had happened to her was somehow happening everywhere else as well.

In fact, Adda realized, it had always been happening since the very beginning of humanity.

With all these thoughts swirling together, the picture was finally completed. Adda stared into this revelation, surprised she hadn't figured it out earlier.

"You can't kill me." Adda said again, her hand slipping into her satchel to trace the indented symbol on the wooden box.

It was burned hot beneath her fingers.

"Because I'm already dead."

7

The silence that followed those words was heavy. It fell upon them like a thick fog, weighed down by a mounting tension. The giant didn't move to refute Adda, he just stood there, an unreadable look on his face. The longer the silence held, the more her statement became concrete, solidifying in her mind as everything she had come across began to make more sense.

The impossibilities of this world started to seem a little less impossible.

"Let her go." Adda said as she took a defiant step toward the giant.

Fear had departed Adda forever as the truth finally shone its light into every recess within her. It chased every dark thought from her until all that remained was the constant, thrumming Certainty. In that moment, Adda became truly free as the limitations she had set around herself were finally torn away.

"Don't come any closer." The Snatcher hissed.

Remarkably, as Adda's mind tore into this new understanding, the giant that was before her began to change. *He* had become an *it*, and it was rapidly diminishing before her. Its once imposing height began to melt away. Soon the thing stood barely above Bethany's head, its fingers still tangled in her hair, the other holding tightly onto its knife.

The details of the creature also began to wisp away, being stolen from it with every gentle breeze that pushed past them. It became shadowy and near translucent, taking on a similar look to the homes in the Snatcher village she had passed through so long ago. The creature's true nature was finally revealed.

Beneath the almost human features that had once adorned its visage, was that of a skulking, cruel looking creature. It was made of tattered wings and bloodshot eyes, with spindly limbs like the branches of a dead tree clawing at the sky. With every movement, dusty feathers would hiss and whisper as its wings would rub together like the legs of a cricket. It had too many arms that seemed to disappear as quickly as they appeared from beneath its cloak of feathers. The thing was vastly different from the grey giant who had confronted her, yet there was no doubt it was the same entity. Every one of its many eyes remained focused on Adda, each wielding that horrible loathing, that personal hatred, like a deadly weapon.

Adda took another step.

Its skeletal arms wrapped around Bethany all the more and the girl began to sob uncontrollably, no longer able to keep it in. The knife settled its point once again on the girl's neck, a frenzied pallor coming over the creature.

"You're so clever." It hissed, extra arms twisting and cracking, wings flexing like a bird trying to make itself look bigger in the face of a predator. "You think you have it all figured out."

Another step.

The creature made a clicking sound, as if a great multitude of heavy beaks or claws were opening and closing rapidly. It was a nervous sound.

"You might know," the creature snarled, its voice becoming more and more deranged.

It shifted its many eyes to Bethany, a cruel sheen flickering like fire deep within its recesses.

"But she doesn't!"

In a single, deft motion, the Snatcher drew its hand along the girl's throat.

The knife followed the act, biting eagerly into the offered flesh. Bethany gave out a strangled cry and her eyes went wide. The Snatcher then gave the girl a shove, letting her fall to the white gravel. Laying face down, Bethany raised her hands to her throat in a vain attempt to stem the flow of blood escaping the gaping wound.

All this happened so fast that Adda hardly had the time to process it. It was a horrible thing to see, but Adda found herself going still. Very still. Adda expected to be taken in by a feeling of panic and fear yet neither rose to meet her. Instead, she found herself filled with a deep sadness.

And, a great anger.

Adda took another step forward. The Snatcher reared up as she approached, holding the wet blade high, threatening to stab at her should she draw too close.

Adda looked at the thing in utter contempt. It had been beaten, its secrets revealed, and yet, in a final, cruel attempt at victory, the creature had lashed out. Did it really think that it could still win? Shaking her head, Adda turned her attention to Bethany as she addressed the Snatcher.

"Leave."

Her voice was calm, even, and filled with an undeniable power. Never in her life had she felt such a commanding tone escape her lips and yet it was her voice that spoke. The words rippled through the air, causing the world to warp around her momentarily as something fulfilled her desire. Adda didn't even have to turn to know that the Snatcher was now gone, whisked away to wherever it had come from.

With a gentle hand, Adda reached down and began to stroke the side of Bethany's face, her heart heavy to see such agony there. It was one thing for Adda to understand, it was another thing entirely to try and get this frightened girl to believe. Bethany's eyes flickered wildly over to Adda's own, tears falling in streams while she gasped for breath. Up close, Adda could see grains of sand crusted onto her face and arms.

"Bethany, it's going to be alright." Adda said, her voice comforting.

She placed a hand over Bethany's own as they clutched against the tide of red.

"I need you to let go."

Bethany made a strangled sound, her forehead screwing together as her body wracked with sobs. She shook her head, trembling in fear. Her face was starting to become extremely pale. Adda then wondered if it was possible for Bethany to die a second time if she believed it to be. What would happen in such a situation? The woman wasn't going to wait around and find out.

"Alright, I'm going to pick you up." Adda said, searching the other's eyes for the spark of understanding. "We're going to get you into the city and get you some help. Just keep fighting for a little longer, ok?"

With a look of confirmation, Adda threaded her arms under Bethany's legs and around the girl's back. Counting to three, she stood, taking on the full weight of the quaking form as Adda got her feet underneath her.

In lifting the girl, Adda's eyes swam as she caught sight of something beyond.

It was Bethany, running as fast as she could, crying as the sound of heavy feet thundered around her. She chanced a look back, seeing a wall of giants charging after her, eager for the hunt as they laughed and taunted her. The hills rolled around her as she ran faster and faster. There was no direction to her flight, it was simply away from the horrid monsters that ran after her.

Adda pushed through the vision and staggered up the hill as she bore this precious burden toward sanctuary.

In response, the sand upon Bethany's body pulled downward with great intensity, gaining weight with every step she took. It didn't collect itself onto Adda, but the grains rolled themselves across the girl's body to form growing clumps. The clumps began to gain mass with every moment, making Adda's task become increasingly more difficult.

One step at a time. Adda thought to herself.

She took a step, then another.

But it was no use.

The weight drove the woman to her knees, slamming them against the white gravel. There was a ghost of pain, but Adda ignored it, letting it slip through her just as the fear had. She no longer belonged to it.

Bethany had gone still in Adda's arms, the blood leaking from her neck slowing down to a thin trickle. It was hot and sticky against Adda's arms and shirt. The poor girl was giving into the pain, falling away into some deeper darkness. Adda remembered Everett, lost in the caves. She remembered the moment she had found him, so confused by the trappings of the past and of how she had helped lift his stone with him. No matter how heavy it had been, she had found just enough strength to push herself forward.

"Hang on a little longer." Adda whispered into the Bethany's ear. "We're almost there."

Setting her shoulders, Adda pushed against the sand, feeling her body strain as it contended with incredible weight. With a grunt, she got one foot under her. Adda rested upon it a moment, catching her breath as she prepared for the next move. With another grunt, Adda shoved upward. She threw her entire strength into her legs, willing them to rise up against this burden. With great effort, Adda stood once more, trembling as though the weight of the world were collapsing in on her.

Despite this, she did not crumple.

She would not fall again.

"Did I ever tell you how much I always looked forward to painting with you?" Adda asked, not meaning to speak, but finding the words spilling out of her as she drew toward the gates at a painstakingly slow pace. "It was the highlight of my week. I loved being able to guide you and watch you grow into your gift. I have so much more I want to teach you."

They approached the gate and Bethany stirred in her arms, letting loose a whimper of pain. Fresh blood spilled free.

"We're almost there, love, we'll get past those gates and you'll finally be safe."

The sand suddenly lunged forward in a desperate bid. It began to pop and fizzle as it came in contact with Adda's skin, being burned away by some inner power. Yet for every grain that crumpled away, two more took its place. They bit into her, needling her with a thousand, tiny cuts. Though the pain was a ghost, unable to actually stop her, the attack managed to slow her progress as their terrible weight increased ten-fold.

When that didn't stop her, the sand assaulted Adda with images of Bethany's life. They bore the girl's every burden like a club, slamming them against Adda's mind over and over again. The world warped, slipping between the gravel path and Bethany's history.

It was growing difficult to not get swept away by the teen's pain.

"Remember that last day in the kitchen?" Adda asked, using the words to stay focused on the moment. "You asked me if we're real or if life was all just a simulation?"

Bethany was growing cold in Adda's arms, her lips taking on a grayish tint. The blood had slowed even more, leaving the poor thing pale and empty. She wasn't dying, she couldn't die again, but seeing Bethany this way tore at Adda's heart.

"The pain, the fear, the death, it's all real. Everything we've been through, every challenge we've overcome, it's all real. But none of those things own you anymore." Tears sprung into Adda's eyes. "Please, hold on, we're so close."

She wasn't certain whether Bethany could hear her or not, but she didn't know what else to do. So Adda kept talking, hoping that some word or phrase might trigger the truth in the girl's mind.

"We died. The day the military came was the beginning of the end." Adda wheezed out.

The crest of the hill blotted the sky before them, but Adda could now see the beginnings of the arch of the gates standing atop the hill. They were so close, only a few more minutes and they'd arrive.

"But it was also the start of something new, something better! I know your body is telling you you're dying, but you have to fight that instinct, nothing is what it was. Come on, girlie, you gotta wake up."

Bethany still didn't respond, her body limp and nearly too heavy to bear. Another step and Adda found that her knees had begun to buckle again. She could feel her feet slowly slipping out from underneath her, unable to keep traction on the graveled surface. They were so close.

Adda came to a halt, unsure of what to do. If she took another step she was sure that her footing would finally give and that she would fall. But Adda also refused to let the girl go, not wanting to risk losing her in a tumble. So the sand and the woman stood at an impasse, both struggling against the other, frozen in place. The sand bit, and burned, and tugged against her. The woman stood there, taking every ounce of punishment with gritted teeth.

Was this her destiny? To be caught so close to salvation as a statue, doomed to stand holding a dying girl for all eternity?

No. Adda thought *This is not the end.*

And so she did the only thing she could think of.

She called out.

Her voice rang out across the world around her, like a bell breaking the sleep of morning to announce a new day. It was a plea, a cry in desperation for the sake of another. Her voice bounced up the hill and tumbled across the walls of pearl that rose before her.

"Help me!"

Even as the words left her mouth, the Certainty swelled within her chest, igniting like a newborn sun, basking the darkness of space in its life giving light. It swelled in her until it reverberated through every cell in her body. Her back straightened, her legs went still, and the sand lurched away as a wave of heat shoved them back from her skin. A well of unfathomable strength opened up within her, flooding every inch of her with its power. For a moment she was tempted to resume her hike, but the Certainty told her to wait, and so, she did.

And not a moment later, her silence was rewarded by the sound of feet crunching across gravel, kicking it up as they moved urgently toward her. From over the crest of the hill a group of people suddenly appeared, running toward the two travelers.

They were nothing like what Adda had envisioned.

It was a group of eight men and women that approached. Adda had expected them to be swathed in white silks and golden broaches, or at least something modern like the clothes she wore. These people were dressed in attire that made them appear that they were on their way to a 1920s themed party. In fact, Adda now wondered if these people actually were from the 1920s.

"Give her here." One of the men said as they approached, his voice gentle.

Without even questioning the request, Adda let the man slide his arms around Bethany and draw her to his chest. The sand still held thick to Bethany, yet the man seemed to not even notice the colossal weight that bore against him.

They moved with urgency, yet none of them acted in a way that would suggest panic. In fact, not even as much as a look of concern appeared on any of their faces as they went about gathering Bethany up.

One of the women unwound a long, beautiful scarf from about her shoulders. She then pressed the fabric against Bethany's throat, clutching one of the young girl's hands in her own. "You're safe now, child, you can wake up."

Adda watched in awe as the girl immediately stirred, making a small sound of distress, her eyelids fluttering as she struggled to lift up her head. The woman's scarf was already beginning to darken against the flow of blood, but miraculously, color was sweeping up across Bethany's face. In a single second, she had gone from looking like a corpse to being flushed with rich life. The girl was extremely disoriented, but had regained consciousness.

"Come on, both of you need to get into the city." The man holding Bethany said.

He spoke to Adda, but his gaze never faltered from the girl, a look that could only be described as familial plastered on his face. Again, in full trust of these people, Adda nodded her head and followed the small group back up the hill toward the city. They gave off the same air as Mike, this easy-going, safe continence, yet with some incredible power stirring just below the surface.

The hill fell away, the path widening to reveal the fullness of the gate splayed open before her. Nothing in life, or after, could have ever prepared her for this view. Even this description, try as it may, cannot accurately describe what lay before Adda, for there are not the words in all the languages in all the worlds that can possibly even hope to capture the smallest fraction of the beauty that resided within the very nature of this city.

Though it can only be a glimpse of what Adda saw, this is what lay before her.

Rising above them, the walls were made of a stone like jasper that was clear as crystal. The walls glowed with some inner radiance, casting out a light so pure it would perhaps blind anyone who looked upon it with eyes made in another world. It acted like a great magnifying glass, projecting a powerful light stronger than that of even the sun. Adda's new eyes had no trouble gazing upon it and drank in every last bit.

The city invited her in, the gate knowing no stranger as it allowed all who walked the path easy passage. The gate basked in the brilliant light all around it, reflecting a rainbow of color in every direction. It was made of thousands upon thousands of ethereal pearls, each one shining with a great radiance.

Ahead of the party, the white gravel reached the edge of the gate before melding seamlessly into the ground, blending completely into the street beyond. The streets on the other side of the gate was made of a substance that shone like gold, yet was translucent like glass. From within that glass, more light erupted in triumphant glory, casting the entire city in a rich, golden color.

While Adda paused to stare in wonder, the woman who had given her scarf to Bethany looped her arm through Adda's own and pulled them close together. The way the woman stood with her made Adda feel as though she were in fact standing with her best friend, rather than a perfect stranger.

The woman smiled at her, and gave a wink. "Would you believe that it's not even finished yet?"

With a squeeze on her arm, the woman guided Adda into the city. Their feet moved away from that familiar, crunching sound from gravel beneath heel and onto the cool surface of golden road. The woman began to walk Adda down a road and to the left, but Adda saw that the rest of the entourage was taking Bethany in a different direction.

"Wait." Adda said, pulling both herself and the other woman to a stop. "Where are they taking her?"

"She's going to be fine." The woman assured and tugged on Adda's arm.

Adda reluctantly allowed herself to be led away though not without casting a few looks after the retreating group. As if sensing Adda's hesitation, the woman continued.

"Your friend is stronger than you think. She managed to beat the valley and the mountain, all with the Enemy hot on her trail. Besides, she, like the rest of us, is beyond harm. Now, there will be plenty of time to catch up, and see her again, but there's somewhere you need to go to first."

"And where's that?"

"To your party, of course!"

8

The woman walked with Adda, speaking on all manner of things as though they had been friends an entire lifetime. There was a knowing there similar to the one the Snatcher held, but instead of malice, this woman spoke and acted with love. She also danced around whatever questions Adda might have, eventually cutting her off by saying.

"You'll see!" In a secretive, playful, tone.

Realizing that none of these people were inclined to share with her the things she wanted to know, Adda lapsed into silence, instead drinking in the sights around her.

Everywhere Adda looked, she saw beauty. The buildings were all as big as mansions, crafted out of gold and pearl, and shone with that same, brilliant radiance. In each, life came bursting forth in the most colorful ways imaginable. Friends and families gathered within these places in great numbers. They laughed, and ate, and drank, speaking loudly with warm voices.

Out front of one home, Adda saw a group gathered around a

table, playing a game of dominos as they sipped on mugs of steaming liquid. A group of kids ran through the street, kicking a ball between one another and shrieking with joy. Through passing windows, Adda would see people from all manner of trades and crafts working upon their individual skills. It caught her eye, that it appeared through one open door, a class of people gathered, canvases sitting on easels, brushes at the ready, while an instructor at the end of the room talked passionately about the dance of brush, color, and stroke, all coming together in harmony to create a masterpiece.

Adda wished to walk into the room and take a place at one of the tables, eager to put her hand to the canvas once more. But the woman gently nudged her, guiding them both deeper into the city.

"Here she comes!" A voice cried from further up the street.

The crowds turned to look upon the strolling pair. A lifetime ago, Adda would have found such attention to perhaps be uncomfortable or strange, but instead she found it to be welcoming. For these eyes didn't see scars, or wounds, or mistakes. They looked and they saw Adda.

A cheer was roused and everywhere she turned she found smiling faces. The crowd whistled and whooped as if celebrating the return of a hero thought lost to war. A procession formed behind them as they went, people continuing to chant and cheer her on. Ribbons and banners unfurled on balconies, welcoming her home. The crowd swelled in, never suffocating Adda, but moving in close to shake her hand or give her a hug. It was strange to Adda as she had never been one to attract a crowd, yet the genuine smiles and warm welcomes put her immediately at ease.

As they moved, Adda found that more and more of the people

were now dressed as the initial entourage of people that had come out from the gate. The crowd was becoming thick with sequins, flappers, vests, and bowler caps. They were also no longer just following her, they were heading in a singular direction.

Before Adda had time to process even this, the woman was now leading them up the steps to the great doors of a sprawling residence that would put any earthly home to shame. The woman pulled Adda about, grasping her hands in her own.

"You've done an incredible thing and the King wanted to honor your walk. He has much to discuss with you, but please, enjoy this, it's for you." The woman reached a hand to cup Adda's face. "I am so proud of you, Adda."

Without waiting for Adda to respond, the woman turned then and opened the doors. With a gentle push, Adda was ushered into the great hall beyond. The woman then stepped back and closed the doors, leaving Adda alone in the strange house.

Fear did not appear, apprehension did not form, yet Adda could feel some kind of nervousness suddenly spark inside of her. She knew who she was on her way to meet and it made her hesitate a moment by the door.

Was this really happening? Adda thought, not out of disbelief, but just out of the sheer magnitude of what she was witnessing.

The woman squared her shoulders then and stepped forward.

Beyond the front door was a foyer magnificent to behold. The floor was made of wood a deep gray. It had been polished and cleaned with the utmost care that brought forth a brilliant shine.

Throughout the room were many large windows, each graced

435

with flowing, blue curtains that darkened the room pleasantly. It was a jarring contrast from the brilliance that adorned the world just outside, but Adda found she loved it. The golden light was still present here, it now just felt like a quiet friend sipping tea in the corner rather than the boisterous voice of the party.

Off to her right and left were other doors. These ones were quaint in size and design, boasting of nothing. Still, they drew Adda's curiosity as they coyly hid whatever lay past their blue frames.

Front and center was a double staircase fit for royalty. Each step was wide and inviting, it was painted white in-between the same, gray wood the floor was made of. Ribbons were laced around the bannisters and railing, flanking the wide steps all the way to a further door above her. That door was a double door, wide and inviting. It urged her to come to it and see what mysteries it hid.

Part of Adda just wanted to wander and explore, but she resisted the urge. She didn't know whose house this was and besides, she had a meeting with the King.

Adda began to walk up the steps, running her hand along the railing as she ascended. She had a momentary flashback, a memory of when she stood in her little kitchen making the same motion along the sill of a window. The sound of her nails running along wood brought back a fond nostalgia.

How much has changed. Adda thought.

Once the stairs were ascended, Adda pushed against the door and found it opened easily to her touch. Just beyond was a hallway that ended in another door. It was long and wide, and was of a similar style of the foyer behind her. She followed the hall, moving closer to its end and saw there were many rooms that ran adjacent to it. The doors were left open to allow Adda to pause at each one and peek in.

One was a library, another a drawing room with a beautiful baby grand sitting before a curtained window, and in another were wide, bay windows that allowed that honey light to spill in unabated.

This room in particular stood out to Adda. The floors here were made of a beautiful, dark wood that radiated an earthly richness. Heavy, blue curtains hung on either side of the massive windows, each embroidered with little white birds along the hem. Above, a modern take on a crystal chandelier hung over the room, catching and recasting brilliant gold to every corner. On either wall to her left and right were many cupboards and cabinets that were such a white as to invite a skilled brush to give them a dash of color.

All these things and so much more were worthy of her attention, but they paled as her eyes settled on what sat center stage in this place. To many others, it would perhaps just be another fixture of the room, but to Adda, it stood out over everything else.

In this room was an easel, waiting patiently for someone to come and give its canvas form.

No, not just someone. Adda thought.

It was put there for her.

That's when Adda realized that this place, this massive home, was hers. It had been built specifically for her. The thought caused tears to brim in her eyes as the reality of where she was began to truly settle in. The emotions were almost too much to handle.

Just as she was about to walk into the room, the door at the end of the hall creaked open and a man in a vest poked his head out. He grinned when he saw Adda, to which he tipped his fedora at her in a way that would suggest he had probably lived his life wearing a cowboy hat instead of the one on him now.

"Party is this way, darlin'! Plenty of time to explore later, so c'mon in!"

Adda cast another look back at the room before she turned and walked toward the man. As she drew near, Adda could hear the swell of music sneaking out from behind the open door. At first, she wasn't quite sure what she was hearing, but as she got closer, there was no doubt what kind of music was mounting to a jovial, frenetic pace in the room just beyond. It was the music that she listened to when she painted, when she felt herself falling apart, and needed something to realign herself.

It was that big-band, toe-tapping, swing that she loved.

Adda grinned then and just about ran to the adjoining room.

The man pushed open the door, letting light spill out over her. She blinked for a moment in the doorway, nearly again overwhelmed by her emotions.

Before her was a long, rectangular room. Its floor was made of a beautiful, dark wood that glinted in the light pouring down from crystal chandeliers. They hung on either side of the room every ten feet or so, sparkling brilliantly in one another's aura. Unlike the room that had held her easel, these chandeliers looked like they had been taken right out of a black and white picture of a 20s dance hall.

The walls of the room held tall, glass doors composed in a way to make them double as windows with silken curtains pulled aside to reveal a large balcony encompassing the outside world. The walls between each door were painted a pearly white with a golden trim that was used to enhance and pull forth the details of its design. They shot straight up before turning into a gentle curve that angled out to become the ceiling up above.

The ceiling was painted in dark colors; blues, blacks, and purples coming together to create the feeling of gazing into the heavens. Peppered along its length were tiny stars winking out of the night sky. The light that was reflected by the chandelier and wood floor made the stars appear to actually glow as though one was looking up at the firmament.

And beneath it all, a turning, whirling madness ensued.

Bodies rotated, tapped, twirled, and danced, feet clicking along the floor to the beat of swelling music that was originating from the other side of the room. There, at the end, was a large stage with huge, red curtains waiting on either of its flanks for the end of the show. Upon the stage were a group of men and women, instruments in hand as they blasted forth their upbeat, jaunty music to keep the room swirling with activity. Hands flew with the expert motions of individuals who had spent countless years refining their practice to then come together and create something truly spectacular.

It was the most beautiful thing Adda had ever witnessed and she couldn't help but stand and stare at the room before her.

Fabric rustled around her legs and looking down, Adda saw she was no longer wearing the same clothing she had on for her entire journey. She was now dressed in the same garb and style as many of the other women in the room. It was black with silvery sequins glinting from amid its form like the stars from the masterpiece above her head.

Her shoes and hair had all been styled to go alongside the theme.

Did I do that? Adda thought in a daze.

"She's here!" A voice cried out, which brought forth a cheer.

A pair of young men dashed up to her, taking her by the arms and leading her out onto the dance floor. And then, after everything she had been through, after everything she had overcome, Adda did the only thing she could think of in the face of such a change in pace.

She danced.

Surrounded by these people, in this place, Adda had a peculiar sense she had never really known back in the life before. She was finally home. That moment of revelation brought into her a peace she struggled to fully understand. All she knew was that this was where she was supposed to be, the place she belonged more than anywhere else.

Hours went by, but she didn't tire. Food was brought out on silver trays to be placed on silk-clothed tables. Glimmering lids were removed to reveal a feast of finger foods perfect for a quick snack before returning to the dance floor. Though Adda didn't hunger, she found that she could still enjoy every bite. Regardless of what she ate, Adda found each morsel was packed with a taste so divine she realized that she had never truly understood flavor until now. Everything before these had been like slop by comparison.

The party blustered on and Adda was no longer sure if it had been hours, days, or even weeks, but apparently it didn't matter. The people around her didn't seem to have anywhere else to be. They all were fully committed to taking this party as long as they wanted.

Perhaps this all would have gone on for an eternity if a gentle hand hadn't taken Adda by the arm, breaking her away from the floor and off to one side of the room. It was the woman who had met her and Bethany out on the path, the one who had lead her to this very house.

She was smiling broadly. "Well you sure know how to throw a party!"

"It's like a dream come true!" Adda yelled over the music, her face flushed and wide with a grin. "Have you ever tried swing before?"

"Oh I've seen myself across many a dance floor in my time." The woman laughed, "But I must say, you dance like the best of them!"

"Thank you, I used to dance a lot in my kitchen." Adda looked back over the room. "This is definitely better than the kitchen."

"There's no doubt about it. Well I don't want to take you from it long, dear, but there's someone who would like to talk to you."

It was like a switch was flipped inside of Adda's mind. The music seemed to quiet, the world slowed, and the lights dimmed. Her attention was pulled toward one of the glass doors that lead onto the balcony, and to the shape of a man standing just beyond, waiting.

Walking from the woman, Adda pushed her way out the door to the outside.

To her surprise, she found that it was night as she stepped past the door. Additionally, the balcony didn't overlook the city, but rather the mountain that she had previously conquered. It rose in the distance, looking less imposing from this side. With no perpetual storm raging about its peak from this angle, the mountain looked far more inviting than it once had.

There was a group of people further down the balcony, heads close together in deep conversation over crystal glasses. Next to her, leaning over a marble railing, was a tall man wearing a stylish tux. He didn't turn to her as she approached and stood alongside him. Adda glanced down, seeing the man's hands rested upon the railing. Her eyes trailed over a pair of wicked scars that marred the back of both of his hands.

"It really is you." Adda said, shifting her eyes back up toward the man.

"Did you have any doubt?" He asked.

"Well I'm here, aren't I?"

The man chuckled at that, turning now toward her. His eyes shone with a golden light that was like staring into the heart of the sun.

"Yes, I suppose you are."

They lapsed into another silence and Adda felt as though he was waiting. She had had so many questions but now it seemed they'd all fled her mind. In light of where she was, it seemed childish to voice them.

Yet still he waited.

"My stone was already at the tree." Adda finally spoke, taking the opportunity given. "If I already bore my burden, why did I have to go back through all of that?"

"Your journey was to give you perspective, but it served another purpose." The man replied.

The words that Mike had spoken to her atop the mountain popped into her head.

"The second is that not all of this journey was about you."

Everett's face flashed through her mind. His hollow eyes and gaunt face floated by like a specter that flitted quietly through the night. They had overcome so much in their journey. The young man had gotten so close to the turning point before he had abandoned their quest.

It wasn't just him though.

Adda thought back to all the other people left in the town. Bethany's parents, Keith, Mrs. Dunton, Scott, and all the rest of the people left behind. They had all attempted to claim such a tiny corner of this world, stubbornly ignoring their dwindling numbers. They were giving themselves to death even as they fought desperately for life.

"But none of them came with me." Adda said. "Well, at least not all the way."

The man nodded his head, "You're absolutely right."

They lapsed into another silence. She wondered what he was getting at, but it seemed that he was quite content with not sharing that information with her. It was as if he wanted her to come to the truth on her own. He knew he couldn't just tell her, because it would be taken as a command, rather than a choice.

"I need to go back out." The words slipped from Adda's lips, solidifying into a purpose even as she spoke them.

She turned to the man, searching his face for any kind of reaction, any look of approval, but he revealed nothing, simply turning to pose a question.

"And why do you think that?"

"They need a guide." Adda spoke, talking to both herself and the man as she navigated her jumbled thoughts and orchestrated them into order.

In her mind, she was back in her home, always the outsider,

always the one to be held at arms length. That suspicion had then turned into looks of pity. There had been a constant reminder she would always be seen as this long-suffering, broken thing that was considered much too fragile to handle. Among them, she was once the least.

How the roles had changed.

"I was made for this." The Certainty bubbled up in her.

Adda turned her head back toward the mountain. It stood still in the distance, no clouds marred its ashen slopes, no dark caves burrowed beneath the stone, and no meadow ensnared those who had come so close, but couldn't make the summit.

This face was far more peaceful.

Yet, if she looked hard enough, Adda could make out the flicker of lightning illuminating the edges of the mountain, a reminder of what lay just on the other side.

"They could only see weakness." The man offered, "But here, true strength finally has its opportunity to shine."

"So then I have to leave?"

"No, you don't have to." He smiled gently at her, placing a hand on her face.

His hands were rough, calloused, as though he had spent a life working as a craftsman.

"You can stay here if you want, the choice is yours to make."

This was no test, no trial to see what she would do in the face of such an offer. The man truly meant what he said, it was entirely up to her on what she would do. The desire to stay was strong. It certainly didn't help that she could still hear the swelling music from within the dance hall rolling out into the night sky. She was finally in a place that she was at true peace.

Could she really leave?

Looking back to the dance hall, Adda paused to see the figure of another man through the glass doorway. The figure stood on the far side of the room from her, near a table where he held a small plate of food and a glass of champagne. As if sensing eyes upon him, the figure looked up and over toward her. Their eyes met through the glass, latching onto one another with a great intensity.

Those eyes sparkled just like she remembered them, they had been so vibrant even up to the very end. It had been so long that Adda had forgotten the deep color that leapt to life there, but seeing them again was like coming back to a familiar street that one had spent their childhood exploring. Those feet would never forget every twist and turn, memories carved deeper with every step.

The more she looked, the more she remembered, and the more her heart filled with warmth. It had been too long since she had seen him, but what was any length of time when compared to eternity? It seemed as though the world was still in that moment. Her hand dropped into her bag then, tracing the wooden box with absent-minded fingers, finding the crevice with the carved symbol.

Then, the figure smiled, raised up his glass in a simple greeting, before turning about and vanishing from view.

In her heart, Adda knew then what she truly wanted. She had spent a lifetime waiting for this moment, she would not shy away from it. The city and the people here would never fade, so they would all be here upon her return, but for now, there was work to do. Turning back to the man she stood with, the man with scars on his hands and light shining from his eyes, Adda made her choice.

"I always wondered what my purpose was. I never thought I'd find it after."

"Adda, the purpose of after is to answer the calling in every person's heart, but calling is placed upon you long before the end of your earthly existence." The man replied to her. "Never underestimate the value of what you did in your life."

He turned once again toward the mountain.

"This journey will be different. You now know the full truth, but the people you are returning to have abandoned it. The trials you will face are no longer from the valley or the mountain or any of the powers that dwell there. Your challenge will come from the hearts of your fellow-man."

"I'll get them, I'll bring them home." Adda said in an adamant tone.

The man smiled warmly.

"I know you will."

Epilogue

Eyes fluttered gently like butterfly wings dancing on the wind as the sleeper began to rouse. It was slow going for she had gone through much, but in every passing moment, she came to herself. Soon, her lashes whisked open, allowing for warm light to chase away the dregs of slumber.

It wasn't piercing rays that struck at her sleepy eyes, rather it was a honey gold of fresh dawn, gently bringing her to wakefulness. It filtered itself through ivory curtains that fluttered gently in a passing breeze. It was perhaps the most pleasant way she had ever awoken and the girl leaned into the moment.

As she lay there, she became aware of how much her body ached. Every muscle felt cramped and stiff, yet somehow she had never felt lighter in her life. Something dreadful had been removed from her, but what it was, she couldn't remember.

The girl stretched out her body, letting out a happy groan as her muscles loosened. It was a good stretch, the one well earned after a deep sleep. A heavy yawn rolled out of her mouth as she settled into her bed, content to let the whole day pass her by.

It had been so long since she had been able to rest.

But then, as the last bits of sleep finally filtered away, she remembered.

Her entire journey flashed past her in an instant. She remembered closing her eyes in the valley, ignoring those who called out to her. She remembered stumbling through the caves, ghosts and ghouls nipping at her heels. She remembered the meadow and the fear in those people as they saw what pursued her. She remembered miles and miles of mountain as she scrambled on the white gravel, hoping someone would come.

It felt like decades of running and hiding, yet it had been to no avail.

She remembered when it caught her. She remembered how it dragged her down the side of the mountain to stand upon the road once again. She remembered the way the knife hovered for a moment, glinting in the sun before it swung down eagerly to bite into her neck. She remembered the pain, the blood, and then, the dark.

She sat up, bringing a hand to her throat. Shaking fingers traced along the delicate skin of her neck, but found nothing. To her surprise, not even a scar remained as evidence to what had happened. It was as though it had never happened.

Yet the experience of that agony hung around her thick like a shroud.

The girl brought her knees up to her chest, a light blanket covering her from the waist down. She wrapped her arms around her legs, resting her head against them, and began to cry.

She hadn't meant to start crying, but this was the first moment that everything had slowed down enough for her to even begin to process it all. Her shoulders shook as she released wave upon wave of the terror that had been building for so long.

"My child," a warm voice cut through her despair, "why do you cry?"

The girl's head lolled up and she peeked through tear-heavy lashes at the one who spoke.

She found she was sitting in a small room that looked something like a hospital. There was a bed with white sheets that she was laying on now. On one side of the bed was a side table that currently held a vase filled with blooming flowers. The flowers were rich and vibrant in their coloring. Past the table was a window with white, silken curtains that continued to filter the golden light from outside. On the opposite side of the room, sitting in a simple chair between the bed and the far door, was a man.

He smiled warmly at her, reaching out a hand and brushing the tears from her cheeks in a fatherly way. The motion was so gentle and knowing that the girl found herself leaning into the gesture. She had no idea who this man was, but there was something familiar about him just the same.

"I- I don't know what's happening." The girl said.

"All will be made clear." He replied, "For now, just know that you're safe."

The girl found herself comforted in that knowledge. Though the man had yet to give her any reason to trust him, she realized that she did, with her whole heart.

The girl turned once again to look over at the flowers, marveling at their beauty. She had never seen such brilliant colors in her life. For a moment, she was even tempted to think that they were fake, a mimicry of life. Yet as she stared, she realized somehow, every flower she had seen before was actually the mimic and this, sitting in the vase before her, was the real thing. They appeared impossibly alive, a feature that would be undetectable in the previous life. Her eyes lingered there for a moment before they drifted down and settled upon a small book that sat just beside the vase.

The girl gasped, recognizing the book immediately.

It was the one that had been gifted to her, the one that she had shoved in her yellow backpack on that fateful day. She remembered the last time she had seen it. She had been in the valley when meaty hands had caught her pack, trying to drag her backward. She had slipped free of the straps, abandoning it and its contents to the valley floor.

"How?" She asked, lifting the book and flipping over the front cover.

There, just before the beginning of the book was a dedication, the first line just saying.

To: Bethany,

May this book protect you and guide you home…

Then, looking at the bottom of the page, she saw that familiar name.

-Adda Reinhoff

"I thought I lost it!"

"No, my child, this is something you can never lose." The man said, gently taking the book from her hands.

He flipped it open to read a few pages, his mouth twitching into a smile. He looked back up at Bethany.

"Once claimed, it's part of you forever."

"What is this place?" She finally asked.

The man laughed then, finding some kind of humor in her question. It wasn't a condescending tone, rather one that seemed delighted.

"It's a gift I made for you." He said, "*This* is your home."

Home.

The word brought with it a strange mixture of emotions. It gave her hope and comfort knowing that she had made it to the end. It also brought with it melancholy. Her mind fell back to where this all started a lifetime ago. There was the suited figure at her door, the blur of a car ride, and the giants standing on the hills. The last she had seen of her parents was confused terror as she sprinted off, leaving them far behind as her brain screamed at her to run.

And she hadn't stopped. On and on she ran, the ever present foot fall of the giants behind her. There was this thing in her, this Certainty, that drew her on and it was the only thing that had given her strength to keep moving.

"Where are my parents?" Bethany asked.

"They're a little lost at the moment." The man said, leaning back into his chair. "But don't worry, I have the right woman on the job."

The statement caused a memory to trigger. In the midst of her brain scrambling to understand what had happened to her, it had omitted certain details. Now, the pieces were coming back together. They collected into the image of a calm face set with a pair of brilliant, shimmering eyes.

It was Adda, facing off with the giant.

But it wasn't the Adda that Bethany had grown up knowing. That woman was beginning to show her age and seemed more content to dance about and paint then go to war. She was kind, mild-mannered, and inquisitive, a true artist through and through. The woman Bethany had seen standing on the path, was no artist.

She was a warrior.

She wore a helm, breastplate, girdle, and boots that all shone like captured sunlight. Each strap and buckle had been put together with the utmost care, polished so that the winking silver shone like stars. Across her back, a shield of the same composition hung ready for use. It was wide and powerful, capable of withstanding even the mightiest of blows.

On her hip was a long, blue-leather scabbard that hid away a sword's blade. Even covered, light escaped from between the seams and top of the scabbard as the sword glowed with ferocious strength. The hilt of the weapon stuck free, made of the same metal as the shield and armor, but the pommel of the sword appeared to be different. It looked as though it were made of wood instead, with a tiny, indented symbol carved into its surface. The woman rested an easy hand upon the pommel, her thumb idly tracing against the worn carving. Though her entire body seemed relaxed, the woman stood ready to pull the weapon free in the blink of an eye.

She was a person that had looked death straight in the eye and had not balked. She was a person that had carried the weight of so many others on her shoulders, yet somehow still stood up straight. She had walked through the night and had come out wearing armor that shone like sunlight.

As this woman had approached, Bethany could feel sweat forming in the giant's hand and it shift backward away from the powerful entity that was approaching them. Its confidence had waned before this warrior, slicing Bethany's throat in its cowardice before the coming storm.

Though it seemed impossible, there was no doubt in Bethany's mind that this was indeed Adda.

The memory flashed by, leaving only one question reeling through the young girl's mind.

"Who *is* Adda?"

The young man pulled himself free of the water, scrambling onto the gravelly bank to escape the clutches of the deep. He retched, his body forcing out the water that occupied his lungs. Every cough ejected more freezing liquid until not a drop of it remained.

With a groan, he fell to his side and rolled onto his back. His chest heaved up and down as he tried to catch his breath from the ordeal. The weight of his stone had nearly done him in, dragging him down into the darkest depths, yet he had somehow managed to swim free.

The vine's writhed around wetly against his arm like worms on a sidewalk after the rain. They weren't happy with their treatment, burrowing in deeper to his shoulder to escape the chill that now bit into his bones. The stone had nearly been drawn into his arm, the vines doing their best to implant their home beneath his skin. It was only a matter of time before they succeeded.

The flesh immediately around it had become a pale, green color and was starting to smell horrible. The people from the meadow used their flower crowns to offset the cloying scent, but without their aide, there was no disguising the foul odor. The young man wrinkled his nose in disgust, trying not to think about how itchy his shoulder was.

He lay there for a while, his heart rate finally slowing as fresh air calmed the panicked adrenaline caused from nearly drowning. As he fell into a more collected state, he realized that there was something different. It took a moment before he started to understand. Raising his other arm, the one without the stone attached, he regarded it. To his surprise, he found that the clutching sand that had so long been his companion was gone.

With new found energy, the young man sat up, looking himself over. There wasn't even a single grain to drag down against him. No matter where he looked, they had been wiped away. The water had washed clean their great weight. Now only the stone remained and he found himself bolstered with newfound confidence in light of this revelation.

"Liberating, isn't it?" An elderly voice spoke.

He jerked his head up, his whole body becoming tense. Looking about, his eyes settled on the form of an old man seated upon a nearby rock. The stranger sat with legs crossed as though he were meditating, his hand resting on his knees. The man was looking at the other with golden eyes flaring with inner heat. The young man had seen this creature once before, on the day that he had abandoned Adda.

Guilt stabbed into his heart.

The man rose and walked over, his steps light upon the gravel of the path. He now stood over the other and extended a spotted hand.

"Jason Everett, I presume?"

Now seeing the man up close, Everett wasn't even sure why he had run in the first place. Though there was a deep intensity in the man's eyes, there was also an easy warmth. Everett immediately felt himself relax.

"You know my name?"

"I know a lot more than just that." The man replied, waving his hand around, "Are you just going to sit there all day?"

Everett reached out and took the offered hand, surprised at the strength of the old man as he was drawn onto his feet. The man's eyes flicked over to Everett's shoulder to which the younger man immediately felt a pang of shame cut through him. Though he wore the same loose fitting clothes that the others did in the meadow to cover his burden, it was like this old man's eyes could pierce right through the cloth to what was hidden below.

Everett had returned to the meadow after losing Adda, no longer having the strength to continue on. He quickly learned that the people were understanding of his stone only at first. Soon, their disposition changed, treating him as a pariah until he finally covered his stone up as they did. After that had been done, they acted as though they had all been friends for the longest time and he was once again invited into their flower circles.

Everett had quickly learned that one never mentioned the stones, instead pretending such a thing didn't even exist.

"Come on then, let's take a look at it." The old man replied, noting to Everett's sleeve.

Wordlessly, Everett followed the command.

Rolling up the wet cloth, he revealed the infection. The stone had been pulled in close, only about an inch or so of vine still remaining above his skin. The old man leaned in, scratching his chin as he regarded the mass.

"Nasty buggers, huh?" He said to himself before turning his attention to Everett. "The name's Mike, it's a pleasure to meet you."

The man then turned on his heel, bustling up the pathway as he waved an arm at Everett to follow.

"Come on then, you're late as it is, so let's not dawdle!"

"Wait!" Everett called out, "What do you mean I'm late?"

457

Mike didn't stop.

The young man let out a growl of frustration, but still hurried after the other. There was some kind of a- Certainty- that bubbled up into his mind, tugging at him to follow. So, with little else to do, he fell into step.

He followed the man up the path, leading them through a clearing where a cute, little cottage sat. Mike marched past the small abode, leading them ever higher. Though he was curious about the structure, Everett continued after the old man.

The path went up and up, and Everett found that though the sand was no longer there to weigh him down, the stone itself seemed to be dragging harder against him. It did not change in size or weight, but there was indeed a pull that was trying to throw him off balance. Gritting his teeth, Everett pushed past it, leaning himself forward as if walking against a powerful wind.

The vines seemed to understand where they were headed and bit deeper into his skin. They wriggled about and tried to bury themselves completely in Everett's arm. The rock was now smooth against his shoulder and he could feel an immense pressure beginning to build there.

Up ahead, the old man seemed oblivious to this and continued on silently.

In a matter of minutes that had felt like hours, the two finally broke onto the summit. The world stretched out around them in every direction, looking microscopic from such a height. Everett fell to his knees on the path, clutching a hand against the stone that was slipping beneath his skin. His fingers clawed at it, straining against its ridges as he pulled against it, desperate to keep it from its objective.

"You can fight it all you want." Mike spoke, standing with his hands clasped behind the small of his back, his eyes shut as he let the wind buffet against him. He opened those golden orbs, flicking a glance toward the struggling man. "No amount of brute force will ever free you from it."

"Please!" Everett hissed through clenched teeth, a heavy hand of pain passing over his body. "Help me!"

"I can't." Mike said flatly. "The stone is yours to keep or to give away."

"Show me how." Everett whimpered.

Mike raised one of his hands, pointing a long finger toward the very top of the mountain. Everett followed the gesture, his eyes falling upon an incredible sight.

The eternal tree sat before him, towering into the heavens, its branches adorned with every kind of bird. The tree hummed with life, true life, and the moment his eyes had fallen upon it, Everett felt the Certainty thrum like a mighty chord. Without even a thought, Everett climbed back to his feet and stumbled toward the tree.

The stone bit, the vines writhed, and Everett walked.

"Just one step at a time." Everett muttered to himself.

It was like he was in the dark of the cave again, trying to push against the call of the darkness all around him. Adda had said that to him, to just take it one step at a time.

Each step was a challenge, each inch was a trial, all the world seemed to be pushing back against him now. Memories whipped around his mind like a hurricane, pictures of inadequacy and loss tried to hook into him with wicked barbs. He heard his sister's screams, he saw the realization in Adda's eyes as he turned from her. He felt the weight of his comfortable, restless, suffocating life crush against him as he refused to make anything of the time he was given.

Yet through it all, that Certainty pulled him against the onslaught, breaking the intense wind that was set before him.

Everett closed his eyes, focusing on the Certainty, letting himself be drawn into it. He raised his hand, the motion causing the stone to grind against his shoulder bone, but he didn't care anymore. Blindly he marched forward, his fingers playing on the air as they searched.

And searched.

And searched.

And found the rough bark of the tree. He slumped against the trunk, laying his palm flat as he crumpled beneath his great burden. The tree sang beneath his hand, radiating a power and energy like none that he had ever felt. The Certainty connected with something that was emanating from deep within the tree's core. They sang to each other in one voice, vibrating with a song older than time.

"Please, I don't want this anymore." Everett muttered, sweat beading on his brow. "Tell me what to do."

Somewhere deep inside of him, Everett realized something. The vines weren't just holding onto him, he was actually gripping them back. Every inch they had gained was not fought for, but rather given up by their victim. Together, he and the vines had made a bond which no power could break. As much as they held him back, he found he was afraid to lose them. They were his safety, his cycle, his identity, his life. They were the building blocks of his very being and to release them was to let go of everything he had ever known.

To give them up was to expose the wounds that marred his soul.

He almost pulled away from the tree.

He almost turned around to return to the meadow.

He almost succumbed to who he used to be.

But then he remembered Adda. The light that seemed to shine off of her, her ability to walk through everything untouchable, her stubborn march that no trial could sway. The valley couldn't tempt her, the caves couldn't keep her, and the meadow couldn't delay her.

Everett wanted that.

He wanted to be like that.

Let go.

"I'm not strong enough." He cried out, tears streaming down his face.

Let go.

"Please, I don't know how."

A hand was on his, gently pulling apart his fingers that was formed into a tight fist.

Let go.

And then Everett did.

With no great flair or dramatic effect, the vines stiffened. They curled before becoming brittle and shattering into hardened, white pieces that fell to the path below, becoming lost amidst the gravel. The rock dropped unceremoniously from his arm, thudding to the ground and rolling away. It settled among the moss and grass, becoming lost in the field of so many others.

Everett sat there, reveling in the feeling. He had never in his life known such profound peace and was afraid that if he were to stir, that the spell would be broken.

"And there he is." Mike's voice spoke from just behind him, a gentle hand resting on the young man's shoulder. "I'm glad you finally made it."

"I have so many questions." Everett whispered, suddenly aware that tears were cascading down his face. They were not from sorrow rather they were summoned in the feeling of pure relief.

"We have much to discuss before I send you off to the city." Mike said, with a comforting pat then turned and started walking away. "Let's go get you some tea."

Everett rose, intent on following the man. As he did, his eyes swept across the summit and a small burst of color grabbed his attention. Curious, Everett stepped toward it. The young man then froze, suddenly realizing what he was looking at. Turning around he called back to Mike.

"What is that?" He asked the question, yet he already knew the answer.

Mike paused to turn around, flashing a broad grin before beckoning Everett to follow. "It's a gift from a friend."

Sparing it one last look, Everett hurried after the older man. They both disappeared down the side of the mountain, leaving behind the tree and its new companion. There, off to one side, set up to overlook the city and its beautiful neighbors, was an easel. Upon that easel was a canvas that had the entire scene below masterfully captured upon its form. The colors were vibrant, the lines were long and swooping, and there, down in the bottom right-side of the canvas was painted a tiny, red *AR*.

Keith sat in his tower, slumped against his chair with his head facing downward. The furniture beneath him groaned in protest as his swelling form was reaching a weight too great for it to handle, yet he could not find the strength to move. His chin rested upon his girth, his size having inflated to frightening proportions. He had become another creature entirely, one that could not have lived in any other place besides this one.

The tiny room that had become his prison cell was now absolutely infested with vines. They spilled through the open door, crawling up the table, chairs, and walls. They connected the castle to the man, dozens of spiked heads wriggling into Keith's hands, arms, and legs. Day by day they sank deeper into him, replacing every part of him with their own likeness. The weight of them was sickening, yet the man would not fight them, because as much as he loathed them, he found that he loved them more.

Nowadays, Keith would simply let his awareness drift across the town. Within his mind, he found that he could easily observe the people living in the town down below him. Further, he could still influence them with his slithering powers. As such, he would spend his days subtly controlling their pathetic, little lives, gaining sick pleasure from knowing that they still lived within the palm of his hand.

It had been a long time since anyone had seen him, not that he would do anything to change that. After Adda had embarrassed him, Keith had retreated to his tower, giving himself over fully to the castle's other occupant. In his mind, it had been the best decision he had ever made.

His second shadow had gladly taken charge, hooking its tiny, barbed claws deeper into him, pulling out a darkness within his heart that he wasn't even aware was there. He was beyond caring at this point, letting this creature have its way. After all, the more Keith gave to it, the more his power strengthened and mutated. This fact alone was worth any cost.

It was also this power that was causing the man to bloat like an overfed tick. Though he had grown formidable, Keith no longer had the strength to lift himself up. Even if the vines weren't there to hold him down, there was no way he could descend the stairs and walk out among his people.

Not that he wanted to. With his whispering snakes able to travel so far now, he had lost any desire at all to go out and mingle with the common folk that lived beneath his great shadow.

Not even Scott would come visit him anymore, instead taking his absence as an opportunity to seize power for himself. The hulking beast had also increased in size, bullying everyone around him to do whatever he wanted. Little did he know that Keith still pulled the strings, subtly controlling them like puppets.

Sure, Scott had become their king, but Keith was their god.

He liked that idea and had embraced it. The shadow liked it as well, whispering fervently of his own legend into his bloated ears. It feasted off the pride and the fear that came rolling off the man in waves.

So it was for the small town and so it would always be.

Until today.

The shadow, so consistent in its praising, grooming whispers, suddenly froze. Its little claws dug in deeper and Keith could feel its hackles raise like a cat getting ready to fight. It sensed something that it did not like. This roused the man, his senses tangled up in the creature's own allowing him to feel it as well.

Something had changed.

Light began to trickle in through the gaping hole in the side of the tower wall, piercing through the gloomy light the emanated from the stones around him. Keith squinted his eyes and raised a heavy hand to push away the intruder. Never before had sunlight managed to break into his sanctum, yet this golden light continued to grow. In a matter of moments the entirety of his home was filled with it, banishing the darkness in one, fell swoop. From somewhere down below, Keith could hear a high-pitched whining sound followed by a successive popping.

The vines were dying.

They curled into balls like maggots in the fire, unable to resist the mighty power that crashed against them. One by one they hardened and shattered, exploding in the onslaught of heat. The vines buried within Keith strained to hold on even as their exposed bits began to shrivel and crumble.

There was nowhere for them to hide.

Keith lowered his hand, trying to look beyond the light. Once his eyes could finally begin to focus, his jaw dropped as his heart swelled with fear with what he saw. The shadow on his back shrieked wildly, tugging desperately to break free, yet found itself as stuck to Keith as Keith was to it.

At first, Keith thought the hills had become water as they were suddenly shifting and moving in a way the reminded him of the ocean. He leaned forward, fascinated by this abrupt, explosive change to his sedentary life. He soon saw the the hills were still as solid as they had always been, not becoming water as he initially believed, but something had grabbed ahold of them, bending them to an impossible power. This power could not be resisted and so the ground moved away from it.

One by one, the hills rolled to the side, shrinking and collapsing into flat ground before the approaching light. They bowed their mighty heads low, making way for a lone figure that could now be seen walking toward their town. From the figure's feet raced a path made of white gravel. It shot like an arrow ahead of them, its course now made straight by the moving hills. It rolled like living water from out of the ground, only stopping once it had reached the front gate of his home.

All of this was incredible, impossible, awesome but it was not the thing that made Keith tremble in fear- and in hope.

For the figure that marched toward them now, clothed in shining armor and wielding a flaming sword was one that Keith knew well. In his mind's eye, he had always seen her as quiet and weak, needing a strong arm to lean on to make it through life's trials. He had always dreamed that perhaps he could be the one that she could lean on. Now, looking at her, he realized how little he knew this woman. Despite everything, she had gone over the mountain and she had returned for them.

He knew who she was.

Her name is Adda Reinhoff.

A note from the author:

Thank you so much for taking the time to read my book. It humbles me to find that you made it this far into it. Whereas the story of Adda Reinhoff is closed, there are many more stories that I'm writing, so if you're curious about these upcoming works, and want to stay up to date, please follow me @luke_p_hopkins_author on most social media platforms.

Also, if you enjoyed the book it would help me greatly if you took the time to tell someone else about it or give me a review on Amazon. These things are both a tremendous help for me on my journey to becoming a career author.

Thank you again for your interest in this story and I hope to see you in my next novel.

Made in the USA
Middletown, DE
02 July 2022

68299762R00265